THE MAN WHO MC

Authors N
Here is the truth of things, woven into
what I would hope is an intriguing story.
Read and believe and this truth could set you free.......

THE MAN WHO MOVED MOUNTAINS

Peter Minns

Peter Minns

GRANGE PUBLISHING

First published in 2005
by
Grange Publishing
23 Station Lane, Cloughton,
Scarborough.
YO13 0AD
United Kingdom

Cover design and artwork
© Gerald Halliday

*Any resemblance to persons, past or present,
in this reality is purely coincidental.*

First edition 2005
ISBN 0-9546907-0-2

Prepared and printed by:
York Publishing Services Ltd
64 Hallfield Road
Layerthorpe
York
YO31 7ZQ
Tel: 01904 431213; Website: www.yps-publishing.co.uk

Ref No: PR3/181105/K

CHAPTER 1

On the tenth anniversary of his mother's death the dream 'returned' to Senior Technician Richard Travis.

He stood at twilight in a deserted, snowbound graveyard, viewing the tumulus of a solitary grave, without marker or memorial. At the sight of it, the words of the nineteenth century authoress, Emily Brontë, came forcibly to him:

'Cold in the earth, and the deep snow piled above thee!
Far, far removed, cold in the dreary grave!
Have I forgot, my Only Love, to love thee,
Severed at last by time's all-wearing wave?'

At his side stood Death, but that awesome creature of legend held no terrors for the Technician. Why should he? It was he, himself, who was in control of events here, of that he was certain.

Together, the two of them began to remove the piled-up snow which covered the grave. That done, they started on the more difficult task of excavating the frozen soil. Travis found the work slow and exhausting but his companion's seemingly boundless strength more than made up for his own deficiencies. Before very long they had dug their way down to the soil-stained, rough-wooden coffin. With the aid of a pair of stout ropes, the coffin was secured and lifted up onto the side of the grave.

Death turned a cowled head in the direction of a rapidly darkening western horizon, and gave out a long, low-pitched whistle of surprising intensity.

Travis watched as the four jet-black horses, drawing a simple, open carriage, came towards them out of the sunset, their racing hoofs pounding the red glow into a river of fire, the noise of their approach a rumble of distant thunder borne on the wind.

In very little time the team of four were with them in the graveyard. They stood uneasily, with crazed eyes and flared nostrils, clattering out the steps to some macabre dance.

With a soothing word here, and a soft caress there, Death quietened his unruly team. That done, he lifted the excavated coffin effortlessly·

onto the carriage. With Travis settled beside him, he whistled the horses into motion.

The journey was done at a breakneck speed. Racing along deserted country lanes, and careering across barren, snow-covered fields, the pace did not slacken until they neared their destination – an isolated, whitewashed, stone cottage.

The load was carried into the house and up the single flight of stairs to a sparsely furnished bedroom of modest proportions. Here, they laid down their burden.

Wrenching open the coffin lid, Travis took out the corpse and laid it on the bed, which occupied the far corner of the small room. A glance behind told him that his companion had made a silent departure, leaving him alone.

He seated himself on the edge of the bed, the better to view the putrefying mass of flesh laid out. The sight was hideous, the stench appalling, and the body so badly decomposed as to be barely recognisable as a female form. With a calculated movement, he bent over and kissed a pair of grinning lips.

Having first unbuttoned his shirt, he took up a shrunken hand and placed it over his heart, gasping as he made contact with the cold, clammy flesh. With eyes shut tight and a bold blind confidence, he took up the challenge.

A vividly remembered scene from childhood days long ago...... standing at the edge of a lazy sea under a cloudless sky...... golden, waterlogged sands on three sides – he *saw* the liquid sand seeping up between his toes...... frothy remnants of waves lapping his ankles – he *felt* the warm, salt bubbles washing to and fro...... a blazing, golden disc overhead – he *warmed* to the glow on his bare shoulders. He put himself there. He *was* there.

He stood outside the door to his other self, reasoning, persuading, cajoling, and watched as the barrier melted away, giving him access to the unlimited power of his subconscious self.

The technique was sound, the philosophy behind it true, but never had mortal man dared to push matters to this extreme limit, least of all the Technician.

With his mind's eye, he looked deep into the body beside him and worked his will – not by wishful thoughts, or hopeful expectation, but by stern commands born of total conviction.

Vital organs rebuilt themselves and sprang into life. Limbs on the point of dissolution fleshed out anew. Once corrupt and stagnant blood began to course afresh through artery, vein and capillary. The hand clasped to his heart grew warm of its own accord.

After an interval of time, he heard a movement and a sigh. Opening his eyes, he looked full into the face of the young woman, noting the latent beauty underneath remnant blemishes of decay and dissolution. The lips moved: 'Don't leave me. I'm frightened.'

He bent low to press his lips against her ear. A lock of golden hair strayed into his mouth as he spoke: 'Don't be afraid; only have faith and believe and all things are possible.'

He returned to his task, plumping out the flesh, restoring to the skin its natural glow and sheen, and smoothing away the last little imperfections.

He reopened his eyes to find that she had been studying him as he lay there. He noted with surprise that as her eyes drifted to and fro to take in the sight of him they appeared to subtly shift in colour from deepest blue to pale, pure lilac. Not his doing, surely? he thought. He gave her an enquiring look and received a dazzling smile in return. The whole image was unforgettable, as it was meant to be.

'I feel I've slept for an eternity,' she said, stretching languidly.

'Yes, I can well believe it,' he answered.

'My name is Emma,' she said. The smile faded. 'Who are *you?*'

'I am Travis, the Destroyer of Death,' he found himself saying.

'Stay with me awhile,' she pleaded, as he rose to leave her.

'That I cannot do,' he said. 'I must return to my own world.'

He walked to the open doorway, where he half-turned to look at her.

'I shall return. Depend upon it,' he said.

'I shall be waiting. Do not fail me,' she called back.

He walked through the doorway to find himself back home in his flat, sitting bolt upright in bed, his body soaked in a cold perspiration and his teeth chattering uncontrollably.

The dream, he recollected, had first come to him some fifteen years before, in the midst of a childhood illness. Thereafter, it had returned at intervals of two to three years, usually at a time of stress, or some minor crisis. In the past year, however, it had come four times, two of

3

the visitations being in the past month alone. It always unfolded in exactly the same way and the experience invariably left him feeling wretched for days afterwards. Sleep was normally impossible for long hours after waking but on this occasion he was able to resettle himself without too much difficulty. The irrational feeling that matters were coming to a head and would soon resolve themselves into an explanation prompted the difference this time. The thought had a calming affect on his nerves, and having laid himself down again he soon drifted into a dreamless sleep.

Even as he slept, a real-life drama, not unrelated, was being played out on the monitor screens of Provincial 3, a mere half-mile away.

Pine Tree Cottage, Yarm, North Yorkshire; 14th May, 1811.

It had been such a little thing in the beginning: an inexplicable lethargy and weakness, a stubborn, feverish headache, and a general feeling of being unwell.

Doctor Hunter had been sent for but had seen nothing to cause him alarm. He had prescribed a tonic, and recommended rest, in the confident expectation that this would suffice. Over the coming days and weeks, however, the symptoms had persisted and grown steadily worse. None of the medications, prescribed with an increasing frequency by a perplexed physician, seemed to produce anything other than the briefest of respites.

The patient was probed and prodded, medical textbooks referred to, a professional colleague consulted – all to no avail. A 'diagnosis' of 'debilitating ague' had early been fixed upon – a conveniently vague diagnosis with an impressive sounding ring to it. In fact, it was the Doctor's old standby when in difficulties and signified nothing. All the while the patient continued to deteriorate, losing weight at a spectacular rate, developing sudden and alarming nosebleeds, and latterly complaining of a painful ache deep within her bones.

Three months into her illness, Emma Sinclair, alone and dying, stirred restlessly on her sickbed in a vain attempt to get comfortable. That morning she had awoken feeling better than in a long time so a replacement for the night nurse, Mrs Jenkins, who had been called away to attend a sick relative, was deemed unnecessary.

That evening Emma's mother had retired early, as was her custom, but not before she had left a small handbell by her daughter's bedside with instructions that she be summoned if the need arose. By this time Emma was feeling much worse but having no great desire for another useless visit from Doctor Hunter kept the fact to herself. Her hope was that sleep would come soon and see her through the night.

Now, close to midnight, sleep had not come and she felt really ill. Should she summon her mother? she wondered. No, she would not alarm her to no good purpose. In truth, she was beyond help.

Alone with her thoughts, she reviewed her life of twenty years: carefree, childhood days, clouded only by the death of her father when she was nine years of age; teenage years shared with her two brothers, both now gone away to seek their fortunes elsewhere; her awakening to womanhood, and the promise of a full and happy life ahead; her illness, hovering over her these past few months like some black cloud. Once men had called her beautiful, but now......

It was with good cause that men had spoken so. A mass of golden hair framing a face of great beauty left an unforgettable impression on the observer. Perhaps the most striking feature was a pair of large, expressive eyes, which possessed the curious characteristic of shifting and varying through all the shades of blue, depending upon light and shade and the mood and temper of the owner. A lively, spirited disposition served only to captivate further, leaving many a person to marvel at the fact that such an exquisite creature was to be found in so commonplace a setting.

The past three months, however, had taken a terrible toll. The once golden hair, now dull and faded, framed a skeletal face. The wonderful eyes, enormous now in their sunken sockets, looked out dully through half-closed lids onto a disappearing world.

A wave of pain washed suddenly over her, prompting a whispered plea: 'Sweet Jesus, release me! Oh, sweet Jesus, release me!' Fighting back the tears, she reached out a bony hand to the bell. Missing her mark, she sent it tinkling to the floor. It proved to be of little consequence for very soon the pain began to ease of itself. Within half-an-hour she had fallen into a restless sleep.

She awoke for the last time a little before five in the morning. The pain was gone and she felt warm and comfortable. Outside, dawn was breaking, and faintly to her ears came the chirping of half-awakened birds greeting a new day. Barely audible was the sound of a distant cart, rumbling its way to an early market. Strange to think that life would go on without her, she reflected: day in, day out; year in, year out. Hot summer days, autumn fall, crisp winter mornings, and budding spring, would all slip by unseen by her. Strange, too, that perhaps at that very moment, in some distant hamlet, a life was coming into the world even as she was preparing to leave it.

A beam of light lit up the bedroom window and raced across the room. Shadows were shrinking, corners came out of the gloom, distant objects took form and shape, but the world to her eyes was contracting to a glimmering square.

Then it was that the darkness came full upon her, leaving her to dream a very different dream.

'Cut! Can it!'

Observer Czyzun winced at the words. At the twentieth time of telling the joke had long since lost what little appeal it once had.

'You're late,' he snapped, over his shoulder.

'Only five minutes,' pleaded Observer Ellis. 'It's that little woman of mine. Wouldn't let me out of bed until I'd done the necessary.' The voice took on a self-satisfied tone. 'The woman is insatiable.'

'So everyone tells me,' said Czyzun.

'Very amusing,' said Ellis, looking not in the least amused. 'Do I detect a note of disgruntlement? Night shifts getting us down, are they?'

Czyzun gave a grunt of confirmation. 'Seven in a row is too much. I've always said so. I'm glad that's the last for three weeks,' he said, stretching wearily.

Ellis nodded sympathetically, and turned his attention to the viewing monitor. 'That's not Pine Tree Cottage,' he said, sharply.

'We're done with that, probably for good,' said Czyzun. 'The Sinclair girl died a few hours back.'

'It was on the cards,' said Ellis, with a shrug of the shoulders. 'I shall miss that little beauty – not that she was much fun of late.'

'Perhaps it's just as well,' said Czyzun. 'I do believe Ritter was getting suspicious. We must have more coverage of her than the

London Section have of Shakespeare.'

'A slight exaggeration,' said Ellis, 'but I take the point.' He cast a despairing look at the monitor. 'Is that the best you can come up with – the vicarage?'

'None of my doing,' said Czyzun. 'Ritter's already done his morning round, and come up with a twelve hour stint with our Mr Sibley.'

'Eight of which will be down to me,' complained Ellis. 'Why do I always seem to get the most boring assignments – those that wouldn't tax the intelligence of a trained chimp?'

'Perhaps they think you're best qualified,' suggested Czyzun.

The insult was lost on Ellis, who was busy casting hopeful looks about him. 'Anything happening elsewhere?' he asked. 'And don't tell me Ritter doesn't like it when any of us go walkabouts.'

'The Slater woman give birth awhile back,' replied Czyzun. 'They're still covering it on Monitor Three.' He shook his head in disgust. 'A botched job, if ever I saw one, even allowing for the fact it's a multiple birth. It's like a butcher's shop in there. Two dead and one to go at the last count.'

'Put you off your meal-break, did it?' asked Ellis, grinning.

In a hurry to be away Czyzun still found time to give his colleague a withering look. 'Ellis, you *are* ridiculous at times,' he said.

As Observer Czyzun was climbing wearily into his bed after his tour of night duty, Technician Travis was climbing just as wearily out of his. Feeling mentally drained and physically exhausted, he headed for the bathroom, there to refresh himself under a running cold water tap. It was as he was patting himself dry that he became aware of the irritating foreign body in his mouth. A probing tongue failed to dislodge it, but with thumb and forefinger he had more success. The cold night sweat returned in full force as he found himself staring in amazement at the yellow, three inch long strand of hair.

It was a full twenty minutes before he had recovered his wits sufficiently to check out his wardrobe. Here, he found a jacket and casual pair of trousers inexplicably damp to the touch. They hung above a discarded pair of stout shoes, unaccountably caked with mud. On the shoulder of the jacket he found a second strand of hair, identical to the first. The dream, it seemed, was assuming a concrete reality, as never before. Deep in thought, bewildered and perplexed, he lingered over his morning meal. Finally, he roused himself. It was time for him to try and get some answers, he decided.

Retrieving the strand of hair from his jacket, he placed it in an envelope, together with a covering letter, written with difficulty in an unsteady hand. Having sealed and addressed the envelope, he arranged for it to be collected and delivered by hand.

Grateful for the fact that he had a clear four days off work ahead of him, he abandoned his tentative plans for a short holiday in the country, and rested for the remainder of the day, sleeping fitfully late into the afternoon.

Early that evening, he received a reply to his letter of the morning. The covering note, which accompanied the information he had sought, read:

'Dear Richard,

I hope the enclosed is of help. Always glad to oblige, old man. I am *very* intrigued and hope you will enlighten me when next we meet up.

Of course, you may rely on my discretion. Still, wise of you not to use the normal channels of communication. A handwritten note, delivered by hand! How quaint! I am entering into the spirit of things by doing likewise.

Regards,
Carl'

The standard Medical Centre assessment form, duly completed, read as follows:

PATHOLOGY DEPT., LONDON COMPLEX Form A9/C
REF. NUMBER: ——————-
SUBJECT STATUS: ————-
SPECIMEN: Hair, with follicle
ANALYSIS DATA, as follows:
A) RACE: Group A1, Factor 10.
B) SEX: Female.

C) AGE: 20 years.

D) BUILD (disposition to): Slim.

E) HAIR (if applicable): Natural Blonde, not engineered.

F) EYES: Blue.

G) BLOOD GROUP: O, Rhesus positive.

H) GENETIC GROUP: D 24-2725-C, not engineered.

I) GENERAL HEALTH: Poor – advanced lymphatic leukaemia.

J) GENERAL OBSERVATIONS: Racial classification and genetic group indicate a young female from the Primitive Era. A more detailed analysis of the sample, particularly with regard to environmental contaminates, confirms this and gives a dating of 1800, plus or minus 20 years. How, then, does one reconcile all of that with a patently fresh specimen? For God's sake, Richard, there are living cells present within the follicle. I am mystified. Have you been making unauthorised trips on that transporter of yours?

Memories of the past, in particular his early days at London Complex, occupied the Technician's thoughts during the first three days of his short break from work. Exactly why this should be so he did not know, although he guessed that his forthcoming meeting with Controller Dyal was a factor, as was the knowledge that it was nine years almost to the day since he had been enrolled into the Student Faculty at London Complex as an eager, bright-eyed sixteen year old.

Memories of his first full day: one of a crowd of a hundred kindred spirits, gathered as one in the main assembly hall to hear the welcoming address of Principal Chantelle; his feeling of excitement, tinged with a slight apprehension, as each minute of waiting came and went; the odd reverential whisper on either side, as if he stood amongst a party of pilgrims gathered at some sacred shrine; finally, the address, itself – exactly the same year after year, he was reliably informed afterwards.

They had been carefully culled from ten times their number of applicants, they were told, in a tone of voice which seemed to carry with it a hint of reproach, as if they were responsible for the disappointment of the other nine hundred. This made them part of a privileged few, given the opportunity of playing a role in humanity's most audacious enterprise: to view the past as it *really* happened; to record, analyse, and evaluate it; to make the past serve the present, and in so doing shape the future.

The first year of the three year course would be devoted to General Studies, at the end of which time they would be individually assessed and assigned to a particular speciality. Some would be earmarked for the role of Observers, others would find a niche in Programming, or Linguistics, or Data Interpretation. A few – the most promising – would be designated Research Technicians. Almost inevitably, there would be some who would fail to make the grade at the end of the first year. These would be rejected outright, for there were no second chances on offer at London Complex. Principal Chantelle hoped that such rejects would be few in number.

The first year of study would be hard, they were warned, and years two and three would be more difficult still. Dedication, application, and sheer hard work were the three factors which would ensure success. If there were any present who had visions of an easy, comfortable, three year existence ahead of them, they had best think again, or pack their bags and leave that very day. London Complex was the original, and the best, of ten such establishments worldwide, with a proud tradition and reputation to uphold. Principal Chantelle was determined to see that the Student Faculty would play *its* part in upholding that tradition and in enhancing that reputation still further.

She wished all of them success for the future.

Just as vivid as the memory of that occasion was the recollection of the introductory tutorial given the following day by Head Tutor Couzens, one of the great personalities of London Complex, and a seemingly permanent fixture at the Faculty from one generation to the next. Edward Rossler Couzens, who, with an acid wit tempered by a kindly eye, was probably that very day set to launch himself into yet one more of his annual monologues to a fresh sea of eager, expectant faces.

Unlike Principal Chantelle's brief speech of welcome, the memorable content of that first ever tutorial address came back to the Technician well-nigh word perfect.

'The key to a proper understanding of Quantum Time Mechanics lies in a true appreciation of that most difficult of all concepts – the infinite.

'Ladies and gentlemen, we live in a Cosmos that is both eternal in time and infinite in space, a Cosmos of which our own vast universe forms but an infinitely small part; a Cosmos not of infinite possibilities but of infinite *realities,* some identical to our own but most vastly different.

'Now, just as the boundaries of matter are blurred and fudged, so, too, are the boundaries of reality. In both of these domains, The Uncertainty Principle is king.'

Pause to assess the reaction of the audience to these words.

'I see from one or two impolite yawns that I tell you nothing you do not already know, but I do so for a purpose. That purpose is to ask if any one of you has thought the matter through with respect of our work here at London Complex?

'No?...... no, I thought not. Very well, let me spell out some rather startling implications.

'The fact is, ladies and gentlemen, in the eighty two year history of London Complex no viewing monitor has ever displayed a scene from our own Earth's history.

'Yes, I know what the Principal said to you yesterday. In a very real sense that was loose talk on her part, as she would be the first to admit. We are all guilty of it here at London Complex, myself included at times. You may hear careless talk of observations of our past, or time travel into our past, but, in point of fact, such things are impossible. On the other hand, time travel to other realities, identical to our own, or observations of *their* past, well, that is a very different matter.

'So, what *exactly* do we do here at London Complex? To put it crudely, we set the controls, we switch on the viewing monitors, we press the appropriate buttons, and we begin to record episodes in the past history of one earth, chosen quite at random by The Uncertainty Principle, out of the infinite number of earths which exist in this infinite Cosmos of ours. It is never one's own Earth that the observer finds himself viewing – the odds against that possibility are infinitely high – but it is bound to be one virtually indistinguishable from it because the parameters of The Uncertainty *Factor* are so incredibly tiny.

'Does any of that matter from the point of view of our work here?

No, not really. The histories which we view differ from our own history to such a minute degree that, in effect, they are one and the same. So, for example, if the authorities ask London Complex to view some major unsolved crime, this we will do, and pass the information back. What we witness, of course, is the identical crime on some other earth, but the culprit is the same – has to be the same – in both realities.'

Another pause to see if everyone was keeping up, mentally. A few doubts on that score. For the present, no matter.

'If, as I say, none of what we have been discussing matters from a practical point of view, why do I lay such emphasis on the subject in this your first tutorial? Ten years ago I would not have laboured the point but the past decade has seen an accelerating research into a practical transporter – a time machine in the misguided jargon of the popular press when they do one of their 'in depth' reports. These past few years the project has been in the capable hands of Senior Technician Memmling, who will tell you that he has high hopes of attaining the goal of a fully functioning machine within the next few years. Tomorrow, you will meet with the man and view his embryonic machine, and I want no foolish, ignorant questions directed his way. Hence this little seminar.

'To avoid confusion and uncertainty, let us for the present adopt the popular jargon.

'You must understand that to the time traveller, as distinct from a mere observer, The Uncertainty Principle makes a *profound* difference. The former may, if he so chooses, go back in time and save the life of a friend killed in some recent accident, only to find when he returned to his own time that nothing had been changed. Why is that? Well, it is because the life he saved was not in his own reality – The Uncertainty Principle would see to that – but in some other. More than that, saving the life of his friend in another reality would mean that he could not even console himself by returning there at some future date. His actions, you see, have made that reality so very different from his own as to put it well beyond the boundaries of The Uncertainty Principle. Were he to make a second visit he would find himself in an unchanged reality, one in which his life-saving act had not taken place.

'In view of all that, the futility of attempting to change the past can be readily appreciated. We might change an infinite number of realities over a period of time, but that would still leave an infinite number unchanged, including, of course, one's own. Nor would it be possible to view any of these altered realities, let alone follow them up, because, once altered, it would be impossible to access them again. One would not even know if a particular reality change was ultimately for the better.

'In essence, all the time traveller is able to do is to change the present moment and, perhaps, influence the future of some other reality, but these restrictions should not be a subject of regret for it is The Uncertainty Principle working across an infinite number of universes which makes any form of time travel possible at all.

'Now I come to the final point on this subject. In view of all I have said, you may be wondering why we at London Complex are expending so much time, money, and resources in building a transporter. Hedged about with limitations and restrictions as it is, what useful purpose can such a machine serve? We have our window on the past. Is that not sufficient? To that question I would answer: no it is not sufficient; it is not sufficient by far. Can a viewing camera help us to restore the balance of nature by delivering up to us a single living thing from that vast host of plant and animal species lost to us in the past – plants and animals presently being genetically engineered at a painfully slow rate, and at a huge financial cost? No, for that we need more than a window on the past, we need a *transporter*. And what of all those men of genius whose lives were cut short in the chaos and barbarism of the Third Millennium? Would they not be better off here with us? We would certainly be a richer society with *them*. Can a camera bring a single one of them to us, in the here and now? No, indeed, but a working transporter may one day do so.

'All of that lies well into the future. There are immense difficulties to be overcome before such an ambitious programme of transportations can be implemented. The first ever transporter trip will be a very simple affair, and will choose itself. It will be pure science. Its aim will be to furnish proof positive of the workings of The Uncertainty Principle in a Cosmos of infinite realities.'

Little did the speaker realise at that moment in time that the man destined to furnish the proof of which he spoke sat not twenty paces away.

So it came about that in the fullness of time, long after Head Tutor Couzens was dead and all-but forgotten, the name of Technician Richard Travis had a familiar ring to every schoolchild.

The speaker now moved on to deal with other topics, but they need not concern us. Suffice it to say that every student filed out of the auditorium with a basic knowledge of the workings of London Complex, and a clear idea of what was expected of them in the days which lay ahead; but the closing sentiments of the lengthy address have a bearing on our story, and need to be set down.

They were words of warning and advice on Edward Couzens' part.

'Towards the end of your first term here you will see your first raw and unedited video recordings from the archives, the first of many in the years to come. 'Raw' is the word for not a few of them.'

A thoughtful pause to scan the row upon row of faces, as if to seek out the sensitive and the vulnerable.

'Now, it is one thing to read about massacres, and plagues, and famines, and all the vile behaviour of human beings at their worst, and it is quite another matter to view the reality. How to deal with that, as deal with it we must if our work here at London Complex has to have any value? When the spirit falters, and begins to fail, I can only advise that you remind yourself of the philosophy which has replaced all the old religions and which underpins our civilisation today. Pain and suffering - death itself - are for each of us but fleeting sensations in a perpetual existence within an eternal Cosmos. As such, they lose much of their significance. Let us, therefore, restrict our pity to this present reality in which we find ourselves, and not burden ourselves with the passing terrors of an infinity of others.'

Nine years on these closing words still constituted sound advice, as the Technician would have been the first to admit, but, in spite of that ready acknowledgement, he still found himself incapable of taking them wholly to heart. This failing on his part was a constant source of self-reproach and distress to him.

The defect had surfaced at an early stage, putting his future prospects at The Student Faculty in some jeopardy, but an ability on the technical side, which had astonished the teaching staff, was deemed to more than compensate.

'In my opinion, the most promising talent seen at The Faculty in a generation. I expect great things of this young man,' was Head Tutor Couzens' verdict at the end of the three year course.

'We have the brain, if not the heart. I suppose we shall have to settle for that,' was Principal Chantelle's grudging endorsement.

Edward Couzens was not to be disappointed in his expectations. His protégé's record in six short years after graduation spoke for itself:

Technician, 1st Class, at the unprecedented early age of twenty two years; Senior Technician in charge of the Transporter programme a mere two years later, after the untimely death of the great Memmling; the only man in the world to have transported himself into a different time period in another reality - all of this by the age of barely twenty five years.

Now, ten months on, another epoch-making adventure beckoned to the young Technician, an adventure which had its origins in long hours spent far into the night, pushing the boundaries of knowledge to new horizons.

'No, it is impossible,' was his chief's initial response to his 'outrageous' claim.

'I did not say The Uncertainty Principle is overthrown, only that it is possible to circumvent it in a modest way,' the Technician pointed out.

'You are telling me that a man may effect a reality change and return later *to the same reality* and view the consequences of his actions? No, I cannot believe it. The Principle is inherently immutable - we all know that. Why, you proved it yourself last year with the first ever transporter trip, to 18th Century Sussex.'

'Here is the proof of what I claim,' he had replied, handing over the bulky dossier of his research work. 'Check it out for yourself.'

Memories of their subsequent meeting a few days later.
'The Council meets a week tomorrow. I shall be there, as usual, and

intend to make a formal request to put the transporter into a state of readiness,' said Controller Dyal. 'I should be back here by noon. Report to me at half-past the hour and I'll give you their decision. In the meantime, Richard, take some time off - that's an order. You look all-in.'

'Will we get the necessary approval?' asked Travis.

'How can they refuse?' replied Dyal. He was resting the Technician's dossier on his lap as he spoke, instinctively stroking it as one would a small child.

The Technician nodded his head towards it.

'Glad you liked it,' he said, with a smile.

The morning of his fourth day of rest - the meeting of The High Council scheduled for the following morning, his appointment with Controller Dyal little more than twenty four hours away.

Surprisingly, he had for three days successfully contrived to set the dream, which was no dream, to one side, directing his thoughts and energies elsewhere. Chance, and a fresh discovery shortly after waking that morning was to change all of that. Now, in spite of his best efforts, the memory of it refused to go away.

The chance event came when a clumsy attempt on his part to replace a book in his library brought a second volume tumbling from the shelf, to lie open, spine-uppermost, on the floor. Cursing his clumsiness, he bent down to retrieve it.

'An Anthology of Classical English Poetry, Volume 3', he read. Turning it over he glanced idly at the open page, which announced: 'Pope, Alexander (1688 – 1744): 'The Rape of the Lock'. A two line stanza leapt out at him:

'Fair tresses man's imperial race insnare,
And beauty draws us with a single hair.'

Frowning, he turned to the glossary of 'difficult words' at the back of the volume and read: 'INSNARE – to catch in a snare; to entrap (commonly, ENSNARE).'

The unexpected discovery was the finding of yet another strand of golden hair, hidden away in a fold of his jacket.

For a full ten minutes after this discovery, he felt the need to study himself in the bathroom mirror, running a finger all the while over the outline of his lips.

Were these the selfsame lips that had matched the contours of her own – *really* matched them? he asked himself. 'But that is not possible,' he told himself, aloud. 'Perhaps the dream persists, even now, and I shall awaken soon.'

Turning on the hot water tap, he ran it until the steam came wafting up at him. Extending a finger, he put it in the flow of piping hot water.

This is no dream, the finger screamed back at him.

As if to reinforce the point, he stumbled over his shoes – *the shoes* – as he re-entered the living room. They had quite dried out, the encrusted soil from her grave crumbling to his touch and scattering itself on the floor.

The strangest sensation of all, however, was still to come. He had placed the newly found strand of hair on a microscope slide, the better to examine it. Placing an eye to the instrument, he focused on the follicle, and watched as the living cells danced their way across his field of view.

The experience sent a shiver down his spine. Lifting a troubled face, he stared into the distance.

'Who are you?' he pleaded. 'Who *are* you? Why do you haunt me so? What do you want of me? I am Senior Technician Richard Travis of London Complex, not Jesus of Nazareth. *I* do not bring people back from the dead.'

After such a troubled day it is not surprising that the dream returned to him that night, but this time there was a difference. This time, she came to him vibrant and alive from the beginning. She stayed with him but a moment, and the message she brought with her was short and to the point.

'If you want me, you must come and get me,' she said.

CHAPTER 2

The long days of waiting were over. Conscious of the fact that the appointed time had come and gone, he sat impatiently, fidgeting all the while. It came as a relief when the man finally entered the room.

'Sorry to keep you waiting. Only just managed to get away,' said Controller Dyal. Seating himself at his desk, he summarised his feelings. 'I don't know, Richard, I'm beginning to think some of the council members are past it, really I am. We seem to spend the first half-hour dealing with legitimate business, and the remaining hour and a half chewing the cud.'

'But not today, surely?' said Travis.

'No, today I would say it was half and half,' said Dyal, with a smile. ' "Any other business?" demands Chairman Vallis, doing his best to hurry things along. "Yes, one other matter", says I, "authorisation to put the transporter into a state of readiness". That put the cat amongst the pigeons, I can tell you.'

'And when the fur and feathers had settled?'

'Rest easy. We have the necessary authority to proceed.'

'Any dissenting voices?'

'On the question of authorisation, only Wendell's. "This is all very well", he pipes up, when I had said my piece, "but the fact remains that after twelve years of research and the expenditure of untold billions of credits we are still left with a transporter that does not transport".'

'That is hardly fair, or accurate,' said Travis. 'Does the man imagine I transported myself to eighteenth century Sussex last year by waving some kind of magic wand? I suppose he was referring to our long-term goal of the recovery of lost plant and animal species, but I believe we are close to a breakthrough on that score – a fact of which he and The Council are very well aware.'

'We need not concern ourselves with the man,' said Dyal, dismissively. 'His was a lone voice of criticism, as is often the case. No, the only real points of contention were what form the field trips should take, and whether you should be the one to undertake them.'

Travis gave a heartfelt groan.

'We went through all of that a year ago,' he said.

'True,' admitted Dyal; 'but to take the first point, I should tell you that there still remain a few voices which advocate a strictly experimental approach to the exercise.'

'Yes, an exercise which is going to cost the energy equivalent of sixty thousand hours of observation. Is this vast commitment to be made in order that someone may – what? – scratch his initials on some nearby tree and then return later to check that the mark is still evident? It's pathetic.'

'It would serve the purpose,' said Dyal, with a shrug of the shoulders. 'It would be enough to prove that one had returned to the same reality.'

'It would make for poor copy,' answered Travis.

Controller Dyal smiled at the antiquated turn of phrase. A year ago he had been obliged to ask its meaning. Now, he needed no such enlightenment. 'I agree with you, and so do most of the council members,' he said. ' "We have it in our power to capture the public's imagination just as surely as we did a year ago," I reminded them. "A strictly experimental technique may constitute good science, but it hardly makes for a riveting news story," I pointed out. That went down well, of course. "My God, but we could do with some favourable publicity," agreed Councillor Saunderson. "The space programme seems to hog all the limelight these days; why not us for a change?" said Tomassen. Don't concern yourself, Richard. Most of The Council are with us on this one.'

'Good. I'm glad that at least is settled,' said Travis.

'It was never *really* in doubt,' said Dyal. 'No, the real bone of contention was whether or not it be you who will undertake these two transportations.'

'There is no one who comes close to knowing as much as I do about the functioning of the transporter,' said Travis, abandoning for a moment his natural modesty in his eagerness to make his point. 'If there are any last minute gliches once the transporter is operational, who better to sort them out than me? Who, other than myself, has a successful transporter trip already to his credit?'

'And who is there we would less wish to lose?' said Dyal, quietly.

'Sir, I have worked long and hard to make this thing possible,' pleaded Travis. 'I believe I have earned the right to undertake this experiment personally. Am I now to be denied that right?'

'No...... no, The Council has fallen in with your wishes, but when your participation was put to the vote it proved to be a close run thing, and I have to tell you that a number of council members are not very happy with the outcome. As it is, The Council is insisting on two conditions being met with.'

'Which are?'

'First, any plan of action you may come up with must be as risk free as possible, if it is to find acceptance. There is no need for you to *court* danger, Richard.'

'The Space Programme is one of continual hazards and risks,' Travis pointed out.

'Yes, but risks which are, in the main, necessary and unavoidable. We are talking here of *unnecessary* and *avoidable* risks.'

'And who is to decide what is, or is not, an acceptable risk?'

'I am.'

'Same arrangements as last time, then?'

'In essence, yes. The Council is leaving the matter in my hands. I have the final say in what will, or will not be, sanctioned without the need to consult them further.'

Travis nodded, well satisfied. 'You spoke of a second stipulation,' he said.

'Yes, I was coming to that,' said Dyal. Here, he paused, the hint of a smile on his lips. 'The Council insist that you stick to the task in hand once you have left us. You are, for example, not to go pottering about some medieval English countryside handing out 31st Century cures to the sick and infirm.'

Travis stirred uneasily at this reminder of past transgressions. 'I freely volunteered that information when I returned from Sussex,' was all he could find to say in his defence.

'As you were duty bound to do,' Dyal pointed out. The hint of a smile was gone. 'Richard, you should not need me to remind you that if you had broken a leg on that little jaunt of yours and been unable to get back to your entry point in time the transporter link would have collapsed of its own accord at the end of its lifespan. You would have been left irretrievably stranded in the 18th Century. There is no such thing as a rescue mission in our line of business, as you well-know.'

'Sir, the chances of my breaking a leg ——'

'—— were remote, but not impossibly so.'

The smile returned in full-force as he studied the face of the crestfallen technician. 'Well, well,' he said, indulgently, 'that was all gone into at the time. Let us draw a veil over it now.'

His little speech of admonition and warning duly delivered, the speaker moved onto other matters.

'So, assuming as I do that you have anticipated The Council's approval all along, any idea where you may be off to this time? There is an abundance of archive material to choose from, of course.'

'Archive material? No, I think not,' said Travis. 'I believe it would be better if I concentrated on one of our current scans – one I can redirect and manipulate to get exactly the sort of case history I'll be looking for.'

'As you wish,' said Dyal. 'Let me see then. The London Station is working its way through the first decade of the 21st Century. That may do.'

'No, I would prefer to avoid London,' said Travis. 'Too crowded with people, and a bit too much activity on all sides for my liking.'

'Then, that really only leaves Provincial 3. Provincial 1 is Northumberland, last decade of the 8th Century, which is pure mayhem, and Provincial 2, Oxford 1140's, is scarcely any better.'

'Yes, I agree. I had more or less decided on Provincial 3 – Yarm, a small market town on the northern boundary of the old English county of Yorkshire. We are currently seventeen months into the 1810 to 1812 time scan.'

'Georgian England again? I might have guessed it,' said Dyal, smiling.

'It is a period of time I know almost as well as our own,' said Travis. There was a defensive edge to the tone of voice, which did not fail to register with the Controller. 'That will come in useful if I have to deal with any of the locals.'

'Yes, of course,' Dyal acknowledged. 'Provincial 3 will serve the purpose very well. A quiet backwater in a fairly settled period of time is just the thing. So, when do you propose to make a start?'

' As soon as I leave here. Why delay?'

'Why, indeed?' agreed Dyal.

'I would hope to come up with something suitable within a few days, which means I should have a case history to put before you within two weeks,' said Travis.

Having concluded matters to his own satisfaction, the Technician was impatient to be away, but it seemed as if his chief was disposed to talk a while longer. He had picked up the Technician's research dossier, which had been lying on his desk, and now sat thumbing through it casually.

'Memmling considered the possibility of doubling the potential of a transporter link in order to revisit a reality,' he mused.

'I did not know that. He said nothing to me,' said Travis, greatly surprised at this information.

'Well, he did no more than scout the idea on a couple of occasions when we were together. The stumbling block, as we all know, is an energy requirement a billion times greater than that involved in creating a simple two-way link. Your proposed modifications to the transporter will change all that.'

'The potential was always there,' said Travis, modestly. 'Reducing the carrying capacity of the transporter from an absurdly high figure to a modest two hundred kilograms was the key.'

'Memmling used to say that this absurdly high figure, as you put it, was an unavoidable extravagance, inherent in the basic equations.'

'Memmling was wrong on that score.'

'So it would seem,' acknowledged Dyal. He broke off to rummage amongst the papers which littered his desk.

'Ah! here we are. Nearly forgot. You may have need of this.'

Travis scanned the single sheet of paper handed him, and read:

SPECIAL AUTHORISATION
Controller Dyal to all London Complex personnel:
You are hereby ordered to render the bearer every possible assistance, and comply with any request made of you, reasonable or otherwise. This matter is to take precedence over all other work in hand.

Further, the bearer is to be allowed unrestricted access to all departments. Normal formalities in this respect are hereby waived.

The note bore the Controller's signature, and carried his rarely used seal of office.

'I think that's just about everything,' said Dyal, rising from his seat to see his visitor to the door. 'Contact Milo if you are in need of assistance in preparing a case history, and when that's done she will arrange a further meeting between the two of us.' He raised a cautionary finger. 'And remember: no unnecessary risks.'

Technician Travis was destined to occupy the Controller's thoughts a little while longer after his departure. A word of command on his part was sufficient to bring forth the computer data which he sought. Leaning forward, he perused the detailed information which comprised the Technician's personal file. The two 'page' record of service did not detain him nearly as long as the somewhat sketchy information concerning the young man's personal details:

PERSONAL FILE: LCA7628T (Sub-Section)
SUBJECT: Richard Marc Travis
BORN: London, 10. 3. 2997
PARENTAGE: Father, John Wyman Travis (deceased). Mother, Hannah May Travis, nee Tyler (deceased).
NEXT OF KIN: Aunt, Zara Eva Tyler; resident Penda, Wales.
EDUCATED: Westminster, Centre 7; Zeisler Foundation, Harrow.
PERSONAL STATUS: Single; unattached.
RESIDENT: London Complex campus.
HOBBIES/PASTIMES: Amateur Dramatics; Classical Music;
English Literature; Horse Riding. Acknowledged expert on Georgian England.
PUBLICATIONS: 'An Introduction to Quantum Time Mechanics';
'Everyday Life in Georgian England, 1714-1837'.

The information told Controller Dyal nothing he did not already know. Indeed, he was perfectly familiar with every detail of File LCA7628T but found it a never-ending source of interest, not so much for what it revealed as for what it inadvertently concealed.

Thus, the Technician's special interest in a period of history long gone was touched upon, but the few brief words scarcely did justice to the facts. There was hardly a facet of that period in time the young man had not studied and made himself expert in, from the language and culture, to food and drink, manners and customs, the law, costume, social etiquette, the arts - the list was near endless.

This interest was not altogether surprising, given the nature of the work at London Complex. Maye, Section Head of Programming, was well-known as an authority on Roman Britain, and Dyal, himself, had more than a passing interest in the early years of space exploration, but what was unusual in the Technician's case was the sheer depth and intensity of his interest, which at times amounted almost to a passion.

'It is our last glimpse of a settled age before the turmoil and upheaval of the next two centuries changed things for ever', was his not altogether satisfactory response when the Controller had once sought to probe the reason for this partiality.

Nor was this the only peculiarity of the Technician, Dyal had to acknowledge.

Here was a young man at the forefront of pioneering research, one who appeared superficially to be very much a product of the times, but who was, in reality, out of step with it in many respects. This showed itself in a number of ways, from his aversion to several aspects of contemporary life to his tacit rejection of many of the current values and standards. As an example, although many a person within the confines of London Complex experienced a degree of difficulty in treating with detachment the cruelties and suffering which were all too often played out on the monitor scenes, the Technician seemed to have a *particular* difficulty in this respect. While The Council may have swallowed the Technician's lame excuse for his unauthorised actions in eighteenth century Sussex - merely a whim on his part, he had claimed - the Controller, who knew the young man better than most, was not deceived. He knew that the Technician's motives went far deeper than this and were eloquent testimony to his irrational distress at the pain and suffering witnessed in a reality divorced from his own.

Then, there was another matter, of less significance, to be sure, but sufficiently intriguing to claim Controller Dyal's interest.

Technician Travis was a sociable animal, often to be seen in the company of young women of a like age, which made it all the more strange that the record showed not a single physical relationship of any consequence. It seemed that many a bright, young thing within The Complex had set their sights on the young man, only to be met with a kind but firm rebuff when the situation began to promise more than a mutual, friendly regard. Dyal was ready to acknowledge that the sexual appetite may vary from one individual to the next but a near nine year celibacy was altogether something else.

Enlightenment, of sorts, had come only recently to Dyal.

He had occasion to call on the Technician out of office hours, on a matter which could not wait until the morning. Situated less than a mile away from the workplaces of both men, it was, nonetheless, his first-ever visit to the young man's home. While the Technician busied himself with gathering together the documents which had necessitated the visit, Dyal occupied his time by idly wandering the large living room-cum-study.

It was, he thought, as if he had stepped into the past.

Antique bric-a-brac - genuine originals, he felt sure, - lay scattered about the room. In one corner stood a large, free-standing unit, displaying more printed books than he had even seen together in one place, outside of a museum of literature. The information they contained could have been stored on computer discs occupying one-hundredth of the space taken up, but it seemed that the Technician had a preference for the age-old printed word.

Occupying a much smaller space was a veritable library of recorded music, together with stage and cinema productions, stored on micro audio and video discs. In keeping with the books and bric-a-brac, very few of the productions appeared to postdate the 20th Century.

Some distance away, three old-style black and white photographs, each one set in a simple silver frame, sat atop an antiquated wooden sideboard. Two long-dead parents, either side of a very youthful Travis, complemented a second photograph of Travis the Technician, replete with traditional cap and gown, on his graduation day.

The central photograph was a mystery to Dyal. Looking squarely out at him was a strikingly attractive young woman, her dress and general appearance testifying to an age long-gone.

'Who is the young woman?' he asked, nodding towards the portrait.

The Technician barely glanced up from the task which occupied him. 'No one special,' he said.

'Some distant ancestor, perhaps? She must mean *something* to you,' persisted Dyal.

With a sigh, Travis put down his work. 'I told you, sir, no one special. Just a minor movie star from the early years of the cinema.'

'Really? Do I know of her?' asked Dyal.

'I doubt that,' answered Travis. 'She was never one of the 'Hollywood Greats'. Her name was Madeleine Carroll.'

To Dyal, the Technician's words of 'explanation' served only to deepen the mystery.

'Then, why have a picture of an obscure actress, dead these thousand years, in pride of......' He broke off, smiling, as realisation dawned. 'Ah! I believe I have it. It is a picture of the perfect woman in the eyes of Richard Travis, is it not?' He looked long and hard at the photograph, the long, blonde hair, amply-filled blouse, and single red rose held in the hand light years away from the present day female, with her shaven head, male dress, and mannerisms.

'If you are looking for that sort, you will have a long search ahead of you,' he said, indicating the photograph once more.

'Oh, I gave up on that years ago,' said Travis.

So there it was! Although perfectly willing to accept each and every one as a friend and equal, none of the Technician's female acquaintances held any *physical* attraction for him. How could they in the circumstances? It seemed that Technician Travis was out of step with the times even more than his Controller had imagined. The latter, however, in line with society in general, had no doubts concerning the status quo. Why should the present day female be obliged to dress and conduct herself in a manner which pampered to the historic prejudices of the opposite sex? Such was the general viewpoint amongst *both* sexes, but it was now apparent to Dyal that the Technician held a very different point of view. In a way, the revelation completed the picture for him. Here was a young man born out of time, with a brain wrestling with scientific problems in advance of the times, and a heart yearning for a lifestyle abandoned long, long ago.

It was only after he had taken leave of the Technician, and had made his way the short distance to his own home, that it occurred to Dyal just how alone the young man must feel on occasions. He had entered in to a chorus of welcoming voices, young and not so young, and the contrast between that and the quiet and seclusion he had just left was startling.

He judged that the young Technician deserved better. In his estimation, a more caring, kind-hearted fellow one could not wish to meet, and he was not alone in that opinion. He could only hope that, unlikely as it seemed, one day Richard Travis would come home to a household such as the one he had just entered.

In years to come Dyal would often console himself with that thought.

'Perhaps he has simply gone home,' he would tell himself.

The thought was a great comfort to him.

CHAPTER 3

While Controller Dyal was occupied with these thoughts, the subject of it all was threading his way between the varied landmarks of London Complex – past the group of buildings which housed The Random Sweep Station, even at that moment engaged in its task of seeking out promising material for future in-depth research; past the imposing edifice which fronted The Search Station, engaged, as always, in dealing with those still unsolved mysteries of the past; and beyond, to the quieter confines of The London and Provincial Stations. Ten minutes after taking leave of his chief, Technician Travis turned his back on a busy outside world and entered into the relative quiet of Provincial Station, Section 3.

It was a constant complaint of Simone Kennett, Section Head of Provincial 3, that administrative duties kept her all too often confined to her office, but the Technician found this was not the case today, and he was directed to the main observation room.

He found her in the company of her deputy, Kelly Ritter, and the Duty Observer, all three engrossed in front of the main monitoring screen in the building.

'Ah! the man himself,' said Kennett, at his approach. 'We thought of bleeping you, but knew you were in conference with the chief.' Her eyes shifted back to the image on the screen. 'Come and look at this, Richard,' she said.

'We are live, are we?' asked Travis, taking up a position alongside her.

'What? Oh, yes – eleven o'clock in the morning of May 18th, 1811, in the grounds of Grange Hall, about a mile south of Yarm.'

Travis watched as the male figure, back turned towards them, appeared to scrutinise the nearby landscape. He felt a twinge of disappointment at the sight. Were they set to summon him for *this*?

'The fellow's been checking out the boundary fences on his estate for the best part of the morning,' volunteered Ritter. He half-turned to the operator. 'Steady as you go, Czyzun. There's no need to reposition the scan just yet. I've a feeling the man's about to turn around.'

Even as he spoke, the figure on the screen obliging did just that, and Travis found himself looking at a strangely familiar face.

'He looks not unlike me, I grant you,' he acknowledged, 'but the human face doesn't have an infinite potential for variation, you know. We've all seen this sort of thing before.'

'Not unlike you! That's the understatement of the year,' exclaimed Kennett. 'Richard, it's obvious you're not an observer by training, or profession. Come with me.'

Travis followed as she began to lead the way to one of the many computers dotted about the room.

'I hear congratulations are in order,' she said.

'Yes, I got the go-ahead from The Council this morning.'

'And I believe you have our modest little section in mind for your source material?'

'Now, I don't know how you know that,' he answered. 'That was the 'news' I was bringing you. Really, Simone, I don't know why anyone bothers with the normal channels of communication in London Complex. People around here are quite capable of disseminating news at the speed of light without recourse to electronic gadgetry; but, yes, I thought I might have a look at what you've turned up recently.'

'The mortality listing would be a good place to start, if you are looking to change something along those lines.'

'Yes, I thought the same. Anything there that might suit, do you think?'

'You might fancy our Miss Sinclair – everyone else around here seems to,' she said, cryptically.

Before he could reply to this, they had reached their destination, and she was speaking again.

'Here we are,' she said. 'Now, watch this.'

A few brief words of command served their purpose.

'Sir Henry Richard Forres,' she said, indicating the head and shoulder portrait which filled the computer screen. 'Baronet, born 1785, unmarried, and with no real next-of-kin, apart from a much younger half-sister; wealthy, handsome by the standards of the time, and lord of all he surveys at Grange Hall.'

Travis conceded the point with a nod of the head. The still, close-up picture did, indeed, bear a striking resemblance to himself, more so than he had first thought.

'The likeness to yourself is uncanny,' she said.

'It's hardly that,' he protested.

'No? Still not fully convinced?' she said.

With a few further words of command, she eliminated the head of hair completely to match the Technician, toned down the somewhat ruddy complexion, and clinically removed a small scar on the left cheek of the subject.

Travis now found himself looking at his identical twin. He stared at the screen, unable to speak and incapable of looking away.

'He's close to your own weight and height, he has the same colour of eyes as you, and he's your age, give or take a few months. To cap it all, you even share the same given name!'

'Yes, I see it now,' he acknowledged. 'I have to admit that it's......
that it's......'

'*Uncanny*, is the word I believe you are looking for,' she said, laughing; 'but what I find really weird is that the fellow should surface now – not a year ago, or fifty years ago, for that matter, but *here and now*, right at the start of your search programme.'

The same thought had occured to the Technician. Not trusting himself to reply, he merely nodded. The feeling of unease and disquiet, which he had lived with during the past few days, began to grow in intensity. He had the strangest sensation that he was losing his freedom of action, that far from controlling events, *they* were controlling *him*.

He heard, as in a distance, Simone Kennett taking her leave of him...... 'must leave now, or would be late for a meeting of Section Heads'...... 'leave him in the capable hands of her Deputy, who would give him every assistance.'

He nodded, and motioned a distracted farewell in response. It was several minutes before he was able to compose himself sufficiently to start work.

A request for details of all monitored deaths in Provincial 3's programme to date resulted in the computer screening of twelve double-line entries - about one-third of the regions total mortality figure for the seventeen months in question, he estimated. He glanced down the list, mentally rejecting four instances where young infants were involved. Difficulty of access and possible complications in treatment were problems he could well do without, he told himself.

Finally, his eye fastened upon the twelfth, most recent entry. This read as follows:

'Item No.12. Name: Sinclair, Emma; Sex: Female; Age: 20 years; Date of death: 14th May, 1811; Cause of death: Indeterminate; Total of all recordings: 21/60 hours; Ref No: PR3/181105/K.'

So this was the young woman of which Simone Kennett had spoken!

A noncommital entry as to cause of death was unusual and invariably signified some obscure ailment, rare for the time period, about which the computer did not 'feel' competent to make a judgement. Unlike those in The Pathology Department, the computers in the various observation centres had no actual specimen, such as a blood sample, or body tissue, to aid them in their diagnosis - or a strand of hair, for that matter, thought Travis, with sudden disquiet.

She had given her name as Emma. That being so, was it possible? Was it *really* possible?

The total recording time for the subject in question – some sixty hours spread over twenty one separate observations - was another oddity. Perfectly well acquainted with the time period, the name of Emma Sinclair meant nothing to Travis. It was certain, therefore, that Provincial 3 had not been scrutinising some noteworthy celebrity, who could reasonably have been expected to attract this degree of attention.

A creeping unease came upon him as he stammered out a request for a close-up picture of subject PR3/181105/K.

With the picture came instant recognition. He had all but known for certain that it would prove so.

His eyes wandered their way across a face which had haunted him from childhood, finally fixing themselves upon the golden hair, a lock of which had strayed into his mouth when he had bent low to whisper in her ear. This was a young woman dead to the world for twelve hundred years - dead to the world but, seemingly, not dead to him. How was such a thing possible? he asked himself.

The picture was dated 4th June, 1810, and designated 'First Contact'. It was noted as being the first of two computer images, with the second one to follow. This usually denoted a radical change in the appearance of the subject whilst under observation and, accordingly, the computer would show both aspects.

Even as he watched, the picture changed. He saw the limp and faded hair, the compressed, bloodless lips, the eyes dull and listless in their sunken sockets. As Travis stared at the two pictures, flipping remorselessly one to the other, he was reminded of the lines of a still-remembered Victorian poem:

> 'Time, a maniac scattering dust,
> Life, a fury slinging flame.'

With a word, he terminated the painfully contrasting display and brought the mortality listing back onto the screen. Resting his chin in his hands, he paused to collect his thoughts. He would analyse the thing logically, if that were possible.

No man had the ability to take himself off in his sleep to another reality, there to have a *tangible* out-of-body experience. Could it be, therefore, that some being of immense power - some he, or she, or it - was directing events? The whole thing had all the hallmarks of a trap to seduce and ensnare him, but to what end?

'If you want me, you must come and get me,' she had said, but if he went chasing after her there was no knowing how it would end. The sensible thing to do, he knew, would be to put the matter to one side - to go to the archives and select a case history far removed in time and space from early nineteenth century Yarm. The only difficulty was that he *knew* he would not be capable of setting the matter to one side. He now thought of this strange and beautiful young woman almost constantly, in spite of his best efforts to occupy his mind with other matters. Left in peace this not surprising obsession on his part might ease in time but, realistically, he held out little hope for that. Far from tailing-off, her 'visits', if one could call them that, were coming with an increasing frequency.

There was no help for it, he acknowledged to himself. He would get no peace of mind until he got to the bottom of the mystery. His search for a case history was over before it had really began.

The worst aspect of it all was that he could not really unburden himself to anyone. The tale he had to tell was so fantastic, who would believe it?

Having thus resolved to carry on and see the thing through, he found himself drawing comfort from one particular feature. If the whole business was a mere device to entrap him in some way, it seemed to him to be a very obvious one, so much so that it ceased to be a trap in the accepted sense of that word. No, he told himself, this is no trap, it is...... it is...... He searched for the word. This is no trap, he concluded, it is an *invitation*.

Very well, he would take up the challenge, but he would not do so willingly. In spite of the fact that in his heart he knew he was out of step with the world in which he found himself, this was the world into which he had been born and where his duty and allegiance lay, and he had no wish to change it for some other. He could but hope that the 'invitation' was a kind and gentle one, and all would turn out well.

A concerned voice from behind him interrupted his train of thought, startling him with its suddenness.

'Richard, you look pale. Are you well?'

With an effort, he collected himself, and turned to face Deputy Section Head Kelly Ritter.

'I'm fine; a little tired, that's all. Perhaps I've been overdoing things of late. I've had a lot on my plate recently '

He motioned the man closer, and pointed out the final entry on the screen before them.

'No cause of death?' queried Ritter. 'Well, that's not as unusual as you may think it to be. I've seen it a number of times over the years. The computer doesn't always have a lot to go on, you know. Is it important to you?'

'That's not what I meant,' said Travis. Leaning forward, he pointed fixedly at the observation figures, which had so intrigued him. 'A lot of time and effort devoted to a relative nonentity, wouldn't you say?'

Ritter groaned. 'Not you, too,' he said. With a sigh, he pulled up a chair and seated himself next to the Technician. 'Sorry, Richard; it's just that I've had one dressing down already from Simone. That was two days ago and she's still making pointed remarks from time to time.'

'Yes, she floated one in my direction,' said Travis. 'Tell me about it.'

With a word of command, Ritter brought up the first of the two pictures which had so engaged the Technician's attention, and put it on hold.

'There's your answer,' he said. 'Quite a picture, isn't she? One of those faces that would be considered truly beautiful in almost any time period.' Leaving his seat, he moved to curve a hand along the hairline. 'Our own included,' he added.

'What on earth has that to do with it?' said Travis.

'Well, of course, it shouldn't have anything to do with it,' replied Ritter. He resumed his seat and leaned forward, conversationally.

'The public out there,' – here, he waved a hand up and away – 'and a lot of folk here at The Complex, for that matter, think an observer's job to be the most exciting thing in the world – a window on the past, with all that conjures up, under one's personal control. They're wrong, of course. Quite apart from having to view the varied crimes and follies of mankind as they are acted out, the work can be deadly dull, particularly here in Provincial. O.K., The Random Sweep and Search Sections offer work full of interest, but that's not the case with us. Here in Provincial the work can be very tedious, believe me. Petty local life, gossip and tittle-tattle, the great mass of ordinary folk doing the same thing day in and day out in order to earn their daily bread – all this we see. In spite of that fact it's all necessary work in that it enables The Complex to build up a complete picture of past life at all social levels. It's in everyone's interest, of course, to try and liven things up a little, and for that reason we spend a lot of time in and around the parish church, the local inns and hostelries, the homes of local celebrities, and so on. After all, if anything interesting, or noteworthy, is likely to take place it will tend to be in situations such as these. For the reason I've given, however, we are obliged to spend much of our time covering the ordinary, common folk, and here the work can be boring in the extreme.' He paused, awkwardly, before continuing. 'Unless, that is, a very attractive diversion turns up.'

'Are you trying to tell me that your bored operators have expended sixty hours observing a young woman simply because she happens to be pretty?' asked Travis. 'To liven things up a little, as you put it?'

'That's about it,' said Ritter, glumly. 'The operators stumble across someone like her once in a long while, linger longer than they ought to, and keep coming back more often than they should. Well, wouldn't you rather study someone like her than some pompous old prelate, or boring country squire? It's only human nature but, having said that, it shouldn't happen. It's a pure waste of time and resources, but it's not the first time it's happened, and I dare say it won't be the last. I have to admit, though, that this is an extreme example, not so much from the point of view of the time wasted but because...... due to the fact that...'

'Well?' asked an intrigued Travis. 'An extreme example due to what fact?'

'Half of the sixty hours were spent in the girl's bedroom,' said Ritter, visibly embarrassed at the information he was imparting.

Somewhat to his surprise, Travis experienced a pang of irrational jealousy, tinged with real anger, at this revelation.

'Good God, Ritter!' he exclaimed. 'Your operators ought to know that kind of thing is frowned upon more than anything else in our line of work. No wonder Simone was annoyed.'

'She was more than annoyed. When the full facts came to light she was furious. "What am I running here, the world's most expensive peep-show?" was her summing up.'

'You're supposed to oversee these things. A little careless of you to let it go on for as long as it did, wasn't it?'

'That fact has already been forcibly pointed out to me,' said Ritter in an aggrieved tone of voice. 'The fact of the matter is, much of the observation dates from earlier this year when Simone was away for six weeks on extended leave. I took over her role, as well as my own, and found myself with precious little time to oversee the operators. The day Simone got back I found myself seconded to Provincial 1 for two weeks. The upshot of it all was that the operators were left pretty much to their own devices for the best part of two months, within the general scope of the programme, of course.' The aggrieved tone of voice was growing with every sentence. 'I ask you, am I supposed to be in two places at once?'

'Well, I have no real complaint to make against you, or anyone else for that matter,' said Travis, soothingly. 'If I make Emma Sinclair my case history, as I've a mind to, then all of this other business will work to my advantage.'

'A little premature, isn't it?' said Ritter, very much surprised. 'Why, you've barely started on your research.'

'True,' acknowledged Travis, 'but at first sight it looks to be a promising case history. Of course,' he added quickly, 'if any real difficulties rear their head I shall have to look elsewhere.'

The Deputy Head seemed eager to agree with the choice, as well he might. Perhaps some of those many hours of contentious observation could be put to some useful purpose after all. That would go some way in mitigation, were his thoughts.

'What do you have in mind?' he asked. 'Restore the young woman to health on your first visit? Confirm you've returned to the same reality on the second visit by observing her alive and well?'

'Yes, that pretty well sums it up,' said Travis.

'But there's a difficulty, surely,' Ritter pointed out. 'We don't know what killed her. How can you effect a cure without knowing that?'

'Yes,' said Travis, carelessly, 'I need to confirm the cause of death to everyone's satisfaction.'

'*Establish* the cause of death, you mean,' said Ritter.

'What?...... Oh!...... yes, establish the cause of death,' agreed Travis. 'I'll have Central Computer study some of the more relevant tapes and shall be very surprised if it doesn't come up with the answer, and Surgeon Canazaar will let me have his opinion, if I bring him in on this. If both agree on the diagnosis, I think we'll be in business.'

'Richard, they are queuing up to use Computer 1,' Ritter reminded him.

'Then, I shall jump to the head of the queue,' said Travis. He brought out his permit from Controller Dyal and put it in Ritter's hands. 'That should open all doors, I fancy, both here and elsewhere.'

Ritter read it through before handing it back, smiling. 'It's hardly necessary here. You've credit enough with us, Richard.'

'Good! Now, a question and answer session, I think,' said Travis. 'Tell me, what do you have on Sir Henry Forres?'

'Very little, although we plan to change all that. The fact is, the fellow's been in the area for little more than two weeks. Moved here from Lincolnshire, we believe. We have a few distant snapshots of him that first week, so far off we didn't spot the resemblance to yourself, but then he took himself off on a week's fishing holiday and only got back the evening before you saw him just now.'

'And did he and the Sinclair girl ever meet?'

'There was hardly time for that, Richard. When he first arrived at Grange Hall, on May 3rd, she was in the final stage of her illness. He went off again on the 10th, and returned on the 17th, but she had died early on the morning of the 14th. He met the girl's mother, though.'

'Really? How did that come about?'

'It was on the 8th, if I remember correctly. We've only a distant glimpse of the meeting, which was out of doors. They seem to have met by chance, which isn't really surprising considering they were near-neighbours.'

'Were they, indeed?' said Travis. He was beginning to see definite possibilities in all of this, and a plan of action was already starting to take shape in his head.

'Yes, the Sinclair house bordered Sir Henry's estate.'

'A small, whitewashed cottage with a thatched roof?'

'Pine Tree Cottage,' said Ritter, nodding; 'but how the devil did you know that?'

'An educated guess,' said Travis, airily. 'Well, all those small, country homesteads were like that in those days, were they not?'

'No...... no, not really,' said Ritter, visibly puzzled.

Already beginning to regret his few indiscreet words, Travis hastily turned to other matters.

'Right! I think that's all I need to know for the present. For the future, I shall require copies of all your archive recordings which feature Pine Tree Cottage - as soon as you can, please. Send second copies relevant to the subject's illness to Surgeon Canazaar. I'll contact him as soon as I leave here and put him in the picture.'

'I'll get onto it right away,' said Ritter. 'Anything else?'

'Yes. I want to see what you have on Grange Hall and its estate. As for Sir Henry Forres, I shall need a lot more than you have on him at present. I want you to put him under constant surveillance until further notice. Send me each morning what you've gathered during the previous 24 hours.'

'Forgive me for asking, but is all of that really necessary? What has he to do with any of this business?'

'In one sense, nothing,' acknowledged Travis, 'but what if I were to tell you that I'm thinking of putting in an appearance not as Richard

Travis but as Sir Henry Forres?'

'Good Lord! There's a thought!' said Ritter, startled by the Technician's words.

'I've also a notion to force an entry into Pine Tree Cottage at night, in order to gain access to our Miss Sinclair.'

'Risky,' said Ritter, shaking his head.

'But what is the alternative?' said Travis. 'The biggest problem will be getting close enough to the patient to do the necessary. Put it this way, what would *your* reaction be if a perfect stranger came up to you and said: "Although you do not know it, I am here to tell you that you are in the early stage of a terminal disease, which if left untreated will one day kill you. I have here the remedy. Now, would you mind rolling up your sleeve so I may stick this needle in you?" '

'Yes, I see the difficulty,' said Ritter.

'So what is left? Hope to surprise her in some secluded spot, and overpower her? Bind and gag her? Drug her?'

'But surprising her in her bedroom in the middle of the night is hardly any better. The difficulties still remain.'

'Not if I leave matters until a few days before she is scheduled to die. By then, she will be too ill to put up any effective resistance. I shall find her bedridden and at my mercy. All of that means a forced entry at night on my part.'

'But the risks, Richard? Suppose you wake the household and are apprehended?'

'Well, the risk of discovery is there whatever course of action I decide upon, but I believe I minimise the danger by impersonating Henry Forres. Consider this: coming back to Grange Hall after a late night out in town, I spot an intruder breaking into my neighbour's house. True gentleman that I am, I come to the rescue, with no thought for my own safety. Alas, the fellow eludes me and makes good his escape, whereupon I enter the house to satisfy myself that no harm has been done, and to alert the family to what has happened. After a quick look around, I was about to raise the alarm when I found myself cast in the role of the criminal. There, how will that do?'

'It's a bit thin, Richard,' said Ritter, frowning.

'Well, possibly, but any defence is better than none. You do not know the time period quite as well as I do, Ritter, old man,' said Travis, smiling. 'You do not fully appreciate the authority and respect that a titled gentleman like Sir Henry Forres would be bound to command amongst the common folk. No one on the premises would *dare* to detain me against my will. Of course, if I continue in my ignorance of the gentleman in question that could prove a little embarrassing. I would be less than convincing if I couldn't hold an intelligent conversation if need be concerning Henry Forres, or Grange Hall and its estate. Hence my need to be fully acquainted with the man. Hopefully, it's knowledge I shall never be called upon to use.'

For a moment, Ritter was silent. Then, he nodded his agreement.

'It's ingenious, I'll say that,' he said, at length. 'Yes...... yes, I like it. Your physical resemblance to the Sinclair's next door neighbour is there for anyone to see. It would be a shame not to put that to good advantage.'

'My sentiments exactly,' said Travis, rising to go. He did so with a feeling of quiet satisfaction. After days of sitting about, brooding, it would come as a welcome relief to be able to occupy himself in a task which offered the prospect of some answers to the many questions which were plaguing him.

'There's no point in my being continually under your feet,' he said, as he took his leave. 'I can work just as well from home for the most part, but I'll probably drop in from time to time. I only hope we don't encounter any unforeseen problems. I really would like to proceed with this particular case history, if at all possible.'

'Oh, the young woman seems very suitable for you,' replied Ritter, doing his best to sound an optimistic note. 'I think there's every chance she'll prove the one for you.'

CHAPTER 4

During the following ten days Technician Travis immersed himself in a detailed examination of a veritable avalanche of video recordings which descended upon him from Provincial 3. Working ten, twelve, fourteen hours a day, he devoted the first six days to a study of Pine Tree Cottage and its occupants. The knowledge gained was in part encouraging, and in part disheartening.

As he had suspected, the young woman, Emma, give no sign in any of the recordings that she had ever been troubled by a recurring dream. It was clear to the Technician that the dreams were his dreams, were his alone, and she was at best no more than an unwitting participant. Recognition, a friendly greeting, and a trusting compliance on her part would *not* feature in their meeting. He was, therefore, left with no other choice but to come to her at a late stage in her illness, at a point in time when she would be too weak to resist him. More than that, it would have to be in the last few days of her life if his appearance on the scene as the new neighbour, Sir Henry Forres, was to have any meaning, or purpose. As an added complication, an examination of the recordings was to restrict his chosen time of arrival still further – to the last few hours of the patient's life, no less.

The first sight of a night nurse in attendance – a conscientious one, as luck would have it – had prompted a sigh of frustration from Travis. Arriving early, and leaving late, the old lady sat there, watchful and attentive, night after night. Then, suddenly, on the very last night she failed to put in an appearance.

The last night it would have to be, then, but this posed an unforeseen difficulty. At such a late stage in the disease, with the patient literally hours away from death, was a cure still possible? Were the wonders of 31st century medicine equal to the task? To his great relief, a few discreet enquiries brought reassurance on that point. A genetically engineered concoction of great potency could be manufactured to order. A mere twenty years previously such a thing would not have been possible, now it was. It was a very narrow margin of victory.

If the Technician's researches brought to light unforeseen difficulties, they also brought forth unexpected bonuses. The clear, moonless night of the 13th to the 14th of May, 1811, was admirably suited to his purpose, and all he could have wished for. A small copse of pine trees, not forty metres from the cottage, would serve as a perfect screen for the transporter's cone of light, and was more than he could have dared to hope for. At the rear of the property, the somewhat insubstantial back door and the primitive sash windows would have posed few problems to even the most inept of burglars. He could take his choice of either entrance. Best of all, the sole occupants of the house, apart from Emma, turned out to be just the mother - a sound sleeper, and somewhat hard of hearing into the bargain - and an elderly female servant, who slept in the attic bedroom on the second floor.

The earliest recordings had revealed a certain Peter Sinclair, this being Emma's younger brother, but the young man had taken himself off some months previously, seemingly to seek his fortune further afield. Certain it was, he was not at home on the all-important night in question.

Six days into his research, with his file on Pine Tree Cottage all but completed, there had come an experience both eerie and disturbing.

At the outset, Travis had studiously put to one side some thirty hours of recordings, which, he knew, served no other purpose than the sexual gratification of the viewer. These were the sensual bedroom tapes relating to Emma, which had so angered Simone Kennett and pained her deputy.

The very existence of the recordings was a flagrant breach of an unwritten law operating within London Complex: that voyeurism, as distinct from objective study, was beyond the pale, and rightly to be censured. It was a dictate drummed into every student from their earliest time at The Faculty, and scrupulously enforced at all levels within The Complex.

In one sense, the rule was strangely at variance with the practises of the Technician's own time. He lived in an era of permissive openness, in which the sexual act was counted as no more than an enjoyable biological function, but the rule was in place for a very good reason.

'A pure waste of time and resources,' were Deputy Ritter's words, but that was only half the story. Were London Complex to turn a blind eye to such practises it would set out on a very slippery slope, which could end in vast sums of money being expended on personal gratification, on triviality and bad taste, and on titillation that was anything but cheap. Indeed, it would be no exaggeration to say that the entire programme which London Complex had set itself could end up cheapened and debased.

As a responsible Senior Technician, Richard Travis could not fail to heartily endorse these sentiments, but he found, for all that, that it was no easy task to resolutely set to one side the recordings in question, such was the allure of the mysterious young woman who had entered uninvited into his life.

So it was that on the afternoon of the sixth day a passionate desire got the better of a sense of duty, which is no new thing in the way of the world.

The half-hour recording which Travis chose to watch was not picked out at random. A handwritten note which accompanied it read: 'What a curious incident! Of no significance, of course, but no less intriguing for that – Kelly Ritter.' The writer had not seen fit to elaborate further, which made his brief comment even more inviting to Travis.

The recording in question was dated to the evening before Emma's twentieth birthday, at a point in time when she remained hearty and well. Alone in her room late into the evening she made ready to retire for the night, oblivious of the all-seeing eye of the intangible camera which followed her every movement.

Slippers, dress, and undergarments were all removed in turn. For a brief moment before slipping on her nightdress, she stood naked before the dressing-table mirror. The well-developed breasts, and curving sweep of the body from waist to hips were visible proof, if any were needed, of a bygone era. The Technician's civilisation had long since abandoned the practise of natural childbirth ('messy', was Surgeon-General Canazaar's terse judgement on the forsaken practise) and some very necessary female attributes in this respect were being discarded at an evolutionary speed which had surprised the biology experts. How those same experts would have viewed the young woman before him Travis did not know, or care. To him the sight - no, the vision - was perfect, quite perfect.

Twenty seven minutes into the brief recording he had still not spotted anything amiss. She had seated herself in front of the mirror and was occupied in brushing her hair, the eye of the viewing camera so positioned that it looked squarely out at her from the mirrored surface. In truth, the instrument was badly positioned and in need of adjustment. The image which presented itself was one of extreme close-up, the head and shoulders of the subject filling the entire field of view, the eyes seemingly looking into the mirror, *and beyond.*

Suddenly, the picture froze, the hairbrush abruptly terminating its downward stroke, and bewilderment and fear written plain in the eyes of the subject. To Travis, it seemed for all the world that the young woman had sensed a presence, but that was impossible, he told himself, for there was no presence in the accepted sense of that word.

Yet the signs to the contrary continued. Clutching the crucifix which hung low around her neck, she gave a violent shudder, blew out the candle beside her with an impulsive puff, and hurried across to her bed, as if seeking sanctuary.

The whole experience brought to the surface yet another difficulty which the Technician wrestled with from time to time: how could one justify this invasion of privacy, this intrusion into an unsuspecting person's life?

It was true that a one hundred year exclusion zone operated, the recent past, in effect, out of bounds to London Complex. The prohibited time zone was strictly enforced and could only be breached by special sanction from the permanent standing committee which oversaw the functioning of all ten observation centres worldwide. Only the solution to some truly terrible crime, or the explanation for some mysterious, major disaster, qualified in this respect; but were the dead not entitled to their privacy during their lifetime? Travis asked himself at moments such as this.

He had once raised the subject with Samon Canazaar and that gentleman's reply was typically outrageous.

'Eighty percent of our work here at London Complex covers the Christian era,' he had pointed out. 'These people, whose privacy so concerns you, believe implicitly that they are being watched over every minute of every day and the record shows that inhibits them not one jot. As for your own feelings, just put yourself in the place of this god of theirs and you will have no difficulty.'

That night, before settling himself down to sleep, he relaxed with a bedtime book, the picture of an exquisite, naked Emma, sporting only a crucifix on a glittering chain still fresh in his mind. The golden age of English poetry was his favourite reading matter so it is not surprising that he chose the selfsame book which had tumbled from its place a week before. He opened the book at random and found himself looking once more at Alexander Pope's 'The Rape of the Lock.' Since the poem constituted no more than a tiny fraction of the anthology he thought this strange in itself, but stranger still were the first lines that his eyes lighted upon:

'On her white breast a sparkling cross she wore,
Which Jews might kiss, and infidels adore.'

He read no further. Closing the book, he switched off the bedside light and looked upwards into the unseeing darkness. Unlike Emma, he sensed no presence but still felt the need to voice aloud his thoughts.

'O.K., you win. There's no need to labour the point.'

On the following day Travis turned his attention to Sir Henry Forres, and took an instant dislike to the man.

The owner of Grange Hall had not been in his new surroundings beyond a couple of weeks before he had provoked a heated disagreement with one of his neighbours, a farmer by the name of Samuel Gibson. As far as Travis was able to judge, the fault lay entirely with Sir Henry.

The dispute centred on an area of land immediately adjacent to the Grange Hall Estate, known as Brow Rise. The fact that this had long comprised part of his neighbour's farm did nothing to deter Sir Henry from laying claim to it, producing in evidence documents either ambivalent or suspect to support his claim.

More objectionable than this in the eyes of Travis was the man's dealings with the several tenant farmers who leased portions of the Grange Hall Estate. Long-standing privileges and concessions were curtailed. Rents, admittedly held down for a number of years and now a little out of step with the times, were arbitrarily increased to the opposite extreme, with little mercy planned for anyone who defaulted.

A few poor folk resident on the estate, people who had subsisted mainly on the charity of the previous owner, were summarily evicted from their humble dwellings and left to wander the countryside destitute.

In all of this Sir Henry had the willing assistance of a little, sour-faced individual, who rejoiced in the singularly inappropriate name of John Smilie, this being the steward who had accompanied his young master from Lincolnshire. It was Smilie who had set the mantraps in the nearby wood, which resulted in the loss to one unfortunate poacher of a lower left leg.

To the staff of Grange Hall Forres was a hard taskmaster, and within a short time an atmosphere of gloom had descended upon the place, but it was that gentleman's treatment of his stepsister, full ten years his junior, which brought Technician Travis to a personal crisis.

Rachel Forres was a plain, unprepossessing fifteen year old, who acted out her life as if she was permanently conscious of that fact. This, in itself, seemed to call forth a contempt from Sir Henry to this shy and vulnerable creature. A painful-sounding stammer which afflicted the girl, and which Travis rightly diagnosed as an emotional problem caused largely by her stepbrother's treatment of her, seemed especially to infuriate him.

Yet, to the outside world, away from the confines of his estate, Sir Henry Forres presented a somewhat different picture. When he so chose the man could be pleasant and agreeable, and the initial judgement of him in town was not unfavourable. It was a widely-held belief that the previous owner of Grange Hall had been more than a little lax in the exercise of his authority. If the new owner chose to restore order and discipline to the estate, who could blame him for that? Certain it was that the arrival of a handsome, single young man, possessed of a large fortune, and master of his own affairs since the death of his father five years previously, caused a considerable stir in the district. Many a matronly eye was turned covetously in the direction of Grange Hall on behalf of a daughter of marriageable age.

The Technician's crisis came on the evening of Day Ten when he watched as Sir Henry, in one of his not uncommon drunken rages, meted out a savage beating to his young sister. After a moment's viewing, he felt compelled to silence the heart-tugging sound, and followed this by shortly afterwards terminating the recording before its ending. Never before had he been moved to do such a thing, and he could not help but feel wretched at his own inadequacies.

It was the old, old problem: his seeming inability to take to heart the concept of infinite realities, in spite of the fact that he was as certain of its truth as any man. In vain he reminded himself that he was viewing only the one reality, and in others, equally valid, a young Henry Forres was in his turn being cruelly treated by a bullying elder stepsister. The trouble was, as he had once pointed out to Head Tutor Couzens, imagination and philosophical argument have their limits. Certain it was that Travis found himself unable to derive much comfort from the visualised images of some inaccessible reality.

Staring at a blank screen, but with young Rachel Forres' screams still ringing in his ears, Travis came to a decision. He had done more than enough research and it was time now to call a halt.

It took him three days to sift through the accumulated data, collate it, and prepare a draft summary, at which point he contacted Milo Sands, Dyal's personal secretary, to enlist her help in producing a fully documented case history to lay before the Controller. A meeting with Dyal was subsequently arranged for the end of that same week, and another, later the same day, with Surgeon-General Canazaar. This done, he turned his thoughts to the one outstanding difficulty.

The plan of action which he was now set upon was, he was forced to acknowledge, not without risk to himself and although he would do his best to play these down there was a distinct possibility that the whole thing would be rejected, and he would be told to come up with an entirely different case history, something simple, straightforward, and less fraught with danger.

The plan he now devised to deal with this eventuality would, by its very nature, have surprised many who thought they knew and understood the Technician. The plan was both deep and devious, traits of character not generally associated with the young man but ones which he could employ if need be. In short, if his case history was rejected he would offer in its place a shocking alternative, which would make the first seem tame by comparison. Findhorn, 1743, would serve the purpose very well, he reckoned.

He had viewed this somewhat obscure and ancient recording some years previously, and had no inclination to sit through it a second time, but judged that it would be as well to go over it again in his mind. The memory of it came back to him in a fragmented sequence of vivid, still pictures:

The Setting: Findhorn, the Highlands of Scotland, 1743. The two schoolchildren on the highway leading out of the village, blind to the danger lying in wait for them at a bend in the road.
The Danger: A shadow too solid...... eyes yellow and crazed...... muscles taut for the spring.
The Attack: A furious onslaught...... the panic and terror...... death a welcome relief.
The Feasting: A tearing of young flesh...... grating teeth upon bone...... a crimson grass carpet.
The Howling: Howls to no purpose...... sad song to the moon...... a lonely farewell.
The Aftermath: The hunter now hunted...... a turning at bay...... death and a trophy.
The Sequel: The last of his kind......the end of an era...... a wilderness tamed.

Yes, Findhorn, 1743, would do very well, he thought, and quickly put the images out of his mind.

The meeting with his Controller went as Travis had feared it would. The Technician's carefully prepared proposals met with an outright rejection.

As far as Dyal was concerned the matter was easily decided. The plan put before him involved breaking and entry at the dead of night into a house occupied by three people – but did not the Technician know that in those days burglary was a felony, and as such a capital offence? As if that wasn't enough, medication would have to be administered to a conscious and unwilling patient. And what was all this nonsense about Travis taking the place of one of the locals? He appreciated that the Technician had to look like one of the natives, but what was wrong with a little cosmetic surgery, easily reversible, similar to that employed the previous year for the Sussex Experiment?

In vain Travis attempted to counter these objections, as he had done once before in his conversation with Kelly Ritter, laying particular stress on the fact that in putting in an appearance as Sir Henry Forres he was using to advantage a most remarkable coincidence.

The Technician's arguments fell on deaf ears. Controller Dyal, unlike Deputy Section Head Ritter, was not to be persuaded. He regretted the time and effort that the young man had put into this particular case history, but he did not like it, and he would not sanction it. The Technician would have to go away and come up with something different. He reached for one of a number of computer printouts, which lay on his desk waiting his attention. The interview was over.

'I've prepared the outline of a second case history,' said Travis.

Dyal looked up, a little warily. 'When and where?' he asked.

'1743 – a quiet, secluded spot in the Scottish Highlands.'

'That sounds better,' said Dyal, nodding in approval. 'Tell me more.'

'It's a tragedy involving two children, which I would hope to prevent. I would come into contact only with the children, and the whole affair could be settled in no time at all.'

'Now, that's more like it,' said Dyal, encouragingly. 'Put it all together and we'll meet again to discuss it in detail.' He turned back to his work.

Travis lingered for a brief moment before getting up to go. Was the man going to leave it at that? he was asking himself. At the doorway he paused once more. Was he going to let him leave just like that? It appeared he was. Well, it did not really matter, were his thoughts. It would all come out in due course, but it would have been nice to have it settled here and now.

He was on the very point of leaving when he was called back.

'Oh, Richard, I suppose I should ask: what was the nature of this tragedy? What happened to these two young children?'

Travis spoke in a matter-of-fact tone of voice as he turned and walked back into the room. 'It's an interesting story,' he said. 'They were waylaid by a wolf, which killed and ate them.'

Dyal stared at him, as if he doubted what he had just heard.

'Are you serious?' he asked.

'Perfectly so,' said Travis.

'You are telling me that a wolf escaped from some zoo, or menagerie, and then proceeded to kill and eat two children?'

'It wasn't a captive wolf, sir. It was a native British wolf, roaming free.'

'I didn't know they had wolves in Scotland as late as 1743,' said Dyal, wonderingly. 'I thought they were gone centuries before.'

'Well, it *was* the last one, as far as we know, although the species lingered on in Ireland for another twenty years. Totally out-of-character, of course, for that much maligned animal but that's probably because it *was* the last survivor. The wolf is a social animal, and the absence of others of its kind to form a pack, even one solitary female for a mate, would drive the creature to take desperate, almost suicidal —.'

Dyal interrupted him with an impatient gesture.

'Let me get this straight, Richard. You are proposing to go back there and put yourself between this...... this crazed animal and its two victims. You wouldn't be allowed to take a weapon with you, of course, but I suppose you could always wave your arms at it in the hope of scaring it away. If that fails, and assuming you are still on your feet, you might resort to throwing stones at the animal.' The tone was sarcastic in the extreme.

'You overstate the difficulties, sir,' said Travis, imperturbably. 'A number of options would be open to me. For example, I could use a sonic disabling device. With that I could —.'

Another interruption: 'No! No! This won't do at all. How do you know what the animal's response will be, given its state of mind? I'm amazed that you're putting this forward as a serious proposition. It's worse than the first plan, far worse. You must see that.'

Travis drew a deep breath. Now was the time for him to put to good use all those skills developed in his hobby of amateur dramatics. The special relationship which existed between Controller Dyal and his favourite technician was about to be put to a severe test. Not without some misgivings, he launched into his calculated outburst.

'Really, sir,' he said, 'if every proposal I put to you is to be ridiculed without a fair hearing, I wonder you seek my services in this business at all.' He give every appearance of being angry and upset, the voice carrying a bitter tone, quite out-of-character with the speaker.

The Technician was not yet done.

'Why not pay a visit to The Faculty?' he suggested. 'I dare say you could find some student willing to take my place. Have him transport himself somewhere, run up a white flag, and then return an hour later to check it's still flying. The only thing is, don't expect *me* to carry out the necessary transporter modifications to make it all possible.' The sentiments expressed bore all the hallmarks of a barely suppressed fury.

It was a shockingly impudent speech, which should have merited the severest censure, and Travis was inwardly relieved to see that his chief's reaction was one of amazement, rather than anger. Was this the pleasant, easygoing young man who endeared himself to all he came into contact with? Dyal seemed to be asking himself. The outburst was *so* out-of-character that the Controller seemed almost to take it for granted that he, himself, must be at least partly to blame. While he recognised the threat of non-cooperation as an idle one – the Technician was in the employment of London Complex and as such was duty bound to follow orders like everyone else – it was brought home to him at that moment in time just how much London Complex had need of the young man who stood before him, and not as a reluctant and coerced individual but as a willing volunteer, eager to do his best.

The rebuke when it came was mild and conciliatory.

'Richard, be reasonable. You must understand my position in all of this. If anything should go badly wrong it is I who shall have to shoulder the responsibility. I know the safeguards which The Council insist upon must be irksome to you. Perhaps they would be less onerous if we did not place so high a value on your head.'

He reseated himself opposite the Technician and studied the young man's face. The aggrieved look was still very evident.

'I'm sorry, sir,' said Travis, giving all the appearance of not being in the least sorry, 'but we had a similar tussle a year ago arguing the merits of the Sussex Experiment. It all worked out fine when it came to it, just as I said it would. Quite frankly, I'm getting more than a little tired of it all.'

There was a moment's silence before Dyal, with a sigh of resignation, picked up the dossier which he had so recently discarded.

50

'All right, Richard, let us return to plan 'A',' he said. 'Perhaps, as you say, I didn't give it a fair hearing. Talk me through it. What were you saying about turning some of the apparent drawbacks to your own advantage?'

'Well?' asked Milo Sands, looking up from her work at his approach.

'It's all systems go,' said Travis, smiling.

'Really? Well, you do surprise me,' she said. 'He's never stopped grumbling about your case history since he first clapped eyes on it yesterday morning.'

'Well, I managed to convince him of its merits,' he said, happily. 'But I want to thank you for all your help in preparing my case history. I know how much work you have on at present, and I'm grateful.'

She cupped her chin in a hand, and looked at him, evenly. 'That's all right – anytime. You know you've only got to say the word and I'd drop everything for you.'

He caught her meaning and blushed, which was just the affect she had sought. Hardly anyone felt the need to blush anymore in their open, free and easy society, and this was just one of several of the Technician's quaint habits which she found delightful.

'I can't imagine how you managed to get his approval,' she said, with a shake of the head.

He told her about Plan 'B', put forward for just the one purpose, and she contrived to look both amused and surprised at one and the same time.

'You have a devious streak, Richard, which I would never have supposed was part of your make-up,' she said. 'Mind, I don't know you *that* well, in spite of several valiant attempts on my part to rectify that situation. Of course, if Sir ever found out how he had been duped he would be very angry – probably withdraw his approval for Plan 'A'.'

'Yes, I rely on your discretion,' he said, uneasily. She had a strange look in her eyes.

She had leant back in her chair, her hands clasped behind her head, and a half-smile playing on her lips.

'You've made a tactical mistake, you know, Richard. You've told me all about your little piece of subterfuge without first securing my pledge of secrecy.' She paused to eye him speculatively, the tip of her tongue tracing the outline of her lips. 'What's my silence worth to you?' she asked; 'and I'm not talking of money.'

'This is blackmail, you know,' he said, giving a poor imitation of a smile.

'Certainly it is.'

'I can't believe you're doing this to me.'

'I haven't done anything to you – yet.'

'I'm awfully busy just now,' he said, lamely.

She turned back to her work, laughing at his discomfort.

'Relax,' she said. 'I'm only joking.'

She shot him a glance to note his reaction.

'Well! you needn't look *quite* so relieved about it,' she said, crossly.

CHAPTER 5

The year after Richard Travis graduated from Faculty Samon Canazaar became, at the age of thirty two years, the youngest ever head of London Complex's Medical Section. A hugely talented but unconventional individual, Canazaar was not well-liked by colleagues and acquaintances. A conceited, intolerant disposition, coupled with blunt-speaking to the point of rudeness, served only to antagonise. Not that the Surgeon-General concerned himself on that score. With an unshakeable belief in his own superiority, the opinions of others were as nothing to him.

Despite these many failings, the man had a genuine respect for proven talent and ability, qualities which he was quick to spot in the young Technician. A grudging admiration had developed over the years into a genuine affection, based perhaps in part on an attraction of opposites. For his part, Richard Travis, unconventional himself in several respects and always ready to think the best of people, saw beyond the intimidating exterior of the man to a softer, kindlier nature beneath.

His garrulous greeting to the Technician was typical of the man.

'Ah! Richard, it's you. Got the go-ahead, I hear, against all the odds. You've just missed Murrell, our esteemed head of Search Section, so it really would seem to be your lucky day. In the fellow comes, full of complaints, as usual. "I don't know why Richard felt the need to go to Provincial", says he. "We could have found him a much more suitable case history. After all, that *is* our speciality".

' "Speciality, my arse", says I, as I booted him out of the door. "You people in Search couldn't find a skunk in a perfumery." '

There was a momentary pause for breath before: 'So, how did you find our lord and master today? How fares the old donkey? Still trotting back and forth between his office and that collection of old farts who masquerade as our council? I haven't seen him in three weeks, and don't want to. Had a blazing row last time we met, you know, and really lost my temper with the man. He told me at one point that he had never been so insulted in all his life. I said if that was the case he must have led a very sheltered life, and I urged him to get out more. He had the nerve to call me anti-social – *me*, of all people! I put him straight and told him: "I'm not anti-social; I just don't like people, that's all." '

'He gave me this, which I suppose you ought to see,' said Travis, handing over Dyal's authorisation permit.

Canazaar read it through with an ill-concealed contempt.

'Typical! Bloody typical!' he exclaimed. 'You've no doubt noticed that it doesn't even bear your name, so if you were to lose it any Tom, Dick, or Harry, could take possession of it and claim it as their own.' He paused, thoughtfully. 'But what a weapon in unscrupulous hands! Be a good chap and loan it me when you've done with it. It may bring me some long overdue authority and respect around here.' He handed it back with some reluctance before resuming his monologue.

'Anyway, enough of all this. I'm a busy man and can't sit here half the day listening to you rattling on. Let us turn to the business in hand.'

So saying, he produced the dossier which the Technician had forwarded a few days previously and extracted two photographs. He tapped the top one with an index finger. 'Now *this* I like – Emma Sinclair, prettiest thing in a bonnet I think I've ever seen.' He glanced at the second, painful, photograph. 'Not so keen on this one, but if all goes well you're going to change all that – in the one reality at least.' He give an expressive sign. 'Now, why don't they breed them like that anymore, Richard? What do we have today? Conformity, uniformity and equality gone mad – that's what we have. We are breeding out the gender differences in our laboratories, and are on the road to becoming a species of hermaphrodites. Are you and I the only two people in the world who find that objectionable? No, I cannot believe it. Someday sanity will be restored. In the meantime, just be thankful that there are some things the powers that be cannot legislate against. The sexual drive, passion, love, and, yes, lust, too, if you like, are still potent forces and long may they remain so.'

A perfunctory knock at the office door interrupted this flow of words, and heralded the appearance of a young woman bearing a tray of coffee and biscuits. Travis guessed this to be the Surgeon-General's latest personal assistant, one in a long line of such people over the years. A fairly recent arrival, this was his first sight of her. She had made her appearance dressed in a decidedly feminine skirt and blouse, a sufficiently rare sight within London Complex to arouse the

Technician's curiosity.

'Oh, yes, you're not hallucinating. She's real enough,' said Canazaar, noting his friend's interest. 'Give her a quick prod in a few strategic places if you don't believe me.'

'He gets worse, doesn't he, Richard? I may call you that, may I not?' she said. 'It's that sister of his he lodges with that I feel sorry for. We only have to put up with him forty hours a week; she, poor thing, has to endure him all the rest of the week. You'll have noticed he's in a particularly foul mood today. That's because he was made to do some very necessary work in the garden yesterday, something which he hates. Understandable really. He's truly the world's worst gardener – even his weeds grow stunted.'

This said, she began to study the large desk at which the two men sat, looking in vain for a vacant space. With a shrug, she set down the tray in the middle of the floor.

'Just look at the mess, Richard,' she said, indicating the clutter around and about. 'Most of this stuff just seems to sit here from one week to the next, and on no account is one allowed to move things, or tidy up.' She rounded on the cause of it all. 'I thought you said the other day that you were going to tidy things in here?'

'I have,' he protested.

'And is this the best that you can do?' she asked, casting a scornful eye around the room.

'Without making an effort, yes it is.' He waved a hand, impatiently. 'Never mind that. Have a look at this young woman and give us your opinion.' So saying, he handed over the two photographs from the dossier.

She viewed them side by side. 'Yes, I have it,' she said, after a moment. 'These must show your previous secretary, before I started my sentence here. The first one shows her on the day of her arrival, all bright and bushy-tailed, and the second one looks to have been taken about a week later.'

'Do you see what I have to put up with, Richard?' asked Canazaar, appealing to his friend. 'There's no respect for one's elders and betters these days. That's gone out of the window like everything else.' He turned back to his young assistant and pointed to the two photographs in her hand. 'This is only the young lady whom our friend here plans to pluck from the jaws of death. It's all part of his plan to save our Universe – or some such thing.'

'But what is our Universe in the scheme of things?' she replied, with a shrug of the shoulders.

'True,' said Travis, smiling.

'There's no pleasing some people,' said Canazaar, but his words fell on deaf ears. The first of the two photographs was now being scrutinised intently to the exclusion of everything else.

'I feel I should know this young woman,' said his young assistant, talking quietly, as if to herself.

'Would that *I* did,' said Canazaar, taking the photograph from her. 'Now, here we have a *real* woman: pretty, charming, obliging, too, I have no doubt, and above all else, *feminine*. Why can't we have a few of her type around this place?'

'You never thought of taking another partner after Lycia died?' asked Travis, who had sat for the most part silent throughout these exchanges.

Canazaar looked at him in surprise. 'Lycia didn't die,' he said. 'Who told you that? She buggered off and left me – went to Australia.'

'Well, I only got the details third or fourth hand. You never talk of her. It was all before my time here, of course, but I always believed she died not long after the two of you got together.'

'Only spiritually,' came a voice.

'It was fine in the beginning,' mused Canazaar, ignoring this remark. 'I remember our first real date together. We went out for a meal and a few drinks – well, more than a few, actually – and at the end of it she said...... well, can you guess what she said?'

'Time to go? Hand me my white stick?' came the same teasing, playful voice.

Travis stirred uneasily. In all his years at London Complex he had never been witness to such verbal liberties directed against the Surgeon-General. There were few, if any, persons in The Complex who would have dared to speak so, even in jest. To his surprise, however, the gentleman in question merely smiled indulgently and resumed speaking.

'She said: "I've never met anyone like you before." '

'Well, I suppose her luck had to run out sometime,' said his young assistant.

'She had a strange, faraway look in her eyes while she was speaking, which told me she was —-.'

'Pissed?'

'—- in earnest. There and then I proposed a permanent arrangement, whereupon she promptly —-.'

'Threw up?'

'—- agreed.'

'There you are,' said the mischief-maker, turning to the Technician. 'I guessed right.'

'For her part, it was love at first sight.'

'Well, that much is obvious. She was hardly likely to have said 'yes' after a second look.'

'But after that it all turned sour,' sighed Canazaar.

'Probably the next morning when she'd sobered up.' She paused to glance a little apprehensively towards the exit, which lay some way beyond the butt of her jokes. 'Well, I have to go,' she said. 'I can't stay here all day exchanging pleasantries with you two.'

She edged her way warily past her chief, but could not save herself from a resounding whack on the rump. To Travis, the resulting squeal of protest sounded distinctly half-hearted.

'Seven-thirty tonight, your place,' said Canazaar. 'You owe it me after this afternoon's performance.'

'Me and my big mouth,' she groaned.

'And don't you dare effect a change of clothing when you get home,' said Canazaar. 'Leave the blouse and skirt on.'

'Do I have to?' she protested. 'I've never worn this kind of stuff before and I feel strange in it. I'm only wearing it today to please you two characters. It's all borrowed. Milo will want it back.'

'Not today she won't,' said Canazaar. 'From tomorrow I suppose we'll be back to that old boiler suit of yours.'

'You're right there,' she said. 'It's bloody draughty down below, I can tell you.' She lifted up the hem of her skirt. 'Are you sure I'm not supposed to wear anything under this thing?'

'Positive,' said Canazaar, with all the conviction he could muster.

With a nod of doubtful acknowledgement, she left.

Getting to his feet, Canazaar began to occupy himself with clearing a space on his desk for the coffee tray, which still reposed on the floor. Carrying an armful of computer discs across the room, he proceeded to dump them on top of his personal computer. Already piled high to begin with, the mass of material began to shape itself into a tottering mountain. As if in response, the computer control light began to blink balefully.

'Well, what do you think of young Rachel?' he asked, over his shoulder.

'I think you've taken a shine to her,' said Travis.

'Is it that obvious?' said Canazaar.

'She is certainly very free and easy in her manner to you,' Travis pointed out. 'You're the last person in the world to allow such latitude, especially in a junior.'

'The girl has spirit, which is more than I can say for the zombies I normally have to deal with. Besides, we have an arrangement the two of us. She says what she likes to me, and I do what I like to her. I suppose you could say she has the best of both worlds, but that's my generous nature for you.'

'Ah! I wondered what that was all about when she was leaving just now. Actually, I've been looking forward to meeting her ever since Milo Sands mentioned her name in conversation a week or so back.'

'Oh, why is that? Know the family do you?'

'No, nothing like that. It's that name of hers: Rachel Forrester.'

'You've lost me,' said Canazaar.

'My double in this other reality I intend to visit goes by the name of Henry *Forres*.'

Canazaar give an indulgent smile. 'Forres – Forrester; close, but not an exact match. It's hardly an earth-shattering coincident, Richard.'

'He has a half-sister by the name of *Rachel* Forres.'

'Now, that is odd,' said Canazaar, suddenly interested. 'Odd, but no more. It's pure coincidence – has to be. But having aroused my curiosity, enlighten me. How do the two compare? Anything like each other?'

'No, not in the least,' said Travis. 'Not unless you count your young assistant as plain, ungainly, and shy to the point of embarassment.'

'Hardly,' said Canazaar, laughing at the picture painted. Reseating himself, he viewed his friend thoughtfully over the top of his coffee cup.

'You look tired, Richard,' he said. 'I suppose you've been pushing yourself too hard, as usual. Relax! Unwind! Grab yourself a bit of happiness now you have the chance. This Sinclair girl is enough to turn anyone's head, and yours more than most. Why not take your screwdriver, or your can opener, or whatever it is you *do* take to that damn transporter of yours and finally fix things so you can bring her back with you. If she has an elder sister, or a younger one for that matter, bring her along, too, and I'll look her over. Mind you, I can't give any promises in advance. A man like me is bound to be a bit choosy.'

'Oh, yes, the chief would love all that,' said Travis, laughing.

'Fair enough,' said Canazaar, 'but let me persuade you to unwind for a few hours at least. Fancy a foursome tonight? You could bring Milo along with you.'

'Thanks for the offer but I've too much on at present.'

'But you could spare one evening off, surely?'

Travis shook his head. 'Maybe some other time.'

'You always say that, but there never *is* another time. What is wrong with you, anyway? You could take your pick of any woman in The Complex but you act out your life like some bloody old-time monk. I know the presentday female is not to your liking, and I share your feelings to a degree, but they're all we've got, bless 'em, and not all of them have totally abandoned their femininity. Milo is a good example of that.' He shook his head, disapprovingly. 'The way you treat that poor woman is a disgrace. She runs after you, cossets you, wipes your nose for you, and what does she get in return? An occasional pat on the head, by all accounts. I understand she has gone out of her way to help you with your case history. I suppose you'll thank her by throwing your inhibitions to the wind and giving her a quick peck on the cheek.'

'Now you're making me feel guilty,' said Travis, the memory of a certain conversation, little more than an hour previously, still fresh in his mind.

'You should show more consideration for other people, as I do,' said Canazaar, appropriating four of the five biscuits which accompanied the coffee.

'Anyway, enough of this. It's time we got down to business,' said

Canazaar. He picked up the Technician's dossier and tapped it with the palm of his hand. 'Right! You want to know the nature of this young woman's illness? Well, it's lymphatic leukaemia, I'm sure. That name probably means nothing to you since it's just one of over three hundred types of cancer, the vast majority of which we've all but eradicated today. Now, on the rare occasions that we encounter it, it's no more than a seven day irritant with proper medication, but it was a different story twelve hundred years ago. In those days the disease went unrecognised, and was left to run its inevitable course. How this young woman contracted the disease is anybody's guess, but I'm told that the region in which she grew up has a slightly higher than average level of natural, background radiation, which I think is suggestive. Of course, there's no such thing as a safe radiation level, in spite of what those idiots back in the Nuclear Age used to say. What is a perfectly safe level for one person is a potentially lethal dose for another. It's all a question of the body's natural tolerance, which varies enormously from one individual to another and, indeed, from one organ to another in the same body. I'm speaking of I.G.R.M., of course.'

'I.G.R.M.?' queried Travis.

'Inherited Genetic Repair Mechanism – the ability of the body to repair for itself damaged, pre-cancerous cells. Anyway, enough of these technicalities. The problem we face is how to effect a cure in this particular case. Bloody difficult, just about sums it up. You're leaving it awfully late in the day, Richard.'

'I don't have a lot of choice in the matter, as I explained in my covering letter,' said Travis.

'Yes, I appreciate your problem,' said Canazaar, 'and don't worry, it's not an insurmountable obstacle, although I have to admit that it severely restricts the options open to us.'

With these words, he produced a small wooden box, which he opened to reveal an antiquated hypodermic needle and a small glass phial of clear liquid.

'It has to be an old-fashioned intravenous injection, I'm afraid. No other possible technique would suffice at such an advanced stage of the disease. The whole box of tricks, apart from the drug itself, comes courtesy of the Medical Museum. They'll show you how to use the hypodermic, and with a bit of practise I dare say you'll manage well-enough.'

'The main thing is that it proves to be an effective cure,' said Travis. 'You are certain on that point?'

'Oh, yes. The progress of the disease will be arrested within twenty minutes, and a complete cure effected within two hours. There's a regenerative element to the drug which will take care of damaged organs and the like over a period of time, and will also ensure a lifetime of immunity.'

'Any drawbacks? Any side-effects?'

There was a perceptible hesitation on the Surgeon-General's part before he answered.

'Only one that need concern you,' he said. 'I have to admit it's a desperate remedy you have there – a sledgehammer cure forced upon us by circumstances. There's no escaping the fact that you are going to cause the lady in question some considerable pain.'

'In what way?'

'What you have there is a genetically engineered, living culture, which will set up a battlefield in the patient's body. The outcome is not in doubt but for the first twenty minutes the lady will think she's died and gone to hell.'

'As bad as that?' said Travis, softly. He sat silent for a moment, beads of perspiration breaking out on the palms of his hands. 'Is there no alternative?' he said, picking up the glass phial and staring into it.

'Only if you change the ground rules,' said Canazaar. 'Why not do the sensible thing? You are conducting a field experiment, not on some kind of mercy mission. Let me give you a simple blocking drug which will arrest the progress of the disease for a few days. Once you've completed your experiment, what does it matter if the patient dies?'

'No, I must effect a complete cure,' said Travis. 'If I don't, this young woman could continue to haunt me.'

He had not meant to say as much. Canazaar's response to these words was only to be expected.

'Continue to haunt you?' he said, staring. 'What the devil do you mean, '*continue* to haunt you'?'

Stumbling over his words, Travis proffered an explanation.

'I mean...... what I meant was that if I were to do as you advise, the memory of what I could have done but didn't would continue to haunt me…… for a long time.'

'But this other reality shouldn't concern you in a personal sense at all,' Canazaar pointed out.

'Oh, I quite agree there,' said Travis.

'So, you agree with me and yet disagree with me?' said Canazaar. He shook his head in bewilderment. 'You're in a strange mood today, I must say.' With a sigh, he took the glass phial from the Technician, replaced it alongside the syringe, and put the container firmly back into the young man's hands. 'I can offer you nothing better,' he said. 'Richard, there *is* nothing else.'

Travis appeared unwilling to admit defeat.

'Give me something to go with this stuff,' he said. 'How about a sedative, or painkiller?'

'That's definitely out of the question,' said Canazaar, firmly. 'The concoction you have there is potent enough on its own without mixing it with something else. Remember, the patient is on the brink of death and it wouldn't take much to send her over the edge. It would also mean a second injection in all probability, so it's all starting to get a bit messy.'

'What am I to do?' asked Travis, plaintively. 'The last thing I would want is the patient screaming the house down.'

'Richard, it's only pain, for Christ's sake; something which doesn't exist except in the mind,' said Canazaar, irritably. 'Prepare yourself beforehand and help the young woman through it. Hold her close and comfort her. Take some of the pain onto yourself. You're capable of that, surely?'

'Yes, of course,' said Travis; 'but I'm not supposed to linger at the scene.'

'Well, this will give you an excuse to do just that,' said Canazaar, slyly. He sighed. 'You're not very good at this sort of thing, are you, Richard? Curing and healing by using the power of the mind, I mean.'

'I wouldn't say that,' said Travis. 'I'm average, I suppose. I have total belief, of course, it's just that it all seems to take longer than it should, and it leaves me feeling physically and mentally drained. I remember curing myself of a viral infection a few years back and feeling worse after the cure than I had before; but, yes, I wish I were more proficient. You could probably cure our patient completely unaided.'

'Thank you for the compliment, but you grossly exaggerate my talents,' said Canazaar, smiling. He indicated a framed photograph of Jesus of Nazareth on the opposite wall, one of many scattered throughout the Medical Section. 'I'm not in his league, of course, as you seem to think but, then, who is? But seriously, Richard, you *should* be more proficient, and you deceive yourself in thinking that you have total belief in your own powers. There has to be some lingering, deep-seated doubts present, otherwise you wouldn't have these difficulties. You should practice more. Anyway, let us move on.'

The Surgeon-General delved into his dossier and produced another photograph.

'Let us turn our attention to Sir Henry Forres,' he said. 'I may say that when I first saw this I took it to be a photograph of you acting out a role in one of those absurd costume drama productions of yours. Everyone who has seen this agrees that the degree of resemblance between this character and your good self is well-nigh incredible. You're like two peas in a pod.'

'Maybe the mouth is not so close a match,' suggested Travis.

'Really? You think so?' said Canazaar. He studied the photograph, looked up at the Technician, and returned his attention back to Sir Henry Forres. 'No, you're wrong,' he concluded. 'Superficially, there appears to be a difference, but I think one can put that down to mere facial expression. He looks a little severe, and it shows in the outline of his mouth, whereas you are your usual irritatingly cheerful self.'

'So, there's no problem in putting the finishing touches?' asked Travis.

'None at all. Just give us an hour before the off. You'll need a full head of hair, of course, in place of that shining dome. We'll also reproduce the small scar on the cheek. After that, dressed the part, I would defy anyone to spot the difference. I have to congratulate you. It was a neat idea on your part to impersonate the man if the need arose.'

'The chief didn't seem to think so.'

'The man is a fool,' said Canazaar, contemptuously. 'No imagination, that's his trouble. The fellow can't see any further than the end of his nose. Mind you, that's so long anyone could be forgiven for taking that as a compliment to him. Still, give the man his due. His reservations about your chosen case history are fully justified. A pretty task you've set yourself, I must say, and for no good cause, as far as I can see. I suppose it was the time period which drew you to Provincial 3's current programme. Just what attracts you to that barbarous and savage age I shall never know. Jesus, Richard, they used to hang people for picking a pocket, or stealing a sheep!'

'Yes, I know,' acknowledged Travis.

'A man could find himself in bondage for life simply because of the colour of his skin.'

'I know,' said Travis.

'Thousands lived in the lap of luxury while millions went hungry.'

'I know, I know,' said Travis.

'Will you stop saying "I know",' exclaimed an exasperated Canazaar. 'I've noticed you've developed a very annoying habit of late. Everytime I feel like a good argument you suddenly start agreeing with everything I say. It's most off-putting.'

'With all its faults, the time period we are talking of was a more civilised age than what had gone before,' said Travis.

'That's better,' said Canazaar, nodding, 'and by and large I have to agree with that.'

'And what of the two centuries which followed on?' asked Travis. 'What of the mass destruction and institutionalised cruelties of those times?'

'Oh, good point!' said Canazaar, with heavy sarcasm. 'Richard, it goes without saying that *any* age is preferable to the 20th and 21st centuries. A thousand years on and we are still clearing up the mess left behind by that degenerate and irresponsible breed.'

'Then what is left?' asked Travis. 'What is left is seven centuries of chaos followed by two hundred years of recent history, most of the latter out of bounds to us.'

'All right! All right! You've made your point,' said Canazaar, peevishly. 'Why you feel the need to dispute everything I say is beyond me.'

Having lost one argument he saw the prospect of an easy victory in another.

'Well, one thing you cannot dispute is what I was saying earlier. Is the delectable Emma Sinclair really worth the risks you are taking on?'

'I'm confident I can see it safely through,' said Travis, speaking with an assurance he did not altogether feel.

'Are you? I wonder at that,' said Canazaar. 'I'm asking myself if you fully appreciate all the difficulties you'll have to face. For example, you seem to take it for granted that this young woman will lie still and quiet while you do what you have to do – and don't tell me that she's on the point of death. In many cases a dying person is still quite capable of kicking up a fuss if they have a mind to. I think you should prepare yourself for a piercing scream when you jump out at her shouting 'boo'.'

'I would hope to come up with a more subtle approach than that,' said Travis, laughing; 'but I agree that the initial contact poses a problem. How would you handle it?'

'Well, this was an age still permeated by the superstitions of the old religions. To most people God, Jesus, the saints, and angels were very real. Play upon that. Overawe her. Be that 'sweet Jesus' she cries out to. Remember the moment, do you?'

'Do you really think that would work?' asked Travis.

'Given the lady's traumatised state of mind, I believe it would,' said Canazaar. 'At any rate, it's your best option.'

Their business concluded, they had drifted towards the door, but the Surgeon-General was not quite done.

'And no taking liberties with the lady as she lies there helpless before you. Just because you're saving her life doesn't give you any special privileges, you know.'

CHAPTER 6

The following afternoon, with the modifications to the transporter completed and everything in a state of readiness, and with the Surgeon-General's reproaches still fresh in his mind, Travis looked in on Milo Sands. He found her harassed and overworked, so much so that she barely glanced up from a rather late working lunch.

'He's out. Won't be back until tomorrow morning,' was her abrupt greeting.

'It's you I came to see, not the chief,' he said; 'but you look busy.'

'You could say that,' she snapped back at him.

'I suppose that's a late lunch, rather than an early tea,' he said. 'Whichever, you shouldn't bolt your food like that. You'll end up with wind.'

'Good! It may blow some of this lot away,' she said, indicating a desk piled high with work pending. 'Arlene's away for a few days and I'm covering for her. That Mandell is a pain. I don't know how she puts up with him.'

'I bumped into him just a moment ago. He wants to see you when it's convenient.'

'I'm not budging from this chair,' she said, flaring up, 'so he'll have a long wait. I'm going to be here half the evening as it is without him dumping more work on me.'

'Half the evening? Oh, that's a pity,' he said, perching himself on the one bare corner of her desk.

She stopped work and looked up at him. He had sounded distinctly disappointed.

'I was hoping we might spend the evening together at my place. We could open a bottle of wine, have a meal together, listen to some music – that sort of thing. I've everything in hand for tomorrow's off, and I haven't properly thanked you for —.'

He broke off as she got up hurriedly, sending a sheet of paper sailing across the room. One hand sought out his while the other made a grab for her coat. A small portion of sandwich protruded from her mouth. He looked back at her piled-high desk as she pulled him across the room.

'What about that lot?' he asked.

'What about it?' she mumbled, scattering a small cloud of crumbs before her. She led him outside and off in the direction of his flat. He found himself having to break into an occasional trot to keep up with her.

'I wish you didn't live such a distance away,' she said.

'It's only a ten minute walk – two minutes at this pace,' he panted. 'Anyway, I want to make a detour to buy some ingredients for a meal. I've nothing prepared.'

'I'm sure that's not necessary,' she said, firmly. 'No, leave breakfast to me.'

She lay on her side, propped up on her elbow, writing out 'Milo Sands' across his bare chest with a finger.

'I'm going to be old-fashioned since I know you like that sort of thing,' she said. 'So, how was it for you?'

'What? How was what for me?' His voice was distant, his mind elsewhere.

She glared at him, and having completed her name finished it off with a pronounced, a *very* pronounced full stop.

'Jesus! Richard! I ask how it was for you and you don't even know what I'm talking about,' she pouted.

'I'm sorry, really I am,' he said, pulling her towards him. 'I was miles away. That wine's gone to my head – it always does. Forgive me?'

'Crush me, and I'll think about it,' she said.

'Crush you? What do you mean, 'crush me'? Wine gone to your head, too, has it?'

She pulled him on top of her, and proceeded to give him his instructions.

'Open your legs and put them either side of mine...... no, don't take your weight on your elbows like that...... yes, that's better...... put your cheek next to mine...... good, now lie still and let your full body weight press down on me.'

'Quite finished sorting out my bits and pieces?' he said. 'Comfortable, are we?'

'Oh, yes! Lovely!' she said, gasping under his weight.

It had been such a long time: four years to the month since she had stood and waved goodbye to a loved one bound for a dim and distant Epsilon Eridani. A real goodbye, as it turned out. A forever goodbye. Now, four years on, she lay, eyes closed and euphoric, enjoying once more the weight of a man pressing down upon her, warming her, enfolding her, merging with her. After ten such minutes, she gently rolled him off her. She felt winded, she felt bruised, she felt happy.

'What was all that in aid of?' he asked.

'You're a man; you wouldn't understand,' she said.

'I can't linger tomorrow morning,' he said. 'A quick breakfast, then I'll have to be off. Sorry, and all that.'

'I understand,' she said, with a nod of the head. She pointed to the antiquated timepiece, which stood on her side of the bed. 'What time do you want that thing set for?'

'Eight o'clock. Give it here and I'll set it,' he said.

'No, I can manage,' she said. 'It's simple, I'll say that for it.'

Carefully, she set the alarm for seven o'clock before turning off the light and settling herself down.

She lay still and quiet. Soon, he fancied he heard her breathing change to become deep and rhythmic. He was sure she had fallen asleep. He was wrong.

'When do you leave?' she asked.

'Two in the afternoon, our time. I shall be back by midnight at the latest.'

'I'm not looking forward to tomorrow,' she said. 'I wish you didn't have to go. Something could go wrong.'

He leaned over to look down at her, and found her wide-awake. 'Nothing will go wrong. It's a less chancy business than a lot of the space exploration which goes on these days.'

'Yes, but space travel I understand. You go from 'A' to 'B', then maybe onto 'C', and then back to 'A'. That's all straightforward enough. I work for the head of London Complex but, even so, I don't really understand what *you* are going to do tomorrow. You step onto a transporter pad and, as I understand it, you don't *really* go anywhere, yet within a moment you're walking in long-vanished scenes and meeting people who long ago crumbled into dust in their graves. It's all so strange – strange and scary.'

'Put that way, yes it is; but you talk as if I shall be time-travelling into our past, whereas I won't be doing anything of the sort. Such a thing is impossible. What I *shall* be doing is visiting another reality at a point in time when the people which you speak of are very much alive.'

'But how can you take yourself off to another reality? How is such a thing possible?'

'Well, it's all a question of timing. When I step onto the transporter pad I literally cease to exist for a miniscule period of time. In a sense, I die and am born again into another reality, as we all are at the point of death. The period of my nonexistence is of such a short duration, however, that I reappear not as a developing foetus but as you see me now. The theory is simple. It's the application which poses all the problems for us.'

She had listened with a furrowed brow, a study in concentration to what he had been saying. After a moment of silence, she spoke.

'Going back to 18th Century Sussex. Why could you not return to the first reality on the second of your two trips?'

'Because of The Uncertainty Principle. You've heard of that, surely, Milo? Because it would have been a miracle if the second of the two transporter links we set up was to the very same Sussex of 1782 – there's an infinite number of those, and the particular reality I set foot in on each of the two occasions was a matter of pure chance.'

'Besides which, your previous appearance in the first reality would, in itself, rule it out of court for a second visit. It would have put it well beyond the parameters of The Uncertainty Principle.'

'Now you have it!' he said, smiling.

'Let me see then,' she pondered. 'The difference tomorrow is that there will only be the one transporter link, with the potential to take you back to the same reality as before.'

'Yes, that's exactly it, Milo. No one ever thought that could be a practical possibility. Now, it's more than a possibility. It's an important step in the future progress of our work here at London Complex.'

He was smiling at the thought, but it evoked no similar response from her. She had begun to concern herself with his safety once more.

'How I wish we could follow your progress tomorrow,' she said. 'Off you go into the blue yonder of the transporter's cone of light, and we are all left in the dark until you return. Why is that? Why cannot we view you on the monitors?'

'Because the Transporter-Reality link cannot be made instantaneous with the Viewing Monitor-Reality link – and I do mean instantaneous. The result is that both transporter and monitor are locked into separate realities. I am present in the Transporter Reality, not in the reality which the monitors display.'

'Realities, and more realities,' she said, sighing. 'I know that truly is the way of things, but I do not understand why it should be so. Why not just the one reality – our own?'

'Because we live in an infinite and eternal Cosmos,' he answered. 'These fifteen billion light years of matter and space, which we call our Universe, are but an infinitely tiny portion of the whole. Infinite realities are a natural consequence of that. Really, when you think about it, the old notion of a Cosmos confined to a single universe, constrained in extent, was very naïve. Is not an infinite number of universes inherently more probable? I suppose the philosophy was 'this is all I see, therefore this is all there is' dictated matters, but there were pointers to the contrary as way back as a thousand years ago. For example, there was Schrodinger's Cat – two realities, equally valid, staring the scientist in the face.'

'What on earth is, or was, Schrodinger's Cat?' she asked, laughing.

'It's a long story,' he said. 'Someday I shall tell you all about it, but not now.'

'I shall hold you to that,' she said; 'but answer me this: we cannot be the only civilisation equipped with a transporter, so why do we never receive visitors from other realities?'

'Well, theoretically it's a possibility, but incredibly unlikely,' he replied. 'Because there are an infinite number of worlds in our infinite Cosmos the odds against any one of them receiving such a visit are infinitely high.'

Once more she fell silent. Snug and warm in her arms, he began to drift off to sleep.

'The Time Traveller preferred the future,' she said, all of a sudden.

'What Time Traveller?' he murmured. 'Milo, what are you on about?'

'The Time Traveller in that story by H.G.Wells. His hero chose to travel into the future, rather than the past.'

'Milo, that is a work of fantasy, beautifully crafted but with an impossible plot.'

'Why is it impossible?' she said.

'Because one's future at any given point in time does not exist. How can one access something which doesn't exist?'

He watched with some amusement as she struggled to grasp the point.

'O.K., Richard, then tell me in plain English, what would happen if Provincial 3 were to change their current programme from Yarm, 1811, to, say, Yarm, 3811?'

'Nothing would happen. All the monitors would display a blank screen.'

'But Yarm, 3811, does exist somewhere, surely? An infinity of realities, and all that.'

'Certainly it exists, but you are overlooking The Uncertainty Principle, which dictates that we may only view, or travel to, worlds which have an identical history to our own. We, of course, have no history for the year 3811 – it lies eight hundred years into the future as far as we are concerned. Come the year 3812 we will have, and then, and only then, will we be able to do what you're proposing. Set the instruments at 3811 now and they would have nothing to relate to.'

'How beautifully you explain things,' she said, looking at him admiringly. 'I've enjoyed our little discussion.'

Their little discussion was not yet concluded. A moment later, she raised another topic.

'These other Milo Sands, as other Milo Sands there must be, is it really me who acts out these lives, or an infinite number of mere carbon copies?'

'Some at least will be truly you,' he said, yawning.

His words stunned her. 'Do you realise the implications of what you've just said?' she asked. 'You've given me immortality, with a yawn.'

'Yes, I'm tired,' he said.

'Do you really mean what you say?' she persisted.

'I do. I do,' he said. 'I really am tired.'

'That is not what I meant – you *know* what I meant.'

'What I've told you is common knowledge,' he said. 'Really, Milo,

71

I'm surprised you're surprised. Put simply, it's impossible to produce an infinite number of carbon copies of *anything* without eventually getting back to the original. There is a limiting threshold, so to speak. We've proved that in both the field of mathematics and in the field of physics. Let me give you just one example. We have gone below that threshold unwittingly with the new generation of Quantum Computers. We have ten such machines worldwide, including Computer 1 here at London Complex. Wonderful though the machines are, they have a drawback. When one of them develops a fault, which fortunately isn't very often, all ten develop the same fault at precisely the same time. In one sense we have ten computers and in another, very real sense, we have only the one. We are trying to get around the problem by tinkering with them to give each a separate individuality, but if we do that we will inevitably downgrade them. It's a tricky problem, which I'm glad is not down to me to solve.'

'So, I'm going to spend the rest of eternity as Milo Sands, London Complex, circa 3,000 A.D, am I?' she said. She paused, frowning. 'Even though I shall have no knowledge of previous existences, I'm not altogether sure I welcome that prospect.'

'You won't have to,' he said. 'You're thinking of the limitations of The Uncertainty Principle, but that only comes into effect when we make a *forced* reality change, as we'll be doing tomorrow. It plays no role in what we are now discussing. When you die, you'll go into the melting pot with the rest of us. You could come back as anyone – perhaps as a hunter-gatherer roaming a primitive landscape; perhaps playing a role in a society even more advanced than this one.'

'Really?' she said.

'You could come back seriously disabled from birth, or greatly disadvantaged in a hundred different ways,' he warned her. '*Someone* has to live out those roles.'

'We're all in the same boat, so to speak,' she said. 'Yes...... yes, on balance I'd rather have it that way. I shall take my chance along with the rest of humanity.'

'Well said,' he replied, smiling. 'We couldn't have it any other way even if we wanted it.'

'So, the notion of a work of fiction, the so-called novel, is a fallacy, is that not correct?' she said.

This was seemingly such an abrupt change of subject that he drew back from her in surprise.

'A literary work of fiction an impossibility?' he queried. 'Well,...... yes, certainly it is. In this infinite Cosmos of ours only pure fantasy – anything which contradicts some fundamental law – is ruled out as a non-starter. Do you know, that never occurred to me before. One can write fact, or one can write fantasy, but one cannot write fiction.'

'Then I shall go to sleep planning my next existence as I would wish it to be,' she said. 'You must do likewise.'

Ready for sleep as he was, he gladly agreed, but after a few minutes curiosity got the better of her.

'Who are you?' she murmured, sleepily.

'I'm Sherlock Holmes, rattling through the fog-bound streets of Victorian London in a hansom cab,' he replied. 'I'm on the trail of Professor Moriarty.'

'Oh, that is no good!' she protested. 'The man had an aversion to women. We could never be lovers in that reality. Come and join me in mine. Now, the year is 1813, and we two have just met for the first time at a dinner-dance in the Assembly Hall at Meryton. You have publicly humiliated me, you unfeeling brute, by refusing to dance with me, but the time will come, Mr. Darcy, when I shall be able to twist you round my little finger. Recognise the picture? Good, isn't it?'

For no good cause, she awoke a little after two in the morning, her bedpartner still and silent beside her. Within a moment, her thoughts had turned to the conversation of a few hours previous and, in particular, the details disclosed to her about a perpetual existence. 'Common knowledge' was his description of those details, but she guessed he had rather overstated the matter. Common knowledge amongst the scientific fraternity they may be, but not amongst the public at large, she was sure. His few words on the subject had certainly come as a revelation to her, as they would have done to her father.

In spite of all the progress, death still remained a fact of life, as she herself could testify.

Ten years ago she had stood by the bedside of her dying father. At the very end, conscious to the last, he had gently squeezed her hand

and spoke a score of words, which still came back to haunt her in quiet moments such as now.

'You know, Milo,' he had whispered, 'the old saying is wrong; death, not space, is the final frontier. Oh, God! here I go.'

The words would haunt her no longer.

She snuggled close to the man who had exorcised her ghost.

'Death, where is thy sting?' she murmured, as she closed her eyes.

It was time to die, and yet not to die. Time to cease to exist, and yet endure as before. Time to leave one reality and enter another.

Dressed the part, he stood on the transporter gantry, his back to the blue cone of light, surveying the scene below. To the five pair of eyes glancing up at him from time to time he looked composed and assured, his only show of nervousness a gentle, occasional smoothing of his cravat.

The hands were being slowly raised one by one as the last readings were being taken and the final checks made.

One...... Two...... Three...... Four...

He waited expectantly, looking down at Supervisor Caroline de Tournai. She looked away from the panel in front of her and up towards Technician Travis. With a firm movement she raised her arm aloft... Five.

He took a deep breath, turned and walked quickly, but without haste, up to and into the pale blue light, which signified his exit and re-entry point. As he did so, a phrase from a primitive television comedy show, which he had once lighted upon, came to mind.

'And now for something completely different.'

CHAPTER 7

Save for one disturbing incident, it had all gone like clockwork.

Leaving the cluster of pine trees which screened the transporter light, he had stood for a moment looking around and taking stock.

It was a dark, moonless night, the velvet-black sky studded with a galaxy of stars. A gentle western wind, mild and moist, lazily stirred the topmost branches of nearby trees as he moved stealthily towards the rear of the cottage. A moment's work had been sufficient to force an easy entry. Soon, he was passing noiselessly through the building, pushing the inky blackness before him with an outstretched hand.

It had taken him a full two minutes to ascend the small flight of stairs and grope his way through the open bedroom door. With infinite care, he closed the door behind him and took up a position in the far corner of the room. The tiny bedroom window shed precious little light in the room, and the gutted candle on the dresser none at all. Wrapping the darkness around him as a cloak, he stood waiting his opportunity.

He heard the restless stirrings, the sharp intake of breath, the whispered plea to her God, the muffled movement, and the handbell tinkling to the floor. It was time for him to act.

It was not until he had seated himself beside her that she became aware of his presence, a vague, dark outline against an even darker background.

'Who is there?' she asked, and with the asking a new and very different reality was born.

'You called my name,' he said. 'Fear not, my child, I am here in answer to your prayer.'

At his friend Canazaar's prompting, he had rehearsed these opening words of his a score of times during the past few days. Now, for the first time, the words struck him as foolish, his claim preposterous. His friend's advice on this point, however, was to prove sound.

In ordinary circumstances, Emma Sinclair would, no doubt, have thought as he did, but these were not ordinary circumstances. Wearied unto death, confused, and fearful, she did not dispute his claim. Her response, when it came, was one of amazement, but not disbelief.

'You are here? You are here *in person*? *For me*? Is this the way of things? I never dreamed it would end like this.'

Summoning up all her courage, she inched out a searching hand to find and clasp one of his.

'Lord, into your hands I commend my spirit.'

A few seconds later, shocked by her boldness, she withdrew her hand, threw aside the blankets which covered her, and began to struggle frantically in an effort to raise herself up.

'What are you doing?' he asked, in alarm.

'It is not right and proper that I should lie here before you like this,' she said, distractedly.

'Emma, I shall decide what is right and proper,' he replied. Firmly, but gently, he resettled her.

'You know my name?' she said. 'But of course you do.' She give a dry chuckle. 'Silly of me.'

'Yes, I know your name, and much more than that,' he said; 'but what I want now from you is your trust. Do I have it? Will you put yourself in my hands, Emma?'

'With all my heart,' she said. 'But how could I not trust you? I love you. In spite of my many failings, deep down I have always loved you. You who are privy to the innermost secrets of my heart must know that to be true.'

Her words proved too much for him. Almost without realising what he was doing, he found himself tenderly pressing his lips to hers.

A little ashamed of his loss of self-control, he began to busy himself with her comfort, smoothing pillows, tidying bedcovers, and replacing a fallen handbell. With movements of a different kind, lingering and gentle, he wiped away the rivulets of tears and beads of perspiration from her face. His final act was to take up the glass of water from the nearby bedside table, dip in a finger, and trace the outline of her crusted lips. That done, and settled beside her once more, he slipped a hand into one of hers and placed the other flat across her forehead.

Gone in a moment was the debilitating pain, the inward struggle of distress, the fierce impatience with the way of things. In their place there came upon her a calm acceptance and a painfree peace.

'Lord, when are we to leave this place?' she said.

'All in good time,' he said. 'There is something which needs to be done first.'

A moment later and he had done what he came for, the injection proving to be an easier task than he had feared it would be. There was not a glimmer of light to aid him, but none was needed. Several veins in the arm, any one of which would have served the purpose, stood out bold to the touch against the wasted flesh on either side. For her part, she felt little more than a sharp, tingling discomfort, a mere trifle to the pain endured in recent weeks, but all that was to change.

'There will be pain,' he warned her. 'You must be brave a little while longer. I shall help you.'

'I understand,' she said. 'I understand that I must be purged of all my sin and error.'

'Hardly that,' he said, 'but come give me your pain.'

Gently, he raised her up, one arm encircling her waist, his free hand supporting her head. He pressed her close to himself as, with eyes shut tight in concentration, he sought out the corridors of her mind.

The pain came earlier than he had anticipated, and he found himself ill-prepared to meet it, with the result that she bore the brunt of its ferocity alone.

Eyes, ears, and brain flared back in an instant to full awareness as the explosion ripped through her body. The skeletal frame, as if seeking an escape from itself, reached outwards and upwards, and beyond, leaving her wide-eyed and stunned, with a mouth agape in a silent scream. Unthinkingly, he had discarded his jacket, which left her hands free to roam his unprotected back. Her nails pierced his thin shirt to score a dozen tracks across his skin. Belatedly, he strove to help her, drawing upon all the modest powers at his command and silently cursing his inadequacies.

Slowly, her pain subsided as his increased apace. The suffering was far worse than he had expected and it took all his willpower not to cry out. Hardly conscious of what he was doing, he bit through his bottom lip in the continuing struggle to stay silent.

After what seemed an eternity, but was in reality a mere fifteen minutes, the pain flickered and died as suddenly as it had flared into existence. He was left battered in mind and body but quietly triumphant.

Still held in his embrace, she laid a tilted head on his shoulder and began to quietly hum a dimly remembered childhood tune. Her only wish now was to be done with the world about her, a world of imperfections and disappointments. The wish became a longing. The longing became an overpowering, killing desire.

He laid her back down, and occupied himself for a few minutes in combing her hair with his fingers, gently tugging and separating matted locks and smoothing them back into place. She, meanwhile, was exploring the contours of his face, tracing the outline of each feature with a roving hand. When his lips clamped playfully around a probing finger, he heard her laugh softly.

It is difficult to say precisely when blind, unquestioning belief began to give way to doubt and suspicion. The early workings of the drug, bringing with it a new clarity of mind, was certainly a factor, as was the Technician's carelessness in forgetting just whom he was supposed to be.

'The Light of the World' holding her in her arms? The God of Abraham, Isaac and Jacob combing her hair and playing teasing games with her? The sheer implausibility – no, impossibility – of such a thing came to her. No, this was no Divine Being, but a mortal man of flesh and blood, a pounding heart and a sweat-soaked brow testimony to his recent exertions.

'Who are you? Who are you *really*?' she asked, the hint of fear in her voice. 'Why do you come to me with a lie on your lips?'

'It served my purpose to do so,' he said, realising that his little ruse was at an end. 'I'm sorry for it, all the same.'

'Purpose? What purpose?' she asked.

'You were close to death. You know that, don't you?' he said.

'Yes, I know,' she said.

'Well, all that is changed. I brought you the gift of life, *that* was my purpose in coming here. And now, I must go. I have stayed too long as it is. I wish you long life and every imaginable happiness, my dear Emma.'

'You speak as if we shall never meet again,' she said.

'Yes, that can never be,' he said.

He got to his feet and began to move towards the door but she stopped him in his tracks with a near-hysterical outburst.

'No! No!' she cried. 'Do not abandon me. Stay with me a little while longer at least. Tell me we shall meet again.'

He stood, irresolute, glancing nervously towards the bedroom door.

The sound of her voice came with a terrifying loudness to his ears and, he felt sure, to the ears of others sleeping in the building. Should he take to his heels, or return to her side in an attempt to quieten her? Not without some misgivings, he chose the latter course.

There was a hint of desperation in his voice when next he spoke.

'Emma, you do not know what you ask. Please, you are making things very difficult for me.'

'But I must know more,' she sobbed, taking his hand in hers. 'I ask you again: who *are* you? How came you here? Why do you choose to help me, I who am a stranger to you? I know nothing of you – it's so dark in here I do not even have the memory of your face. You must have a name; tell me that, at least.'

'My name is Richard,' he said. 'For the rest, let us just say that I am a man in pursuit of a dream. More than that, I cannot tell you.' He adopted his most soothing tone of voice. 'Sleep will come soon. I shall stay with you until it does. There, how's that?'

He waited for a response, but none came.

'Nothing to say?' he said, gently.

'Only that I have been a fool. How stupid of me not to have recognised the truth before now. This is all nonsense, is it not?' she said, sadly. 'This is the last, foolish dream of a dying young woman. I shall awake in the morning, if I awake at all, to find nothing has changed. But why do I tell you these things? You are but a phantom in that dream.'

'Emma, believe me when I tell you, this is no dream,' he said, earnestly.

'Oh! if only that were true,' she said. 'How I wish I could believe that.'

'And I wish there was something I could say, or do, to convince you that all of this is very real,' he said.

'Perhaps there is,' she said, thoughtfully. 'Yes, perhaps there is. If you reach into that dresser top drawer you will find a finger ring.'

He did as she asked. 'I have it,' he said, after a moment spent fumbling in the dark.

'Give it me, and let me have your left hand,' she said.

Taking hold of his hand, she began a process of trial and error. After a moment, he felt the ring pass comfortably over the knuckle of his index finger, and settle itself snugly below.

'It was my father's,' she said, by way of explanation. 'Now, do you have a keepsake for me?'

'Well, ...no,' he answered. 'I didn't expect this. I came here with little more than the clothes I stand up in.'

'Very well, you must leave your mark on me. Will you do this thing as one lover to another?' she asked.

'Emma, I do not follow you,' he said, shaking his head. 'What *exactly* do you want of me?'

She pulled him down beside her and directed his head to her neck.

'You must pierce the skin, draw blood, and suck hard on the wound,' she whispered. 'Low down, where it may not readily be seen.'

He pulled his head away. 'You are surely not serious in any of this?' he said.

'I was never more serious in all my life,' she answered.

At a loss for words, he made no reply.

'I can well understand your feelings,' she said, answering his silence. 'What man would want to perform such an act of intimacy with a wizened, ugly creature like me. The darkness is a friend to me, but I dare say you have my picture clearly in your mind. But it was not always so,' she added, wistfully. 'There was a time, and not so long ago, when men thought me beautiful.'

'That day will come again, believe me,' he said, gently.

Once more, she pulled his head down to her neck.

'This is not wanton, licentious behaviour on my part,' she said. 'No man has ever done such a thing to me before, and I swear no man ever shall after tonight. Believe me when I tell you that there is a purpose in all of this. You say you are no phantom. Prove it.'

He head her softly gasp as he punctured the skin, but thereafter she lay quiet, apart from the occasional low moan. For his part, with his injured bottom lip complaining painfully at the role it was being forced to play, he began to experience such an exquisite mixture of pain and pleasure as he had never felt before. He found it no easy thing to stop himself from taking matters further.

For not the first time, as once before in 18th Century Sussex, he was glad to be out of reach of any viewing monitor. What would they think of me back home if they could see me now! were his thoughts. This was, for sure, one incident which would not find a mention in his field report.

After five minutes, he raised his head and announced, somewhat breathlessly: 'There! It's done. I don't know how well. I've never done that to any woman before.'

'I'm happy to hear it,' she said, smiling. 'But you can plainly see the wound?' she asked, running a finger over the spot.

'I can see nothing in this light, or, rather, lack of it,' he answered, 'but you may be certain that my handiwork, amateurish though it may be, will be plain to see in daylight.'

'I pray it will be there in the morning,' she said. 'Oh, God! let it be so.'

'My dear Emma, it will be there for weeks to come,' he said, ignorant of her meaning and surprised by her words.

She had turned her head away from him as he had been speaking.

'Go now,' she murmured, sleepily. 'Go quickly; do not speak, or pause, or look back. Only remember.'

In silence, he left her.

He made his way back to his entry point with his mind a turmoil of mixed emotions. There was elation at having safely accomplished the first, and most difficult, of his two part experiment, but there was sadness, too, in the thought that he would never meet with her again. There was joy in the knowledge that he had plucked her from the jaws of death, but it was a joy tinged with sorrow brought on by the realisation that he would never know how she would spend the rest of her days. Irrespective of what he had accomplished that night, the monitors at London Complex were programmed to show the unaltered reality of her all-too brief life, her sad decline, and her early death. The principal reason for his undertaking this particular reality change above all other possibilities had been the hope that it would somehow put a stop to the recurring dream which had haunted him for so long a time. Now, he was not so sure he wanted that, for if his hope was realised the link between the two of them would be broken for ever. All that would be left would be the memory of her, fading and blurring over the years to come.

At the edge of the small plantation of fir trees he hesitated, but only briefly. Grimly resolved to do his duty, he began winding his way between the patchwork of trees, his ears pricked for the slightest sound. All was deathly quiet, however, the only sound the occasional soft snap of some twig or piece of fallen foliage beneath his feet.

There was a difference this time when he stepped gratefully inside the boundary of blue light. As before, in 18th Century Sussex, he was gone in an instant, but this time he did not take the light with him. It continued to shine steadily, just as he had arranged it so. Unbeknown to him, or anyone else at London Complex, however, exactly thirty six seconds after his departure it suddenly shrank to an inert, microscopic size. That was most definitely *not* part of the arrangements.

It was destined to stay in this altered state for some considerable time.

Emma awoke the following morning feeling weak and languid but entirely free from pain. Now was the moment of truth, she told herself, as the memories of the night's events came flooding back to her. Now came the acid test.

'Please, God, let it be so,' she whispered.

Leaning over, she took up the small mirror from the bedside dresser, and with a trembling hand angled it to her neck.

Was it to be life? Or was it to be death?

An ugly – no, a beautiful, an oh! –so–beautiful – blood-red wound, with a tiny pair of puncture marks at its centre, disfigured her neck low down. A feverish hunt through the dresser drawer also revealed a finger ring conspicuous by its absence.

'My God! it was no dream,' she laughed.

She flopped onto her back and savoured her ease and comfort beneath the downy sheets of a bed no longer a prison.

'My God! it was no dream,' she wept.

After a little while, she composed herself and began to idly study the shifting, sun-fringed shadows which sharpened and softened in turn across her bedroom ceiling. With her mind concentrated on the events of the past night, an aching pain of a kind utterly unknown to her a mere twenty four hours before came upon her – the pain of their parting and his continued absence. He had told her plainly that they could never meet again. She would have to come to terms with that.

She would have to live with that, she acknowledged to herself, but it would not be easy. He had wished her long life and every imaginable happiness; if nothing else, she could at least return his sentiments. Looking out of her bedroom window to a distant horizon, she voiced her thoughts

'Long life and every imaginable happiness to you also, my dear Richard,' she whispered.

This is a tale of strange and wonderful events, but read now the greatest wonder of them all. In spite of his words, they were, indeed, destined to meet again. Her response was to spit in his face, after a failed attempt on her part to kill him.

Later that morning she told her mother of all but the most intimate events of the night, but that sensible lady had merely smiled indulgently, nodded her head from time to time, and volunteered only an occasional, distracted 'yes, dear', and 'no, dear', as she busied herself attending to her daughter's comfort. Her mood *did* change towards the end of the tale, however, at the mention of the finger ring.

'By rights, that is Robert's,' she said, frowning and tutting her disapproval. 'Oh, Emma, dear, I hope you haven't gone and lost it.'

The reaction of her good friend Elizabeth Palmer on hearing the tale in full was markedly different, but no less disappointing. Giving no credence herself to the story, she had advised: 'For goodness sake, Emma, keep this matter to yourself. At best, you will be disbelieved and laughed to scorn; at worst, you will be believed just enough for people to label you a disgrace to your sex for allowing some passing vagrant to share your bed with you. For myself, I have no doubt but that you have had an unusually vivid dream, and no more than that.'

'Then, how do you explain this?' asked Emma, pushing back the tresses which hung low around her neck.

'A bite from some night insect,' said Elizabeth, promptly. She looked more closely at the wound, still vivid and fresh. 'At least, I hope it is an insect bite.'

Disappointing though these words were to Emma, she knew in her heart that they constituted sound advice. From that moment she resolved to speak no more on the subject to anyone.

On the day following her appetite returned, and on day six her mother was forced to listen to her first complaints of boredom. On day ten, Sir Henry Forres, recently returned from a holiday spent angling, paid her a visit, and was kind and charming. She had a vague feeling that the two of them had met before but he laughingly denied such a possibility. By this time the wound on her neck was fast fading, despite her best efforts to keep it clearly visible by repeated attempts to irritate the skin around and about.

Emma continued to improve in health and strength and within two months had recovered in full a beauty never really lost. Towards the end of that eventful year, she came to a fateful decision

'It is as he said. He will never return,' she told herself, and settled for what she believed to be a good second best. Had she but known it at the time, the comparison between the two men in question was a travesty. Twelve months after the visit of Richard Travis saw her distraught and fearful for the future as she struggled to cope with the physical and mental abuse.

And so it came about that the Technician's few hours of rest and recuperation after he had left her were as a lifetime to her.

CHAPTER 8

Supervisor Caroline de Tournai was waiting for him on his return.

'Welcome back, Richard,' she said.

He nodded a greeting, and began to head for the sanctuary of the rest-room which had been put at his disposal for the duration.

'The chief's been in touch,' she said.

He lengthened his stride, forcing her to quicken her pace to keep up with him.

'Every twenty minutes, on the dot, since you left,' she continued. 'At first it was: "How's things with you, Caroline?" Next: "Everything O.K. at your end?" Then it was: "Where's Richard? What's keeping him?" As if I could answer that! Oh! yes, the Surgeon-General came through twice wanting to know the latest. I think he's still a bit annoyed that he wasn't allowed to be here in person.'

The Technician give a grunt, signifying his irritation, as they entered into the quiet of his little room.

'Essential Transporter Section staff, only – that's the way I wanted it,' he said. 'It's no different from last year. If Samon was allowed here, there's fifty others who would feel they have an equal right to be present. Really, Caroline, what is the matter with everyone? Isn't it enough that the whole thing is being beamed live into every home and workplace in The Complex, and far beyond, come to that?' He paused to cast an eye about him. 'Incidentally, while we're on the subject, I hope this isn't part of the set-up?'

'No, you have your privacy here,' she assured him. 'So you see, you may unburden yourself to your heart's content. Want to tell me about it? How did it go? You were gone so long we began to get worried.' She pointed to his damaged lip. 'I'd especially like to know how the hell you came by that.'

'It went well-enough,' he said. 'I did what I had to do.'

'And the lip?'

'Self-inflicted.'

'I see. Desperate for a pee, and couldn't find the toilet?'

'Something like that,' he said, contriving a painful smile.

'Back in a minute,' she said.

She reappeared a few moments later bearing one of the standard-issue first aid kits.

She found him in the bathroom annex, where he stood, stripped to the waist, before a handbasin of freshly run cold water.

'It's years since I played doctor and patient,' she said, flourishing the traditional white box marked with the obligatory red cross. 'Having said that, all I can offer you is some salving cream. These kits are next to useless. They look as if they came out of some museum. Why is it that in any public place you care to mention the medical kits are always a hundred years older than any of the other fixtures and fittings?'

She had meant to say more but at that precise moment he half-turned away from her and she caught sight of his back. She stared at the angry-looking lacerations criss-crossing his skin.

'Jesus! Richard, what *have* you been up to? Don't tell me *that* was self-inflicted. You'd need to be a contortionist to do that to yourself.'

'No, the patient did that,' he said.

'Did she? My word, you have been having fun the pair of you. Fighting you off, was she, or fighting to get your clothes off?'

'Neither, actually.'

'Ah! yes, I see. Taking the pain, were you? As bad as that, was it? Well, don't expect me to do the same,' she said, dabbing the ointment onto his lip. 'This is going to hurt you more than it hurts me. The old sayings are the best, don't you think?'

With one task completed, she began work on his back.

'Any other injuries?' she said, hopefully, looking down at his nether regions. 'Groin strain, perhaps? Don't be shy. I'm a doctor, remember?'

'Caroline, you are a Doctor of Philosophy, not a Doctor of Medicine,' he said.

'Now, that's just nit-picking,' she said.

She finished off her work of healing with a flourish.

'So, how did you find the patient?' she said. 'How did she look in the flesh? They say the camera never lies, but there's evidence in plenty that it sometimes flatters to deceive.'

'I can't answer that,' he said. 'The candle had gutted – obviously, something I'd missed when viewing the recordings – and that I hadn't bargained for. That's our viewing monitors, for you. Day or night, they show every detail crystal clear and flooded in light. Still, perhaps it was no bad thing. She never saw my face, which will save embarrassment all round when she meets up with Henry Forres, as meet up with him she must, I suppose. I was never very happy at that prospect, for both their sakes.'

'You were gone an hour and a half. What on earth were you doing all that time? If you went off on some moonlight jaunt, the chief is going to have a fit when he finds out.'

'There was nothing like that,' he assured her. 'The two of us just got talking.'

'Yes, and the rest,' she said. 'Well, if we ever manage to link the transporter to the viewing monitors that will put a stop to these escapades you seem prone to on your field trips. Not that there is any prospect of that.'

'I disagree,' he said. 'I think the coupling will be made in the not too distant future.'

'Surely not,' she said, in surprise. 'For that to happen, the reality link has to be made instantaneous to both the transporter *and* monitor, otherwise we find ourselves with two realities on our hands, not one. Such perfect synchronisation, below the Planck Threshold, is an impossibility, even for us.'

'Perhaps so,' he said, 'but once upon a time faster than light space travel was reckoned to be an impossibility, but now it's commonplace. And how did we achieve that? By a scientific sleight of hand, that's how. As far as Nature is concerned, we haven't crossed that forbidden barrier, but for all practical purposes we have. In our line of business a way forward along those lines may just be a possibility.'

He seemed glad of her company and, moreover, disposed to talk. Thus encouraged, she sought the answer to something which had been puzzling her.

'Richard, why did you choose this particular reality change for your field experiment?' she asked.

'Why not? It was conveniently to hand, and serves the purpose,' he said.

She shook her head, not at all impressed by his answer.

'Given your views on the subject, one might have expected you to choose to do something more significant – prevent a war, stamp out an epidemic, or save the life of some notable figure in history.'

'I've an experiment to carry out, that's all,' he answered. 'Caroline, I'm on a mission, not a crusade. Anyway, Dyal would hardly have been likely to have given his blessing to some grand undertaking.'

He was condemned out of his own mouth.

'A *crusade?* Is there such a thing in our line of work?' she said, gently.

He was beginning to look distinctly unhappy at this turn in the conversation, and she decided not to press the point. Abruptly, she changed the subject.

'So, when exactly is the next jumping-off point?' she asked.

'That pretty well fixes itself,' he said. 'I can hardly call on the Sinclair household much earlier than eight-thirty in the morning – eleven p.m., our time. On the other hand, every minute after that reduces the safety margin. Let's play safe and make it eleven o'clock.'

She was nodding her head as he was speaking. At the risk of him thinking that she was stating the obvious, she felt obliged to say: 'Yes, never lose sight of the fact that we've engineered a reality link of twelve hours, *maximum duration.* Although we may be having kittens here, 1.29a.m. is fine; 1.31a.m. is fatal.'

He was shaking his head impatiently as she was speaking.

'I shall be back within twenty minutes of leaving here,' he said.

'So soon?' she said. 'Will that give you enough time to do the necessary?'

'I believe so,' he said. 'I shall keep it simple, which should please the chief. I'll simply knock on the front door, announce myself, and ask after the patient. We know this young woman died at about five in the morning so if the news at eight-thirty is that she's alive and feeling a little better that, in itself, will be sufficient proof that I've returned to an altered reality.'

'Not necessarily. Not absolutely,' she said, frowning. 'You could end up the victim of misinformation. It may be that someone looked in on her first thing, saw her lying still and quiet, and simply assumed she was sleeping.'

'Not possible, Caroline,' he said. 'Look at the recordings and you'll see that the servant woman found a corpse at seven a.m. At eight-thirty the place was in an uproar. No, I shall either be met with smiles and reassurance, or weeping and gnashing of teeth.'

'The word is that you have a personal interest in the Sinclair girl,' she said, smiling. 'Don't you want to see her a second time?'

'In the circumstances, no,' he said. 'We wouldn't be left alone together, you may be sure of that, and I've no real desire to spend twenty minutes in her company with her mother looking on. Coming after our first meeting, that would be an anti-climax, if ever there was one.'

He seated himself on the edge of the simple bunk-bed, which occupied one corner of the room. Here, she joined him with the easy familiarity of an old friend and colleague.

'Richard, we have only the one transporter link for this experiment,' she said. 'Surely, it is as certain as can be that it will take you back to the same reality which you left half-an-hour ago. *It has to.*'

'Yes, I wouldn't dispute that,' he said.

'So, that being the case, why the need for this experiment at all? I keep asking myself. If the outcome is a foregone conclusion, what purpose does it serve?'

'Looked at in that light, you might say the same of our undertaking of a year ago,' he said. 'The existence of The Uncertainty Principle was never really in doubt but, Caroline, if history tells us anything in the field of science it is that we should take nothing for granted. Because a law of Physics is 'obvious' does not mean it is sacrosanct. No scientist worth his salt would pass up an opportunity to put such a law to the test. As for today's little experiment, there are still a few voices out there which maintain that the outcome is *not* a foregone conclusion, that theory and practise are *not* the same. Let us hope that what we achieve today will convince them otherwise.'

He had laid himself down as he was speaking, preparing for sleep, but she could not leave him without raising one more topic, which had long intrigued her.

'What is it like, Richard?' she said, looking down at him. 'What do you feel when you enter another time and place? Of all men living only you can answer that. I think I would be disorientated, my senses overwhelmed.'

He seemed disinclined to answer, but she persisted.

'What did you feel when you first stepped out into that reality of eighteenth century Sussex? Richard, you must have felt *something.*'

'I felt euphoric – 'intoxicated' would not be too strong a word. It took me a full five minutes to settle myself.'

'And how did you feel when you stood in the garden of Pine Tree Cottage? Was that any different?'

She watched as, with a set face, he turned his head away.

Reaching over, she cupped his face in her hands and made him look at her.

'Richard, I am your friend,' she said. 'Something is troubling you. Tell me what it is.'

It was then that he let her into a secret, one which he had intended to keep to himself.

'Caroline, standing in that garden, I was afraid.'

'I can understand that,' she said, gently. 'You had a difficult task ahead of you, more so than in Sussex, but it was a task of your own choosing.'

'No, you don't understand,' he said, shaking his head. 'It was not exactly my situation which made me fearful.'

'What then?' she asked.

For a moment he was silent, his eyes downcast. When he finally looked into her face she was startled to see a haunted, troubled look in his eyes.

'It was the voice,' he said. 'I was afraid of the voice. I heard it the instant I stepped out of the transporter's cone of light, coming at me out of the pine trees. After a little while I managed to convince myself that it had all been imagination on my part, and I put it out of my mind to a degree. Walking back into that black cluster of trees to come home was to bring it all back, and it took all my courage to reach the safety of the transporter. Deep down, you see, I knew, as I know now, that it was not imagination on my part. Caroline, I heard that voice as clearly as I hear yours now.'

'And what did the voice say?' she said, her face full of concern. 'Did it threaten you?'

'Threaten me? Yes, you could say that. It spoke just three words of greeting.'

She shook her head, perplexed. 'But how can a few words of greeting constitute a threat? Tell me, what *exactly* did the voice say?'

'It said: "welcome home, Technician." '

Ten minutes later, as he drifted off to sleep, she left him.

Deeply preoccupied, she headed for the Transporter room.

The recent conversation had only served to heighten the doubts and fears which had occupied much of her thoughts during the past few days. There was nothing definite, nothing she could put her finger on, only a few incidents, akin to the one that her friend had just related, allied to a vague feeling of unease.

One such incident, innocent enough in itself but disturbing to her nonetheless, had occurred only the day previously. The Technician had asked her to witness his recently drafted will.

'Putting everything in order, are we?' she had asked, jokingly.

'Hardly that,' he had answered, 'but I suppose there is one chance in a thousand that something will go badly wrong tomorrow. Anyway, every responsible person should make out a will. Any solicitor would say the same, Caroline.'

All of that was true, she acknowledged to herself. Years before, she and her partner had made out their separate wills in each other's favour, but neither of them had any expectation, still less hope, of coming into their legacy for many years to come. Even so, it still struck her as odd that the Technician had been moved to make out his will when he had. If he was really sincere in what he had said, why had he not felt the same need at the time of his epoch-making Sussex experiment?

Another curious incident had occurred the previous morning in the Transporter room itself.

They had been in the process of setting up the reality link when, not altogether unexpected, a technical difficulty had reared its head. Here was an old problem, partially resolved but not yet fully sorted out. There had been a similar hiccup in the setting up of the Sussex link a year before. Then, it had taken twenty hours of hard work on everyone's part to set matters right but this time, unaccountably, the problem seemed to resolve itself in a matter of minutes. Everyone present, the Technician included, was disposed to regard this as a lucky omen, but she was not so sure. To her mind, it was almost as if some immense, invisible force had weighed in with some very useful but unasked-for help. As the dismal prospect of long hours of overtime and a delayed experiment receded into the distance, a relieved operator had cried out: 'The gods are with us, I think.' There was general laughter at this, but she had not been disposed to join in.

Then, there was the case history itself.

Was she alone in viewing with unease the physical resemblance between the Technician and Sir Henry Forres? That there was such a perfect match between the two was remarkable enough. That the titled gentleman should choose to reveal himself at the precise moment in time that he had was well-nigh incredible in her estimation.

She had similar reservations with regard to Miss Emma Sinclair.

Here was a young woman with all the attributes that could be expected to appeal to the Technician's partiality. The result was that her friend had tacitly abandoned that objectivity essential to the task he had set himself. Moreover, what was striking, what was eerily striking, was that this temptress should just happen to be a near-neighbour of the look-alike Sir Henry Forres. No, she did not altogether trust Emma Sinclair. 'Beauty is truth, truth beauty', the poet Keats had written, but in this instance at least she preferred the little-known variant to the poet's words: 'Beauty is truth, but she does not always speak it'.

More disturbing than all of this, however, was an indefinable sense of foreboding, which had plagued her ever since her first involvement in the experiment. She had experienced the same feeling of an impending catastrophe seven years previously, shortly before the air disaster in which her father had died.

The scene in the Transporter Room as she entered brought a measure of reassurance. The transporter's cone of blue light shone sure and steady, its pale glow seeming to radiate a calming influence. Her little staff of operatives moved each one about their business with a quiet confidence, or so it appeared. If anyone shared her own nervous apprehension it did not show.

She retired to her nearby office and tried to occupy her mind with routine tasks, but to no avail. With a sigh, she put aside her work. In five hours time she would rouse her friend. After a light meal, he would begin to prepare himself for his departure.

Five hours to go and counting. Five hours to go and counting – counting, oh! so slowly.

She had half-expected him to be up and about when the appointed time came, but was not altogether surprised to find him still sleeping. That he could sleep so soundly on an occasion such as this did not surprise her unduly. On his own admission, he had slept little the previous night and had arrived back at four o'clock that afternoon looking exhausted.

Having gently shaken him awake, she looked on in silence for a moment as he began to dress himself in the period clothes and replacement shirt.

The time had come to voice her doubts before it was too late.

'You've only to give the word and we can abort this experiment, here and now,' she said.

'We've come too far to turn back,' he said. 'I have to see this thing through.'

She shook her head. 'I can't seem to get the thought of that voice you told me about out of my head. I've thought of little else these past few hours. It's weird. It's inexplicable. It's frightening.'

He nodded his understanding, but went on to say: 'Well, having slept on it, I'm rapidly coming to the conclusion that it was all a flight of fancy on my part. It was pitch-black in the middle of that cluster of pine trees, and what with that and the thought of what lay ahead of me, my nerves were stretched to breaking point. This next time it's going to be different. I'm going back in broad daylight and with a much simpler task ahead of me.'

'Yes, that's true,' she acknowledged, reassured by his words. 'Incidentally, tell me in the language of nineteenth century English, what exactly will you say to whoever opens the door to you at Pine Tree Cottage?'

He spoke a score of words, but they did not bring enlightenment to her.

'I can scarce make out one word in three,' she said, laughing.

'No, I wouldn't expect you to,' he said. 'The English language is not some static thing. It has a life of its own and expands, contracts, and modifies itself with each passing century. A full quarter of the people employed by London Complex are concerned with linguistics for that very reason.'

'But you, I know, are truly expert in the language of 18th and 19th century England,' she said.

'I flatter myself I am, and in the language of ancient Greece and Rome,' he said.

'Why so?' she asked. 'The first I can understand, but it's news to me that you've a special interest in the Classical Period.'

'I don't especially,' he said, 'but I've an abiding interest in literature through the ages. The ancient Greeks were the first to refine the art of literature, and it's much more rewarding to study the works of Plato and Plutarch in the language in which they were written than peruse some modern-day translation.'

'That's what I like about you,' she said, draping an affectionate arm about him. 'You're so accomplished in so many fields, and yet modest and unassuming with it. You're a celebrated figure on the world's stage, akin to that man who was the first to step out onto the moon's surface a millennium ago, for no one has done the once what you are about to do a second time. That would be enough to turn any man's head, but not yours.'

'Caroline, will you stop this?' he said. 'You're embarrassing me.'

'Everyone loves you here at London Complex, you know that don't you?' she said, ignoring his request. 'Even the Surgeon-General, who loves no one but himself, has a real affection for you. I *know* why you have difficulty in coping with the tragic events of other realities – it is common humanity on a rare scale. You know my sexual preferences lie in quite the opposite direction to the majority of my sex so I've no ulterior motive in saying what I do say.'

He stopped what he was doing and turned to face her.

'This is beginning to sound like my eulogy,' he said.

In the circumstances, it was entirely the wrong thing to say. With barely a pause he attempted to correct that. 'Caroline, will you please stop rambling on about nothing of consequence and come and help me with this damn cravat thing? I've been tussling with it for the past ten minutes and it still looks like a dog's breakfast.'

She did as he asked, and with the task done to the satisfaction of them both, she began a gentle tugging at his hair.

'Is this real, or simulated?' she asked.

'It's the real thing, alive and growing by the day,' he replied. 'Permanent, too, if I so wish. I had a similar mop removed after Sussex, as you know, but I've half a mind to keep this lot when I get back.'

This casual remark on his part pleased her. It appeared that the Technician had no doubts, himself, about his safe return. For the umpteenth time that day she told herself that she was worryingly unduly, but with more conviction this time.

The business with the cravat meant that he was now several minutes behind schedule. Accordingly, he declined the cold buffet prepared for him in favour of a quick cup of strong coffee and a more leisurely supper on his return. The coffee consumed, Technician and Supervisor headed directly for the Transporter Room. Here, they parted company, she taking up a position behind the four operatives seated at their control panels, and he climbing the score of steps to the metal gantry, where he took up a position close to the blue light of the transporter link.

Now that the decisive moment had come, her fears for his safety returned to her in full force.

The confident nods of the four operatives as she moved from one to the other told her that the transporter's cone of light give every indication of being in perfect working order. Indeed, her practised eye told her that for herself. So, everything must be in order...... must it not? They could not probe the exit point, where the Technician would rematerialise, but since there was only the one cone of light, which existed simultaneously in both realities, that must mean it would look the same from that other vantage point...... wouldn't it?

One by one the hands of the four members of her staff were being raised to give the green light to go. One...... he had shaken hands with all four operatives on entering the room, which now struck her as odd since he had never done such a thing before. Two...... now, he was standing and looking around intently, as if he wished to imprint the scene on his memory. Three...... he was waving goodbye to her, the act seeming to carry with it an air of finality. Four...... her turn next.

She wavered. She saw him staring at her and begin to shake his head at her hesitation. She tried to raise an arm but it seemed to have a will of its own and refused to move. She saw him shifting restlessly as he looked down at her. She saw the operatives turning round one by one and looking at her with an air of curiosity. With a mind-sapping effort, she raised an arm. Five!

He stepped into the blue light and disappeared instantly, leaving her to stare at the empty space where he had stood.

Of her future life in her current reality Caroline de Tournai was now certain of one thing above all else. In that instant of time it came to her with an absolute conviction.

'I shall never see him again,' she said, as the scene before her began to mist over.

CHAPTER 9

In the garden of Pine Tree Cottage the microscopic, long-dormant cone of light flared accommodatingly back to its original state with the arrival of Technician Travis. The explosive transformation was of much too short a duration to register on his consciousness, but that mysterious sixth sense, which comes to the aid of all of us on occasions, made him vaguely aware that something unusual had happened. He stepped outside the boundary of light, and viewed it with a critical eye. In shape, size, and intensity, however, it appeared perfectly normal.

One glance about him, however, was proof enough that something had gone wildly wrong. He had timed his arrival for early morning, but in place of a rising sun in the eastern sky was a setting sun close to the western horizon. Morning had become evening.

The warm, humid air served to reinforce the clear impression of high summer, evident in the lush greenery on all sides. Spring had been transformed into summer.

Both the nearby cottage, dark and silent, and the unkempt, overgrown garden in which he stood give every appearance of abandonment. Most shocking of all, the transporter's cone of light stood no longer in the midst of the small plantation of fir trees, but shone clear and plainly visible to any passerby in a small area of bare soil separating garden and trees.

Down on his hands and knees, he was quickly able to establish that the transporter link had not, in fact, moved at all but that someone had cut back the copse by felling a score of trees – stumps and vestiges of stumps left no doubt on that point.

It seemed clear that he had returned not after the planned seven hours but some two to three *months* later.

He looked in wonder at the transporter's light, deeply puzzled that it had survived for so long a period time, presumably escaping detection all the while. He could only assume, and rightly so, that it had remained shrunken and inert until his passage had reactivated it. How this could possibly have happened was a mystery to him.

Warning bells were telling him that he should immediately terminate his visit by stepping back into the cone of light, and so return to his own world. That would, of course, scupper the experiment irretrievably.

The same unswerving determination to personally carry out the experiment now persuaded him to linger a little while and investigate. Something had gone badly wrong, and any clues he could unearth as to why this should have happened could be of vital importance to any future research. He moved stealthily towards the cottage, resolved to give himself twenty minutes of time but also determined to bolt back to the safety of the transporter if any danger threatened.

As he approached the rear of the cottage he saw he had been mistaken in his assessment that the building was unoccupied. A dimly flickering light was moving from room to room on the rear upstairs floor. Someone was in the building, moving about with a lantern, or candle.

He switched his attention to the front of the house, approaching it silently via the small side-garden. Here, no light was visible, and the picture which presented itself was one of quiet desolation, as elsewhere. He spent a full ten minutes searching for some clue which would help solve the mystery which confronted him, but found nothing. With a despairing shake of the head, he began to make his way back to the rear garden.

Meanwhile, Sir Henry Forres, lantern in one hand and bunch of keys in the other, was leaving by the rear door. He was on the point of locking up when he was startled by an unearthly shriek no great distance away. Leaving the bunch of keys hanging from the lock, he whirled around just in time to see the pale, ghostly form of a barn owl glide into the shadow of the nearby trees. It was then that he spotted the pale blue light of the reality link. Full of curiosity, holding the lantern aloft in front of him, he moved towards it.

Travis exited the side-garden in time to see a puzzled Henry Forres step into the middle of the cone of light.

Time seemed to stand still for Travis as he watched in horror the scene before him. His passage home began to flicker, dimming and brightening in turn, as if the light was possessed of human faculties and was debating with itself as to whether this was the returning Technician, or not.

Because it used up precious energy, the in-built scanning device was not made terribly sophisticated. Its sole purpose was to deny access to some passing stranger who might blunder into its zone of influence. It did not really cater for the remote possibility of some identical twin from another reality doing likewise. Travis, of course, had been well-aware of just such an identical twin in the shape of Henry Forres, but if everything had gone to plan the man would have been seventy miles away in the wilds of Northumberland. He had, therefore, deemed any refinement of the scanning device as quite unnecessary.

The light resumed its steady glow. Sir Henry seemed on the point of stepping out of the circle of light. Travis began to breathe again.

'Move away,' he whispered. 'For pity's sake, move away.'

Perversely, his passage home responded to this plea by blinking out of existence, taking a frozen Henry Forres with it.

He was stranded. No, more than that, he was lost for ever. His years of experience and his store of knowledge hammered out the message in his head: Senior Technician Richard Travis, ex-London Complex, you are lost for good, and no power in the known Cosmos can bring you safely back home.

It is true that he had half-expected some such catastrophe but, all the same, he found himself ill-prepared to meet it. Noble thoughts of self-sacrifice in the familiar surroundings of London Complex was one thing, but here was the hard reality and he had not bargained on the tide of desolation now sweeping over him. He sank to his knees, fighting to keep control of his emotions as the evening twilight closed in upon him.

In time, his personal crisis began to ease. He must act. He must do *something*, were his thoughts. He got to his feet, and with a firm step walked the short distance back to the cottage. The door at the rear of the building, the very door he had used himself once before, swung open at his touch. With no fixed purpose in mind, he entered into the gloom of the interior. Aimlessly, he wandered the empty rooms, his eye noting the dust and decay of long neglect. His first thought had been to spend the night there but he found not a stick of furniture within and an atmosphere so depressing that he speedily abandoned the idea and was glad to quit the place.

Outside once more, he secured the door. Through the fast-fading light, he squinted at the tie-on label attached to the bunch of half-a-dozen keys.

'*PINE TREE COTTAGE*', said the one side.

'*JAMES BUCKLAND, ATTORNEY AT LAW, YARM*', announced the other.

He needed time, he reflected. He needed time and peace and quiet sufficient for him to recover his wits and to work out what was best to be done for the future. As for the *immediate* future, spending the coming night under some wayside hedge was not an attractive proposition. If he did that, he would awake in the morning cold, hungry, destitute, and with nothing resolved upon. Sir Henry Forres had vanished from the face of the Earth for good, that much was plain. Very well, if only for a few days breathing space, he would take that gentleman's place.

He had chosen to eat very little during the past twenty four hours, and the first pangs of hunger coinciding with the first spots of a summer shower decided the matter.

Pocketing the bunch of keys, he turned his face towards the certain comfort and dubious safety of Grange Hall.

He saw a single downstairs' light and a scattering of lighted windows upstairs as he approached the building via the curving, gravel driveway. It was now quite dark and he estimated the time to be about ten o'clock.

Taking his courage in both hands, and praying that no one had paid particular attention to the clothes Sir Henry Forres had been wearing that evening, he pushed open the front door. Entering the hallway, he made straight for the main staircase, thankful for the time and effort he had spent in memorising the layout of the place. A footman, whom he did not recognise, came suddenly through a doorway and out into the hallway. At the sight of him, the man stopped, bowed courteously, and passed on his way. With a thumping heart, he ascended the staircase, meeting no one until he breasted the landing. Then it was that he came face to face with Rogers, the butler.

He surprised himself with his own outward show of calmness.

'Ah! Rogers; I know it's late, but would it be possible to arrange for a cold supper to be sent up to my room? Nothing elaborate – a green salad, with bread, and a little drinking water would suffice.'

If Rogers was surprised at this request he did not show it, but with a polite bow of acknowledgement stated that he would see it attended to at once.

Travis sought the sanctuary of what he knew to be his bedroom, closing the door behind him, gratefully. He noted that the candles had been lit, the curtains closed, and the bedsheets turned down. With a sigh of relief, he laid himself down and began to take stock of his situation.

It was clear that the trap set for him, which he had half-suspected all along to be the case, had been sprung, but he did not propose to spend any great deal of time wrestling with the complexities of that particular puzzle. He had spent many fruitless hours during the past few weeks debating the matter with himself, and had lighted on no new insights, and had reached no firm conclusion. If the sole intention of it all had been to divorce him from his work at London Complex that had been achieved. There was absolutely nothing he could do to rectify the situation and, in truth, he had no complaints, for he had walked into his present predicament with his eyes open.

As for his future life in the early nineteenth century, he had a clear choice of two alternatives. Either, he could withdraw into himself and wallow in self-pity, or he could resolve to make the best of things and begin to build a new life for himself. The first alternative could offer him nothing but a miserable and purposeless existence. Surely, anything was better than that, he told himself.

He did his best to look on the positive side. Was his situation so terrible? he asked himself. No, he thought not. No time castaway was better qualified to deal with life in the year 1811 than he was. Moreover, there would be compensations. New adventures and experiences, novel emotions and delights, old-world recreations and pursuits, and a breed of women more suited to his tastes – all these things beckoned. Apart from his work, half-a-dozen true friends, and even fewer distant relations, was he leaving so very much behind? No, he was not, he concluded. The loss of his work would be the hardest blow to bear, but he would find other challenges, and set himself different goals. Moreover, this was *her* world and he was now a part of it.

Or, was it her world?

Had he entered into some variant reality in which she did not feature? No, he could not believe that. Pine Tree Cottage existed, as did Grange Hall. Present, too, was Rogers the butler, and until very recently Sir Henry Forres. Where, then, was Emma and her little family? Here, was a mystery.

It was not so very strange, he acknowledged, that he had encountered Sir Henry Forres, with such disastrous consequences to them both. Grange Hall lay little more than a stone's throw from Pine Tree Cottage. As a near-neighbour, there was nothing remarkable about Forres occasionally frequenting the cottage, but what was the fellow doing there at that time in the evening, and carrying with him the keys to the property? Stranger still, why was the building deserted? Above all else, where was Emma?

These and a dozen other questions occupied his thoughts and he knew that he would not be able to rest easy until he had the answers. Finding the answers would occupy his time during the coming days, as would making the necessary adjustments to life in the year 1811. It was important that he occupied his time. Sitting about with time on his hands, brooding and feeling sorry for himself, just wouldn't do at all.

A somewhat timid knock at the door roused him to alertness. At his bidding, a young girl entered the room carrying a tray of food and drink. With a large shawl draped over her shoulders and bare toes peeping out from below her nightshift, she give every appearance of having been abruptly roused from her bed in order to bring him his meal. She left the tray as he directed, dipped a curtsy, and moved hurriedly towards the door.

He realised he had been given an unexpected opportunity to obtain some useful information.

'Do not go just yet,' he called out to her.

She froze, motionless, her back towards him.

'Well, turn around, girl,' he said, kindly. 'Come closer and let me look at you.'

Slowly, reluctantly, she did as he asked. As she did so, he saw that she was in an extremity of fear. From her mouth there came a peculiar drumming sound, which he realised with a start were her teeth chattering.

'Please, sir......,' she said, in a helpless tone of voice.

'Don't be afraid, child. I'm not going to harm you,' he said. 'Now, tell me your name.'

'Mary – Mary Moore, sir,' she replied.

'And how old are you, Mary?' he asked.

'Fifteen, sir; I'm only *just* fifteen years,' she said, with what he thought was undue emphasis.

'You're fairly new here, aren't you? How long have you been with us?'

'Three months, sir.'

The fact that he did not recognise her, didn't seem to know her at all, did not surprise her. She was a scullery maid, the lowest of the low, with a function in life to be neither seen nor heard by those she served but simply to do what she was bidden.

'And what is your position here, Mary?'

'I'm a maid in the scullery, if you please, sir.'

'Very good. Now, Mary, I want to see how well you have learnt your duties. Tell me, whom do you serve at Grange Hall? Apart from myself, of course.'

'Miss Rachel, sir, and......'

'And who? Who else, Mary?'

'And...... and any guest who may be staying at the Hall.'

Her answer came out in an unconvincing gush of words. He felt sure this was not what she had originally intended to say, but he wanted to deal gently with little Mary Moore and decided not to press the matter.

'Do we have any guests staying at the moment?'

'No, sir.'

'Good; very good, Mary,' he said, reassuringly. 'Now, then, take me through your working day, starting from when you first get up.'

By dint of such questioning, he quickly confirmed the daily routine of the house and the names and brief details of most of the staff, some already known to him, some not. It was an encouraging start for him, he thought.

Glancing at the clock on the nearby mantelpiece he saw that it was very nearly eleven o'clock. The girl was expected to be up at five a.m. and at the thought of it he felt a twinge of guilt at having interrupted her night's rest.

'I'm sorry for having kept you from your bed, Mary,' he said. 'Will you forgive me?'

Forgive? What did he mean? No one in her life had ever asked for her forgiveness. She mumbled a confused reply, eager to be away.

'You have my permission to stay in bed until seven o'clock,' he said. 'I'm sure the rest of the staff will manage well-enough without you for a couple of hours. Tell cook, or whoever it is who does come to wake you, that this is my express wish and I shall be angry if I'm not obeyed in this matter. Do you understand?'

'Oh! yes, sir. Please may I go now, sir?'

He made her wait a moment longer. Picking up a shilling coin from a pile of loose change to be found on the dresser top, he presented it to her. She took it from him, only to offer it back instantly.

'Oh! please, sir; I beg you, no,' she cried, on the verge of tears. It was clear that she thought she would be expected to give something in exchange.

'As you wish, Mary,' he said, gently. 'You may go now.'

She made a rush for the door, but paused before leaving to ask: 'Shall I rouse Sarah, sir?'

The question had all the hallmarks of a tactful suggestion, the significance of which was lost on him. Bemused, he shook his head, and watched her leave.

Turning his attention to the meal brought him, he found it consisted of greens, cheese, and pickle, together with a generous helping of some kind of meat, which he guessed was mutton. In addition, there were two thick slices of brown bread plus the water he had asked for.

His civilisation had long since abandoned the practise of eating animal flesh. Inevitably, therefore, this portion of the meal was left until last. A creeping horror assailed him as he put the tiniest morsel of meat into his mouth. The gagging sensation which came upon him threatened to develop into a full-scale retching. Hurriedly, he shoved the plate away. The thought came to him that he must have a word with cook before many days passed, otherwise he could well see himself fading away.

The events of the past twelve hours now began to take their toll. Wearily, he undressed and got into bed, but not before he had carefully stowed away the one item which he had brought from his own world. Shrink-wrapped within a slim, plastic wallet was a six-capsule, three day course of treatment for the disease of tuberculosis.

Why had he brought it with him? he asked himself. Why, when he had given an undertaking to his Controller not to indulge in any unauthorised action, had he felt the need to raid for the second time in a year the assets of The Medical Museum at London Complex? Unlike his Sussex venture, he had no plans to use such a medication, so why had he done it? He could not answer that, except to admit to himself that it was done at the bidding of the voice – the voice in his head incessantly urging him: 'Take it; who knows, you may have need of it, and where's the harm?' It was all a part of that mysterious period of time, with its bizarre portents and inexplicable events, and it had been easier to give into the voice than attempt to fight against it.

The result was that the cure to a disease extinct in his own time, but increasing apace in this world of 1811, now rested incongruously out of place amidst the trinkets and paraphernalia of the early nineteenth century in a Georgian dresser drawer.

Accompanying it was an item of a personal nature. After some hesitation, he decided to remove the finger ring given him by Emma, some ten hours ago by his reckoning.

Ten hours. Was that all it was? His visit to the dying Emma seemed a lifetime ago. So much had happened it was difficult to credit such a short interval of time. Now, here he was, lying in a strange bed, amidst even stranger surroundings, at the start of a new life. He felt a rising tide of apprehension and excitement at the prospect of the challenge which lay ahead.

Was he equal to that challenge? he asked himself. Could he slip into Henry Forres' shoes and play the part well-enough to carry it off? Would he be allowed the breathing space of perhaps a week or two to sort out his life? The more he considered the question the more sure he felt he *could* successfully carry it off. There were three aspects to consider, and he pondered each in turn.

First, and most important, was the degree of physical resemblance between himself and the man whose place he had to take. On this point, he had no doubt. He more than resembled Henry Forres, he was the man's exact double, even down to the small scar on the left cheek.

Second, was the degree of similarity in speech and mannerisms. Here was no natural affinity but one that must be engineered. Using his talents as an actor, he had spent many hours imitating both features and prided himself that he had achieved a good match. It was not a perfect one but it would have to do. The ease with which he had already deceived some of the staff at Grange Hall give him cause for optimism. In truth, danger threatened from very few individuals to a man only recently arrived in the district. He would have a half-sister to contend with, and a few old retainers brought from Lincolnshire, and that was about all.

If appearance, speech and mannerisms posed few problems, the same could not be said of character. Here, the difference between the two men opened up into not so much a discrepancy as a yawning chasm. The Technician, gentle, kind-hearted, and considerate, was the very opposite of the violent, severe, and self-centred Henry Forres.

He knew that to play the part well he should modify his natural disposition so as to come close to that of the owner of Grange Hall, but he shrank from the prospect of having to do this. 'To thine own self be true,' ran the old saying. He would not, *he could not*, surrender his principles in an imitation of Henry Forres.

This decision on his part would, he knew, bring difficulties, but there was no help for that. There could well be gossip and whispered comment behind his back, but none of that would constitute danger. There was only one individual who had the power to denounce him as an imposter and he had not the means. Henry Forres was as dead to this world as he was to his own. All the same, he resolved to guard the secret of his identity with his life for it would be ironical if he was to prove to be the instrument of his own downfall.

As for the man whose place he was about to take, Travis could only wonder as to how *he* would fare in *his* new life, and what London Complex would make of him; but such speculation on his part was quite useless, he acknowledged. He would never know how the man would fare.

These thoughts turned his mind back to his own world, and to that little band of people he had loved and lost.

He tried to envisage the arrival of Henry Forres in the Transporter room: the short-lived joy of Caroline de Tournai on his seemingly safe return; the consternation and dismay which must inevitably have followed once the true situation revealed itself; and the recriminations which would plague The Complex thereafter.

He thought of the pain and sorrow which his loss would cause to those he had been close to: of a discredited Dyal having to unfairly shoulder the blame for the disaster; of the irascible Canazaar, with one more grudge against the way of things, turning further in on himself; of the grief of Milo Sands, who now had to learn to live with a second loss. In spite of his best efforts, he felt the tears welling up, misting his eyes and stinging his cheeks.

Enough! Enough! He had chosen his future path in life, yet here he was barely started on his journey and already taking a wayward fork. He would dwell no more on London Complex, on Senior Technician Richard Travis, and on the shattered dreams and blighted hopes of former days. From this moment on, he was Sir Richard Forres of Grange Hall. The dropping of the name of Henry would be the one gesture he would make to his past, a tiny concession which he felt due to him.

Tomorrow would be the first day in his new life, and he would make a start by calling on one 'James Buckland, attorney at law, Yarm'.

One final puzzle came to him as he drifted off into an uneasy sleep. Why had the transporter 'hesitated' before accepting Henry Forres as the returning Technician? It was true that the time displacement of a few months would have slightly aged and subtly altered the man, but hardly to *that* extent. By Travis' reckoning, the man should have been recognised and accepted instantly. Here, then, was another mystery.

It was just as well he was ignorant of the true explanation, otherwise even the fitful, restless sleep which now came to him would have proved impossible.

CHAPTER 10

Richard Forres (for as such we shall now know him) was awoken at eight o'clock the following morning by the drawing back of his bedroom curtains, the rays of the sun, already high in the sky, shedding instant light and languid warmth into every corner. A welcome cup of freshly brewed lemon tea steamed invitingly by his bedside. He propped himself up, teacup in hand, and studied the slim, lithe figure of the dark-haired servant girl who had entered his room. She answered his friendly greeting with a glowering look and the briefest of responses before leaving abruptly with what he thought was a quite unnecessary display of noise. If little Mary the previous evening had given the impression of being terrified of him, his morning's visitor had given every sign of displeasure.

Oh, dear! he thought, what have I done now?

He dressed quickly, anxious to be out and about as soon as possible. He had yet to meet his self-appointed stepsister, Rachel, and as he approached the door of the breakfast room he steeled himself for the meeting. On entering, however, he found that she had already breakfasted and left, judging by sprinkling of crumbs and discarded items of crockery, which littered one end of the breakfast table. Although he knew the meeting could not be long delayed, he was, nonetheless, relieved at this temporary reprieve.

He lifted the lids from an array of hotplates, and baulked at their contents. Eventually, he settled himself happily beside a large rack of freshly made toast and a pot of what proved to be a delicious raspberry preserve.

After a few moments, a manservant, whom he recognised as Simpson, the under-butler, entered with a dutiful bow and the morning's greeting, and set down a further serving of tea to accompany the toast.

'Ah! Simpson, it's you,' he said. 'Tell me, do you know where Miss Rachel is this morning?'

'It's Wednesday, sir,' came the reply, as though this explained everything. Fortunately for the questioner, he went on: 'She is in Stockton for the day, and will be back at the usual time, I believe.'

'Oh! yes, of course,' he said, smoothly. 'Thank you, Simpson.'

An hour later saw Richard Forres entering Yarm High Street after a short but disconcerting walk from Grange Hall. His fellow pedestrians had grown steadily in number during the journey, from an infrequent passerby to a fair crowd of people in the centre of the small but bustling market town. Their behaviour towards him had been, with the odd exception, universally the same. His words of greeting had been pointedly ignored, and his nods of recognition disregarded. His friendly looks into the faces of those he passed had been repaid with stony stares, or averted eyes. It came as a relief, therefore, when he arrived at his destination and entered into the relative privacy of attorney Buckland's place of business.

The young clerk who received him was formally polite, and profuse in his apologies for the fact that his employer was engaged with another client and would not be available for another half-hour. Would Sir Henry care to wait, or would he prefer to call back later? was the question put to him. The man appeared distinctly relieved to learn that the new arrival would prefer to call back.

He left the place and headed for 'The George and Dragon', an old coaching inn situated on the east side of the High Street. It was important that he test himself by mixing with the locals, and twenty minutes spent in that busy establishment would serve the purpose very well. The visit was also likely to provide him with the latest news and gossip, and other useful titbits of information.

In this expectation, however, he was to be sadly disappointed. His frosty reception on his way into town was to continue in 'The George and Dragon'. As he entered, the noisy buzz of activity and gossip abruptly ceased, and he found himself approaching the bar in a near-sepulchral silence. He was solved the problem of deciding what to order by the opening words of the publican: 'Good-day to you, Sir Henry; the usual, is it?'

As he sipped the drink set before him, he tried time and again to strike up a conversation with his host, but all his efforts were to prove in vain. The man seemed bent on being civil, but no more than that. All the while, a large, stout, fair-haired lady, whom Forres took to be the publican's wife, hovered in the background. She was openly hostile, ignoring him completely, and shooting her husband furious looks every time the man seemed on the point of unbending a little. The fact was, the two of them had argued several times in the past concerning the owner of Grange Hall. To her, he was a callous brute, who ought not to be allowed across the threshold. To him, he was a disagreeable but valued customer, who spent freely with them – and was he, or was he not, running a business?

Forres was glad to leave after barely half his allotted time, winding his way past customers abruptly silent once more. As he walked out onto the street he heard the hubbub of noise return, and was left to marvel at the fact that in the space of a few short months since his arrival Sir Henry Forres had managed to antagonise so many people.

He headed towards the nearby River Tees, and was soon strolling along the busy wharves, which fronted the south bank. All was activity and noise, with boats small and large loading and unloading, but he knew that already the little port, deep inland, was in decline, loosing trade steadily year by year to the new port of Stockton, some five miles downstream. Within fifty years Yarm would become a quiet backwater, the river silted up in places and the now busy wharves silent and deserted.

It was here on the waterfront that at last he found a few friendly faces. Several times he was greeted by shouts of welcome from some of the lower class of folk who found employment there. It seemed that Sir Henry Forres had, considering his station in life, peculiar tastes in his choice of friends.

With much food for thought, he made his way back to the attorney's offices. Within a moment of his arrival he found himself being ushered into that gentleman's presence.

Always immaculately dressed, as befitting his occupation, James Buckland was a small, daper, balding gentleman in his early fifties, with a friendly, open face, and an easy going disposition. His one peculiarity, a source of some amusement to friends and family alike, was the curious habit when agitated, or upset, of preening and cosseting in meticulous fashion nonexistent locks of hair on a shiny scalp. The friendly, open face was not, however, much in evidence when he proceeded to greet his visitor with an icy politeness.

He viewed this reception with a sinking heart, but his present position of almost total ignorance with regard to his state of affairs he found intolerable, and he remained resolved to proceed with his carefully thought-out quota of guarded but probing enquiries. These were based on the supposition that Sir Henry Forres had been looking around Pine Tree Cottage with a view to buying the property.

It was clear that something had happened to the Sinclair family, which had resulted in the cottage becoming vacant. The son, he knew, had left home some time ago and he thought it likely that the mother, who was known to be in ill-health with a weak heart, had died, leaving a house much too large for daughter and solitary servant. Emma must have removed herself elsewhere, whilst entrusting the sale of Pine Tree Cottage to attorney Buckland. For his part, Sir Henry Forres, as a near-neighbour whose land abutted that of the Sinclair property, had become a prospective purchaser. Perhaps the man was hoping to extend his estate, or perhaps he had thoughts of housing his steward, or some other employee, in a building conveniently to hand.

It was a carefully worked out and entirely reasonable scenario, given the known facts. It was also totally wrong and its use as a working hypothesis was soon to result in an excruciatingly embarrassing scene in James Buckland's office.

'I have here the keys to Pine Tree Cottage,' Forres began, handing them over.

'Thank you, Sir Henry. I'm obliged to you,' said Buckland. He dropped the keys into a desk-drawer and looked at his visitor in a marginally more friendly fashion. 'All done, then?' he said. 'Everything in order?'

'Yes, perfectly so,' said Forres, 'although I have to say that the cottage looked a little forlorn standing empty and silent yesterday evening. Quite a change from the old days, what?'

'You could say that,' came the unhelpful reply. Was it the listener's fancy, or was there a hint of censure in the voice?

He leaned forward towards the attorney in a casual, friendly fashion. 'And it is your opinion that the asking price is fair, is it not?'

James Buckland teased an invisible lock of hair 'back into place', a frown of disapproval darkening his face. This was typical of his visitor, absolutely typical, he was thinking. He made a determined effort to remain polite and businesslike. 'Sir Henry, we agreed the asking price here in this office a month ago,' he said. 'Mr. Williamson is meeting that price in full, and I have verbally agreed the sale on your behalf. At this moment, my clerk is drawing up the contract of sale, and I would hope to have everything completed within the week. Are you suggesting that I approach Mr. Williamson's solicitor with a view to extracting more money from his client?'

So, he was selling the place, not buying it, which was a surprise. He had assumed all along that the cottage had been the property of the Sinclair family but perhaps it had only been leased from the neighbouring estate. Either that, or Sir Henry Forres was taking a quick profit on a property only recently acquired. The man's visit yesterday evening must have been for the purpose of a final look around.

Hurriedly, he sought to placate the attorney.

'You mistake my meaning, sir,' he said. 'I only question if the price is a fair one to Mr. Williamson.'

This was the first time in twenty five years of legal practice that James Buckland had heard a client at the point of sale question an asking price to his own detriment, but if his visitor's apparent concern on this point surprised him he contrived not to show it. 'The asking price is fair to both parties,' he said, patiently.

Forres moved with relief onto what he believed to be firmer ground. The state of neglect of Pine Tree Cottage could only mean that the property had remained empty after the Sinclair family had vacated it. That being so......

'I came across a few trifling possessions belonging to the previous occupants,' he said, casually. 'They seem to have been overlooked by everyone concerned, myself included. I shall see that they are returned to the family, if you would oblige me with a forwarding address.'

James Buckland's reaction to this apparently innocuous request was nothing short of astounding to Richard Forres. He watched as the man sat bolt upright with open mouth, disbelief, amazement, and anger chasing one another in rapid succession across his face.

'I ask only the present whereabouts of the Sinclair family so that I may perform this small service on their behalf,' said Forres, feebly, all-too conscious of the fact that he was guilty of some terrible faux-pas.

James Buckland's first thought was that this was some puerile attempt at humour, in appallingly bad taste, by his visitor but this quickly give way to a belief that a somewhat transparent attempt was being made to extract information from him, information which he knew his client would love to be in possession of. Finally, came the conviction that the fellow's dissipated lifestyle had, at last, caught up with him. The smell of port on the man's breath had not escaped his notice, nor had the cut and swollen lip – this, presumably, the result of some drunken fracas. The fellow was the worse for drink, which explained his piece of foolishness with regard to the asking price of Pine Tree Cottage. Either he was intoxicated, or drink was beginning to addle his brain. It was all too much, thought the attorney. It was intolerable. He felt one hand clenching up while the other worked feverishly across his scalp.

Finally, he spoke. 'You wish to know the whereabouts of the Sinclair family? Is that correct?' The voice was quiet, the tone menacing.

Richard Forres could only nod in reply, not at all sure he now wanted to know.

'You surely cannot mean to enquire after the *entire* family?' the attorney said. The tone of voice was now heavily sarcastic, the significance of which was lost on Richard Forres.

Anxious not to draw attention to his particular interest in Emma, he replied: 'Why, yes, Mr. Buckland. Is there a difficulty?'

In James Buckland's opinion, his befuddled visitor was asking for it. No, more than that, he was sitting up and positively begging for it.

'Very well, Sir Henry, since you press me,' he said. He looked up towards the ceiling, his face a picture of mock concentration. 'Let me see. Where to begin? Well, the mother and elder son are resting six feet under the ground in the parish churchyard, put there by your own abominable handiwork. Young Peter Sinclair is, I believe, now back in the district, living on the outskirts of Stockton, I'm told; but if you value your safety I would strongly advise that you steer clear of that young man.'

Having spoken his piece, James Buckland waited for the angry response, which he was sure must follow. None came, the silence hanging heavy on the air.

'You look surprised, Sir Henry,' he said, after a moment of awkward silence. 'I cannot imagine why that should be. I only say to your face what the whole town says behind your back. Unprofessional of me, I grant you, but, then, you did press me on the matter.'

Forres suddenly felt an urgent need to put some distance between himself and the speaker, but there had been no mention of Emma, and he could not leave things as they stood.

'And Emma? What of her?' he croaked.

'Ah! now I do believe we are getting to it,' said Buckland. 'With regard to Emma, I can truthfully say that I have not the slightest notion as to her whereabouts, and I rejoice that despite your best efforts you seem to be in the same state of ignorance as myself.'

It was done. It was all said, and he was glad of it. The little speech was long overdue on his part, he judged. As for his client's patronage, he was welcome to take that elsewhere anytime it suited him to do so. He walked across the room and opened wide his office door.

'I am a busy man, Sir Henry,' he said, 'and I really do not have the time to play foolish games of cat and mouse with you. You may expect my cheque in respect of Pine Tree Cottage a week from tomorrow. My clerk will deliver it by hand. I bid you good-day, sir.'

With a burning face and feelings which would be difficult to put into words, Richard Forres made good his escape.

Once outside, he set off to walk the short distance to the parish church of St. Mary Magdelene, thoroughly confused by what he had just been forced to listen to.

Buckland had spoken of an *elder* brother, in addition to young Peter Sinclair. How was it possible that Emma had *two* brothers? In fact, as he quickly realised, there were only two possibilities: either, he was in a somewhat different reality to the one he should be in, or the information available to London Complex had been incomplete. With everything else to date dovetailing to the known facts, he could scarcely credit the first possibility but the second one was more than plausible. By the standards of London Complex, the coverage of Emma had been extensive, but coverage of the Sinclair family *as a whole* had been much more restricted. If the elder of the two brothers had left home before the programme of observations had begun, as seemed to be the case, his existence could very easily have been overlooked.

In a sense this was a minor matter. What troubled Richard Forres more was James Buckland's claim that the man whose place he had taken had been implicated in the death of this elder brother, as well as that of the mother's. If that were true, attorney Buckland had been offering sound advice when he cautioned him with regard to young Peter Sinclair, but less easily explained were his words concerning Emma. Why had the owner of Grange Hall been using his 'best efforts' in an attempt to discover Emma's whereabouts? Had the man been conducting some kind of hateful campaign, or vendetta, against the Sinclair family? He hoped with all his heart that this was not the case.

Preoccupied with these thoughts, oblivious to the stares and slights of more townfolk, he entered the churchyard to seek out the Sinclair family grave. A stunning surprise greeted him when he eventually located this and read the inscription on the modest granite memorial:

'SACRED TO THE MEMORY OF ELIZABETH SINCLAIR, WHO DEPARTED THIS LIFE 30th FEBRUARY 1813, AGED 51 YEARS'

Below this, an inscription slightly different in style, and clearly a later addition, read:

'AND TO ROBERT SINCLAIR, DIED 28th APRIL 1813, AGED 27 YEARS'
'*I know that my redeemer liveth.*'

1813? February and April, 1813!

He had taken it for granted, had assumed all along, that he had returned in the summer of 1811 because a discrepancy of more than a few months was unthinkable, but the unthinkable had happened. He was not a few months astray, he was more than two years late in his arrival. How such a huge discrepancy in time was possible he could not begin to imagine.

The true date of his return explained a great deal. He marvelled no longer at his hostile reception in town. The thoroughly unpleasant Henry Forres had been given ample time to make himself almost universally disliked. He wondered no longer at the transporter's 'reluctance' to accept the man. The intervening two years had physically changed Henry Forres, not to the human eye perhaps, but certainly to the more sensitive eye of the transporter's in-built scanning device, which had come within an ace of rejecting him as its designated passenger. Finally, he ceased to puzzle over a surprisingly crowded sequence of events: of a young woman fully recovered in health and long gone; of a major change to the landscape of the garden at Pine Tree Cottage; of a house which had in turn been occupied, vacated, and now all but sold. There had, in fact, been time enough for all these things.

It was a major setback, he acknowledged, ruefully. The irritating ignorance of relatively recent events, to which he had been resigned, had suddenly turned into a catastrophic 'memory loss' extending back more than two years. If he was to play the part of Sir Henry Forres successfully, he must bring himself up to date with regard to his present situation as quickly as possible.

Help came in the shape of Vicar Sibley, as he saw the familiar figure of that clerical gentleman making his way the short distance from vicarage to church. Seizing the opportunity, he hurried to intercept him.

The 'greeting' extended to him when they came face to face was, as before, polite, formal, and bleak. It was also brief. Sibley, it seemed, had no great desire to linger long in the other man's company. Richard Forres was forced to come straight to the question he had been hoping to lead up to.

'Would you oblige me, Mr. Sibley, by making the parish registers available to me?' he said.

'To what purpose?' said Sibley, curtly.

He had anticipated the question.

'I have felt the need recently, vicar, to engage myself in some useful occupation. To that end, I have begun work on a history of our little town. The parish register would, of course, furnish me with much useful information. I understand that you have the keeping of them, and that they go back in time to the year 1649.'

It was a not unreasonable request. The writing of town, or county, histories by gentlemen of leisure, detailing all manner of topics from antiquities to zoology, and including year by year birth and mortality statistics, had become quite the fashion in recent times. What surprised the Reverend Sibley was that a labour of love such as this should be seriously contemplated by the man before him, but if the owner of Grange Hall was at long last about to engage himself in a useful – no, a laudable – pursuit, he was the last person in the world to discourage the man.

His countenance softened a fraction as he nodded his assent. 'Come with me, Sir Henry,' he said.

The would-be author was led through the body of the church to the small vestry at the far end. Here, Sibley motioned him to a table and chair. Unlocking a large, antique cupboard, he indicated row upon row of neatly arranged volumes.

'Just the most recent years to begin with, I think,' said Forres.

Two slim, clothbound books were placed before him, together with paper, quill, and ink. Sibley nodded in approval as his visitor set to work.

'I shall leave you to it, then,' he said, after a moment. The tone of voice was now almost benign.

Eagerly, as soon as it was safe to do so, he sought out the burial entries for Elizabeth and Robert Sinclair, but found these added little to the information inscribed on their gravestone. With a sigh, he turned his attention elsewhere.

For very nearly an hour he busied himself in copying out selected entries, dealing in turn with burials, then baptisms and, finally, records of marriages performed. It was all useful information, much of which would have been known to Sir Henry Forres, and which should, accordingly, be known to him, but he had to acknowledge that it was hardly furthering his own quest. All that was soon to change.

He was occupied in copying out an entry dated 9th August, 1811, detailing the marriage of James Buckland's only daughter, when his eye, straying a few lines down the page, caught sight of an infinitely more relevant entry. He averted his eyes for a few seconds before returning to it, all the while doubting his senses, but the entry was real enough in recording the marriage of one, Sir Henry Forres, bachelor and gentleman, resident at Grange Hall, to one, Emma Sinclair, spinster of the parish.

Married! In the eyes of the world at least, he was a married man. More than that, much more than that, he was married to *her*.

Yet, was it so strange, so wonderful? he asked himself. No, he thought not. The two parties had been near-neighbours, both single and of a marriageable age, the one rich and handsome, and the other beautiful and desirable. He did wonder as to how Emma could have been so deceived with regard to Sir Henry's true character but reminded himself that the gentleman in question was adept at presenting two very different faces to the world. It was all-too likely that, flattered by the attentions of a young man possessed of wealth and social standing, Emma had been blind to Sir Henry's true nature.

With a shaking, useless hand, he put down his quill pen and began to go over in his mind all that he had learnt that day. He found he had little difficulty in reconstructing the history of the past two years, at least as far as Emma and Henry Forres were concerned.

Some little time after his visit to a dying Emma she had taken up with the owner of Grange Hall. After what appeared to have been a short engagement the two had married. All-too soon afterwards the gentleman's vicious character must have revealed itself to Emma.

Weak and in ill-health as she was, her daughter's misery must have hastened Elizabeth Sinclair to an early grave – that much was clear from James Buckland's remarks. Just how Henry Forres had been implicated in the death of Robert Sinclair remained a mystery to him, but he realised it would be very odd if this, too, had not come as a consequence of Emma's treatment at the hands of her husband. Perhaps Robert had sought to protect his sister and there had been a falling out between brother and husband, with disastrous consequences to the former.

The rest of it was not in doubt.

Shortly after her brother's death, Emma had fled her husband and gone into hiding. Motivated either by a desire for revenge, or else out of wounded pride, Henry Forres had been bent on reclaiming his wife. Finally, it was clear from his own reception in town that morning that the man's dissolute ways, and his treatment of both wife and stepsister, had thoroughly alienated the good people of Yarm.

He had thought to fill in the gaps in his knowledge of recent history in easy stages over a period of a few weeks but the information he had been seeking had all come irresistibly flooding in during the course of a single day. He should be rejoicing at this easy success but in the circumstances it was impossible for him not to feel sick at heart at what he had learnt. By his actions he had saved Emma's life, but for what? For a life hardly worth the living.

What to do for the best? that was the question.

The problems he now faced if he continued in his present role were ones he could well do without as he struggled to adapt to an alien environment. That being so, should he not wash his hands of the whole business? Would it not be for the best if he were to slip quietly away to London, there to build a new life for himself as a free agent? Given his special talents, he did not doubt his ability to thrive and prosper in what would be to him a mecca of opportunity, but where would that leave Emma and Rachel, not to mention the host of people who were dependent on the continued existence of The Grange Hall Estate? Towards Emma he felt a particular responsibility, so much so that he shrank from the thought of abandoning her, alone and unhappy and locked for goodness knows how many years to come in a loveless, mockery of a marriage.

Should he continue to play the part of Sir Henry Forres but leave Emma to her own devices – in effect giving that young woman her freedom? The thought did not appeal to him, for he realised that his own future happiness at Grange Hall depended in no small measure in making amends to Rachel, and building a new and better relationship with all around him. He was, understandably, very reluctant to leave Emma out of that process of reconciliation.

In the final analysis, the question he had to face was a simple one. Did he, or did he not, want Emma as his wife? As Technician Richard Travis, he had never felt the need, or inclination, to take a permanent partner, but already, as Richard Forres, he was beginning to view things in a different light. As things stood, it was a lonely road which lay ahead of him. How wonderful it would be, he thought, to have by his side a lifelong companion, one whom he could turn to when the memories of a lost existence rose up like ghosts from the past to haunt him, as haunt him they would on occasions.

Who better to fill that void than the wife already provided for him? Who better than the one remaining link to his previous existence? Who better than the one who had brought him here? But could he possibly repair the damage done by his predecessor?

At first sight, it seemed a hopeless task. How she must fear and loathe him. One certain fact, however, give him hope for the future. Emma's real husband was gone from the scene and he was there in his place. If he had to turn the other cheek to atone for the man's past misdeeds, he would do so. If he must needs return the enmity and hatred of all those injured, or offended, with kind words and deeds, he would do precisely that. If there are mountains to be moved he would move them, and through it all he must guard with his life the secret of his true identity. Like some small child, he found himself whispering a promise: 'I shall be good. I shall be better than good.'

So it was that in the quiet of that small, secluded spot Richard Travis, consciously and deliberately, took upon himself the sins of another.

'You look unwell, Sir Henry. Does anything ail you?' came a voice.

Engrossed with his thoughts, he had failed to hear the return of the Reverend Sibley. The man stood just behind his shoulder, looking down at him, the eyes taking in the pale, drawn face of his visitor.

He slipped easily into the role of Henry Forres.

'No, I am well, Mr. Sibley,' he answered, 'just a little low in spirit, that is all. To own the truth, my mind has been straying from my task. I have been looking back over the events of the past two years and viewing with shame the part I played in them. Is there any hope for one such as me, do you think?'

Sibley made no reply, but pulling up a chair seated himself close by. How often in the past had he sought out the young man to remonstrate with, or censure him, and all to such little effect? Now, for the first time, the man had come to unburden himself.

'I have met with open hostility in town today,' said Forres. 'Kind words and friendly gestures have been few and far between.'

'Can you wonder at it?' asked Sibley, an acid tone to his voice. 'By your conduct, you have managed to achieve the single-handed destruction of very nearly an entire family.' He paused to view the affect of his words. If young Forres had come with a sympathetic hearing in mind he was going to be disappointed. 'The Sinclair family were very popular hereabouts,' he went on. 'Emma, in particular, had a fair host of admirers. You talk of hostility, but if it were not for the protection which your social standing affords I fear you would long

120

ago have met with far worse.'

'Do you hold me responsible for the deaths of Elizabeth and Robert Sinclair?' asked Forres.

Sibley considered the question for a moment, determined to be fair and objective in his response.

'Not directly, no; but indirectly, yes, certainly. Elizabeth Sinclair succumbed to a long-standing heart complaint, but there can be little doubt that your abominable treatment of her daughter hastened her decline. I was with her at the end and I can tell you that it was the only thing which occupied her thoughts. Her distress was pitiful to watch.'

'And what of Robert?' asked Forres.

'The two Sinclair boys always were headstrong and impetuous,' said Sibley, with a sigh. 'We all know that Robert deliberately set out to provoke you that evening in 'The George and Dragon', and that when attacked you did little more than defend yourself. It was no fault of yours that he stumbled and fell, splitting open his skull. All the same, had it not been for your infamous conduct towards his sister the foolish and tragic events of that evening would not have taken place and Robert would be alive today.'

'But was my conduct towards my wife so *very* bad?' asked Forres.

'How can you speak so?' cried Sibley, visibly loosing all patience at the question. It was time, he thought, for some plain speaking. 'Your treatment of Emma, and that of your sister – let us not forget her in this matter – has been nothing short of deplorable. More times than I care to remember Emma has come to me in despair, black and blue from some drunken beating at your hands.' He paused for a moment, struggling to control a rising temper. 'Oh, if you are sober and so inclined you can conduct yourself well-enough, Sir Henry, but you are the Devil himself when the drink is upon you.'

This said, he walked over to the vestry window, and stood looking out at the summer scene before him. 'I do not make you out, sir, I do not make you out at all,' he said, quietly. 'You have every advantage in life: health, wealth, a good intellect, and social standing. You also had once the love of a young woman for which many a man in these parts would have sold his soul. And how have you used these God-given gifts? By leading a life of gambling, drunkenness, and debauchery – that is how. It pains me to say it, but if you were to die tomorrow you would be surely damned, sir.'

'But a man may change for the better, may he not?' said Forres; 'and does not your bible say that there will be more rejoicing in heaven over one sinner that repenteth than over ten such people who have no need of repentence?'

Sibley turned and approached him, nodding his agreement. It was only later, much later, that the words '*your* bible' were to strike him as odd.

'Yes,' he acknowledged, 'but it must be a *true* repentence, and not one forced upon you by your present circumstances and adopted in the hope of some personal advantage.'

'May I ask if you have had any news of Emma?' said Forres. 'How does she fare? Does she lack for anything?'

'I have seen her just the once since she left Yarm, but we correspond at intervals of time. She keeps tolerably well, but is deeply unhappy, which should come as no great surprise to you. Apart from other considerations, she misses the company of your sister, Rachel. As you know, the two of them became firm friends within a short time of their first meeting.'

'I take it all her regard for me has now gone?' The voice of the speaker carried with it the faint trace of a hoped-for contradiction, but a telling silence on Sibley's part served as answer enough.

'If you were to perceive a change for the better in my conduct, would you speak to Emma about a possible reconciliation? It is your duty to promote that, is it not?'

With these words, Forres unwittingly touched upon a particularly troublesome matter to Vicar Sibley. That man of God took the marriage vows which he administered very seriously even if, sadly, that was not the case with some of his parishioners. 'For better, or for worse. For richer, for poorer. In sickness and in health' – so ran the words.

'*For better, or for worse.*'

It was for this reason he had several times in the past urged Emma to remain with her husband when she had been on the point of leaving him. It was for this reason that he had joined forces with Emma's uncle a year ago, when she had fled her husband the first time, to successfully urge her to return. The result each time had been for her more pain, more grief, and more despair. He was not prepared to proffer such counsel again unless he was very sure of a real and lasting change in the young man before him. In spite of his deeply held beliefs in the sanctity of marriage, he could not, in all conscience, urge Emma's return to what would be more suffering. Not that she would listen to him even were he to do so. Too much had happened. Too many loved ones had been injured, or destroyed. No, Emma was lost for ever to Henry Forres, of that Sibley had no doubt, but he could not bring himself to say as much to the sad figure of the man beside him.

They sat in silence together for a few moments, Sibley noting that although he had not responded to the young man's plea for assistance that had brought forth no complaint, or reproach.

'Will you oblige me in one respect at least?' said Forres. 'Will you from this day on address me as 'Richard'? I have done with 'Henry',' he added, with real irony in his voice. 'I would be grateful if you would also let your parishioners know of my wishes in this matter – quietly, as the opportunities present themselves.'

It was, Sibley thought, a strange request, and he could not begin to understand the reason which lay behind it, but he sensed the matter was important to the young man.

'Yes, if that is your wish,' said Sibley. 'It is, after all, one of your two given names.'

'For the present, I think I shall shelve my local history project,' said Forres. 'I believe I would be better employed in putting my life in order.'

'In the circumstances, I agree,' said Sibley. 'So, what are your future plans? What *will* you do?'

'What *can* I do?' said Forres. 'I shall be myself, Mr. Sibley. I shall be *myself*.'

'That can hardly be said to have served you well in the past,' Sibley pointed out.

'Yes, but the future will be very different,' said Forres. 'A day will come when all those who detest the sight of me will be proud to own me as a friend. I shall not rest until it is so.'

Sibley raised an eyebrow at these bold words, but contented himself with saying: 'It is quite a task you set yourself.'

'An impossible task is what you are thinking.'

'I did not say so.'

'No, but you thought it, and I cannot blame you for your scepticism, in view of all that has gone before.'

'I only mean you have a mountain to climb.'

'Or, a mountain to move,' said Forres. He picked up a bible lying within easy reach, and began to leaf through its pages. Within a moment he had found the passage he was looking for and was reading out to his surprised listener:

'Mark, chapter 11, verse 23 – *'For verily I say unto you that whosoever shall say unto this mountain, Be thou removed and be thou cast into the sea, and shall not doubt in his heart, but believe that these things which he saith shall come to pass, he shall have whatsoever he saith.'*'

Setting the book to one side, he said: 'Now, Mr. Sibley, what is your interpretation of that passage of scripture?'

'Why, that through faith, and with God's help, a man may achieve the seemingly impossible,' answered Sibley.

In different circumstances Richard Forres might have taken exception to the phrase 'with God's help', but as things stood he was happy to nod his agreement.

'Then, I shall be that man, Mr. Sibley,' he said. 'I shall be the man who moves mountains.'

With these enigmatic words, Richard Forres departed, leaving a puzzled Vicar Sibley staring thoughtfully after him.

CHAPTER 11

He arrived home to find a letter awaiting his attention. Having broken the seal, he unfolded the single sheet of paper and read:

'I need to see you urgently. Meet me at noon by the second stile on the footpath leading into Bluebell Wood. Come alone and on foot, and you will learn something to your advantage.

J. G.'

Puzzled and intrigued, he began to read the message through a second time, addressing Simpson as he did so.

'When did this arrive?' he asked.

'Shortly after you left,' Simpson replied.

'Did you take delivery of it personally?'

'No, it was handed to Mostyn, who was working close to the entrance gate at the time. He tells me one of the street urchins from town brought it.'

With a nod, Forres dismissed the manservant and headed for the dining room for a spot of late lunch. His morning's business had occupied him for very nearly four hours, so it was now a few minutes after one o'clock. It would seem, therefore, that J.G. – whoever J.G. was – must have had a long and lonely vigil at the designated time and place, but that was no fault of his. If the matter was as important as the writer implied, he, or she, would, no doubt, be in touch again. With more important matters to occupy his mind, he pocketed the letter and instantly forgot about it.

The first task of Richard Forres after lunch was to undertake a thorough examination of his room and adjoining quarters. He had learnt much that day, but there still remained gaps in his knowledge of how things stood at Grange Hall. A searching examination of the family living quarters would, he hoped, help to fill in some of those gaps.

There were eight bedrooms, his own included, opening onto the first floor passage which ran the length of the house, with the servant's quarters occupying the second floor of the handsome, brick-built

Georgian building.

Two of the eight bedrooms he found empty and unfurnished, whilst three others, fully furnished but showing no evidence of permanent occupation, were clearly intended to serve as guest rooms. The room next to his own, however, was different to the five previous. In a large, custom-built wardrobe he found a whole range of female apparel, ranging from coats and full-length gowns to small accessories, such as gloves and kerchiefs. He turned up little of a truly personal nature, however, apart from a small jewellery box containing a modest range of inexpensive decorative items. The telltale signs of *current* occupation were absent, clearly pointing to the room being Emma's hastily abandoned quarters.

The room directly opposite give every indication of current female occupation, and was clearly that of 'his' half-sister, Rachel. Having no wish to pry, he contented himself with a cursory look around before turning his attention to his own room. Here, he was quickly drawn to a small chest of drawers, tucked away in the far corner.

The first two drawers produced little of consequence, but the locked bottom one promised more. It took a twenty minute search to find the key, but he eventually located it in a tiny, concealed compartment tucked away at the back of the antique chest. Unlocking the drawer, he drew it out completely and carried it across to the bed. Seating himself down beside it, he began a systematic examination of the contents.

His first major surprise came with the discovery of a large leather purse containing Treasury notes and gold guineas to the value of £840 – a substantial sum of money for the time period. Together with the cash was an unredeemed I.O.U. for 150 guineas in Sir Henry Forres' favour. The pledge was in the name of one, William Harker. Still outstanding after six weeks, it appeared that the said gentleman was not very prompt in honouring his debts, but in that he was not alone, as Richard Forres was soon to discover.

At first sight, all this seemed to augur well for the continuing prosperity of The Grange Hall Estate, but further discoveries were to disprove this. First, was a large sheaf of seemingly unpaid bills from suppliers and tradespeople, some of them dating back more than a year. Second, and even more revealing, were several communications from Sir Henry's accountant urging financial restraint, and prophesying a gloomy future if the proffered advice was not acted upon.

Notwithstanding the large amount of ready cash, it appeared that the late Sir Henry Forres was heavily in debt. The discovery puzzled Richard Forres for it was a known fact that Sir Henry had come to Yarm possessed of a substantial fortune, bequeathed to him by his father. Moreover, the purchase of The Grange Hall Estate, with its large acreage of good arable land and its many tenant farmers and smallholders, all contributing to the estate's coffers, should have proved to be a sound investment.

The discovery of a black, leather-bound notebook, with page after page of detailed entries, brought forth the sorry explanation.

For the best part of two years, in almost nightly visits to Stockton, Sir Henry had been gambling recklessly. The notebook detailed a full record of winnings and losses, the latter more in evidence than the former. Certain it was that estates more lucrative than Grange Hall would have struggled to cope with such financial profligacy. At the very end, however, it appeared that luck had turned in Sir Henry's favour, the last three pages of the little black book, covering a period of some two weeks, detailing winnings in excess of a thousand pounds. All of that still left the estate in debt to the tune of ten thousand pounds by Richard Forres' estimation. It seemed that in addition to everything else, he had inherited a parlous financial legacy.

The discovery was all he needed, he thought, bitterly. It was the final straw. It put the finishing touch to a thoroughly discouraging day.

Two more finds were to come his way, the one potentially useful, the other poignant and disturbing.

First, came the discovery of three entires, all bearing the York postmark, and all addressed to the owner of Grange Hall. An examination of these quickly established that the sender, one Doctor Johnathon Sinclair, of Micklegate, York, was none other than an uncle of Emma, a gentleman whose existence had been hitherto unknown to Richard Forres.

It was evident from the contents of the letters that Sir Henry had been in contact with the Doctor in order to obtain information with regard to Emma's whereabouts. No less evident was the fact that Johnathon Sinclair had long since lost patience with his niece's husband, and had no wish to either volunteer information, or tender support.

The first letter, dated May 20th, detailed a long list of Sir Henry's past misdeeds, which were put forward as justification for Emma's desertion, and ended with a claim of ignorance as to her present whereabouts.

In a second letter, dated June 14th, this claim was repeated. There was also a stinging reminder of how the writer had helped Sir Henry in a similar situation a year before only to be let down by the gentleman's rapid return to his former lifestyle. The final paragraph requested Sir Henry 'not to opportune me further in this matter'.

This request had clearly been ignored, as a third letter, dated July 4th, made plain. Brusque and to the point, it read:

'Dear Sir,

I write this as a consequence of your uninvited and unwelcome appearance here yesterday. My purpose in writing is to repeat for the last time that I have no knowledge of my niece's present whereabouts. I would only add that even if this were not the case, I would be the very last person to divulge such information to you.

Please note that I shall not favour with a reply any further communication from you on this subject

yours,

Johnathon Sinclair.'

It was plain to see that Henry Forres had refused to take 'no' for an answer, and had persisted in his enquiries, even to the extent of calling unannounced on his exasperated relative. It seemed that he had not believed Johnathon Sinclair's protestations of ignorance, and neither, after due reflection, could Richard Forres. The Doctor was, in all probability, Emma's sole surviving relative, apart from young Peter Sinclair. Alone, vulnerable, and without any independent means of support, it seemed highly unlikely that Emma could survive in the world without the active help and support of her uncle.

In spite of the thoroughly discouraging tone of the letters, Richard Forres began to make plans to visit York at the earliest opportunity. The fact of the matter was, he had no other leads to follow for he was resolved not to press Vicar Sibley for further information, and a visit to Emma's sole surviving brother would more likely than not prove both fruitless and hazardous. His conduct, and his method of dealing with Johnathon Sinclair, would be very different from that of Henry Forres, and there was a chance, slim, it was true, that the old gentleman would reciprocate in like-fashion. Within a short space of time his tentative decision to go to York became a firm resolve. Tomorrow, he would go into town and book passage on the southbound coach for the day following.

He was brought back to the present by the sound of an approaching carriage. From his bedroom window he watched as a chaise and four drew to a halt to disgorge its passenger.

Rachel Forres, soberly dressed in a plain, dark costume, alighted from the coach and stood in the driveway below looking about her, and blinking in the bright summer sunshine. With haunched shoulders, and nervous bobbing movements of the head, she looked to Richard Forres like some small, defenceless bird, alone in the world and wary of it. Hair shaped into an unflattering, tight bun, and a pair of large, functional spectacles, completed a picture of youth not so much lost, as never aspired to. Had he not known differently, he would never have put her age at a mere 17 years.

He could not help but feel pity for the girl when he thought of all she must have suffered at the hands of her brother. They would meet for the first time at dinner that evening, and the thought that in the days to come he would overwhelm her with kindness and affection, give him a warm glow of pleasure anticipated.

Returning to his task, he began to replace the varied contents of the drawer back into proper order. Then it was that he made his final, shocking discovery. From a large, chamois-leather bag, which he had thought empty, there tumbled out an object more eloquent than the hoard of cash, more revealing than the sheaf of correspondence, and more disturbing than the little black notebook. It was not the buckled and twisted oval gold frame of the painted portrait miniature which caught his eye, nor the tiny daggers of glass which clung to its inner edge, but rather the butchered remnant of a face – *her* face, he was sure

– set in crazed enamels. The portrait had been heavily scored – 'savaged' would not be too strong a word – by the hand of someone in a furious, blind rage, so that now a single eye, set within a noseless, mouthless face, gazed out at him in mute appeal.

The discovery plunged him into a fresh bout of despair, which lingered with him until he stirred himself to dress for dinner. This took him longer than it should have – would he never master these damn Georgian cravats?

He arrived late to the dining room, to find Rachel already started on her meal. She looked up timidly, greeted him with a few hesitant words, and with eyes downcast hurriedly resumed eating.

He was seeing her for the first time close up in the flesh and her appearance saddened him. A large, ugly bruise, mottled yellow with the passage of time, disfigured her face below the left eye. Thinking he may be deemed the cause of it, he lacked the courage to mention it in conversation.

A close scrutiny of her face revealed it to be pockmarked, not badly so but certainly noticeable from where he sat. This legacy of childhood smallpox was a feature of her appearance which he had missed in his cursory study of her at London Complex. It was, he guessed, a source of much misery to the sensitive, vulnerable young woman sat opposite him. She looked pale and anxious, and old beyond her years, and it pained him to see her so.

Their first meal together was not the pleasant occasion he had hoped for. He struggled through the main course, picking his way around the meat and its juices but finding it impossible to entirely escape the flavour. Fortunately, the first course had been a vegetable broth, and there had been a glacé sweet to finish, but he still felt hungry at the end of it all.

He made several attempts, with all the gentle kindness he could muster, to engage his 'adopted' sister in conversation, but met with little success. Was she well? Had she had a pleasant day? What had she brought back from her day out at Stockton? What were her plans for tomorrow? To all such enquiries she stammered the briefest of replies. Eventually, he was forced into silence.

The meal at an end, she gave every sign of wishing to be away. He had half a mind to detain her, but decided against it. He must not force the issue, he told himself. He was not going to change things overnight, and he must be patient. He watched in silence as she left him.

Tired out after his busy day, he went to bed early to dream of home and Milo Sands. They were curled up together, she awake, and he in that altered state of consciousness between sleeping and waking, only vaguely aware of what she was doing. He felt her hands, warm and sensuous, exploring his body.

'Milo,' he murmured, sleepily; 'Milo, what are you doing *now*? Go to sleep.'

He heard an exclamation of derision, followed by: 'Never mind her. Why do you interest yourself in a foolish child when you may have a grown woman?'

The dream was very real. In truth, it was no dream at all. Sitting up, he saw dimly in the moonlight filtering through his bedroom window a recognisable female form.

'Sarah? Is that you?' he said, peering closely. 'What the devil are you doing here?'

'You did not send for me last night, nor tonight, for that matter,' she said, accusingly; 'and don't think I don't know the reason. Eleanor told me you were closeted with Mary for a full half-hour last night. Rogers should have woken me to bring you your meal, not her.'

'She's a child, barely fifteen years of age,' he protested. 'Do you really believe anything untoward happened between the two of us?'

She sniffed, derisively. 'It wouldn't be the first time. Considerations of that kind have never stopped you in the past. All I know is that it doesn't take half-an-hour to deliver a supper tray.'

'We got talking, the two of us, that's all,' he said.

'I find that hard to believe,' she said. 'What can the two of you possibly have in common? Anyway, if the girl means nothing to you, why did you call her name just now?'

'Did I? ...... Oh! that. I was saying 'Milo', not Mary,' he said, unthinkingly.

She raised herself up to look more closely at him. 'Who the hell is Milo? Is that supposed to be a name?'

He ignored the question, as ignore it he must, and scanned the angry, pretty face looking down at him. She was young, pleasing to the eye, and there for the taking. In the situation which he now found himself, lonely and friendless in an alien world, he was sorely tempted for a moment, but, no, it wouldn't do. It wouldn't do at all. For the best part of two years the master of Grange Hall had mistreated his wife, had slighted her, and cheated on her. He had taken on the role of her husband and he would not, he *could* not, tread a single step along that same path.

Mary's suggestion the previous night, that she be allowed to bring Sarah to him, and the latter's behaviour the following morning – inexplicable incidents at the time – were now explained. How long this affair between master and maidservant had been going on he did not know, but it must stop now, he resolved.

'Sarah, I believe we should put an end to this affair,' he said, firmly. 'I am now determined on a fresh start in an attempt to win back my wife, if that is still humanly possible. It will hardly further my cause if I continue to be unfaithful to her. And consider: what future is there for you in any of this? You should find someone whom you can love openly, and who is free to love you in return.'

It was, perhaps, a measure of his predecessor's known character and reputation that these soft-spoken and reasoned words did nothing to placate the listener, who simply took it for granted that he had found another mistress more to his liking, if not Mary then someone else she could not guess at.

'Do you think you can discard me when the fancy takes you with a few honeyed words?' she hissed. 'Do not imagine I can be so easily disposed of.' Her intimate relationship with her late master had, it appeared, made her bold, and uncaring as to his temper.

It was late, and he had been through an exhausting, traumatic day. He had done his best to deal gently with a problem which was none of his making and it was now time to assert his authority.

'I want you to go back to your room – *now*,' he said, wearily.

She made no move to comply, but continued to lay taut and tense beside him.

'If you do not leave, I shall summon Rogers, and have you forcibly removed, which will probably arouse the whole household,' he warned her. 'Is that what you want? Do you wish to be publicly shamed and humiliated?'

Reluctantly, she got out of bed and began to put on her nightshift, which lay discarded on the floor. She was crying quietly and, not for the first time, he silently cursed Sir Henry Forres.

She looked back at him before leaving. 'Am I to be dismissed?' she said.

He sat up and stared across at her. 'No, of course not,' he said. 'I would have you as a friend.'

She thought this a ridiculous statement coming from a master to a lowly servant but, all the same, could not refrain from replying: 'You ask too much.'

He could not help but groan in frustration after she was gone. He had managed to make an enemy of one who, in all probability, had been the only friend and companion he had in the world. He wished with all his heart for some success in his planned visit to York. He could not help feeling he was due some good fortune for a change.

CHAPTER 12

Jane Gaskell was a young lady much addicted to that class of sensational literature which has come to be known as the Gothic Horror Novel. Very much in vogue at the time of our story, these lurid tales seemed to hold a particular fascination for the seventeen year old, the attraction being that they offered a ready escape from a mundane world of daily routine and ladylike duties, all of which she found irksome at times.

Her favoured reading opened a window on a very different world from the one in which she moved. Here, was a world of decaying towers and crumbling spires, crowning architectural piles. Here, were long forgotten lumber rooms, covered in the dust of centuries and reeking of unspeakable horrors. Here, were ghoulish retainers, looking every bit as ancient as the stone and mortar which surrounded them, serving their terrible young master. Here, presiding over all, was that young man: cruel, unprincipled, pitiless in his anger, and as handsome and virile as his coal-black, favourite stallion.

In her imagination, a varied set of circumstances, each one, in truth, highly unlikely, brought her to live in such a place, there to fall into the power of its youthful owner, whose sole purpose in life, according to local gossip, was to seduce as many young virgins as possible – young innocents like herself.

Let us picture the scene as Jane pictured it to herself, one dark and stormy night a week after her arrival. He, the worse for drink, but not inebriated, and certainly not incapable (that would never do!); she, alone in her room, listening, terrified, to his approaching footsteps. Maddened by her repeated rejection of his advances, he was about to take matters into his own hands.

See there his mad pursuit of her from room to room; her panic-stricken tumble down the staircase; her broken, bleeding body lying at his feet; her face as pale as pale, whiter than the scanty white nightdress which covered her; her limp body carried in his arms, a trailing hand brushing the delicate cobwebs on the winding stone staircase leading to his room.

The following morning she awoke to find a pair of anxious eyes looking down at her. Over the next few days, as he nursed her back to health, her beauty and goodness forced a change in him, until one night, as he tiptoed from her room, she found herself calling out to him: 'Do not go; stay with me through the night.'

In the fulness of time, they forsook that castle of gloom, seeking pastures new. Behind them they left a local legend – the ultimate tale of the triumph of good over evil.

Such was the make-believe world of Jane Gaskell, a world of the imagination oddly at variance with her real character, for in all other respects here was a young woman with her feet planted firmly on the ground, and displaying a pluck and daring to a degree rare in one of her sex. Not that Jane paid much heed to the social conventions in that respect. The so-called 'male preserve' she refused to recognise. In modern parlance one could fairly describe her as a 'tomboy'.

Now, it is an odd fact of life that such creatures tend to be pretty, and in this respect Jane was no exception. It is also true that females of the likes of Jane Gaskell are by no means unattractive to many men. The combination of beauty, a frequently displayed boyish teasing, and a *seeming* unavailability can be a potent combination. The seventeen year old Jane exuded a sexual appeal, a fact of which she was well-aware and was not averse to taking advantage of on occasions in order to get her own way.

In her heart, Jane never imagined that she would be given the opportunity to act out her fantasy, but on the night of July 29th, 1813, she came close to doing just that.

A more unlikely companion for Jane could not have been found but in the shape of Ruth Harker, yet the two of them were firm friends, and had been for four years within a short time of their first meeting at Miss Jenkinson's school for young ladies in the town of Wetherby. Plain in appearance, demure, and with a proper ladylike reserve, Ruth was in many respects the very opposite of the confident, outgoing Jane. Their schooling now behind them, they had resolved that their friendship must continue. Accordingly, in addition to regular correspondence, it had been arranged that Jane would spend the coming month of July with the Harker family in Yarm, while the following December would see them together again in the Gaskell household in Leeds.

For three weeks Jane had spent a pleasant enough time with her friend, her only complaint being a situation a little too quiet for her liking. In the middle of the second week, however, there had come a rare flutter of excitement when Ruth had pointed out in town one morning the notorious owner of Grange Hall. Along with the identification had come a lurid commentary, of which 'lost to God and man' would be an accurate summary. Such a description, of course, was one guaranteed to arouse an intense curiosity in Jane. She stared at the handsome face pointed out to her with an intensity sufficient to provoke an embarrassed dig in the ribs from her friend.

Here was the villain-cum-hero of her fantasies, if ever that man existed in real life: a wickedly handsome face, just as she had always pictured it, and a terrible past, just ripe for conversion. Even Grange Hall, pointed out to her on an especially grey and dreary day, appeared not too different from her fantasy castle. Of course, there *were* some differences. In particular, Henry Forres had a wife, but a wife could be set aside, especially one guilty of desertion. If Jane Gaskell had been better acquainted with the gentleman in question it is likely that she would not have harboured such foolish thoughts, but the man was a stranger to her and friend Ruth had spared her the most sordid details of his life-history out of feelings of delicacy. Intrigued, Jane had suggested that they call at Grange Hall on some pretext or other, a suggestion which had horrified Ruth.

In the final week of her stay Jane began to notice a change in her friend. Constantly preoccupied with her own thoughts, it was clear to Jane that something was troubling her. After a few days, her persistent enquiries paid off when Ruth decided to unburden herself.

It seemed that master William, the young man of the house, had, not for the first time, run up gambling debts which he could not honour. In sheer desperation, he had come to his young sister, but she could offer him nothing except her modest savings of fifteen guineas to add to his own meagre five pounds. The debt was for 150 guineas, and payment was, even now, overdue. To make matters worse, the I.O.U. in question was held by the odious Sir Henry Forres.

'I have asked for more time,' William had told his sister, 'but he says that if the money is not forthcoming by midnight on the 29th, father will know of it by nine the next morning.'

'Can William not go to his father on his own account?' Jane asked.

'Impossible!' exclaimed Ruth. 'Jane, this has happened twice before, though not with that evil man Forres. On the last occasion father settled the debt but give William fair warning that if it happened a third time he would be cast off from the family.'

'Surely, he did not mean that?' said Jane.

'I believe he meant exactly that,' said Ruth. 'He give a promise at the time that this is what would happen, and I have never known father go back on his word. One may provoke him only so far. Beyond that point he can be both ruthless and inflexible.' She turned to her friend, the tears streaming down her face. 'Midnight two days hence is all the time left to William, with no hope of even one-quarter of the sum being found. Oh, Jane, what is to be done?'

It was then that the true qualities of Jane Gaskell showed themselves.

'Give me all the money, yours and William's,' she said. 'I have a little of my own to add to it.' She took her friend's arm in hers. 'You will leave this in my hands. In my hands, you understand? No! no questions, I beg you. Trust me, Ruth, trust me.'

Going to her room, she took up pen and paper. Within ten minutes the brief note was finished. The following morning she made arrangements to have it delivered by hand to Grange Hall. Late the same morning she went alone to the secluded spot a little way out of town, which she had offered as a meeting place, but her quarry failed to put in an appearance. She waited a half-hour after the appointed time before giving up.

Her failure to effect a meeting was irritating in the extreme. In theory, thirty six hours grace still remained, but in reality the time was a lot less. Prior arrangements necessitated an excursion to Stockton that afternoon in the company of Ruth. Here, at the house of her friend's aunt and uncle, they were to remain until the afternoon of the following day. She could do nothing more until her return to Yarm. Suddenly, the deadline set by Sir Henry Forres began to loom uncomfortably close.

As she made her way back to the Harker household the solution came to her, such a perfect solution that she wondered why it had not come earlier. Immediately upon her return the next day she would pay a call at the Vicarage and explain the situation to Mr. Sibley, whose discretion could be relied upon. He could escort her to Grange Hall with the utmost propriety, and might even be persuaded to lend her moral support.

Alas, for the best laid plans!

She arrived at the Vicarage at three o'clock the following afternoon to find the man she sought not at home. He had left an hour earlier, bound for Darlington on some business or other, and was not expected back until very late that evening.

Only one option remained.

She set her face towards Grange Hall to make the journey alone. Uninvited and unaccompanied, it would mean the ruin of her reputation, but that was not something which weighed heavily with her. The very next day, before the gossiping tongues had really got to work, she would be on her way home, some fifty miles distant.

She had not gone a hundred yards before she turned back. She may not have to suffer the consequences of what she had in mind but Ruth would surely suffer in her place. Any improper action on her part would reflect on her friend, indeed on the whole Harker household. What price, then, the keeping secret of William's disreputable conduct?

No, her journey to Grange Hall would still have to be made, but it must be made in secret and unobserved. To accomplish *that* it would have to be made under the cover of darkness.

She retired early that evening but surprised Ruth by entering in upon her at ten o'clock fully dressed.

'I knew you would still be awake,' she said.

'Who can sleep at a time like this?' cried Ruth. 'Oh! Jane do you still have no news for me? Is all hope gone? William is weeping next door. Can you not hear him?'

'I hear him,' said Jane, distractedly. She opened the bedroom window and looked down into the darkness below. 'Your father is still moving about downstairs, and we are fast running out of time, so it has to be the bedroom window. Sorry to disturb you, my dear, but the branches of that pretty little garden tree of yours don't reach as far as my window.' Gathering up her dress and petticoat, she tucked them into the voluminous pair of Mrs Harker's drawers, which she had put on for just that purpose. She swung a bare leg over the windowsill. 'Wish me luck,' she said, with a grin. 'Tell William, no peeping, although on second thoughts best not tell him anything.'

Almost before Ruth was aware of it, her friend was gone.

She rushed across to the bedroom window and leaned out.

'Jane, this is madness,' she cried. 'Come back, dearest, this instant, or you will surely injure yourself.'

'Would it surprise you to learn I've done this before?' came a voice. 'This very tree, I mean. I shall be perfectly safe. Go back to bed, but don't close the window.'

'Go back to bed?' cried Ruth. 'Do you imagine that I shall be able to rest easy for a single moment until your return? I believe I know where you are off to. Oh! Jane, come back, I implore you.'

The plea went unanswered. With her heart in her mouth, she listened to her friend's descent. Suddenly, there came a most unladylike string of oaths interspersed with a few words of cultured English.

'What is it? What was that you said?' demanded Ruth.

'I said, that was one thrill I could well have done without,' replied Jane, petulantly breaking off the offending twig and throwing it to the ground.

Ruth watched as a moment later a ghostly form flittered across the lawn and away from the house. Dizzy with shock and fear, she collapsed onto her bed to await the return of her remarkable friend.

It had been another busy and eventful day, reflected Richard Forres as he made ready to go to bed. In the morning he had gone into town to book passage to York for the following day. A reservation was not the only thing he secured from James Blenkinsop, manager of the stagecoach office. A ten week old King Charles Spaniel was his other purchase.

Arriving home just in time to take lunch with Rachel, he had surprised her by placing the squirming bundle of fur into her hands.

'It's Charlie!' she exclaimed.

'Yes, Mr. Blenkinsop said that you had taken it upon yourself to give every pup in the litter a name,' he said, smiling. 'I hope I've made the right choice.'

'Oh, yes; they are all equally lovely,' she said; 'but do you mean he is mine? Mine to keep?'

'Yes, of course,' he said. 'I knew I was doing the right thing when Mr. Blenkinsop told me how many hours you've spent during the past ten weeks in his upstairs' room with Meg and her puppies. He tells me there were times when you could barely tear yourself away.'

'I'm surprised he was disposed to part with him,' she said, suddenly thoughtful and serious.

'But why should he not? Is Charlie not come to a good home?' he said.

Later, Rachel's remark was to strike him as doubly odd. It was odd in itself, but it also confirmed a vague feeling which came to him when he was making the purchase, a feeling that the owner was, indeed, not too happy to part with Charlie.

He had spent the afternoon making arrangements for the smooth running of the estate in his absence, and the evening hours in packing for his journey. Somewhat to his disappointment in view of his gift to her, the evening meal with Rachel had been another subdued, awkward affair.

Now, alone in his room, he was thinking of undressing for bed when there came a startling interruption.

She entered silently, closing the door behind her. Leaning up against it, she looked across at him, saying nothing. Her dress, her demeanour, and the manner of her entry, told him in an instant that here was no servant.

'Who the deuce are you?' he asked, when he had recovered from his shock.

'Jane Gaskell, at your service,' she answered, coolly.

Suddenly, her composure evaporated.

'Oh, Lord!' she gasped, clutching in vain at her dress.

He watched, mesmerised, as a pair of white cotton drawers settled themselves snugly around his visitor's ankles.

'I must say, I like your way of greeting people,' he said. 'We must meet more often.'

'Turn around so I may put them back on,' she said, blushing. 'No, not like that,' she protested, as he completed his pirouette. 'Turn your back on me...... now, stay like that until I give you the word.'

'Leave them off, I don't mind,' he said, glancing over his shoulder; 'only let me open a window, first.'

'I shall put them back on, thank you very much,' she said, indignantly.

In truth, she was tempted to take up his suggestion. Mrs Harker's capacious drawers, about six sizes too large for her, had given her endless trouble in her walk to Grange Hall, but she had been forced to wear them in order to negotiate her way down from Ruth's window. Her descent had only been made possible by tucking the reams and reams of material which went to make up her dress and petticoat into an item of underwear sufficiently large for the purpose.

At a word, he turned to find her glaring at him.

'Well, they're not mine,' she said. 'They belong to Ruth's mother.'

'I see,' he said. 'Your pair in the wash, are they?'

'Do not be insulting,' she said, 'and will you stop staring at my ankles?'

'Just watching on the off-chance,' he said. 'The suspense is killing me. But tell me, for whatever reason, wouldn't it have been easier to wear a pair of trousers?'

'Don't be absurd,' she exclaimed. 'Whoever heard of a woman in a pair of trousers?'

She glanced about her.

'It would help if I could sit down,' she said. 'Don't you have a chair handy?'

'No, funnily enough I come upstairs in order to sleep, not to sit down. There's the bed, of course. Try the horizontal position. They're not likely to come down that way – well, not on their own accord, that is.'

'Now you are being impertinent,' she said. She give a gesture of annoyance; 'and once and for all, will you stop looking down at my feet? It is very disconcerting talking to the top of your head.'

He was slow to respond, causing her to cry out: 'Oh! I cannot stand this. I shall tie a knot in it. Yes, that will serve the purpose.'

'I say, steady on,' he said, backing away from her.

'Turn around again,' she said. 'No, not like that...... yes...... now, stay there.'

Lifting up her dress, she drew the surplus material of her underwear together and succeeded in tying a knot, thus taking up the slack.

'Well, thank you for calling, Miss Gaskell,' he said, when she had done. 'We must do this again; it's all been great fun. Give these shows nightly, do you?'

'You did not keep to our appointment,' she said, ignoring his remarks.

'Ah! the mysterious J.G.' he said; 'but don't you mean *your* appointment?'

'If the arrangements were not to your liking you might at least have sent a servant to Bluebell Wood to acquaint me of the fact,' she said.

'There was no way I could do that,' he said. 'I spent most of yesterday in town and had already left here when your letter arrived. Really, Miss Gaskell, you might have anticipated some such thing. I do not sit around waiting for cryptic messages to arrive, you know.'

'I was certain that you had received my note in good time,' she said. 'I made the boy promise to see that it was delivered into your hands.'

'Well, he has dunned you out of whatever fee you paid him,' he said. 'He did not even make the front door. He handed over your letter to one of the gardeners. By the time my under-butler took possession of it and came looking for me, I was long gone.'

She appeared not to be listening to him. Her eyes were darting about the room, taking in every detail. In truth, Jane Gaskell was feeling a little disappointed. No ghoulish retainers hovered in the background, no caged raven caught her eye, and the fearsome young owner of the place was proving anything but fearsome. Her eye took in a disappointingly well-lit room, tastefully furnished, and with all modern conveniences, but perhaps appearances were deceptive.

Going across to the bed, she peered underneath.

'No ravished virgins cowering out of sight?' she said. 'No, I see not, only a you-know-what. Having a night off, are we?'

He stared at her, uncomprehending. It was several seconds before he found his voice.

'What I would like to know is how you got here?' he said. 'I didn't hear a carriage pull up; and who let you in?'

'No carriage; I walked,' she replied; 'and I let myself in. They haven't locked up downstairs as yet.'

He was staring again.

'You mean, you simply walked in through the front door and up the staircase without anyone stopping you?'

'That's very nearly the size of it,' she answered. 'Saw one young fellow in all that livery stuff.'

'That would be one of the footmen. How did you deal with him?' he asked.

'I just give him an imperious stare, and walked on,' she said.

'An *imperious* stare?' he said. 'Pray tell me, what is that? Show me.'

She drew herself up to her full height and give him a look of disdain, as if looking at something undesirable on the sole of her shoe.

'Always works,' she said. 'It's no good creeping about looking guilty in these sort of situations. One has to give the appearance of owning the place.'

'I see. I must remember that,' he said, smiling.

'Also saw a fat little chap, bandy-legs, balding dome, dressed up to the nines.'

'That would be my butler, Rogers,' he said, cringing a little at her description. 'He must have stopped you, surely?'

'Yes, he told me where to find you,' she said.

'He told you *what*?' he asked, in surprise.

'Told me where to find you,' she repeated. 'I put my finger to my lips when he challenged me, and simply said in a confiding whisper: 'secret assignation with your master. Surprised he didn't mention it to you. I don't want to walk into the wrong bedroom. Can you help me?' I took a chance, of course. He may have got out his checklist for the night and asked me my number, but he didn't.'

Once again, he found himself staring in silence.

'May have overdone things a little with your man, Rogers,' she said, thoughtfully. 'He was walking away from me, quite satisfied, when I leant over the banister and said: 'not a queue tonight, is there?' Careless of me. That remark wasn't necessary.'

'Is my reputation that bad?' he said.

'Terrible, by all accounts,' she said.

'But you are not afraid of me?' he said.

'I'm afraid of no one,' she said, jutting out her chin.

'Miss Gaskell, you are a wonder,' he said, shaking his head and smiling. 'I never knew there were young ladies like you in this day and age.'

This remark seemed to please her, but conscious of the fact that time was pressing, she decided to come to the object of her visit. Producing a small leather pouch, she opened it up and tipped out the contents.

'Twenty four guineas,' she said, spreading the coins out with her fingers, 'the balance to come in monthly instalments over the next six months. I refer to this business with William – William Harker. Are you agreeable?'

Here, then, was the reason for her visit. She had come in an attempt to stave off disaster to that young man. The repayment was long overdue, and there could be little doubt that Sir Henry Forres had been pressing for the money, with dire threats as to what would happen if it was not forthcoming very soon.

'Is there an attachment between William and yourself?' he asked.

'Certainly not,' she said. 'He does not even know I am here. I have come out of regard for Ruth, his sister and my friend.'

He could not help but admire the loyalty of his visitor to her friend, but the situation posed a problem for him.

He had already decided that he wanted no part of Henry Forres' gambling activities, that he would burn the little black book, and not press for payment on the money owed him. That did not mean, however, that he should tamely hand over the pledge, for that would hardly be in keeping with his predecessor's known character. Not that he had any desire to imitate the man, but he must resist the temptation to fly off to the opposite extreme. He would hand the pledge over, but not as a carefree gift. How to do that?

'Come, take the money, Sir Henry,' she said, breaking into his silence. 'Agree to the terms on offer and you will get the full amount in due course. If you confront Mr. Harker tomorrow morning, William will be disgraced and you will end up with nothing but a worthless piece of paper.'

'I do not believe that to be the case,' he said. 'I believe the father will honour his son's debt on two counts. First, Mr. Harker, as an honourable man, will look upon this as a debt owed by the family, which must be settled. Second, even if that were not so, he must know that the only way to protect the family's good name is for him to buy my silence with the repayment of his son's debt. So, Miss Gaskell, can you give me one good reason why I should accept your terms when I can reasonably expect to have this business settled and done with in the course of a single day?'

She could not. He watched as she bit her lip in frustration. It was, he thought, an interesting face. Attractive rather than pretty, it was one well-suited to her character.

He had been casting about for a solution which did not involve a total capitulation on his part, and just such a solution came to mind. He would find out just how far she was prepared to go in order to achieve success. If nothing else, the exercise would at least be an entertaining one.

He went over to the small bureau by the door, and returned flourishing a deck of cards.

'Do you gamble, Miss Gaskell?' he said.

'Certainly not,' she said, indignantly; 'but I am fond of a harmless hand of cards on occasions.'

'So you know how to cut a deck to advantage? To decide who shall call trumps, for example?'

'Oh, yes, of course,' she said. 'Ace is high, then King, then Queen, and so on down to a Two. Whoever draws the highest card wins the cut.'

'Well, I have an early start to the day tomorrow, and I dare say you have no wish to linger here longer than you have to, so let us keep it simple. We shall each draw a card and compare the two. If you win the point, I shall make you a present of Master William's pledge. You may even keep your twenty four guineas.'

'And if I lose, what then?' she said.

'Why, then, you may still have the pledge and your money.'

'I do not understand,' she said, frowning. 'You must want *something* from me, otherwise where is the point of it all?'

He took out his watch and indicated the time to her.

'A quarter to eleven,' he said. 'Come what may, we must get you safely home before daybreak. If the victory is mine, you shall agree to spend the next five hours here.' He pointed to the double-bed standing invitingly close by. 'Room for two,' he said.

It is a measure of Jane Gaskell's naiveté to say that she was shocked by his proposition. She should not have been, of course. Alone with a man in his bedroom at such an hour, and a man of Henry Forres' reputation at that, what did she expect?

If pressed, she would have found it difficult to answer that question. Perhaps she had believed that her feminine charms, tantalisingly displayed, *but no more than that*, would succeed where William Harker's modest talents of persuasion had failed, or perhaps she had hoped to manipulate the man she had called on as she had manipulated so many of his sex in the past.

But what price now her foolish daydreams? Here was no gothic castle, but the parallels were striking, nevertheless. In particular, there stood her villain-cum-hero as she had always imagined him – tall, handsome, enigmatic, and with a suppressed goodness beneath his outward show of villainy, she was sure.

Except, she did not wish to act out her fantasy. When it came to the test, she discovered that make believe was one thing, and reality quite another. The first was acceptable to her, the second was not. No, she would return home and tell Ruth that......

Oh, God! Ruth. What *would* she tell Ruth? 'Leave this matter in my hands,' she had told her. 'Trust me,' she had said. How could she return to the waiting Ruth and tell her she had failed? For William she felt little pity. She had never really taken to that rather foolish, self-centred young man, but had tolerated him for her friend's sake. No, William had brought his ruin on himself, and invited no pity, but with Ruth it was different. How could she bear to witness her anguish knowing it had been in her power to prevent it? Suddenly, she felt trapped in an impossible situation, and it was all her own doing.

For the first time, she began to consider the alternative, lifting her eyes to look squarely into the face of the man before her. It really was a generous offer he had made her. Win, or lose, she would return with what she had come for, and there was a fifty-fifty chance that it could all be had for nothing, absolutely nothing.

For his part, he stood watching the struggle taking place within herself, ready to suggest a lesser forfeit if she refused him.

'Very well, I accept,' she said. 'I suppose I can only lose it the once.'

She did not need to explain herself. He understood perfectly what she meant by those words.

Without further ado, before a change of heart on her part was possible, she walked over to where he had placed the deck of cards and cut them. She found herself staring at the Two of Hearts, conscious of the fact that she could not have drawn a worse card.

'Oh, bad luck,' he said, looking over her shoulder.

She did not wait for his turn. Seating herself on the edge of the bed she began to undress.

'What happens if we oversleep?' she said.

'Sleep? Who said anything about sleep?' he said.

She began to shake violently, her fingers hardly equal to their task

'Are you any good at knots?' she said.

Things had gone far enough, he decided. Taking her by the hand, he led her back to the deck of cards.

'Do not despair, Miss Gaskell,' he said. 'All is not yet lost.'

She shook her head. 'The best I can hope for is that you also draw a Two. That would mean I would have to draw again. I do not believe I have the courage for that.'

He considered the matter for a moment.

'Very well,' he said, 'let us say that the Two of Hearts beats any other deuce. How would that be?'

'You will not draw a Two,' she said.

'Don't say that,' he said. 'It is in your power to make me do so.'

'In my power? How can that be?'

'You must picture, let us say, the Two of Spades in my hand. You must do the thing properly, and picture me in your mind's eye holding the card just as vividly as you can. You must *will* me to draw the card.'

'That sounds like nonsense,' she said.

He shrugged. 'But you have nothing to lose by it. Come, why not do as I say?'

'Why are you doing this? Why are you trying to help me?' she said. 'Don't you want to win?'

'All I want is for you to remember me with affection,' he said.

Puzzled, she sought his eyes, seeking an answer to a mystery. She was finding it hard to believe that a man such as this could be responsible for even one-tenth of the crimes ascribed to him by her friend. For her part, she could neither see, nor sense, anything in the least sinister about him. All that was apparent to her was a kindly humour and an effortless patience. How different, she thought, from the callow, immature, young men who sought to court her back home. If and when she ever willingly give herself to a man, it would be to a man such as the one before her.

He was a little surprised to see her turn and stare at the bed standing behind her.

'Very well, I shall do as you advise,' she said, turning back towards him. She closed her eyes in concentration.

He did not think to attempt to join his mind with hers in order to help her. There was no point, were his thoughts. It really didn't matter what card he drew. He stood, waiting patiently, until she finally give him the signal to proceed.

In fact, he drew the Ace of Hearts, the sight of which made him smile inwardly. He had thought it just possible that she might have an untapped, natural ability for this sort of thing, but that now appeared highly unlikely, to say the least.

'Two of Spades,' he said, in the tone of voice of one bitterly disappointed. 'Well, I'm blowed. It doesn't always work.' Hurriedly, he replaced the handful of cards on top of the rest of the pack, being careful not to let her catch sight of the card in question.

'You'll want that piece of paper,' he said, going across to the chest of drawers, where it was still housed.

Disbelieving, she looked from pack of cards to his bent figure at the other end of the room, and back again. In his haste, he had not replaced the cards he had taken particularly well. They lay at a distinct angle to the rest of the pack.

With her fingernail, she carefully separated the two halves and looked at his chosen card. The sight astonished her on two counts. Here, was an unexpected truth, and an unexpected lie. Was it possible she had misjudged the cut? She felt sure she had not, and an examination of several other cards, preceding and following on from the Ace of Hearts, confirmed her belief. The Two of Spades did not feature at all.

She opened her mouth to protest, but thought better of it. If that is how he wanted it, so be it. Quickly, she tidied up the pack.

She was barely in time. A few seconds after she had done he was coming towards her with the I.O.U. in his hands.

'Shall we burn it?' he asked, stopping at the cluster of candles which lit up the room.

'I had rather Ruth and William had sight of it as proof of my success,' she said, eyeing him, thoughtfully.

'Yes, of course,' he said, handing it to her. He glanced at his watch. 'I think it's high time we got you home.'

They walked in silence for a few minutes until she decided she could not leave matters as they were.

'Why the play-acting back there?' she said. 'You didn't draw the Two of Spades at all.'

He began to protest his innocence but she cut him short.

'I shall tell you exactly what your chosen card was,' she said. 'It was the Ace of Hearts, was it not? It was careless of you not to leave the pack neat and tidy. I found your card without any great difficulty. So, were you merely toying with me all along?'

'In one sense, yes,' he said, sighing; 'but in another sense, no. There was a part of me which wanted, which wanted very much to possess you. It was no easy task on my part to fight against that inclination, believe me, but tomorrow I set off to York in the first step on the road to recovering my wife. I owed it to her, I owe it to myself......'

'Yes, I understand,' she said. 'Ruth tells me that Lady Forres is very beautiful. She says also that you have treated her very badly. I intend to scold her for that, for I know that cannot be. Are you aware of these scurrilous stories which are whispered behind your back? Do they not make you angry, these lies which are told concerning you? They would me, if I were in your place.'

'Are you so sure of my character?' he said, smiling. 'Perhaps the townsfolk are right, and you are wrong.'

'I refuse to believe that,' she said. She linked an arm in one of his, and give him a sly look. 'So, no regrets about letting me off so lightly this evening?'

'Only the one,' he said. 'Do you know, Miss Gaskell, I have always wanted to wake up with a virgin. I suppose you find that an odd remark?'

'I find it beautiful,' she said, softly. 'Now, I *know* the townsfolk are wrong.'

They stood beneath the tree which grew beneath Ruth's bedroom window.

'What a remarkable young lady you are,' he said, peering up at the path she had to take. 'Are you sure it's safe?'

'Quite safe,' she said. 'There's a stout branch, easily able to take my weight, which reaches to within two feet of the windowsill. I could show you a dozen more difficult climbs back home, safely negotiated.'

'So, you make a habit of it?' he said, laughing. 'But tell me, what is the point? Why climb a tree, for heaven's sake?'

'Why, to get to the top, of course.'

'Ah! yes, silly of me,' he said. 'Do you know, that never occurred to me? But we are wasting time.'

'Yes,' she said, 'let us say farewell, but not with a handshake.' She indicated with her eyes his cut lip, still far from healed. 'That's a nasty injury. How did you come by it?'

'It's a long story.'

'Well, I shall be careful,' she said. 'Open your mouth a little, and try to curl your bottom lip down. This is going to be more of a suck than a kiss.'

'Where did you learn to kiss like that?' he asked, when she had done with him.

'I have a very affectionate horse back home,' she said. 'I've missed Toby this past month.'

'I can well believe it,' he said. 'But do take care, Jane, I beg you.'

She glanced upward. 'Don't worry. I shall be perfectly safe.'

'I was referring to this business with your horse.'

'Toby is a gelding,' she said, laughing.

'Oh, I say, what rotten luck.'

'Behave yourself, sir,' she said. 'Really, you should learn to conduct yourself with propriety, as I do.' She hitched up her dress and petticoat to her midriff. 'My hands are cold; any good at knots?'

Laughingly, he obliged, and watched as a moment later she began her ascent. She paused, ten feet up.

'I could do this in the dark,' she said.

'You *are* doing it in the dark,' he reminded her.

'Yes...... well, there you are, then,' she said.

Eventually, she reached the safety of the open window, where her friend stood ready to help her inside. He saw William Harker's pledge change hands, and smiled at the joy of Ruth, visible in the flickering light of the candle which she held.

Now Jane was leaning out of the window to address him one last time.

'That was an amazingly successful card trick you taught me,' she called out, softly. 'I wonder William did not end up owing you far more than 150 guineas with an ability like that at your command.'

'It's not a trick,' he called back; 'but, Jane, you do surprise me. You were willing me to draw a Two and I turned up an Ace. Where was your success in any of that?'

'Who said I was willing you to draw a Two? I never said that I had a Two in mind,' she retorted.

Surprised by her words, he was at a loss for a reply. His silence prompted her to burst out laughing.

'Oh! my dear Sir Henry, what a dunce you are,' she said. 'Have you not guessed the truth of it, even now?'

CHAPTER 13

The so called Yarm to York Post comprised only a small section of the main Edinburgh to London stagecoach route, itself one of many which networked the country as a whole.

The popular image of the stagecoach as a slow, lumbering, and very uncomfortable vehicle, rattling its way through a countryside infested with highwaymen, was a far cry from reality in the nineteenth century. The early part of that century saw the high watermark of this mode of transport before its gradual demise at the hands of the steam locomotive. By the year 1813 the heyday of the highwayman was long gone, and a major programme of road improvements had resulted in a stagecoach service which bore little resemblence to that which prevailed a half-century before.

So it was that a little over four hours after boarding the coach at Yarm, in a journey which included a change of horses at Thirsk, and a halt at Easingwold, Richard Forres found himself alighting from the vehicle at the old coaching inn 'The Black Swan', in Coney Street, York.

A second reading the previous day of Johnathon Sinclair's letters had given rise to a belief that here was a name which rang a distant bell. His extensive knowledge of the time period included the hazy recollection of a noted local worthy who went by that name. The man had resided in the North Country (where exactly he could not recall) and had flourished at the beginning of the nineteenth century. The journey to York had given him ample time to search his memory so that by the time he arrived at his destination he was fairly sure that he would soon be in the company of a man of letters, a lover of science and technology, and a notable humanitarian and free thinker. He was left praying that his memory had not played him false for all this promised to present him with just the opportunity for which he was looking.

The forthcoming meeting raised the question of how much scientific knowledge in advance of the times he should divulge in conversation. After giving the matter much thought, he resolved to say nothing of consequence, for there was no need. A display of intellect equal to the best scientific minds of the time would be more than sufficient for his purposes. The pace of technology was accelerating fast enough – bringing benefits, it was true, but also bringing huge social problems – without his added intervention to complicate matters.

He took a late lunch in 'The Black Swan' before setting off on the short walk to the Doctor's residence. This proved to be a pleasing, three storey town house, situated close to the city wall.

A decrepit old servant, eighty years if he was a day, he thought, answered his summons. Squinting all the while at the caller's name card, the old gentleman announced that his master was taking his customary afternoon walk, but was expected back in half-an-hour. Sir Henry was welcome to wait, if he so wished. Gratefully, Forres accepted the invitation. He was shown into a large and particularly fine drawing room, where he was left to his own devices.

Within a short time he was able to confirm that his knowledge with regard to Johnathon Sinclair was correct. Scientific papers, in what he recognised as the Doctor's own hand, lay scattered about the room. He was not expecting such proof of identity to be so readily to hand, but guessed that were he able to roam at will throughout the building he would find similar proof in other rooms, and, indeed, it was true that the Doctor, a confirmed bachelor with all the bohemian traits of that class of gentleman, was prone to taking his work with him as he moved about the house, picking up and discarding papers as he did so.

Scarcely able to believe his good fortune, he put the next half-hour to good purpose by sifting through the Doctor's work, appraising it as he did so.

He was momentarily disturbed ten minutes into the exercise by a subdued but animated discussion beyond the closed door of his room.

Faintly, there came to him the sound of a shrilly-reproaching female voice, punctuated at intervals by an apologetic-sounding, deep, male voice, which he thought he recognised as belonging to the elderly manservant who had admitted him. At one point he fancied he heard his own name mentioned. It seemed as if the old fellow was in trouble over some matter, and he wondered if he was the cause of it. No one came to disturb him, however, and after a few minutes the house fell silent once more.

Doctor Johnathon Sinclair stood looking at the calling card handed to him with a frown of disapproval darkening his face.

It was, he reflected, a most unfortunate set of circumstances which had resulted in the entry into his home of a gentleman whom he had hoped never again to set eyes upon. Saunders, his manservant, was away for a few days, one of the principal guests at some nephew's wedding in Durham, and to fill this temporary void he had engaged his predecessor, retired some years ago but still living no great distance away in the city. Following on from their recent confrontation, he had issued instructions to his modest staff of servants that should his niece's husband put in another appearance he was to be turned away at the door, but he had not thought to caution his old retainer. As luck would have it, this second, most unwelcome, visit had come on one of the rare occasions when Saunders was not on duty, and at a time of day when he, himself, had not been present to deal with the matter. It was, he reflected, all the more annoying that, with his gout troubling him more than usual, he had very nearly cancelled his customary afternoon walk, but a lovely summer's day had succeeded in tempting him out.

The result of all this was that Sir Henry Forres had been invited in, and was even now, no doubt, making himself at home.

He laid a hand on the arm of his troubled manservant.

'Do not make yourself uneasy, Jordan,' he said. 'The fault is mine. I should have given you fair warning. You may go now. I shall deal with our visitor.'

In point of fact, the whole unfortunate business was not *entirely* unwelcome to Johnathon Sinclair. After giving the matter some thought, he had recently come to the conclusion that his way of dealing with his niece's husband had been at fault in the past. It had been brought home to him that his protestations of ignorance as to Emma's whereabouts were not having the desired effect and some deliberate misinformation would serve her better.

Entering the drawing room, his ill-humour was not helped when he found the cause of it reclining at his ease, surrounded by his own private papers.

He give the briefest of nods in response to the friendly greeting and came straight to the point he wanted to make.

'I fear you have had a wasted journey, sir,' he said. 'My latest information is that my niece is now engaged on a tour of the Continent and is not expected to return for some considerable period of time.'

Richard Forres was not deceived. He thought it unlikely that in her present circumstances Emma would wish to undertake some grand tour of the Continent. Moreover, the speaker, a man to whom subterfuge did not come easily, had been less than convincing in his manner of address. In short, he had been a little *too* prompt, a little *too* eager, in volunteering his 'information'.

To Johnathon Sinclair's surprise, his visitor waved a dismissive hand in response, as if the whereabouts of his wife was the last thing on his mind. Instead, he brought over a page of mathematical calculations and tapped it with a finger.

'Forgive me, sir, for the liberty of occupying my time in your absence in a study of some of your scientific papers,' he said. 'I share the same interest as yourself in these matters so, naturally, your work attracted my attention.'

'Indeed, sir,' said Johnathan Sinclair, raising an eyebrow. It was news to him that his visitor had any worthwhile interests at all.

'Would you permit me to bring to your attention an error at this point?' said Forres, indicating a line of equations a quarter of the way down the page.

Johnathon Sinclair give a disparaging look in response, but condescended to take up the paper in question and cast an eye over it. It happened to be a treatise which had given him a great deal of trouble during the past month. The mathematical proof of the theorem which he had been seeking should have been a straightforward enough task, but it had not proved to be so. He had checked and rechecked his calculations, and had reappraised and partially rewritten the paper, but all to no avail – a successful proof still eluded him.

His visitor picked up a quill-pen and a sheet of paper, which lay to hand, and proceeded to rewrite the offending line. 'This is the correct progression to line eight,' he said, handing over the paper. 'I think you will find everything follows on naturally from that point.'

The error in question had been a subtle one, but important for all that. Hitherto, the author had failed to spot it all along, but he saw it now.

'May I be so bold, Doctor, as to suggest that the mathematical method you have employed is unnecessarily complicated,' Forres continued. 'Allow me to show you a better approach.'

He picked up the quill again and began writing, his hand fairly racing across the page with a speed seemingly restricted solely by the motion of quill to inkpot, then to paper, and so on back to inkpot. In a very few minutes his handiwork was being scrutinised.

Johnathon Sinclair read it through twice before glancing at his own effort by way of comparison. The new mathematical proof was both concise and elegant, the hallmarks, he knew, of all the finest work in that branch of science. It comprised little more than half-a-page, in contrast to his own laboured effort of very nearly two pages. He barely had time to look up before another example of his work was being thrust under his nose.

'For your sanity's sake, Doctor, I would suggest you give up on this one. That which you seek is incapable of mathematical proof, although I grant you that may not always be the case.' For the third time he took up quill and paper, this time to outline the reasoning behind his statement.

Giving Johnathon Sinclair barely enough time to read and digest this, he moved on to another matter.

'There are a few documents I chanced upon which relate to the field of scientific invention, entirely new devices in some instances, or improvements to existing ones. I found these of special interest. I must take issue with this one, however, which relates to an improved lifting mechanism for heavy loads. I have taken the liberty of sketching a new design alongside your own, which I flatter myself would serve the purpose better, but I would value your opinion in the matter.'

A somewhat dazed Johnathon Sinclair turned his attention to the two sketches. In the one, pulleys had been redrawn, blocks and tackle repositioned, and levers and gears redesigned.

There could be no doubt as to which of the two devices promised more. In this new light, his own contraption now looked to be positively medieval.

Throughout the whole of this period of revelation, Johnathon Sinclair had said barely a word. Now, he put to one side all of the papers which had been brought to his attention, and stood staring at his visitor in silence. To say that the gentleman before him had surprised him would be an understatement. He was astonished beyond measure, and at a complete loss for a suitable response.

Richard Forres anxiously returned the gaze. 'There are references in some of your papers to working models,' he said. 'If you do, indeed, have a workshop where some of these models are to be found, I would esteem it an honour to be allowed to view them.'

The Doctor found his voice at long last, although it was so charged with emotional turmoil he scarcely recognised it as his own.

'Yes, of course, Sir Henry. Yes, certainly,' he stammered. 'Pray, step this way.'

In the passage of time which followed Johnathon Sinclair quite forgot that he was in the company of one whom he had long regarded as a disagreeable and troublesome relative. The man had become instead a fellow scientist, and it was on that basis that the two men made their tour of the Doctor's laboratory, dealing with each and every mechanism in turn and amicably arguing the merits of them all. The younger man scattered both praise and constructive criticism in his wake, volunteering an improvement here, suggesting a modification there, praising the imaginative and the inspired, and casting a honest doubt when need be.

The Doctor handbuilt all his own models and, irrespective of their intrinsic merit, his visitor was fulsome in his praise of the craftsmanship which had gone into the making of them, praise which brought a flush of pride to the elder man. By the time they had completed their tour of inspection, a dozen new and exciting possibilities for the future filled Johnathon Sinclair's mind. Half-completed, abandoned work could now take on a fresh impetus. Seemingly impossible obstacles were obstacles no longer, and several differing mechanisms now lent themselves to improvement, or refinement.

A glance at his watch told an astonished Johnathon Sinclair that a full two hours had elapsed since the two of them had entered the room. He felt a pang of genuine remorse. All told, his visitor had been in the house some three hours and had not been offered so much as a cup of tea by way of refreshment. Immediately, he sought to put that right.

'You will join me in my evening meal, will you not?' he asked.

They partook of their meal for the most part in silence, each man engrossed with his own thoughts.

For his part, Richard Forres was feeling pleased with himself. He had made the journey to York not so much to learn the whereabouts of Emma – such an achievement in view of all that had happened was, he realised, not possible in a single visit – but rather to show by word and deed that Sir Henry Forres was a changed man. He guessed that the Doctor was one of the few people in regular contact with Emma. That being so, if he could enlist his support in securing her return to Grange Hall he would be more than satisfied. He felt he had come a long way in achieving this, and there still remained one further service he could perform for Johnathon Sinclair which could only add to his own standing.

Johnathon Sinclair's thoughts took a different form. He did not know his visitor as well as he perhaps he should, having met with him on only the four previous occasions. Most of his knowledge of the man, in fact, had come via his niece. From this limited experience, he had always held his wayward relative to be an intelligent individual, well educated, and widely travelled, but, even so, he had that day been astounded by the sheer range and depth of learning of the young man. This must be, he thought, the supreme example of the proverbial saying 'hiding one's light under a bushel', and it saddened him to reflect on how greatly his niece's husband had squandered his talents over the years. By rights, such a gross misuse should make him more angry than ever but he could not help feeling a debt of gratitude for all the encouragement and help so freely extended to him that day.

More than this consideration was a very definite feeling that he was playing host to a man changed out of all recognition. He had effected a reconciliation between his niece and her husband once before, but he had been conscious of the fact all the while that the gentleman concerned was going out of his way to be pleasing and agreeable, and he had been left to hope rather than believe that Henry Forres had changed for the better. Now, he had no such qualified feelings. The kind word, the friendly gesture, the charming manner on view today, all seemed spontaneous and natural rather than calculated and premeditated. He was forced to conclude that here was a man really changed for the better – either that, or else the fellow was, on top of everything else, a consumate actor.

In the interval before dinner he had overheard his visitor engage himself in friendly, familiar conversation with both Jordan and his maid, Constance. Aware of their master's aversion to the man, but ignorant of the reason for it, the two of them were now giving *him* looks which seemed to say: 'Why on earth do you hold this gentleman in such low esteem?'

Only one thing was spoiling an unexpectedly pleasant day for Johnathon Sinclair. His troublesome gout was becoming more and more painful as the day wore on, and was threatening to give him a restless night. A particularly nasty twinge made him wince with pain and carefully reposition his legs.

These signs of distress were not lost on his guest.

'Damn gout,' said the sufferer, by way of explanation. 'Today it's been especially troublesome. I think I shall have to take some laudanum, and retire early.'

'That substance is habit forming, as I'm sure you must know,' said Forres.

'Indeed, it is, Sir Henry, but it is the only thing which brings me some measure of relief.'

'These days, all my friends address me by my middle name of Richard. Will you not do likewise? Sir Henry sounds so formal.'

'Grown tired of Henry, have you?'

'Yes, you could say that.'

'Saul become Paul?'

'In a way.'

'A change of names, in itself, signifies nothing.'

'I realise that. It is but a token.'

'I believe I understand you. Well, then, 'Richard' it is.'

'Good! That's settled. Now, we were talking of your gout. If you so wish, we shall retire to the lounge after our meal, and I shall take away your pain.'

'Take away my pain? I do not follow you. Have you something better to offer me than my laudanum?'

Richard Forres put down his knife and fork and spread out his hands. 'A little massage, a technique picked up on my travels, will serve you better, I believe. Will you put yourself in my hands?'

'Why, yes; if you think you can help me.'

'I do not think it, I *know* it. Therein lies the secret of success,' said Forres, smiling.

If it had not been for the astonishing events of earlier that day it is unlikely, to say the least, that Johnathon Sinclair would have consented to divest himself of shoes and stockings and place himself at the disposal of his guest, but he sat now, quietly expectant, with outstretched legs, and bare feet resting comfortably on a small footstool. That a massage session could in any way prove beneficial to the complaint of gout seemed to him improbable, but his curiosity, present here as in so many aspects of life, had been piqued by his guest's quiet, confident assurances. So it was that he took on the role of willing patient readily enough. He watched, intrigued, as Forres took up a kneeling position before him, and began to flex the fingers of both hands.

'The pain will leave you within ten minutes, but to be really effective I shall need to carry on a little while longer,' he was told. 'All I ask is that you do not disturb my concentration by speaking until I am done.'

With these words, the would-be healer laid a hand on each of the patient's ankles and began a gentle massage of both feet, working his way in a gradual progression from ankles to toes. In the wake of these hand movements there came a blessed relief from pain for the sufferer.

For twenty minutes the healing hands worked on, probing and prodding, kneading and pressing, and Johnathon Sinclair's astonishment increased apace. There were times when his affliction bore down so severely upon him that he could not bear the pressure of a shoe during the day, or the weight of bedclothes at night, and the present exercise should, by all past experience, be causing him excruciating pain, yet he felt not the slightest discomfort. Nor did the pain start to seep back when eventually the numbness began to melt away, bringing with it feeling and sensation.

At length, with a somewhat weary sigh of satisfaction, Forres rose a little unsteadily to his feet. Throughout the entire exercise he had been crouched, head bent and with a face hidden from view, seemingly lost to the world in total concentration. Johnathon Sinclair's words of wonder and thanks were cut short at the sight of him. The young man looked to be exhausted, his face wearied and pale, but his only words of explanation as to the cause of it hardly seemed adequate.

'Yes, it taxes one – more than it truly should,' he said, sinking gratefully into his chair.

The evening was now well advanced, and learning that his visitor had made no arrangements in the city for an overnight stay, Johnathon Sinclair was insistent that he remain the night.

'Very well,' said Richard Forres, 'but I have a mind to take upon myself that early night you were talking of a short while back.'

Johnathon Sinclair was not, himself, late in retiring for the night and before he did so he looked in on his guest. He found him in bed, but awake and sitting up. Fussing over him, and in the eyes of the Doctor taking an inordinate length of time over what appeared to be quite unnecessary tasks, was his young maid, Constance.

'That will do, Constance,' he said, firmly. 'I think it's time we allowed our guest to settle himself for the night.'

He watched her leave before sitting himself down at the end of the bed.

'I expected to find you asleep,' he said. 'You look fatigued, to say the least. You should have sent Constance on her way.'

'No, there is too much going on in my mind to rest easy,' said Forres.

Johnathon Sinclair nodded. He felt exactly the same. Deep in thought, he looked intently at the other man, and under this close scrutiny Forres stirred uneasily. His growing alarm was not eased by the sudden question: 'Is it really you?'

'None other,' he said, forcing a laugh.

'I have been asking myself: is this the thoroughly disagreeable young man who called here but a few weeks ago, visibly the worse for drink? Is this the same individual of whom I have had such unfavourable reports? Can this be the same person who has physically abused his wife and sister these two years past?'

No defence was possible, and the accused man did not attempt to offer one, but lay silent with downcast eyes.

'Your behaviour today has left me utterly confused with regard to my feelings towards you,' continued the Doctor.

'May we not put aside the past?' said Forres.

'For my part, yes, in time that may be possible,' said Sinclair. 'I may even learn to forgive you for the way in which you have all this time squandered talents which I never knew you had until this day. My niece, I cannot speak for. She has not only injuries of her own to resent but those inflicted on ones near and dear to her.' He shook his head, perplexed and troubled. 'But separated from you, what sort of life does she have to look forward to?'

This was true, as Richard Forres, himself, was well aware.

At the beginning of the 19th Century a man took possession of a wife almost as one took possession of a chattel. Thereafter, she could be slighted, ignored, abandoned even, with very little chance of redress, although the reverse did not really apply. A woman who deserted her husband, for whatever reason, became one of society's rejects, an object of censure and scorn, condemned to a lonely future existence.

'I ask for one last chance to redeem myself,' said Forres, earnestly. 'Given that chance, I promise to take away all the hurt, and all the pain of the past two years.'

'Richard, it is not in my power to give you that one last chance. Only Emma may do that,' said Sinclair. 'But I must own to an untruth when first we met today, for which I make no apology. Emma has no plans to travel the Continent. In fact, she is settled at no great distance from Grange Hall. I will not furnish you with her address, but what I shall do is to promise to write to her, inform her of your visit here today, and stress the very favourable impression which you have made upon me. I shall ask her to consider a return to Grange Hall. More than that I am not prepared to do. She has been hurt too often in the past for me to put her at risk again.'

Forres nodded his thanks, grateful for these words of encouragement.

Sinclair indicated his legs, which hung comfortably over the edge of the bed.

'In return for my best efforts on your behalf, when this cursed gout starts to trouble me again, I shall send you word express in the hope that you will visit here and treat with me again. How long, anyway, before the benefits of your strange treatment wear off? May I at least look forward to a comfortable night's sleep?'

'You may dispense with your cane, Doctor, if you wish,' said Forres, smiling. 'You shall have no further need to slit your shoes. You may drink your port as the fancy takes you. I have brought you no mere temporary relief but a lasting cure.'

'No, sir, you jest,' said Sinclair, startled by these words. 'Such a thing is not possible. You forget, I was a medical man in former days, and know full-well that such miracles just do not happen.'

'I believe in miracles no more than you do, and certainly make no pretence of dispensing them,' said Forres, smiling; 'but I speak the truth, all the same.'

'No, I cannot believe it,' said Sinclair, flatly.

'You have a healthy scepticism,' said Forres, 'and I am glad on that account I took the precaution of promising you no more than a temporary relief. Had I promised more, your lack of faith in what I had in mind to do would have made my task infinitely more difficult, not to mention the added distress to myself.' He patted the bed either side of him. 'Comfortable though this is, I would not have enjoyed the prospect of a week beneath the sheets, even with your delightful Constance in attendance.'

Johnathon Sinclair could not free his mind of the many extraordinary events of the day, with the result that he did not, after all, get the restful night he had been hoping for. It was two o'clock in the morning before he drifted off to sleep.

He was roused as usual at eight o'clock, but went promptly back to sleep and did not stir himself until nearly an hour later. He dressed quickly, but not before he had spent a few minutes in a critical examination of his feet. They looked and felt perfectly normal, passing all the tests which he put them to, including a bearing down with all his weight upon his toes – an exercise which had been beyond him for many years. It seemed as if he was truly cured, but how exactly that could have happened he could not begin to imagine. There were only the few vague clues which his guest had hinted at to help him, and these were hardly sufficient.

He entered the breakfast room to find his young relative well into his morning meal. With no thought of food himself, he immediately broached the subject uppermost in his mind.

'A permanent cure, you said. You still hold to that?'

'Certainly, I do,' said Forres.

'But how can you be so sure?' persisted Sinclair.

'Because I was sure in my own mind of success from the outset. If I'd had any doubts on that score I would not even have attempted to do what I did. Besides, one instinctively knows when the thing is accomplished.'

'You speak as if you have done this kind of thing before.'

'You could say that,' said Forres, evasively. 'Let us just say that I've met with a few modest successes in the past.'

Sinclair shook his head in bewilderment.

'This is beyond me,' he said. 'You speak of *modest* successes. Is that how you view what you accomplished yesterday evening?'

'It was a modest achievement in comparison to, say, eliminating a cancerous growth, or restoring sight to the blind. Not that I would attempt such feats, you understand, for I know them to be beyond me.'

'No, I do *not* understand,' said Sinclair. 'Young man, I am determined that you shall not leave here today until you have fully explained yourself.'

Richard Forres considered these words for a moment before coming to the conclusion that whereas the disclosure of scientific knowledge in advance of its time was one thing, the information now being sought was quite another matter. All the facts were there to be gleaned and acted upon, if a man would but open his eyes and free his mind.

'As you wish, Doctor,' he said. 'I have a little packing to do before I take my leave, but I shall be free in half-an-hour, and shall meet with you in your library. Be so good as to make available a copy of The New Testament, preferably in the original Greek text, and a suitable English-Greek lexicon. We shall have need of them.'

For the present, he would say no more.

At the appointed time in the library, Johnathon Sinclair found himself watching with a growing impatience as his visitor quietly occupied himself in taking down copious notes from the two works of reference placed at his disposal. After some twenty minutes of this the

Doctor could contain his impatience no longer.

'You spoke a short while back of restoring sight to the blind, and of ridding the body of a malignant tumour. Surely, here at least you were not serious?'

'I was perfectly serious in what I said,' answered Forres. 'A man may raise the dead, if he has a mind to, and I shall shortly tell you how.'

This outrageous claim was made with such a quiet but firm assurance that Johnathon Sinclair found himself quite incapable of giving voice to his incredulity.

A deathly quiet now seemed to descend upon the room, the only sound the measured tick of the clock on the nearby windowsill. With the quiet, there came upon the good Doctor a creeping sensation that he stood on the brink of a stupendous revelation.

At length, Richard Forres put down his quill-pen and looked smilingly into the eyes of the elder man.

'So, let us begin,' he said.

CHAPTER 14

Richard Forres was speaking.

'I am sure as a medical man you would be willing to acknowledge the role of the mind in a person's *physical* well-being, and also the influence, for good or bad, which that mysterious entity exerts on those about it.

'In the first instance, take two patients facing some terminal illness. Let us assume that the first sufferer lapses into a melancholic, pessimistic frame of mind, while the second individual accepts his illness with a positive attitude and a determination to fight the disease. The almost inevitable outcome is that the first patient enters into a rapid decline and is soon gone, whereas the second individual continues to enjoy life, within his limitations, often for a length of time beyond any reasonable expectation.

'With regard to the second aspect, consider for a moment two physicians, the one outwardly confident and reassuring, and inspiring trust and respect in his patients, and a second practitioner who, for whatever reason, generates no such confidence in those who come under his care. Now, you will find that although both may be equally expert in the field of medicine, even to the extent of treating identical ailments in identical ways, the first will have a slight but significantly higher rate of success than the second.'

'I think there are few in the medical profession who would dispute any of that,' said Sinclair. 'There can be little doubt that the mind exerts a powerful influence, especially on the body it inhabits.'

'Just so,' said Forres, 'but let us extend this discussion to see if we may put a limit on what the mind is capable of achieving.

'You are aware, are you not, of travellers' tales concerning the African witchdoctor, or Haitian voodoo priest, who seemingly have the ability to cast a spell, or curse, to such good effect as to make the unfortunate victim sicken and die? Here, of course, we have the power of the mind being put to evil effect, and to such a degree that a healthy human being is done to death effectively as if that person was the object of some murderous assault. Of course, you and I know that the witchdoctor's spells are, *in themselves*, harmless – mumbo jumbo, if you like – but the fellow is held in such awe by his tribe that mere words on his part are enough to seal the fate of the poor unfortunate victim.'

Richard Forres leant back in his chair to study the effect of his words.

'Now, Doctor, is that not a most extraordinary thing when one thinks about it?'

'I have no firsthand knowledge in this matter, but there are accounts in plenty from seemingly trustworthy eyewitnesses, I grant you,' said Sinclair, thoughtfully. 'No, I do not doubt what you are telling me, and, yes, it is a quite remarkable business.'

'So, we progress,' said Forres, smiling; 'but now let us consider so-called 'miracles' – miracles of healing in particular.

'Down the ages we have testimony to such things. Every civilisation we care to think of bears witness to seemingly inexplicable cures and acts of healing. In our own time, there is a welter of evidence which hints at some indefinable power inherent in meditation and prayer, in mesmerism, acupuncture, faith healing, and in a dozen other practises in the field of what may be termed 'alternative medicine'. Thus, the pilgrim has his shrine, or holy place, to inspire him; the faithful have their guru, or religious leader, to look up to; the mystic has his crystal, or talisman, to gaze upon, or touch; the country folk have their herbs and potions by which they swear; and so on.

'Now, the vast majority of so-called 'miracle cures' reported in these many and varied fields are undoubtedly bogus – the testimony exaggerated, embroided, or plain untrue, but can they all, without exception, be such? It is worth pointing out that we have need of only the one irrefutable 'miracle' to allow us to rethink the whole dogma of scientific scepticism which we have taken upon ourselves in this respect.'

'But how can these things be?' interrupted Sinclair, impatiently. 'What is the mechanism whereby miracles work? How can a miracle, which flies in the face of Nature's laws, have any kind of reality?'

'It is a presumption to say that a miracle flies in the face of Nature's laws, rather one should say that it flies in the face of Nature's laws *as we know and understand them.* There is all the difference in the world between those two statements."

'I believe I can guess what you are leading up to,' said Johnathon

Sinclair. 'You are about to tell me that the power of the mind lies at the heart of this business, are you not?' He shook his head in disbelief. 'Do you seriously claim that my cure last night was brought about simply by the working of your will?'

'That is precisely what I am saying,' said Forres. 'I see that surprises you but why should it, Doctor? Remember our African witchdoctor and ask yourself: is it such a huge step from killing a man by the fear which you induce to healing another by the faith which you inspire?'

'It is an incredible claim you are making,' said Sinclair, 'and yet......' He paused in mid-sentence to glance down at his feet. 'And yet, I have the evidence before my eyes.'

'Yes, you do,' said Forres; 'and consider this: these topics we have touched upon, from the working of some spell to the placebo effect of an intrinsically useless medicine, are very diverse, are they not? Yet, for there to be any sense, or meaning, there has to be some common thread which runs through it all. That common thread is the working of the mind; and the degree of success depends upon the degree of conviction that what one is doing will ensure success.'

'But if that is all that's involved one would expect miracles to be commonplace,' protested Sinclair. 'How is it they are met with so rarely?'

'Because the belief in what one is striving to achieve must be complete,' Forres answered. 'There must be total faith in the process without a shred of doubt, even in the deepest recesses of the mind, for doubt is the great enemy. Faith of such high order is very difficult to achieve, but not impossibly so.'

Sinclair shook his head, still far from convinced.

'One would expect this power of the mind to be demonstrable in the scientific laboratory,' he said. 'Clearly, it is not or we should all have heard more about it.'

'My dear Doctor, with the sole exception of an openly hostile audience, the sceptical, rigorous atmosphere of a science laboratory is the worse possible place for a demonstration of the power of the mind. The very act of testing, as if there were some doubt about the matter, is sufficient, in itself, to inhibit the process. But let me tell you a story, the truth of which I can vouch for.

'There was once a youth who suffered from a severe and distressing skin complaint, for whom the doctors could do nothing. To put it plainly, the young man's condition was untreatable by the medical science of the time. Eventually, he was taken on as a patient by a practitioner of mesmerism, or hypnosis as I prefer to call it, who was unaware of the fact that he would be dealing with a skin condition which was quite simply beyond help. Within a short space of time he had effected a major improvement in the patient's condition, which astounded the medical men. One of these gentlemen then made the mistake of enlightening the hypnotist as to the true nature of the young man's skin complaint. The result was, all the subsequent efforts of the healer proved quite useless. In short, the youth failed to respond, as he had once done. The doctor concerned, you see, had unwittingly sown a fatal seed of doubt in the mind of the would-be healer.'

The tale finished, Richard Forres picked up the copy of The Gospels which had been put at his disposal.

'This is without doubt the richest source of case histories which relate to what we have been discussing,' he said. 'It was for that reason I asked you to provide a copy – that and the fact I know you have extensively studied these writings pursuant to your interest in the origins of Christianity. Here, we have a book more widely read than any other literary work. Countless millions of the faithful have read and revered every chapter, verse and word. In more recent times, a growing number of sceptical academics, such as yourself, have looked at it through very different eyes, but here and now, in the quiet of this room, you and I are going to do what no man has done before. From the outset of our study we are going to make two seemingly contradictory assumptions: first, we shall take it for granted that the many healing miracles which are recounted are records of historical events, which really did happen pretty much as described; second, we are going to assume that these wonders were performed by a mortal man, and not by God incarnate. Let us see whether this unique approach leads us into the light of revelation, or into the darkness of confusion. In short, we shall put to the test my theory of the power of the mind. Remember, I contend four things: first, a man's faith in his own powers can enable him to perform so-called 'miracles'; second, anyone with the necessary degree of self-belief can work his will;

third, this faith, or self-belief (the two words are essentially the same in this context) must be untainted by doubt, so much so that it is virtually impossible to work a miracle in a sceptical, or hostile, atmosphere; fourth, there really is no limit to the power of the mind.

'Now, I should state at the outset that I find it difficult to take seriously the point of view of the out and out sceptic who would have us believe that these miracle stories are all legendary. They are more often than not related in a quite matter-of-fact fashion, with convincing little touches and asides, with casual titbits of gratuitous information, and plain-speaking dialogue, all of which has the ring of truth about it. In short, they do not read like those fantastic myths and legends which we find in other fields of ancient literature. Would you not agree, Doctor?'

Johnathon Sinclair was forced to concede the point. Although in essence a sceptic and an agnostic, he was fair-minded enough to admit that he had, himself, been troubled on this very point.

'The theories of the rationalists are scarcely more credible, in my judgement,' continued Richard Forres. 'The notion that ancient Palestine was littered with psychologically disturbed people suffering from hysterical blindness, or nervous paralysis, or whatever, seems unlikely, to say the least. Far from being common, such psychologically induced conditions are really rather rare in all time periods. Moreover, many of the stories do not lend themselves to a strictly rational explanation. These latter stories are, of course, conveniently ignored, or discarded, by advocates of this line of reasoning. We should also note that the disbelieving Jews did not doubt the fact that Jesus performed miracles. They simply ascribed his powers to sorcery, or devilry. This is made plain in The Talmud, and is confirmed by their scornful jibe in chapter 3 of Mark: '*By the prince of devils he casteth out devils.*'

'Now a striking feature of these miracle stories is how often faith, or belief, is mentioned, if not as a prerequisite for healing then at least as a very desirable thing, which is, of course, what I've been maintaining all along. True, it is not a topic which is brought up in every story but, then, we would not expect that for all the tales are abridged to a greater or lesser extent, and many cover no more than a few verses, but it is there as often as not and must be counted as a remarkable feature.'

This said, Richard Forres began to work his way through the notes he had made.

'Matthew, chapter 8, verse 10, translating from the original Greek: Jesus, speaking of the centurion who had asked him to cure AT A DISTANCE one of his servants – *'When Jesus heard it, he marvelled, and said to them that followed, verily I say unto you, I have not found so great a faith, no, not in Israel.'*

'Note, Doctor, that we are here dealing with a pagan Roman soldier, so the faith which Jesus is speaking of has to be the simple belief of the centurion that Jesus, as a healer of repute, is able to do what is being asked of him. In other words, religious faith does not enter into it. The response of Jesus is interesting: *'Go thy way and AS THOU HAST BELIEVED, so be it done to thee.'* It would appear, then, that the depth of belief of the centurion is going to have some bearing on the effectiveness of the cure.

'Matthew, chapter 9, verse 28: Jesus speaking to the two blind men who had come to him asking for the gift of sight – *'BELIEVE YE THAT I AM ABLE TO DO THIS?'* Receiving a positive response, Jesus then goes on to perform the miracle with the words *'ACCORDING TO YOUR FAITH be it unto you'.*

'Mark, chapter 5, verse 34: Jesus, speaking to the woman with a chronic discharge of blood, who has crept up on him unawares and been cured by touching his robe – *'Daughter THY FAITH has made thee whole'.*

'Are we justified in saying that the woman has essentially cured herself? I think we are. So what do we have from all three stories? What we have is belief, or faith if you like, and a healing cure inextricably linked, with the faith of the sufferer almost as important as the healing powers of Jesus.

'I see you shake your head at that, Doctor, but read Mark, chapter 6, verses 1 to 6 and you will find that even Jesus could fail in the face of unbelief. In the countryside of his boyhood, in his home town where the people who had known him as a child were not prepared to believe in his powers of healing, we read: *'And he could there do no mighty work...... and he marvelled because of their UNBELIEF.'* Note that we are not told he *would* not effect any miracles, but that he *could* not. In essence, he tried and *failed*. If that does not confirm what I was saying earlier about the power of the mind faltering in a sceptical atmosphere, then I don't know what does.

'I also spoke of fear, doubt, and uncertainty imposing severe *restrictions* on the power of the mind. Let us look at a few Gospel incidents which illustrate that.

'Mark, chapter 5, verse 36: Jesus, speaking to Jairius before attempting to raise his daughter from the dead – *'Be not afraid, only believe'*

'Matthew, chapter 17, verses 14 to 20 relates the healing by Jesus of a deranged and dumb boy. Before Jesus arrived on the scene, we are told, his disciples had been trying to heal the boy but had failed dismally. After Jesus had taken over and effected the cure, the disciples ask Jesus why it was that the same feat was beyond them. Jesus reply was: *'Because of your UNBELIEF'*.

'Now, let us pause awhile to ask ourselves what exactly Jesus meant by those words?'

'I suppose the logical interpretation, Richard, is that the disciples did not really believe that God would answer their prayers and cure the poor unfortunate.'

'But is that so terrible?' said Richard Forres. 'There is a counter-argument which would say that it is somewhat presumptious to take it for granted that God will do whatever one asks of Him. But we are splitting hairs here, Doctor. In plain words, the disciples, deep down, did not really believe themselves capable of this act of healing, and because they were not expecting anything to happen, nothing *did* happen. For his part, Jesus seems to have learned from experience that a total belief in matters such as this was an essential requirement.'

'Still, I suppose one could argue that to ask God to do something without fully expecting Him to comply is a kind of betrayal of one's faith.'

'Yes, and it is a point of view which I find singularly unconvincing. Is the Christian believer supposed to order God about with expectant demands? What is so wrong about a hopeful request?

'But we were speaking of the destructive effects of fear and doubt. Let me direct your attention to Matthew, chapter 14, verses 28 to 31. Jesus is walking *on* the water of The Sea of Galilee, and at his bidding

Peter attempts to walk towards him. At first, Peter succeeds, but growing afraid, we are told, he begins to sink. We then read in verse 31: '*And immediately Jesus stretched forth his hand, and caught him, and said unto him, Oh thou of little faith, WHEREFORE DIDS'T THOU DOUBT?*'

'Now, Doctor, could one have a better example of the destructive effect of doubt, even when a miracle is in actual progress? Peter did succeed initially, did he not? But let me come to my final point: that there really is no limit to the power of the mind if the necessary belief is there. Jesus, himself, said as much to the father of the deranged and dumb boy when he said: '*If thou canst believe, ALL THINGS ARE POSSIBLE TO HIM THAT BELIEVETH*'. But let me quote you one passage of scripture that will admit of no uncertainty.

'Let us turn to Mark, chapter 11, verse 23, and read the words of Jesus himself: '*For verily I say unto you, that whosoever shall say unto this mountain, Be thou removed and be thou cast into the sea; and shall not doubt in his heart, but believe that these things which he saith shall come to pass: he shall have whatsoever he saith*'.

'There is a similar passage in Matthew, chapter 17, and another to the same effect in chapter 21 of that gospel.'

'The moving of a mountain could fairly be regarded as hyperbolic, Richard, and is not meant to be taken literally, as for example, the passing of a camel through the eye of a needle.'

'Indeed, it could, and we shall not dispute the matter, but what is a hyperbole if not the deliberate exaggeration of a real truth in order to make a telling point? You must surely grant that, if not to be taken literally, the passage certainly means that through faith very little is impossible.'

They sat together in silence for a moment, a silence which was eventually broken by Johnathon Sinclair.

'My Christian friends would argue that the matter is a simple one. They would say that Jesus was able to do these things because God was working through him, and that he asked only that people acknowledge that fact by having faith in him.'

Richard Forres shook his head.

'No, that will not do. It does not *really* explain this constant harping on about belief, or faith, by Jesus to the almost total exclusion of any other consideration. It does not take into account Jesus' dealings with a *pagan* Roman soldier. It does not explain Peter's failure to walk on water, even in the presence of Jesus and with his master's encouragement. Most important of all, it does not begin to explain how it is that miracles are to be met with outside of the Christian faith, often in a purely secular context.

'What has the Christian dogma to do with the Javanese native who barefoot walks uninjured across a white-hot bed of charcoal? Of what relevance is it to the Indian fakir who can injure himself in the most dramatic fashion with sword, or spike, and yet feel no pain? How can it touch upon the story of our hypnotist friend and his boy patient? Of what bearing has it on maledictions, apparitions, poltergeists, telepathy, hypnosis, mind over matter, and a host of other phenomenae? The power of the mind, and that alone, is the key to our understanding of the miraculous and the inexplicable.'

'Going back to miracles of healing, one is bound to ask oneself how it was that Jesus was so much better than anyone else in what he was able to achieve?'

'Because, Doctor, his belief in his own abilities was *total*. He believed himself to be The Son of God, and that God was working through him, and would grant all that he asked. For God, of course, anything is possible, for he is by definition omnipotent. You and I do not have that same advantage of total belief and are only too well-aware of our limitations. We should also remember that Jesus was a most remarkable man, perhaps the most remarkable man who ever lived.'

'That is true,' agreed Johnathon Sinclair. 'For myself, I see now why you promised me no more than relief from pain last night. The last thing you would have welcomed would have been my natural scepticism if you had promised more, but why did that healing exercise have the opposite affect on you? That, I do not understand.'

'These things always come at a cost,' said Richard Forres. 'That cost is a drain on mental and nervous energy which puts definite limits on what a man is able to achieve. For example, were I to seriously take on a task that was beyond me I would run the risk of real, self-inflicted harm. People more proficient than myself in these things, those with a natural ability, can, of course, achieve more with less effort, but the exercise took its toll even on Jesus, and we read how he had sometimes to go away to a quiet spot in order to renew and refresh himself. Remember the story of the woman with a discharge which we touched upon earlier? She crept up unawares on Jesus in order to touch his robe but, as St. Mark tells us, Jesus knew that 'power had gone out of him'. For 'power' read 'mental and nervous energy', and all will be plain to you.'

Johnathon Sinclair picked up the book which had formed the basis of their discussion and spent a few minutes glancing through it and voicing his thoughts.

'It is a beautiful theory which you expound – simple, elegant, and beguiling. We make the one basic assumption – that the human brain is a far more potent force than is generally supposed – and, at a stroke, in a dozen different fields of human experience there is the promise of enlightenment, where hitherto there has been ignorance, or uncertainty. I cannot fault the logic of your argument, or the plausibility of the points you have been making, and I am left to wonder that none of this ever occurred to me, at least as a possibility. I have studied these ancient writings for thirty years without it seems appreciating their true import.'

'Do not be too severe upon yourself,' said Richard Forres. 'You are but one of a vast company in that respect. The trouble is there has only ever been two points of view concerning these stories of miracle healing. Either, they are the unexceptional actions of God and, as such, have no need to be critically examined, or they are legendary tales centred on a deluded man, and there's an end to it. This was never more so than with the last of the miracle stories with which we shall deal. I am speaking of the raising of Lazarus, as recounted in chapter 11 of St. John's Gospel.'

'I am surprised you bring that up for discussion,' exclaimed Johnathon Sinclair. 'You surely do not count that incredible story as an historical event?'

'Now, Doctor, we must not descend to the level of our opponents, on both sides of the argument, who conveniently misinterpret, ignore, or discard the written evidence to fit in with their preconceived ideas. Of course, with an approach like that a man may 'prove' anything. No, we shall not descend to such a level, and shall treat the story as an historical event, which is what it purports to be. In so doing, we shall solve two Gospel mysteries, which have puzzled scholars for eighteen hundred years.'

'I was not aware of any mystery, apart from the tale itself,' said Johnathon Sinclair.

'No? Well, you do surprise me. I see I shall have to begin at the beginning.

'Let us remind ourselves of the details. Jesus is sent word that his friend, Lazarus, is lying close to death in the village of Bethany. Instead of hastening to his friend's aid, Jesus chooses to loiter where he is for two days until he is sure that Lazarus must be dead. Only then does he act. Jesus had determined upon a miracle, and has decided to make it as spectacular as possible for the testimony it will afford. He tells the disciples plainly that he was glad for their sake that he was not with Lazarus earlier, so they may better believe. Sure enough, when the little party do finally arrive in Bethany they find that Lazarus had been in his tomb four days. Ignoring, *as best he can*, the weeping and wailing of the friends and neighbours of Lazarus, who have turned up on the scene, and disregarding the angry reprimands of the sisters of Lazarus for his dalliance in coming to their brother's aid, Jesus proceeds to bring Lazarus back to life.

'Now, let me draw your attention to the state of mind of Jesus at the scene outside the tomb, as detailed by the gospel writer. He twice tells us that when Jesus saw the crowd of onlookers weeping and lamenting he was 'deeply moved in spirit, and troubled.' That is how the emotion is expressed in the standard English translation but it somewhat understates the case. The word in the original Greek which is translated as 'deeply moved in spirit' has very definite connotations of *anger*, does it not?'

Johnathon Sinclair consulted his Greek-English lexicon, and after a moment's study exclaimed in surprise: 'Yes, you are perfectly correct.'

'So, Doctor, why should the very natural mourning of the onlookers have excited feelings akin to anger in Jesus? It seems a totally inappropriate emotion on the face of it, does it not?'

There was a long silence while the Doctor wrestled with the question. Finally, he spoke, but not with any great conviction.

'Perhaps Jesus was annoyed at their lack of faith in him...... in his ability to bring back to life a man four days dead.'

Richard Forres said nothing, but give his friend an expressive look.

'No, that will not do at all,' admitted Johnathon Sinclair, sheepishly. 'Since his own disciples and the sisters of Lazarus did not anticipate what he was going to do, he could hardly expect a crowd of strangers to know better.'

'Exactly so,' said Richard Forres, 'and yet I believe you to be half-right. In a sense, it *was* their lack of faith which irritated Jesus. But let us turn our attention to the Greek word which is translated as 'troubled', which is equally puzzling in this context. If you consult your lexicon again you will find that this Greek word is not simply a passive one but points to the trouble as something which arose *within and from Jesus*. The literal translation is *'he troubled himself'*.

'How odd! How strange!' said the Doctor, glancing from gospel to lexicon, and back again. He shook his head, despairingly. 'I can make neither head nor tail of all this.'

'You disappoint me a second time,' said Richard Forres, smiling. 'I would ask you to picture the scene. Jesus has set himself the task of performing what would be, even by his own standards, a prodigious miracle, but all about him are people who are loudly mourning what they regard as the *irreversible* death of this man, Lazarus.'

The light dawned on the elder man. 'Yes, of course,' he exclaimed.

'Take your mind back to yesterday evening in the light of the points I have been making. Ask yourself, what would have been *my* reaction if you had been surrounded by friends and acquaintances whose behaviour clearly showed that they thought your gout incurable? What would have been my feelings if all of this had been going on while I was contemplating a cure for you?'

'You would have become irritated with my friends. You would have become annoyed.'

'And if they had persisted with their scepticism, what would have been the further affect on me?'

'Their attitude would begin to really trouble you. The self-doubts would begin to creep in. You would be in danger of doubting you could really effect the cure which you had in mind.'

'Yes, I believe you could fairly say that I would begin to *trouble myself.*'

'Good heavens!' breathed Johnathon Sinclair.

'I believe it is significant that immediately before Jesus called Lazarus out of his tomb he felt the need to offer up a prayer, a very unusual thing for him to do before effecting a miracle. There is, too, an interesting disclaimer within the prayer: '*Father, I thank thee that thou hast heard me. I know that thou hearest me always, BUT I HAVE SAID THIS ON ACCOUNT OF THE PEOPLE STANDING BY.*' These spoken words were needed in order to counteract the negative sentiments of the onlookers. If that were not so, why mention these people at all?

'Of course, if the whole incident is dismissed as a fable the points I am making carry no force, but if that is the case it is very odd, is it not, that a made-up story should confirm in so subtle a way the theory I've been expounding to you?'

'Very odd indeed,' agreed Johnathon Sinclair, 'but if we hold the story to be true, we must grant the divinity of Jesus. Even if we take your theory of the power of the mind to its extreme, no mortal man could bring back to life a man four day's dead.'

'Because a man performs supernatural feats does that make him one with some pre-existent God of the entire Cosmos? I think the matter is at least debateable in view of all we have talked of concerning the power of the mind. And consider: can an all-powerful God fail in *anything* he does, as Jesus did in his hometown? But here we stray into the realm of Theology, pure and simple, and an arena of debate which I would sooner avoid. Remember, this is not meant to be a theological discussion. We are only dealing with these gospel stories in so far as they have a bearing on our topic of the power of the mind in achieving so-called miracles of healing.'

'On that point, I am very nearly convinced,' said Johnathon Sinclair, 'but you have yet to explain how the process works. How is the mind able to effect a physical cure, particularly in another person?'

This was a difficult question for Richard Forres to answer without recourse to subjects such as antibodies, the body's auto-immune system, brain-wave functions, and other like concepts, the discovery of which lay far off in the future. Still, the Doctor was deserving of a reply.

'The evolved human brain is one of the most powerful objects in our Universe, and we function from day to day using but a tiny fraction of its full potential. With the proper stimulus, it is quite capable of turning some of this tremendous unused potential into regenerating tissue, repairing damaged organs, strengthening the bodies natural defence mechanism, or producing highly complex chemicals to order so as to combat a specific disease. Belief, or faith, is the driving force, while doubt and fear inhibit the process. The brain must believe that what is being asked of it is reasonable and attainable, otherwise the healing process never gets off the ground.

'Therein lies the stumbling block. Our brains have critical faculties, developed over many thousands of years, which are essential to our well-being. Without them we could all too easily be persuaded into doing all kinds of foolish things, and we would be a gullible and easy prey to every charlatan, quack, or rogue. In this business, however, these critical faculties have a powerfully negative affect, for we have all been conditioned to the belief that miracles do not happen, or if they do they certainly do not emanate from within ourselves; and yet one's brain will only achieve results if it feels that what is being asked of it lies within its power.'

'I wonder, then, that anyone is able to obtain the necessary level of belief of which you speak,' said Johnathon Sinclair.

'Oh, it is possible,' said Richard Forres, 'but it takes both time and persistance, and a firm resolve at the outset not to be discouraged by initial failure, or subsequent setbacks. These must be acknowledged truly and honestly as the product of a still inadequate faith, rather than as a result of some inherent flaw in the basic theory.

'One needs to go over and over again in the mind the kind of positive evidence which I have been presenting to you today, so that one's faith may be strengthened. One needs to get into regular contact with this subconscious 'other self', which guards our critical faculties, and reason with it. There are a number of ways of achieving this but I have found the best approach is by the use of self-hypnosis, which allows our conscious self to make contact with our subconscious self. One may then make a start on some fairly easy task, such as relief from mild pain, or discomfort, the better functioning of the digestive system, or the improvement of a skin or hair condition. Success *will* follow, even for the beginner; a modest success, to be sure, but important for all that in so far as it will enable one to build on these little 'victories', increase one's faith, and allow one to move on to more ambitious undertakings'

They talked on together for a little while longer, at the end of which Johnathon Sinclair felt bound to ask one more question.

'Richard,' he said, 'who taught you these things? How did you come by this knowledge?'

'I have been a witness to such things', is what he should have said, but did not. 'Three generations of my people, myself included, have watched as a 1st Century mortal man from Palestine performed immortal deeds through simple acts of faith', is what he should have said, but could not. Of all the revelations to come out of the programme of observations at The Cairo Complex, indeed any of the ten such centres worldwide, this had been far and away the most revealing, the most compelling, the most *surprising*. Within a decade, the new knowledge had been shaped into full-blown theory, and within a generation it had evolved into a working philosophy. The healing powers of Richard Forres, which had so amazed Johnathon Sinclair, were, in fact, unexceptionable by the standards of his time, although it would be fair to say that even the most gifted of the Technician's fellowmen could not hold a candle to the man from Palestine.

Saying nothing of this, Richard Forres evaded the question in a time honoured way.

'Heavens! Look at the time!' he exclaimed, pointing to the room clock in a show of surprise. 'If I'm not away from here very soon, I shall be in danger of missing my transport home. We shall continue this discussion on another occasion.'

'I wish I could persuade you to stay another day,' said Johnathon Sinclair.

'No that cannot be. A mountain of work awaits my attention back at Grange Hall, but we shall meet again before too long.'

Johnathon Sinclair, revelling in his new-found freedom of movement, insisted on accompanying his guest on the short walk into town to see him safely aboard his homeward bound coach.

They walked together for the most part in silence, giving the Doctor the chance to review the events of the past twenty four hours. It came to him that the greatest wonder he had experienced was not the amazing revelations made to him in laboratory and library, nor even the easy, painfree way in which he was striding into town, the tapping cane in his hand now transformed into some flourishing wand, but that all these wonders had been imparted to him by his niece's husband, *of all people.*

He took his leave of his guest outside 'The Black Swan' but had not gone a dozen paces before a sudden thought made him turn around and retrace his footsteps.

'Promise me one thing,' he said. 'Promise me that when you do return here you will do so as my friend, Richard, and not as Sir Henry Forres.'

Richard Forres leaned out of the carriage window and looked down into the anxious face of the speaker. His future prospects were very uncertain, so much so that he had a natural reluctance to begin making promises which he might find difficult to keep, but he was more than confident that here was one promise he could safely make.

'Have no fear on that score, Johnathon,' he said.

Returning home, Johnathon Sinclair's first task was to put pen to paper and write to his niece, as follows:

'My dear Emma,

            I have had an unexpected visit from your husband, who astonished me greatly every moment I was with him.

I have never in my life seen a man so greatly changed for the better in so short a space of time. My strong impression is that this is no mere passing phase, and I rejoice in the fact that the young man seems at last to have come to his senses and in future means to do justice to those wonderful talents which he saw fit to reveal to me. The full details of the visit will have to wait until next we meet, although I doubt you will credit the half of it even on my testimony.

My dearest Emma, in the light of all this, and recognising the unsatisfactory nature of your present situation, which can hardly continue indefinitely into the future, I cannot help but urge you to turn your thoughts to a meeting of reconciliation.

I remain,

Your affectionate uncle,
Johnathon Sinclair.'

He despatched the letter by express post and three days later was holding in his hands Emma's reply. It was a furiously angry letter, a mixture of hatred for her husband, and bitterness towards her uncle for what she clearly regarded as a betrayal of her in favour of his recent visitor.

It read:

'My dear uncle,

It was with feelings of amazement and dismay that I read your most recent letter, which arrived yesterday evening.

I do not know by what sordid means my husband has contrived to worm his way back into your favour, but I do know that if I were foolish enough to agree to the reconciliation which you urge upon me my husband's pretence of charm and good humour would be speedily discarded.

You write that you believe he has changed for the better, but if that is so the change must be of recent occurrence for when last I saw poor Rachel she was sporting a fresh injury inflicted by that brute of a brother.

You give it as your opinion that this so-called change is of a permanent nature, but I would remind you that such improvements in the past have been of but short duration before the vicious character of the man reasserts itself. A meeting between the two of us, still less a return to Grange Hall on my part, is out of the question. My whole being cries out against such a thing. You may have forgotten the injuries which he has inflicted on our family and on myself these two years past but I have not, and I tell you plainly that I would rather die than return to him.

I count you not only an uncle but also a true friend, one of the few who remain to me, and a source of aid and comfort. I have lost so much, am I now to lose you?

Your Emma'

Johnathon Sinclair resealed the letter, and redirected it to Grange Hall, but not before he had added a few lines of his own:

'My dear Richard,

I know the enclosed will cause you pain but I feel you have the right to read in its entirety Emma's letter in response to my own.

Perhaps I am partly to blame for promoting your cause a little too eagerly, but I had no idea that my niece's prejudice against you had progressed to the stage of a distressing, deep-rooted hatred. I shall, of course, write her a conciliatory reply, assuring her of my continuing love and support, but for the present I can do no more on your behalf. To attempt to do so would put at risk her regard for myself, the loss of which would benefit no one.

Be patient, my friend, and all may yet turn out well.

Johnathon Sinclair'

CHAPTER 15

Richard Forres arrived home five hours after his departure from York. Rachel was nowhere to be seen. Nor, for that matter, was Charlie, but he thought little of it at the time.

It was not until he entered the dining room for his evening meal that he was able to meet up with Rachel.

He began his meal, chattering happily all the while of his visit to York, but within a few minutes it dawned upon him that something was badly wrong. Rachel had not said a word, even to the extent of not returning his greeting when he had entered the room. Now, she sat with eyes downcast, a trembling spoon hovering reluctantly over the bowl of soup before her.

Determined to get to the root of this latest disappointment without further ado, he dismissed the servants in attendance with a few brief words. It was only after they had left that a sudden thought came to him.

'Has Charlie been behaving himself?' he asked. 'Where is he, anyway?'

It was the moment she had been dreading.

He watched, astonished, as she got up hurriedly, overturning her chair in the process, and fled to the far corner of the room.

'Do not hurt me, brother,' she cried, cringing away from his presence as best she could, and with a hand held defensively against her face. 'Oh, do not hurt me, I beg you,' she wept.

'Rachel, I would not hurt you for the world,' he said, as he approached her; 'but I must know what has happened. I ask you again, where is Charlie? He is at the bottom of this business, is he not?'

She could not avoid his questions. Come what may, she must answer him, and get it over with.

'I gave him back to Mr. Blenkinsop this morning,' she said, in a tone of voice listless to the point of apathy. 'He has refunded the purchase price. You will find the money in your room.'

'Gave him back!' he exclaimed; 'but why, Rachel? For heaven's sake, why?'

He watched as she closed her eyes.

'I did it for Charlie's sake,' she said. 'I saw what you did to Sparkle, you see, and could not bear to think of Charlie suffering some similar fate.'

'And what *did* I do to Sparkle?' he asked, dreading what her answer would be.

'When Emma left here a year ago, in her haste to be away she left Sparkle behind. On the second evening of her absence, I watched from my bedroom window as you dragged that poor creature out into the courtyard below and proceeded to beat it to death.' She shook her head in disbelief. 'I have never heard a dog *scream* before, or since. I would not have thought the animal capable of such a sound. You gave out that Sparkle had met with an accident and you had buried him in the grounds. On her return, Emma chose to believe you, and to spare her feelings I did not think to enlighten her. It was very late in the evening and quite dark and I feel sure I was the only witness to what had happened. I am glad on that account for Emma's sake.' She paused, weary and uncaring. 'And now you may do your worst,' she said.

Richard Forres had already resigned himself to defend the former owner of Grange Hall on occasions, if only to serve his own interests, but he could not defend the indefensible. His appetite gone, he turned away and headed for his room. Seating himself down on the edge of his bed, he began to weep bitterly.

An hour later, he entered into Rachel's room, putting her instantly at ease by holding out to her a large bunch of blood-red roses.

'From the garden,' he said. 'I cut them myself not ten minutes ago.'

She took the flowers from him and held them close to her face, savouring their fragrance.

'No one has ever given me flowers before,' she said, wistfully. Putting them to one side, she looked at him in surprise.

'You have been weeping,' she said. 'I can see plainly that you have been weeping.'

'Yes, I've been weeping – much good it will do me, or anyone else, for the matter.' Seating himself down, he buried his head in his hands. 'I hope I do not shock you, but I feel like Christ crucified. Oh, Rachel! what is to be done? Even God cannot change the past, so it is said.No:

'The moving finger writes, and having writ,
  Moves on: nor all your piety, or wit

Shall lure it back to cancel half a line,
Nor all your tears wash out a word of it' '

'Beautiful,' she said. 'The words, I mean. Beautiful.'

'Beautiful, yes,' he said, 'but tragic, too.'

She took up a position alongside him. He felt a hand steal into one of his.

'I sense a change in you,' she said. 'I *see* a change in you. I cannot put it into words, but you look subtly different. And what has happened to your voice? It carries with it a soft and gentle tone, and there is a slightly husky quality there which I never noticed before.'

'But how often have you seen me like this?' he said. 'Hardly ever, I dare say. My voice is emotionally charged, that is all.'

'Yes, of course,' she said, satisfied with his 'explanation'.

'Rachel, will you do something for me?' he said, squeezing her hand. 'Will you go to Mr. Blenkinsop tomorrow morning and ask him to hold onto Charlie for, say, a month – or two, if he is agreeable? When you are quite certain that Charlie will come to no harm at my hands will you then go and reclaim him? I promise not to press you into a quick decision. Indeed, I shall not raise the subject at all. I shall leave it entirely to your discretion as to when it is safe to bring Charlie back home. Will you do this for me?'

'Yes, if that is what you wish,' she said.

'That is what I wish,' he said; 'but if I am powerless in this matter of Charlie, it is not so with you.'

'What do you mean?' she said.

'Only this: I know I have no right to ask your forgiveness for all that has gone before, so I shall not ask it of you. I know the forgiveness which I seek must be earned. So be it. I shall earn it, and more than earn it. Believe me when I tell you that from this day forth I shall love you to the point where you cannot fail to love me in return.'

She had placed her arms around his neck as he had been speaking, and he felt her tears on his cheek. He had made her cry, as so often in the past she had been made to cry, but this was a different kind of weeping and the tears of joy lifted his spirits. Gently, he raised her bowed head and began to kiss away her tears, and in the salt moistness he found a sweetness.

'Oh, Henry,' she murmured.

'Richard,' he said. 'The name is Richard.'

Richard Forres spent the first few days after his return to Grange Hall familiarising himself with the workings of the estate. In so doing he found a great deal not to his liking. His low spirits induced by this depressing survey were not helped by the receipt of Emma's letter, forwarded from York. He had been careful not to build up his hopes too high following on from his little excursion but, even so, the content and tone of the letter filled him with dismay. After due reflection, he came to the conclusion that for the present he could do no more in that direction, and that it was now time to turn his attention to putting the estate into good order.

With the somewhat grudging assistance of his steward, he initiated a whole series of reforms. Ill-timed though it was from his point of view, he nevertheless saw to it that the rents of his long suffering tenant farmers were reappraised and reduced to more realistic levels. Debts due to the estate were rescheduled, or written off if simple justice demanded it. Properties emptied by callous evictions were handed back to the previous occupants, with new leases which were fair to all concerned. In keeping with his beliefs, generous incentives were offered to tenant farmers engaged in animal husbandry to make a gradual change to cereal growing. Most demanding of all, work was put in hand to rectify long-standing instances of neglect to land and property.

For two weeks he worked from sunrise to sunset, implementing his plans at breakneck speed and cajoling, bribing, and bullying all about him to labour likewise.

His steward, a sour, ferret-faced individual by the name of Smilie, seemed bent on thwarting him at every turn, and he was tempted on more than one occasion to dismiss the man. It was clear to Richard Forres that the fellow had his own fixed ideas on how the estate should be managed and, having been given a more or less free hand in the past, did not take kindly to his master's seemingly new-found interest in his own property. Loathe to start his new regime by dismissing his right-hand man, he persisted with his recalcitrant employee and by sheer persistence saw his reforms implemented.

A case in point was the keepering of the estate. Apalled at the sight of dozens of separated heads and feets of owls and birds of prey nailed to barn and kennel doors – fully in keeping with the times, it must be admitted – he had lost no time in abolishing the post of gamekeeper.

'The pheasants will have to fend for themselves from now on,' he told a protesting Smilie. To Rachel, who was a witness to the episode, he merely said: 'Rachel, I shall never understand the mentality of the man who enjoys killing living creatures for the fun of it.'

In the midst of all this, he found time to visit his next-door neighbour in an attempt to settle a still unresolved boundary dispute affecting the two properties, the origins of which he had viewed at what seemed a lifetime ago at London Complex.

The Gibson farm, a modest holding of some thirty acres, devoted principally to sheep farming, abutted part of the western boundary of The Grange Hall Estate. A pleasant, fifteen minute walk one gloriously sunny afternoon brought him to the rambling, stone-built, grey-slated farmhouse.

His knock was answered by a dour, middle-aged serving maid, small of stature but otherwise amply proportioned. In spite of her modest height, she still contrived successfully to look down on him with an air of disdain.

'Aye, I ken who you are,' she said, cutting short his few words of introduction. 'You 'ad best come in, I suppose. Wipe your feet, mind.'

She led the way into the front parlour, muttering her disapproval of the unwelcome visitor.

'Wait here while I fetch the master. Dinna' touch anythin', mind.'

Pleased with herself at this calculated insult, she left, only to reappear a moment later outside the front window, running across the adjacent field as fast as her fat, little legs would carry her. The entrance of Samuel Gibson at the same instant told Richard Forres that the woman was bent on carrying the news of his arrival to some third party.

Samuel Gibson, owner of Fold Farm, was a typical example of the local breed of farmers who had worked the surrounding countryside for generations past. The sturdy frame, and craggy, weather-beaten face, mirrored inner qualities of solid dependability and honest frankness. At fifty years of age, a generous mass of prematurely snow-white hair contrasted oddly with a sunburnt, nut-brown face. He motioned his visitor to a chair but pointedly ignored the hand of friendship extended to him.

For a short while Richard Forres sought to voice the customary pleasantries concerning the weather, farm work, and local gossip to a taciturn audience. He was eventually interrupted in mid-sentence by his unwilling listener.

'Why have you called, Sir Henry? What is it you want?' he was asked.

'Yes, to the point. I am here to settle this dispute between the two of us. A falling out between neighbours is never a pleasant thing, especially when it is over such a trifling matter as a small strip of poor grazing land.'

'This falling out is none of my making, and this small strip of land which you allude to is nigh three acres in extent. That may be a trifle to you with your rolling acres, but to me it represents a full tenth of my little property, but I am always open to suggestions, Sir Henry. What is it you propose?'

'I would be willing to waive all claim to the land in question, and acknowledge your undisputed right to it in law.'

'Indeed? And what do you want from me in return?'

'I want nothing save your future friendship and goodwill.'

Samuel Gibson's words of surprise at this unexpected offer were cut short by the violent opening of the parlour door. A young giant of a man, stripped to the waist save for a sleeveless, cotton bodice, filled the doorway and glared at Richard Forres.

'Flora brought me news of our *gentleman* visitor. Just give the word, father, when you want him thrown out,' he growled.

He entered into the room, and to Richard Forres it seemed to abruptly shrink in size.

'Take a seat, Harold, and calm yourself. Our visitor has come here with a pleasantly unexpected offer.'

'Oh, aye? And what may that be?'

'He is prepared to relinquish all claim to Brow Rise, and asks for nothing in return save our future goodwill.'

These words appeared to take the wind out of the sails of young

Harold, and he contented himself with a bull-like snort of disbelief.

'Well, Mr Gibson?' said Richard Forres. 'Do you want me to have Mr. Buckland put the thing on a proper legal footing and have this matter settled for good in your favour?'

'Yes, of course, Sir Henry; but I'm bound to ask: why this sudden change of heart after all this time?'

Inspired thoughts did not come often to Harold Gibson but one came to him now, and he did not hold back to hear their visitor's reply.

'Because, father, he has heard from the lawyer fellows that he stands no chance in this business. To make the best of a bad situation, he comes here to curry favour and to impress us with his *generosity*.' He got to his feet and give Richard Forres a look of contempt. 'Well, none of this cuts any ice with me. Do you imagine a gesture forced upon you, and a few fine words concerning mutual goodwill can recompense my father for all the grief this business has caused him these two years past?'

'Sit down, Harold; you are out of order,' said the father, sharply. 'We have the concession. Let that be enough.'

'So, that is settled,' said Richard Forres; 'but there is another small matter.'

'Oh, yes?' said Samuel Gibson, frowning.

'Is that your broken-down, old horse I saw out there, struggling under its load?'

'Old Tom? Yes, but the load is modest enough, I'm sure. Truth is, the animal is past twenty years of age and fair worn out, I fear.'

'Then, is it not time the animal was retired?'

'Retired? What do you mean, 'retired'?'

Richard Forres shrugged the question aside. It was clear to him that in this matter at least the two of them were not on the same wavelength. He tried again: 'Is it not time you bought a replacement animal?'

'Do you *know* what a good working horse costs these days, Sir Henry? Fortunately, a small holding such as this one makes but modest demands on such an animal but, even so, as far as Tom is concerned I fear his days are numbered. When he goes we shall simply have to make do without a horse.'

'May I ask what business this is of yours?' demanded Harold.

'None, really; but I have a fine, strapping three year old shire surplus to my needs, and I was thinking we might effect a straight exchange.'

Doubting his senses, Samuel Gibson could only reply: 'Let me get this right. You are offering me a three year old shire in a no-strings-attached exchange for my Tom?'

'Just what is your game, sir?' growled Harold.

'I have no ulterior motive,' said Richard Forres, with a shake of the head. 'I merely thought this would afford you some recompense for any distress our dispute may have caused.'

'It is a most generous gesture, which I'm happy to accept,' said Samuel Gibson.

Harold was not so easily won over. A second flash of 'inspiration' came to him.

'I have it! Of course! It's our Nancy, is it not? You seek to impress her and secure her good opinion with gestures of this sort.' He had risen to his feet as he had been speaking. 'Do not imagine that your lewd looks, and impertinent remarks behind her back when you catch sight of her in town have gone unnoticed.'

Nancy? Who the devil is Nancy? were Richard Forres' thoughts.

As if in answer to his question, a pretty, red-haired girl of twenty years or so suddenly burst in upon them. A kitchen apron draped across her front, arms bare to the elbow, and hands liberally dusted with flour, told plainly from where she had sprung.

'A pretty gathering we have here – noisy, too,' she said, scornfully, her eyes sweeping the room.

'Nancy, have you been listening?' demanded her father.

'Listening? *Listening?* Who needs to cock an ear with this big oaf sounding off?' she exclaimed, indicating her brother.

'That will do, Nancy,' said Samuel Gibson. 'This is business talk and does not concern you.'

'If the matter does not concern me, why is my name mentioned?' She turned to her brother. 'Harold Gibson, I heard you speak my name. What have you to say about me in my absence?'

The big fellow shrank back in his chair, a look of apprehension on his face.

Good God! the brute is afraid of her, thought Richard Forres.

He had been made to suffer several insults at the hands of Harold, the unfriendly giant, and he now seized upon the opportunity which had presented itself for some mild revenge. A loose, *a very loose*, summary of Harold's words would serve his purpose.

'Your brother fancies that I have called today because I am courting you. He relates strange stories of meetings between the two of us in town, in which the boundaries of decorum and propriety are exceeded. It is all nonsense, of course, Miss Gibson, but I beg you will not be too severe on him for I am sure he has your best interests at heart and believes he is only saving you from yourself.'

This little speech provoked a mixed response. Samuel Gibson, who was well-aware of what their visitor was about, was doing his best to hide his amusement. For his part, Harold Gibson was looking thoroughly confused. He was a clumsy fellow in word and deed, he knew, but had he really said what had just been recounted? If he had, he must have expressed himself very ill.

An outraged Nancy Gibson give voice to her thoughts in no uncertain fashion.

'You great clod!' she cried, glaring at her brother. 'What are you about? Do you seek to ruin my reputation? I've half a mind to box your ears here and now.' She indicated their visitor. 'Do you imagine I could ever take up with a creature such as that?'

It was another insult, but from a different quarter. The offended party decided it was time for him to employ more verbal gymnastics.

'Pray, do not distress yourself, Miss Gibson,' he said. 'Your low opinion of me is well-known hereabouts and should leave no room for doubt in this matter. As for my own feelings, your brother's notion that I could somehow see you as an object of desire is, of course, quite ridiculous. Is all of that not so?'

She nodded, doubtfully, agreeing in essence with what he had said but not at all happy with his turn of phrase. She was left with the distinct impression that she had been insulted once more.

'Come now, Nancy,' said her father, laughing, 'the gentleman is here today simply to inform us that he is waiving all claim to Brow Rise, which is welcome news, indeed.'

'I see. Come to the conclusion this is one legal suit he cannot win, has he?'

Harold Gibson came to life again.

'That is my judgement too, sister,' he said, eagerly.

'Really? Then clearly I must be mistaken in what I say.'

'I can add two and two together,' he said, sulkily.

'Yes, and make three, or five, of it every time, I dare say.' She turned to her father. 'I heard Tom's name mentioned. How does he come into this matter?'

'Sir Henry and I will effect a change of horses, very much to our advantage, I might add.'

'What, then, will become of Tom?' she said.

'Sir Henry will dispose of him as he sees fit,' said Samuel Gibson, with a shrug of his shoulders.

'You mean he will end up in Sam Bolton's bone and glue yard? Is that how we repay poor Tom for twenty years of faithful service? Father, my earliest memory is that of being gently carried around the farm by Tom. The two of us grew up together. Is he now to be discarded like some piece of rusted, useless machinery? I am sure our visitor will not insist on taking possession of his acquisition. Can we not, therefore, keep both horses?'

'Nancy, how can we?' asked her father, gently. 'Be practical, girl. It is difficult enough to make a living hereabouts without taking on the upkeep of *two* horses, one of which serves no useful purpose.'

'Miss Gibson, I have no intention of allowing Tom to end up as you describe,' said Richard Forres. 'I have two horses of my own come to the end of their working lives. He may join them in a happy retirement, and you may visit him at Grange Hall whenever you wish.'

'You would do this for us? *For me?*' said Nancy, in surprise.

'No, for myself,' he said.

She stared at him, deeply puzzled. Was this the notorious owner of Grange Hall who was speaking? she was asking herself. Was she dreaming, or had the man taken leave of his senses?

'I have a notion,' she exclaimed.

Before anyone knew what she was about, she had swept across the room and was bending over him as he sat there, her face inclined and moving to close with his. He felt sure she was going to kiss him and, unaccountably, like some silly girl, he closed his eyes. The action was not lost on her, and his discomforture came swiftly. She tapped him on the nose with a dusty finger, leaving behind a whitened tip.

'I'm grateful, but not *that* grateful,' she murmered, under her breath.

Her nose came to rest a couple of inches from his lips, at which point she give two melodramatic sniffs. She held her position above him, and turned her head to address her father.

'No, I was mistaken – stone-cold sober.'

Samuel Gibson flushed with embarrassment, but his angry reprimand died on his lips at an outburst of laughter from their visitor. Nancy joined in the merriment, and even the big fellow in the corner managed an awkward grin. The father found himself smiling and nodding indulgently.

'Oh, dear!' said Richard Forres, a little breathless from his laughter. 'Do you know, Mr Gibson, I came here today with – dare I say it? – feelings of compassion and pity for your good self, but with a bear and tigress to defend your interests, feelings of dread and apprehension for my poor self would have been more appropriate.'

'You must excuse my daughter's familiarity,' said Samuel Gibson. 'Since the death of my wife three years ago she has been mistress of the house and terrorizes us all.'

'I see. Well, I pity the man she marries, assuming anyone will take her.'

For some reason, this seemed to touch her on the raw and her good humour vanished in an instant.

'Well, I would not have him treat me as some men treat their wives,' she said. She was looking pointedly at their visitor, her meaning clear, but as if to dispel any doubt in the matter added: 'Speaking of which, how is Lady Forres these days, do you know, sir?'

Samuel Gibson sprang to his feet, his face dark with mortification.

'Nancy! That is a private matter between Sir Henry and his wife, which in no way concerns us. You will apologise this instant to our visitor.'

Richard Forres held up a restraining hand, and rising from his chair walked slowly over to where the girl stood. She sought to evade his eyes, but he lifted up her chin and made her look at him. His eyes gazed full into hers and she found herself quite unable to look away.

'I...... I'm not afraid of you,' she said, uncertainly.

'Mr. Gibson, I venture to suggest that your daughter is in need of a good spanking,' he said, his eyes never leaving hers. 'If you are loathe to perform this very necessary duty, I would be more than willing to put her across my knee.'

She jumped back, wide-eyed and open-mouthed.

'You wouldn't dare,' she gasped.

'I believe you are right, sir,' said Samuel Gibson, with a sigh. 'I must confess the same thought comes to me on occasions, except I fear it is too late and she is beyond the reach of amendment.'

By now, Harold Gibson had heard enough. He got to his feet with a characteristic snort.

'You three may have time for this foolish dalliance,' he said, 'but some of us have work to do.'

This said, he clumped noisily out of the room.

'If my brother gives you any future trouble just come to me,' said Nancy, lightly, a little ashamed now for her loss of temper and anxious to make amends. She paused before continuing, apologies not coming easily to her as a rule. 'I really am grateful to you with regard to dear old Tom. Will you forgive my remarks of a moment ago? I know I say and do foolish things on occasions.'

'We are all guilty of that at times, Miss Gibson,' he said, smiling; 'and, yes, you are forgiven. For myself, I must own that I jested when I spoke of correcting your behaviour. I would not dream of chastising you in the manner I described – unless, of course, you asked me to.'

She blushed deeply at these provocative words but, strange to tell, did not see fit to reprove the speaker.

Her father coughed discreetly. He was now very much indebted to their visitor, but he had no wish to see his daughter become emotionally entangled with a man of the likes of Henry Forres.

The man in question took the hint and made to leave, taking Nancy with him as far as the garden gate. Samuel Gibson watched with mild interest as the two of them engaged in conversation for a few moments.

Having returned to her father's side, the two of them stood watching the departing figure dwindle into the distance.

'His middle name is Richard, did you know?' she asked.

'Yes,' he said. 'Why do you ask?'

'He says he prefers the name to Henry, and would be so addressed in future by all his acquaints.'

'To be sure, I never heard of anyone who refers to him by that name. Still, that is not to be wondered at. The fellow can have few friends to oblige him so.'

'Yes, the man cuts a rather sad and lonely figure.'

'Why do you say that, child? He did not strike me as such. He laughed, and jested, and entered into the conversation readily enough. I wonder only at his forebearance at your teasing and Harold's ill-humour.'

She shook her head at this.

'He had the appearance of a player acting out a part, or so it seemed to me. He was one of us, and yet not one of us, if you take my meaning.' She pursed her lips, thoughtfully. 'You did not look full into his eyes, as I did. I saw an almost unbearable loneliness, and a sadness, too.'

'A woman's intuition?' said Samuel Gibson, smiling.

'Yes, call it that if you will,' she answered.

There was a moment's silence before the father spoke again.

'Nancy, I would wish to caution you not to be quite so free and easy with that gentleman in the future as you were today. We have just seen him in a high good humour, so much so that I marvel at it, but I would remind you that the fellow has an evil reputation. I would not wish to see you hurt.'

She laughed, lightly, and shook her head.

'Henry Forres – or should I say 'Richard Forres'? – has no special regard for me, nor I for him, although if he continues as we saw him today I believe I could easily get to like him as a friend.'

'Since you tell me it is so, I do not doubt your own sentiments, but I wonder you can speak so readily of his feelings towards you.'

'He loves his wife, father. It's that simple.'

'Then, he has had a strange way of showing it in the past. How can you speak so?'

'We talked concerning her before he took his leave of me. He is impatient for her return.'

'We all know that, Nancy. It signifies nothing save wounded pride at her desertion.'

'No, you are wrong, father, I'm sure. There were tears, *real tears*, in his eyes when he spoke of her.'

'Well, that's as maybe. For myself, I can think only of how the fellow conducted himself today. It was so greatly out-of-character.'

'I do not agree,' she said, frowning.

Later, on mature reflection, this instinctive observation was to puzzle her as much as it did her father when it was first made.

Left alone, she continued to gaze thoughtfully for several minutes in the direction of their departed visitor. More than once she felt the need to moisten a pair of inexplicably dry lips with the tip of her tongue, as all the while her hands worked unthinkingly to act out the drama which was unfolding in her mind's eye.

Returned to the kitchen, she was scolded by Meg, the cook and housekeeper and the one person in the house who was not backward in taking her to task if the need arose.

'Child, what have you been doing to yourself?' she demanded, turning Nancy around and indicating the seat of her dress all covered in flour.

CHAPTER 16

Hand in hand with the reorganisation of the estate, there came changes in the day to day running of Grange Hall itself. Here, innovations designed to lighten loads and sweep away little injustices, together with a display of genuine concern for the well-being of all the household staff, were to serve him well. Within the space of a few weeks, Grange Hall became a very different place from the somewhat gloomy abode it had once been.

An air of ease and informality now ruled, apparent even to the most casual of outside observers. The powdered wigs and stiff, starched livery of all the male servants within the house were quickly dispensed with in favour of less formal attire, while all the maidservants, without exception, were soon going about their duties in modest but pleasing uniforms, designed by their master.

For his part, Richard Forres soon abandoned the almost obligatory top hat, except on the most formal of outdoor occasions, and went everywhere bareheaded. 'I'm heartily tired of trying to balance those ridiculous chamber pots on my head wherever I go,' were his words to Rachel. Moreover, he refused to be cosseted and waited on every minute of the day. 'Why ring for a servant to perform a simple task which I can do myself in a matter of seconds?' he had said to Rachel. It pleased him to see that she swiftly began to follow his example.

The household staff responded in like kind. Even the once sullen and resentful Sarah was soon showing signs of a placid resignation to her altered status, while with the trusting, impressionable Mary he struck up a special relationship, in spite of her lowly position within the household.

His one failure, in spite of his best efforts, was with his cook, Helen, on whom his future well-being depended in no small measure.

The eating of flesh from the corpses of dead animals and birds was anathema to the civilisation into which he had been born. He readily acknowledged to himself that he must adapt in order to survive and flourish in his new environment, and had already done so in a hundred different ways, but this was one custom he had brought with him which he could not set aside. Although he had compromised his principles to the extent that he now consumed dairy produce, the eating of flesh from another sentient creature was simply beyond him.

In a later age this vegetarian preference would have posed few problems. Two hundred years into the future the practise was widespread and people like him were well-catered for, but in 1813 the non-meateater was a real rarity and the situation was very different. Meat, in all its varied forms, was to be found in sauces, broths, and stews, besides comprising an important part of more substantial meals. It was rare, therefore, for him to be able to consume a complete meal. He often went hungry and was conscious of the fact that he was losing weight.

A way out of the difficulty, one would have thought, would be to explain the problem to a sympathetic cook and have her prepare special meals. This was fine in theory, but he found his own particular domestic decidedly *unsympathetic* to his needs, this in spite of the fact that he dressed the problem up as a medical one, and in terms which could reasonably be expected to excite concern and understanding. It was not that Helen refused to comply with his wishes – she could hardly do that – but he sensed her indifference to his problem during their several meetings together, an indifference that was clearly apparent in practise. His carefully drafted menus were implemented with little thought or care, while his verbal requests and suggestions were for the most part ignored. He faced, therefore, the same kind of non-cooperation which he had encountered with his steward, but with the one added difficulty: while he could effectively oversee his steward to ensure his instructions were carried out, he could hardly stand over his cook for hours at a time in the kitchen. As with his steward, he had a natural disinclination to take drastic action, but felt the time was fast approaching when he would be left with no other option.

The reason for Helen's hostility he could only guess at. His only credible supposition was that she had perhaps been closer to Emma than most of the other servants and her resentment at the past treatment of her mistress still lingered on. The true cause of it all, however, proved in the end to be quite another matter, the details disclosed to him by Mary. It was an affair of the heart in the form of a mutual affection between Helen and Rogers, his butler. The affection had blossomed into an engagement, and plans for a marriage. That the ceremony had not taken place long ago was due entirely to Sir Henry Forres.

The attitude of the upper class towards the employment of married couples as live-in servants varied from household to household. There were obvious problems where younger domestics were involved, not least being the accommodation of the offsprings of such couples within the family home, but most employers were more tolerant with regard to older servants, with the wife beyond the age of childbearing. When, therefore, some months previously Rogers had broached the subject of a marriage between Helen and himself he had been hopeful of his master agreeing to their continued employment at Grange Hall after the match had been made. He had been in the employment of the Forres family for twelve years and believed he was due some consideration on that account. Besides, with a wife approaching fifty years of age there could be no complication in the shape of children.

Typically, Henry Forres was not agreeable. Both butler and cook must continue to live in – it was impractical that they reside outside Grange Hall – and he was not going to set a precedent for others to follow by giving his blessing. In short, if they wished to marry they must forfeit their positions.

Rogers had taken the ruling philosophically and, gentleman's gentleman that he was, continued to faithfully carry out his duties without complaint, but Helen could not so easily hide her disappointment at this unexpected obstacle, nor conceal her displeasure with the man who was the cause of it.

The trouble was that unless their master had a change of heart the proposed marriage was effectively blocked for all time. The couple lacked the financial means to terminate their employment, and while an experienced cook could readily obtain a position elsewhere, such was not the case with a butler. Further, the two positions would have to be in the same household, and an accommodating one at that, otherwise there would be no advantage in the change.

Richard Forres learnt all of this from Mary, and the information pleased him. Such a matter was easily resolved and he lost no opportunity to do so. That very day he raised the subject when Rogers entered the room in which he was sat.

'Rogers, when are you going to make an honest woman of Helen?'

he said, casually, from behind his newspaper. 'Time passes and neither of you are getting any younger.'

For once, Rogers professional calm left him. Uncertain of the meaning which lay behind the remark, he was lost for a response. Was his master hinting that Helen and he should marry and quit the place? Was he wanting to be rid of them both? He knew that of late his master had been experiencing some difficulties with Helen – he had, himself, cautioned her on several occasions about her disposition – but if their employer wanted them to go why did he not speak out plainly and say as much?

'We would not wish to go against your wishes in this matter, sir,' he answered, diplomatically. 'Above all else, we would like to remain here at The Grange.'

'And so you shall,' said Richard Forres, putting his newspaper to one side. 'I would be happy to see the pair of you married and remain with us.'

A month previous Rogers would have been astonished at these words, but his master's conduct had been so pleasantly out-of-character of late that he found himself more pleased than surprised at this change of heart.

'I think you had best give Helen the good news immediately,' said his master, cutting short the profuse thanks being directed his way, and anxious that his cook be acquainted with the changed situation as soon as possible.

An hour later, disregarding all the norms of social convention with a complete indifference, he went downstairs to the kitchen bearing a large bottle of champagne. He found the place in uproar. Helen, her work temporarily forgotten, was pacing the floor, clearly much affected by the news recently brought her, while Mary paced beside her attempting to exert a calming influence. Martha, the formidable daily help, stood with her back to the sink, waving a large, dripping ladle as if she were conducting some discordant choir, and loudly airing her views in the matter. Only the shy, placid Eleanor appeared to be going about her work as normal.

All four had bobbed a curtsy at his appearance, Mary accompanying hers with a warm smile, Eleanor hers with a downcast look, and

Martha giving vent to a doubtful nod. In the considered opinion of the last named, it was improper for a master to seek out a servant in this fashion; if he wished to speak with one or more of them on a particular matter, he should summon *them* to *him*.

Once she had recovered from her surprise at this sudden appearance of her master, Helen burst into a flood of tears and a torrent of words.

'Bless my soul! if it's not the master come to see me, and with a few kind words, I don't doubt; but, goodness! if I don't declare, it should by rights be the other way about; and 'how does he find me?' I ask myself: why, pacing the floor like some silly girl not half my age, with no thought of work and duty, but only foolish thoughts going round and round in her head, and a weakness in her legs, and a flutter in her stomach – and if only my poor mother were alive to see me now; goodness me! what would she not say at the sight, and rightly so, for she was never one to pass over in silence the foolish ways of young folk – and I'm so happy,' she wailed.

She paused for breath, giving Richard Forres the chance to speak.

'I thought we might celebrate the good news in the proper fashion,' he said, placing the bottle on the kitchen table. 'Eleanor, do you get five glasses, while I draw the cork.'

Martha frowned. She did not approve of intoxicating liquor, but condescended to take a glass. Soon, all but one of the five charged glasses were being raised in a celebration toast.

'Come along, Martha, do not spoil the occasion,' urged her master. 'You have real champagne from France there.'

Martha's frown deepened. She did not approve of that country over the water.

'I wonder you possess it at all, sir,' said Mary.

'It's a vintage bottle laid down long before the war, Mary,' he replied.

Mention of the seemingly never-ending war with France served to mollify Martha a little, and she consented to take a sip. She quite approved of wars for they were invariably waged against foreigners, of whom she did not approve.

'So, Helen, is there a date fixed upon?' said Richard Forres.

The lady thus addressed, having nicely recharged her lungs, burst forth once more.

'No, not as yet, sir, though we have a mind to six weeks next Saturday, but we must first speak with Mr. Sibley and arrange matters. Six weeks! Oh, Lord! and so much to do; a hundred and one things to manage; I do declare, it fair makes my head spin to think about it; and all so sudden, there's the wonder of it, for along comes Mr. Rogers and begs me to stop what I'm about, then sits me down and breaks the news in one great gush of words – or so it seemed to me – which fair made me faint away, the like of which I never did before.'

She rambled on in this fashion for a full two minutes before being interrupted by Martha, her sweeping ladle held aloft once more, threatening all present.

'Well, far be it for me to dampen festive spirits, but this poor lamb has my sympathies. Three husbands I've buried in my time, and each one left me poorer than when he found me.'

'You surely cannot mean that all three died?' asked Richard. A humourless Martha confirmed gravely that such was the case, then watched in surprise as a grinning Mary began to whisper in her master's ear. This brought the frown back to Martha's face, for here was evidence of a surprising familiarity between master and scullery maid. One hardly needs to add that Martha did not approve of familiarities.

'We must alter the sleeping arrangements at the proper time, Helen,' said her master, mischievously. 'I would not have you, or Rogers, creeping about at the dead of night from one room to the other disturbing the household in the process. There is a large, double room spare which will serve the purpose perfectly. All I ask is that you do not so tire Rogers as to make him unable to satisfactorily carry out his daily duties.'

This reminder of her future husband's conjugal rights and the role she would play in them conjured up images which poor Helen was quite unable to cope with. She collapsed heavily into a handily placed chair, her eyes wide-open in her plump, flushed face, and her gaping mouth gasping for air like some stranded fish.

'Oh, Lord!' she gasped, 'how you do tease a poor woman, sir. It fair makes me giddy to hear you speak so, but I would do my duty as any good wife should, and he the same for his part, I'll be bound. Lord, but it's hot in here with no sweet air to cool a body down.' One hand clutched at her throat, while the other waved frantically to and fro before her face. 'Come and assist me, Mary, before I swoon clear away,' she croaked.

Mary, grinning broadly, seized up a towel and began to waft it ostentatiously before Helen's face.

Martha stood viewing the scene before her with a look of deep disdain before fixing her eyes on her master as the cause of this most recent commotion. For his part, he was somewhat unnerved to see that she had exchanged her ladle for a large rolling pin.

'Men!' she exclaimed; 'a poor woman's body is their chief concern.' Rather late, she remembered just whom she was addressing, and forgetting he was the object of her reprimand added, illogically: 'Present company excepted, of course.' She sighed in exasperation. 'I have had endless trouble in that respect all my life. Even now, though five years a respectable widow, I am continually pestered by a host of lewd and idle fellows.'

Richard Forres could only stare in surprise at this last remark. He had six strapping Irish labourers temporarily employed in work on the estate whom he considered positively frail and feminine in comparison to Martha. He wondered for a moment if she was being serious before finally concluding that she was.

Now, if the new owner of Grange Hall had a fault it was a fondness for teasing, especially when confronted by the pompous, or the ridiculous. Martha possessed both of these 'attributes' in abundance and boasted, he knew, the added attraction of taking literally anything he might choose to say to her.

'These unwelcome attentions are your own doing, Martha,' he said, gravely. 'Oh, I do not mean to imply that you deliberately court these distressing liberties, only that you possess in too great an abundance those feminine charms which fire a man's passions and, alas, all too readily excite his carnal desires. I have often remarked upon the fact.'

'Oh! have you, sir?' she gasped.

'Indeed, I have, and not I alone,' he said, knowingly.

'Oh, heavens!' she stuttered.

She give a positive glare in the direction of Mary and Eleanor, who had taken to giggling uncontrollably, before turning thoughtfully back to her work.

The scenes she had witnessed had not pleased her, but she was prepared to overlook the behaviour of Helen in view of that poor woman's situation, while her master, after some initial foolishness had redeemed himself at the end by speaking much sound commonsense. As for the conduct of Mary and Eleanor, well, that was only to be expected for they were two foolish young people. The frown returned to her face. She did not approve of young people.

Helen had meanwhile calmed down sufficiently for her master to take her quietly to one side.

'Helen, about those instructions I gave you for specially prepared meals,' he began.

'Oh! yes, sir,' she said, hastily, her face full of dutiful concern, 'they should present no difficulty, no difficulty at all.'

With an appointment to see his banker that same afternoon, Richard Forres took an early lunch, all the while reflecting that as one problem was sorted out another rose up to take its place.

Two years of profligacy on the part of Sir Henry Forres had taken its toll, to the extent that the estate was now in a grave financial position. The reforms to the estate which he had implemented combined with a modest lifestyle would, he felt sure, rectify the situation in time, except he was fast running out of that particular asset.

He had used the proceeds from the sale of Pine Tree Cottage together with half the hoard of cash he had found to pay off his most pressing creditors. The balance of the cash would, inevitably, be swallowed up in payment for the very necessary work of restoration and repair which he had put in hand. Within the month, therefore, the last of the cash would be gone, leaving him a potentially sound and viable estate, it was true, but also a legacy of debts to the tune of £9,000, a very considerable sum of money. In short, he needed to raise more funds, and the need was urgent.

All was not lost, however, for during the past few days a still as yet half-formed plan to deal with the crisis had been taking shape in his head. To that end, he had begun making a few discreet enquiries concerning a certain matter. Not that he would divulge his budding plan to his banker, or to his accountant, or to anyone else for that matter. The sole purpose of his day's business in Stockton was to buy a little time for himself.

As he mounted Star, his favourite horse, and set off at an easy trot along the riverside bridleway to that town, other problems crowded in upon him.

He had lately become conscious of the fact that the strange, untypical behaviour of the master of Grange Hall had made him a major topic of conversation and gossip, not only in the town of Yarm but in outlying districts also. He had half-expected this but the *degree* of such unwelcome attention had surprised and disturbed him. His reception in town was now markedly different from that of a few weeks previous. Many still held aloof, declaring his recent conduct to be unreal and would not, indeed, could not, last, but many others were better disposed and now greeted him with an increasing warmth and friendliness. That was gratifying, to be sure, but it had all happened a little *too* quickly for comfort. Former cronies, those that Sir Henry had gambled and caroused with, were deeply puzzled by this changed conduct and made no secret of their feelings. A joking remark which he had overheard the previous day in Yarm, to the effect that the master of Grange Hall had been whisked away to be replaced by some long-lost, benign, twin brother, had come shockingly too close to the truth in his estimation. Fortunately, a ready solution to the problem was at hand in the shape of Rachel Forres.

For two weeks Grange Hall and its estate had occupied all his waking hours, but he now felt free to turn his attention to Rachel. Quite apart from the fact that he believed she was owed something after all she had suffered at the hands of her brother, was the thought that the transformation which he had in mind for her would serve as a perfect diversion from himself. The supposed change in Sir Henry Forres, which had so engaged the attention of the local populace, would be as nothing to the very real change in the man's sister. If all went well, in ten days time it would not be he who was the main topic of conversation amongst the idle and the curious, but Rachel. The process would take him a week, he judged, and he would make a start that evening.

All of that still left unresolved the problem of Emma. How to win her back? was the question. Here, he could see no easy solution. Certainly, blundering around in some fruitless search for her, and antagonising people in the process, was not an option. He could only hope that, as the once and future Mr. Micawber was apt to declare, something would turn up.

For the rest, it give him a feeling of self-satisfaction when he reflected on how well he had managed to adapt himself to his new life. He flattered himself that no other person from his own time could have done as well. Of course, his profound knowledge of all aspects of the time period had been of immense help – that and a disposition which found pleasure in the simple things in life, and eschewed many of the trappings of a higher civilisation.

It was true that there were a score of things the loss of which he felt keenly, from basic amenities such as running hot water, and instant light in the darkness at the touch of a switch, or a word of command, to more important considerations, such as the abrupt termination of his work at London Complex, but he tried not to dwell on such things for he knew that were he to do so it could ruin all his hopes for future happiness. Like some shipwrecked castaway of old, he would put to better purpose what remained to him. If there were losses, there were also gains to balance the account: a beautiful and still relatively unspoilt countryside; horses, for which he had a real love, to be met with at every turn in all their varied forms; a society of people spanning the whole range of humanity, in stark contrast to the dull uniformity of his own time; the slow and easy pace of life, which suited him, and, above all, the exhilarating unpredictability of a primitive existence.

One thing he longed for above all else was for the companionship of another human being like himself. What would he not have given to have within easy reach a friend, or acquaintance, from his own time? What would he not sacrifice to have the company of a fellow traveller, someone he could truly converse with and confide in, and whom he could seek out when at times, in spite of his best efforts, the pain of his unique loneliness became almost unbearable?

With a mind occupied with these mixed emotions he rode into Stockton. After stabling his horse, he made to keep his appointment, looking out all the while for a glimpse of Rachel. She had left home that morning for her weekly shopping excursion to the town, and he thought it possible that they may run into each other and spend some time together. He failed to spot her, however, and once his business was concluded he decided on a little shopping of his own.

A chance remark made to him at his second port of call, a haberdashery store which he had entered for the purpose of purchasing for Rachel a surprise gift of material for the making of a bonnet, was to have momentous consequences. He had completed the purchase when the proprietor, well-acquainted with the Forres family, observed how seldom of late had he seen Miss Rachel, although once she had been a regular customer.

Richard Forres thought this a very strange remark. From the little that Rachel seemed disposed to tell him of her weekly excursions to Stockton, he had been led to believe that she was a regular caller at the shop in which he now stood. Puzzled, he went out of his way to call at a few more of the High Street establishments where she could reasonably have been expected to shop. In each he made discreet enquiries concerning her, and in every case received the same answer: Rachel Forres, although at one time a regular customer now called very seldom. Furthermore, when she did pay one of her infrequent visits it was *never* on a Wednesday.

It was a perplexed and troubled traveller who made his way home late that afternoon. There could be no doubt from what he had been told that wherever Rachel went each Wednesday it was not to Stockton town centre, as she claimed. Her curious reluctance each Wednesday evening to talk much of the day's events was, thus, explained, and the implausibility of an outing to a town less than six miles away consuming eight hours of time now came to him for the first time. It was no wonder, he reflected, that she had put him off when he had suggested the previous evening that they meet up the next day and travel home together; but why the untruths and deceit on her part? Furthermore, if she was not spending each and every Wednesday as she stated, just what was she doing?

He considered the possibility of secluded meetings between Rachel and some secret admirer, but quickly rejected the idea. He thought it very unlikely that the shy, unprepossessing girl boasted some secret admirer. Perhaps, however, she was meeting with a friend of whom she knew he would disapprove? Peter Sinclair, he knew, lived in the vicinity of Stockton. Was it possible that she was meeting with him?

No, he thought not. There was no evidence, absolutely none, of an attachment between the two of them. The dashing, devil-may-care Peter Sinclair had nothing in common with poor Rachel, apart from a mutual love of Emma.

Good God! Emma!

The thought when it came so startled him that his horse shied at his reaction and he found himself having to pat the animal reassuringly before he could continue on his way.

Was it possible? he asked himself. Could it be that Rachel was meeting with Emma?

The more he thought about the matter the more convinced he was that this was the true state of affairs. He knew from Vicar Sibley and from others that the two young women had been firm friends at Grange Hall. What could be more natural than a mutual desire to keep in touch after they had been forced to part company? He remembered Johnathon Sinclair's words to the effect that Emma had removed herself no great distance from Yarm. Surely, all of this pointed to Emma being settled in the general vicinity, not too far away from both brother and sister-in-law? A final, telling point came to him when he recollected that Rachel did not make use of one of the estate's carriages for her weekly excursion, but was conveyed there and back in a chaise and four owned by Colonel Palmer, supposedly carrying his own daughter on the same 'shopping errand'. The Palmers, he had been reliably informed, were long-standing friends of the Sinclairs, and of Emma in particular, but had no special attachment to Rachel. If there was a secret to be kept from him, as seemed to be the case, the use of a carriage from the Palmer's stables rather than one from Grange Hall could be viewed as a very necessary precaution.

Firmly convinced that he was on the right track, he turned his thoughts to how best he should deal with the situation. What would be his best course of action? he asked himself.

Being loathe to put at risk the relationship of mutual affection and trust which he had so painfully built up with Rachel, he shrank from the thought of a confrontation with her. Besides, he was no Henry Forres and was incapable of bullying the girl if she proved stubborn. No, Rachel was due to make her journey again in seven days' time and he would uncover the truth of the matter by the simple expedient of following her coach. He would be patient and bide his time, using the coming seven days in carrying out his carefully laid plans for Rachel.

That night, for the first time since his days at London Complex, she entered into his dreams. Strangely, she looked a generation older, although still beautiful in his eyes. Different too, was the situation. They sat together on the bank of a small stream. Little children splashed and frolicked in the shallows, while young adults hovered around and about. A youthful, second Emma, subtly different somehow, stood by his side. He stared at his reflection in the water. As he did so, away in the distance a steam locomotive sounded its' whistle.

He awoke with a start. Reaching out, he took a pillow into his arms.

For a little while he sought in vain to rekindle the dream, but eventually reconciled himself to simply the haunting memory of it.

CHAPTER 17

Rachel Forres was not, in point of fact, quite the unprepossessing young woman many a casual observer judged her to be, as her 'brother', himself, had gradually come to appreciate. A close scrutiny revealed both a face and figure which were studies in contrast. An unflattering pair of spectacles, a seemingly permanent fixture in spite of their mere occasional need, served no real function other than to obscure a large pair of fine, hazel eyes, fringed by long lashes and framed by two perfectly shaped eyebrows. A disagreeably sallow, pockmarked complexion effectively drew one's eye away from a finely proportioned nose, pleasingly generous mouth, and well-modelled chin. The fine head of rich, chestnut-coloured, shoulder-length hair drew no admiring glances when drawn back into the large bun she invariably sported – a severe hair style which, in truth, few women can display to advantage. A stooping, round-shouldered posture, together with drab, functional clothes, completely masked a long-legged, slim, curvaceous figure.

Richard Forres had come to the conclusion that he had set himself no great task in seeking to transform Rachel's appearance. Discard the spectacles, unbind the hair, and change the clothes to advantage, and a very different young woman would begin to reveal herself. Indeed, he reckoned there were only two difficulties worth the mention. First, was the girl's complexion and skin texture, which would require a lot of work and effort on his part to change but was certainly not beyond his powers. Second, was Rachel's disposition – her personality, no less – which showed itself in a dozen different ways, from her bad posture to her shy reserve, and still occasional stammer. A physical change for the better without a changed personality would not suffice. Of course, an increased confidence in her appearance was bound to have a beneficial affect, but it would not be sufficient in itself to bring about the truly radical change he had in mind for her. To achieve *that* he would have to resort to some old-fashioned hypnosis, something he was capable of but hesitated to put into practise. The reshaping of her personality would inevitably involve an invasion of her privacy, yet he could see no alternative if he was to leave Rachel with a well balanced nature to match her looks. How far to take matters before calling a halt would be a delicate matter of judgement. He hoped that he would be able to gauge things correctly.

On the evening of his return from Stockton he made her sit beside him in the lounge, and took her hand in his.

'Rachel, will you put yourself in my hands in the coming few days?' he said. 'I wish only for your happiness, and believe you would enjoy life all the better if I effected a few changes in you.'

'You find fault with me. Well, I do not wonder at it,' she said, unhappily.

'Indeed, I do not find fault with you. I could love you, I *do* love you, just as you are, but I rather think you find fault with yourself, and I sense you are not happy. I want to change that for the better. Perhaps it would please you if you were beautiful?'

'Beautiful? Me?' she exclaimed, incredulously. 'I am ugly, and am despised and rejected by society on that account.'

These words shocked him. He had not fully appreciated the depths of her feelings of inferiority and inadequacy. Any doubts concerning the morality of what he was contemplating were now dispelled.

'Do not speak so. Do not even think it,' he said. 'Let me prove you wrong.'

He removed her spectacles, and carefully unbound her hair to send it tumbling down her shoulders. She stirred uneasily but raised no objection to what he was doing.

Thus encouraged, he drew ever closer to her.

'Now, I want you to clear your mind completely, and look full into my eyes.'

She did as he asked and there followed a moment of perfect stillness and quiet.

'Tell me what you see, Rachel,' he said, the soft murmur of his voice barely breaking the silence.

'Eyes...... your eyes...... grey-green as the sea...... enormous...... filling my whole vision.'

'Nothing else? Look deeper, Rachel. Look beyond those eyes.'

'Yes...... I see tenderness...... but I see a sadness, too...... no, sadness is not quite the word, or if it is it stems from...... from a terrible form of loneliness.' Her eyes drifted fractionally away from his. 'How is it that you are so very lonely?' she said.

'Concentrate more,' he said, smiling. '*You* are the object of this exercise, not me. Look deeper, Rachel. Search out my inner self. Search for it.'

A moment more and he saw her eyes glaze over.

'*Now* tell me what you see,' he said.

'Wonderful things,' she whispered. 'I see cities, clear as light and stretching to the far horizon...... towers of glass reaching beyond the clouds...... I see a race of people, not unlike you and I and yet different...... strange clothes...... not a head of hair in sight...... all are as one...... where are the old, the infirm, the ladies and gentlemen of fashion?'

'That is good,' he said, with quiet satisfaction. 'Now I want you to blot out that scene and I shall paint a more familiar one for you. Picture a gathering of people in splendid surroundings – a room full of men and women, all dressed up in their finery. There is music, and dancing, and merriment. See there the long sidetable sagging under the weight of food and drink. See there the chandeliers casting a hundred shifting shadows. In the centre of the room there stands a young woman. She is beautiful, Rachel, oh! so beautiful. All men know it. She is the centre of attraction wherever she chooses to go. She knows it herself, and revels in the knowledge. See how she moves amongst her admirers. See the toss of her head. See the sway of her hips. 'She walks in beauty as the night, of cloudless climes and starry skies.' Is she not beautiful, Rachel?' he asked, invitingly.

'She is. Oh! but she is,' she gasped.

The fingers of his hand sought out the pitmarks on her face. Easing into them with his fingertips he began a series of tiny, circular movements.

'These have no business to be here,' he said, 'for that young woman we talked of is you, Rachel. You are looking at yourself. Do you not see that? Do you not understand what I am saying?'

'Yes, I understand. Yes! Yes!' she exclaimed.

'Then tell me in plain words what it is you understand,' he said.

'I understand that I am beautiful,' she answered.

So it was that he found himself dealing with the ideal subject: willing, impressionable, pliant – *too* willing, *too* impressionable, *too* pliant, more so than even he realised.

In the days that followed the staff at Grange Hall watched in surprise as a quiet wonder unfolded before their eyes. No one was privy to exactly what was taking place, save for the two actors in the drama. Others were aware only that each evening brother and sister spent a great deal of time closeted together, and that each succeeding morning there emerged into the light of day a brighter, more beautiful young woman.

In less than a week the transformation was complete: the disfiguring spectacles discarded completely, the drab clothes exchanged for a fetching new outfit, which revealed a voluptuous figure; the hairstyle remodelled to show to advantage the mass of glossy red-brown curls; the face, with its lustrous, smooth skin and striking hazel eyes, changed almost out of recognition; the smile, winning; the look, confident; the posture, graceful; the disposition, playful and appealing; the whole, alluringly feminine.

That Tuesday, they went into town together after an absence of some time. She created a sensation, while he was barely noticed. In the days that followed she became the main topic of conversation on every gossiping lip, while his imagined transformation played very much second fiddle. It was exactly as he had planned. It was just what he had hoped for.

The carriage which was to take Rachel on her weekly outing entered the gates of Grange Hall at a few minutes before nine o'clock the next morning. Mounted on horseback and watching from the protecting screen of a cluster of nearby trees was Richard Forres.

Having picked up its sole passenger, the vehicle came back into view, passed out of the Hall gates, and turned right onto the main road into Yarm. A moment later, Richard Forres urged his horse forward and set off to follow at a discreet distance.

Within ten minutes, the vehicle had clattered through the cobbled centre of Yarm and was crossing the county boundary into Durham, via the old stone bridge which spanned the River Tees.

The first surprise of the day for the rider in pursuit came near the top of the hill on the northern outskirts of Yarm when Rachel's carriage swung left off the road into Stockton and began to head west, in the direction of Darlington, a large market town some twelve miles distant. Assuming some strange, roundabout route was not being taken, it seemed as if the intended destination was not to be Stockton, or anywhere very close to it; but perhaps he should have anticipated this he told himself. That particular town, although an ideal place of residence for Emma in her present circumstances, was a little *too* close for comfort to Grange Hall, as she, herself, must have appreciated.

Soon, Yarm had been left behind, and here, out in the country, travellers were much fewer in number. The rider adjusted his distance accordingly and settled down to his task of calculated pursuit. The relatively few turn offs, mostly minor tracks to hamlets, or isolated farms, and the level, open landscape, came to his aid, and he found he had little difficulty in keeping in touch with his quarry at a safe distance.

A little more than an hour after setting off saw both carriage and horseman speeding through the outskirts of Darlington. Two minutes later they entered into an avenue of early Georgian town houses, situated a quarter of a mile from the town centre. It was here that Rachel's carriage, slowing all the while, came to a gradual halt outside a modest, three storey dwelling.

From a safe vantage point, Richard Forres watched as Rachel alighted from her carriage, pass through the small wrought-iron gate which give access to the property, and began her approach to the front entrance along a narrow gravel pathway. He saw the front door open at her approach, and the figure of a young woman, blonde, tall and slim, go forward to greet her.

Clearly, Rachel had been expected and her arrival watched out for. Fascinated, he continued to watch as the two figures engaged in a moment of conversation before entering the house, arm in arm. Meantime, Rachel's coach had taken itself off, back to the Palmer's residence, he assumed. A glance at his watch showed the time to be very nearly ten-thirty.

On day twenty seven after his arrival into his new world, he had found what he had been looking for, but what to do next? he asked himself.

He set off to ride the short distance to the town centre, where he stabled his horse.

Lingering over a drink in the nearby tavern, he pondered his options.

Should he return more or less immediately to the house and confront Emma and Rachel? Should he return later that day, after Rachel had left for home? Would it be best to take a more cautious approach? Perhaps he should return to Grange Hall without further ado and over a period of time patiently seek to enlist Rachel's help in arranging a meeting between Emma and himself? If he told Rachel of the day's events, laying stress on the fact that he had left Emma in peace, surely that would stand to his credit?

His instincts told him that this last course of action was the most sensible of the three options open to him, but a fierce impatience to have the matter resolved sooner rather than later, and a burning desire to meet with Emma at long last, carried the day. He would not distress Rachel by announcing himself in her presence, but neither was he prepared to simply collect his horse and head back home. Rachel, he knew, arrived home each Wednesday afternoon promptly at five o'clock, which must mean that she took her leave of Emma shortly after half-past three. To be on the safe side, he would call on Emma at four o'clock. In the meantime, he would spend the coming five hours shopping and sightseeing in town.

So it was that he came to a disastrous decision, which was fated to lead to a near-tragic sequence of events.

Like Richard Forres, Emma, too, was having an eventful day. She had been fully expecting the arrival of the Palmer's carriage that morning, but had certainly not anticipated walking out to greet her sister-in-law only to find herself in the arms of an apparent stranger.

'Rachel? Is it you?' she gasped, freeing herself from her visitor's embrace.

'Either me, or a very bold stranger,' answered Rachel, with a laugh. 'Of course it is me. Have I changed so *very* much?'

'Changed? This is no change, it is a transformation,' said Emma. 'I was never so astonished in all my life. What *have* you done to yourself?'

'Come inside and I shall tell you all about it,' said Rachel, linking the elder girl's arm in her own and leading her back towards the house.

216

There was a spring in her step and a jauntiness in her carriage which did not fail to register with Emma.

'It is a weird and wonderful tale, and I am none the wiser on several counts,' said Emma, shaking her head, when Rachel had told her story. 'Mind, I always held you to be your own worst enemy in that you did not do yourself justice. I have told you so often enough in the past, but you were never disposed to listen.'

'It has been my own doing,' acknowledged Rachel. 'I took your counsel as words of censure. I lacked belief in myself, you understand. My brother has given me that self-belief.'

'I marvel at that,' said Emma. 'It is certainly a novelty that he should concern himself with anyone other than Henry Forres.'

She continued to study Rachel in disbelief. 'It is amazing. It is truly amazing, and although it grieves me to own it I suppose I must give my husband some credit in the matter.' She reached out a hand to run her fingers down Rachel's cheeks. 'But *this* is not possible, at least not in the space of a single week. Yet, I can *see* the colour and sheen, and I can *feel* the smoothness.'

'That part is a mystery to me, also,' Rachel admitted. 'I have the knowledge of what happened without the understanding. But enough of myself. What news do you have for me?'

'I have nothing to relate which remotely bears comparison. It continues quiet here. I did have a visit from John Sibley on Friday last, and a letter from my uncle yesterday.'

This information was imparted with so little enthusiasm that Rachel felt bound to say: 'I would have thought such diversions would be welcome to you.'

'They should be, Rachel; they should be; but these days my uncle sings my husband's praises a little too often for my liking. His letters are full of hints concerning a possible reunion. He credits Henry with curing his gout, you know. What nonsense! He obtains some relief because of the fine weather we have been enjoying. It is no more than that, I'm sure. I'm surprised he has allowed himself to be so easily deceived.'

'And Mr. Sibley? What of him?'

'He is more guarded in what he has to say, but I believe he is tending to the same good opinion of Henry.'

She got to her feet and began to pace the floor in an agitated manner.

'Oh, Rachel, is it not unfair? My husband's past sins are, it seems, all but forgotten and I am held to be the guilty party in leaving him.'

'But my brother is changed, Emma. Truly, he has changed for the better out of all recognition.'

'So I am told on all sides, but you and I have seen this all before, have we not, and more than once at that?'

Rachel shook her head impatiently. 'It is different this time, really it is. I believe the change in him *will* last this time. Do not ask me how I know that, I just do. I have forgiven my brother all his past injuries to me. Can you not find it in your heart to do the same?'

'No! I cannot! I will not!' cried Emma. 'I have suffered too much at his hands these two years past. Deplorable as his conduct towards you was at times, it does not compare with my own suffering. Remember, I shielded you whenever I could and more often than not bore alone the brunt of his anger, or drunken fury.'

'I have not forgotten,' said Rachel, quietly.

'You must also bear in mind that if I were to return home my situation would be very different from your own.'

'Not so very different, surely?'

'But it would be, Rachel, it would be. In a few years' time you will come of age and be free of your brother for ever, if you so wish. You will come into your inheritance and be as free as a bird. If Henry's present good humour was to change tomorrow, you have that happy prospect of release in the not too distant future. My own prospects would be very different. I am the man's wife, and am bound to him for life. There would be no release for me in a few years' time if his present conduct was to revert to what it has always been in the past. Remember, also, that a wife has certain duties which are not encumbrant on a sister. Yes, I see you take my meaning. In short, the prospect of having to live with a man I loathe and fear for perhaps the next thirty or forty years appals me. Quite frankly, I would rather die than face that.'

She had begun to pace the floor once more, struggling to control her emotions, fighting to hold back the tears.

'What care I if he *has* changed? Can he undo the past and bring Robert and my mother back to life? I shall never forgive him for what he has done to my family – never! never! never!'

Rachel made her sit back down, and put a sympathetic arm around her shoulders. For several minutes they sat together in an emotionally charged silence, a silence which was eventually broken by Rachel.

'What a sorry pair we are today,' she exclaimed, getting to her feet. 'A diversion will drive away the gloom, I fancy. Emma, what do you say to a walk into town?'

'You know that is not possible,' Emma replied. 'If I were to be recognised and news of my whereabouts noised abroad......'

'But you cannot stay closeted here every minute of every day,' said Rachel. 'Let us risk it. We shall go into town, find ourselves a couple of handsome young beaus, and put ourselves under their protection.'

'No thank you,' said Emma. 'I have had my fill of men to last me a lifetime.'

'But, Emma, not all men are the same, and think of the sport the four of us could have together.'

'I imagined you spoke in jest,' said Emma, 'but I see you do not. Rachel, what has come over you today?'

'I make one condition,' said Rachel. 'The thought was mine, so I claim first choice of any gentlemen we may light upon.'

'That is a scandalous suggestion,' Emma protested.

'Calm yourself, dearest,' said Rachel. 'I was not serious. We shall, of course, toss a coin to decide who has first choice.'

'Rachel, if you do not stop this at once I shall take myself off elsewhere and leave you to your own devices,' said Emma.

'Oh! very well,' grumbled Rachel. She flopped heavily back into her seat and give a heartfelt sigh, signifying her boredom.

'Let us do some embroidery,' suggested Emma. 'I shall go and get my workbasket.'

'Yes, why not do that? Let us live dangerously,' said Rachel. 'Stone me, is that the best you can come up with?'

'I've never heard you speak so,' said Emma, bewildered by these words. 'It would seem that your appearance is not the only thing to have changed.'

'Well, you know I dislike needlework,' said Rachel, sullenly.

'I know nothing of the kind,' protested Emma.

'Well, you know now,' said Rachel; 'but I have a better suggestion to make. Go and get Cato. He will lift our spirits.'

Emma left the room, to reappear in a few minutes bearing on her outstretched arm a splendid specimen of an African Grey Parrot. She perched the bird on the back of a chair, where it settled itself happily, pleased at this change of scenery.

'Hello, Cato,' said Rachel, brightly.

'Merry Christmas. Good evening, sir,' replied the bird, promptly.

Rachel shook her head in disbelief at this. 'Really! I would not have thought it possible to make three factual errors within the compass of five words. Cato, you are a stupid creature – what are you?'

'You are too severe with him,' said Emma, laughing. 'He is, after all, only a bird.' The incident brought back to her a pleasing tale she had recently heard, which served to add to her amusement. 'Your words of censure call to mind a joke recently told me,' she said.

'A joke? Oh! do tell. I love a joke,' said Rachel.

'Well, then...... let me see...... oh! yes. There was once a certain traveller, who stopping off one day at the local inn was astounded to see one of the customers deeply engrossed in a game of chess with a mongrel dog. The animal, hard-pressed, was making a valiant defence of the white queen.

' "What an amazingly clever animal you have there," said the traveller, when he had recovered his wits.

' "Indeed, sir, you are mistaken," said the man. "The fact is, my Brutus, here, is a rather stupid creature."

' "How *can* you speak so?" said the traveller, very much surprised by this remark.

' "Very easily," replied the man. "He hardly ever wins."

'There is only one problem in having Cato with us,' said Emma, when they had recovered from their laughter. 'I had some needlework in mind, but that is impossible when he is present.'

'Oh, why is that?' asked Rachel.

'Because he attacks the thread, and picks at the stitches made. It is useless to try and continue,' said Emma.

Rachel had a sudden change of heart concerning the bird.

'What a clever boy! Oh, my, what a clever boy!' she said, fussing him.

Gradually, with Cato present and intent on showing off, the gloom was lifted, and together they spent the remainder of the day happily enough.

Eventually, at the appointed time, Rachel's carriage returned and she took her leave. Emma made her way to the kitchen, where she busied herself with several tasks until a knock at the front door heralded a visitor.

Trembling with a barely concealed nervousness, Richard Forres stood waiting for a response to his knocking. He now had a clear plan of action in mind. He would claim an acquaintance with Mr Sibley, which was true, bearing a message from that gentleman, which was certainly not true but which would be sufficient to gain him an entrance. Once inside, and face to face with Emma, he would plead his good intentions. He would make no attempt to persuade her to return to Grange Hall, still less would he force her return. He would ask only that he be allowed to visit her from time to time, perhaps in the company of Rachel, after which it would be up to him to regain her affections.

Such was his plan, but it all came to nothing when the maidservant who came in answer to his knocking let out a piercing scream at the sight of him. It seemed that at least one member of the household, apart from Emma, knew him by sight and reputation.

The ground floor plan of the house was such that the long passageway he looked into led directly to a large kitchen at the far end. Three doors, into the drawing room, the lounge, and the dining room, fronted the left-side of the passageway, while a staircase leading to the upper floors occupied the right hand side, a little distance away from the front entrance.

Looking over the shoulder of the maidservant, who now stood bobbing and weaving in front of him in an attempt to bar his entry, he caught sight of Emma. She stood at the open door of the kitchen, looking in his direction, drawn there by the commotion at the front door. Briefly, their eyes met, and he saw her face transform itself with fear at the sight of him. He watched as she momentarily stepped back into the kitchen to retrieve some object which he could not see before fleeing to the staircase, and the comparative safety of some upstairs' room.

He thrust the maid to one side and was soon following in hot pursuit, ascending the stairs two at a time and calling out her name. She had fled to the furthermost bedroom on the second floor and was attempting to bar his entry when he burst in upon her, sending the flimsy, inadequate barricade she had hastily constructed clattering across the room. She retreated to the far corner of the room, where she turned to face him, defiantly. The kitchen knife she held in her hand had a blade a full ten inches in length and glinted razor-sharp in the sunlight which streamed in through the ceiling fanlight.

He approached her with an outward show of calm, which belied his inner turmoil. Stopping some six feet away, he stood looking at her.

Disregarding their meeting in the inky blackness of Pine Tree Cottage, this was their first meeting in the flesh, although she had come to him often enough in his dreams – or was it rather he had come to her? No matter, here for certain was reality. Here, in vivid, living colour was the dream come true. Looking at her in silence, the oddest of sensations came over him.

'Oh, my dear Miss Sinclair,' he began, 'do you know, I have the strangest feeling that all my past life, all I have ever thought, or said, or done, has been but a prelude to this moment.'

The intervening two years had, he thought, brought her beauty to its full maturity. Standing there, knife in hand, she had all the appearance of some wayward, errant angel. He swallowed hard. 'What a delight to see you so well recovered,' he said, softly.

She stared back at him, bewildered by this bizarre greeting.

'Keep back,' she hissed, as he made the slightest of movements towards her. She waved the knife threateningly before his eyes. 'I shall use this if I have to.'

'I wish only to talk,' he said, mildly.

'But I do not wish to talk,' she said. 'I have nothing to say to you.'

The commotion downstairs came loud to his ears, and he fancied he heard the first footsteps on the stairs. Throwing caution to the wind, he decided he must close with her.

He sprang forward, seeking a hold on her threatening right hand, but fast as he was she proved faster. The knife snaked out, slicing through the left arm of his light summer coat as if it were made of paper and ripping the flesh beneath. He felt no great pain but drew back from her, vaguely aware that he had been wounded.

The uproar below was by now much closer. For the first time, he thought he heard a man's voice in the distant ground floor passageway. With it came the realisation that if he were to be seized and held while Emma made her escape to some other hiding place, all his efforts would have been in vain. It was then that he saw her eyes leave his and fix themselves on his wounded arm. Fascinated, she stood watching the first flow of blood as it ran down his hand, trickled along his fingers, and fell pattering to the floor in huge drops.

Taking advantage of this distraction, he lunged forward once more and succeeded this time in seizing hold of her right wrist. Locked together, they grappled with each other.

'Emma, there is no need for any of this,' he managed to gasp. 'I mean you no harm.'

Her answer was to force the hand which held her own towards her face and bite savagely into it. He winced with the pain of it but continued to hold on until, twisting her wrist around in a violent movement, he succeeded in sending the knife spiralling to the floor. It was at this point that she leaned forward and spat in his face.

This stunned him far more than the two injuries suffered, and the shock of it made him release her. He took a step backwards and looked at her in silence, appalled at what she had done.

Engrossed in the furious struggle of the previous few minutes, he had failed to hear the stealthily approaching footsteps and stood oblivious to the arm raised high behind his back. He felt a terrific blow to the back of his head, and with it came a headlong fall into some black, bottomless pit.

CHAPTER 18

He came back to consciousness with the sound of a raucous voice demanding a kiss ringing in his ears. Opening his eyes, he gazed in wonder at the anxious face which looked down at him. The stranger took his meaning, and indicated with his head their noisy third party, which stood on its open perch behind his back.

'Our Cato,' he said. 'If he disturbs you I shall remove him.'

'Give me a kiss,' repeated the bird in shrill tones, as if annoyed at the continual lack of response to this very reasonable request.

'No, let him be,' said Richard Forres. 'To be frank, he makes the best offer I've had in a long while.'

The bird shuffled along to the very end of its perch, craning its head to get a better view of their visitor.

'Good morning, vicar,' he said.

'How are you feeling?' said its owner, anxiously.

'Bruised and battered. I have no sense or feeling in one arm.'

The man nodded. 'The wound is not deep but it is a full five inches long. Your coat sleeve took the main force of the blow. I have a ligature on the arm to restrict the bleeding, but I shall loosen it briefly to allow the circulation to return.'

He busied himself with this task, speaking all the while.

'You have been dead to the world these two hours past. Doctor Waterhouse called and stayed half-an-hour, but then had to leave. He was more concerned about your head wound than with either of the two other injuries. I am to test you on the matter and have him call back if need be.

'So,' he continued, leaning back to give the invalid a better field of view, 'look across the room and tell me if you see well, or no.'

'I see well-enough,' said Richard Forres, casting an eye about him.

'Everything sharply focused, then? Nothing blurred, or indistinct? No?' He held up a hand. 'How many fingers do you see?'

'Six,' came the prompt reply.

The man give a visible start. 'You count *six* fingers on the one hand?'

'No, not really. I said that to worry you. I see plainly two fingers
—'

'How many?'

'—and a thumb.'

'Ah! I see you still have your wits about you. I do not think we have need to trouble the good doctor further.

'Now, I should tell you that I have sent word to Grange Hall, and shortly expect a carriage to convey you back there – we have no vehicle here at our disposal, you understand. I assume you came here on horseback. Well, I shall see that the animal is recovered and returned to you. Clearly, you are in no fit state to ride back on it.'

He stood up and walked over to Cato, who had lapsed into a sullen silence. The bird brightened instantly at his approach.

'I am William Jamieson, master of this house,' he said. 'Cato, here, you know, and my wife, Agnes, you see over there.' He indicated a large, stout lady, who had that moment entered the room. She came towards them slowly, ruefully examining the wreckage of a copper bed-warming pan held in her hands.

'I am sorry for the ruin of it, madam,' he said, guessing this was the weapon which had floored him.

'I wish it had been a loaded gun,' she said, glowering at him.

This remark brought a pained expression to her husband's face as he made his way back to sit on the edge of their visitor's makeshift bed.

'You must excuse my wife,' he said. 'She has a high regard for Emma, and looks on her almost as a daughter.'

'Your good lady wields a powerful arm, Mr. Jamieson,' said Richard Forres, gingerly touching the back of his head.

'No! No! That was none of her doing,' Jamieson protested.

'Then, I should like to meet the amazon responsible, if woman she be.'

'She is gone – fled.'

'And Emma with her, I presume. I take it you are not going to enlighten me as to my wife's present whereabouts?'

William Jamieson looked at him in silence. Although he had been endeavouring not to show it, he was, in reality, deeply worried by the day's events. The man who lay prostrate before him was a prominent, titled gentleman, who could exert a great deal of power and influence should he choose to do so. In his own house, here at Darlington, and at the hands of his maidservant, the man had been so severely injured as to be rendered unconscious. It was true that the fellow was an uninvited visitor who had forced his way into the house, but that would count for little in the circumstances. The man was, after all, only attempting to reclaim his wife, as he had every legal right to do so, from a family who were harbouring her and aiding her in her desertion.

'Let me ease your fears, Mr. Jamieson,' said Richard Forres, noting the anxiety written plain across his face. 'You befriended my Emma when she was in distress. You took her into your home and have treated her, I have no doubt, with every consideration and kindness. I bear you no ill-will. On the contrary, I am indebted to you.'

This gracious little speech thoroughly confused the listener. Was this the monster of Grange Hall, of whom he had heard so much? he was asking himself. It did not seem possible. He began to feel guilty and more than a little ashamed at the young man's violently hostile reception. If only he had been present when the man had come calling perhaps events would not have got quite so out of hand, he reflected.

'I wish you had not come here today, sir,' he said, unhappily. 'Something could have been worked out, I'm sure, if you had acted with more discretion. As it is, I am left to regret not only the loss of Emma's future company, but also your present injuries.'

'I wager your regrets are not half as painful as my own,' said Richard Forres, looking ruefully at his throbbing wrist. 'As for Emma, I see now the folly of my actions, but you must believe me when I tell you that I came not to carry her off against her will, but only to reason with her and ask for her company from time to time. You must tell her this and convince her it is safe to return here. I would not have her abandon this comfortable home for one less to her liking.'

'I shall pass on your message,' said Jamieson, 'but, in all honesty, I have to say that I do not think she will believe you. The sad fact is, she fears you too much to take you at your word.'

'Yes, I have been blind and overconfident all along,' sighed Richard Forres. 'I have been blind to the evidence I had in plenty of Emma's very real hatred of me, and overconfident in my abilities to overcome those feelings.'

This sad observation was suddenly interrupted by a veritable torrent of words from Cato. Sundry greetings to one and all were interspersed with observations on the weather, and solicitous enquiries concerning everyone's state of health. The speaker concluded his outburst with assertions of his own handsomeness.

'You have a remarkable bird there, Mr. Jamieson,' said Richard Forres, setting aside his gloomy thoughts.

'I have refused a hundred guineas for him from Squire Henderson,' said the owner, proudly. 'He has a vocabulary of more than eighty phrases.'

'And not a crude, or intemperate, saying amongst them, I dare say.'

'I should hope not,' said Jamieson, shocked at the thought. 'We have a little trouble with the Cole children, three doors down. They are regular visitors to see the bird and I have had cause to reprimand them on more than one occasion for the odd rude word or two. Being children, they lose patience with the bird from time to time. They do not understand that even a bird such as Cato, clever though he is, cannot be expected to respond promptly whenever they wish it, but I would be loathe to forbid their visits for the bird enjoys their company as much as they do his. Fortunately, Cato seems not to have fastened onto anything coarse, or improper.'

As he finished speaking, the outpouring of words from Cato was replaced by a very passable mimicry of a barking dog.

'You keep a dog, I take it?' asked an amused Richard Forres.

'Yes, a spaniel who answers to the name of 'Splash' – he is fond of water, you understand. He is about somewhere, I fancy. But see there the reason for Cato's latest outburst.' He indicated a large black and white cat, which had entered the room and now sat contentedly inside the doorway, grooming itself with its paw.

'Is Cato afraid of the cat, then?'

'Lord! bless you, no,' laughed Jamieson. 'If anything, it is the other way around. No, Cato does it to tease the animal, but Tabs is not as stupid as Cato believes him to be and knows full-well what the bird has in mind.'

'I think I shall test my legs with a turn about the room and in so doing become better acquainted with your entertaining bird,' said Richard Forres, swinging his legs over the side of the couch on which he lay. He approached the bird slowly on a pair of unsteady legs, reaching out a hand as he saw Cato obligingly lower his head to have it fondled. At this point, there came a warning call: 'Take care, sir, and do not be deceived by appearances. Cato does not take readily to strangers.'

The stranger in question choose to ignore this advice and began to trace with a finger the silky outline of the bird's head and back.

'Well, I'm blowed!' exclaimed Jamieson, in surprise. 'He does not normally allow such liberties, except with a favoured few.' He walked across the room to join man and bird. 'Come and see this, Agnes,' he called out to his wife.

Richard Forres turned his attention to the bird's breast. A moment later, he was looking with self-satisfied pride at the bird's owner. It is well said, however, that pride comes before a fall, and it did so now. Perhaps looking on this further familiarity as an unasked for liberty, or more likely having successfully lulled the visitor into a false sense of security, the bird fastened a razor-sharp beak onto the offending finger with lightning speed. His former admirer jumped back with a startled yelp of pain and was left nursing an instantly bloodied finger.

'Serve you right,' cried Cato, who then proceeded to spoil the effect of this fine piece of reasoned diction by immediately adding, incongruously: 'Another scone, vicar?'

Agnes looked at the streaming finger before glancing at their visitor's other injuries.

'My! we are in the wars today,' she exclaimed, rubbing her hands together with brisk satisfaction.

Having roundly scolded his pet, and received a bored yawn in response, William Jamieson led the crestfallen young man back to the couch, there to attempt repairs to the wounded finger.

'I'm exceedingly sorry for this latest injury, Sir Henry,' he said, 'but I *did* caution you.'

'The fault is mine,' said Richard Forres. 'I'm too trusting, that is my trouble. But I think you may safely boast, Mr. Jamieson, that you have there a pet whose bite is worse than his bark.'

Agnes, in spite of her prejudice, was forced to chuckle at this observation, while her husband roared with laughter until the tears rolled down his cheeks. He had barely regained his composure when the sound of an approaching vehicle heralded the imminent arrival of the carriage from Grange Hall.

A moment later Rachel Forres burst into the room with Simpson at her heels.

'Mr. Jamieson, what is all this?' she demanded. 'Has something happened to Emma? Your note said only that......' She broke off, noticing for the first time her brother sitting pale and woebegone at the far end of the room. 'Good God!' she cried, in alarm.

'Do not concern yourself on my account, Rachel,' he said, attempting to make light of things. 'I have had a mishap, or two, but am not seriously injured. Indeed, I have a few toes on the left foot which are quite undamaged.'

'But what has happened?' she cried. 'How came you here, of all places? Where is Emma?'

He watched in silence as Agnes pulled Rachel to one side and began to talk to her in an animated manner. Little glances in his direction, and the occasional pointed finger, left him in no doubt that the details of his visit were being divulged. He noted, glumly, that the looks which Rachel was giving him were gradually changing in character from ones of anxiety and concern to stony stares of dismay and anger.

For William Jamieson, it was the first sight of the new Rachel.

'Heavens above! Sir Henry, is that your sister?' he asked, disbelieving.

Richard Forres acknowledged that it was.

'This is, indeed, a day of wonders,' said Jamieson, with a shake of the head.

The two gentlemen having taken their leave of each other, the wounded party enlisted Simpson's help to reach the carriage waiting outside. His sister, he noted, was still deep in conversation with Agnes.

Cato, who had enjoyed a thoroughly entertaining day, watched with interest as the battered figure of their visitor, supported by his manservant, moved painfully towards the door.

'Thank you for calling,' he cried out.

With Simpson seated beside the driver, he was left alone in the carriage to await the appearance of Rachel. Eventually, she joined him, only to sit as far away as possible and in total silence. Ignoring him completely, she proceeded to stare fixedly out of the carriage window. They rode for fifteen minutes in this fashion until he could endure it no longer

'Rachel, I'm sorry,' he said.

'*Sorry? Sorry?*' she exclaimed. 'You spy on me; you follow me; you drive away my sister and best friend, and all you can say is that you are sorry?'

'Mr. Jamieson is fully acquainted with Emma's new situation,' he said, soothingly. 'I am sure he will take you to her when next you visit, so, you see, there is no reason why Emma and you should not continue to meet with each other. Do not be angry with me, Rachel. I have had a terrible day. I have four injuries to nurse as my punishment.'

'So few?' she replied. 'Serve you right, is what I say.'

'Yes,' he sighed, 'those were Cato's words.'

While this somewhat limited dialogue was taking place, an altogether different conversation was in progress in the Jamieson household.

'I must say, Emma's husband is not at all as I imagined him to be,' said William Jamieson, thoughtfully. 'On the evidence of today, I should say that one would have to go a long way to meet a more agreeable fellow. I can scarce believe this is the same person whom Emma complains of.'

His wife grunted, doubtfully, not at all convinced that this was the case.

'Come now, Agnes,' he protested, 'you must own that he fair treated us as his equal. There is not a trace of conceit, or condescension, to be seen in the man, and I never in my life saw anyone who took an injury, or a jest, against himself with a better humour. How can one reconcile all of that with what we have been told about the man?'

'As I understand it, much of Sir Henry's bad conduct stems from an overfondness for drink,' said Agnes. 'We saw him today sober and eager to please. Had this not been so, we could easily have been witness to a very different kind of behaviour and be regarding him now in an altogether different light.'

'Yes, I dare say you are right,' acknowledged her husband. He had put on his coat as he was speaking and now gathered up his hat and riding crop. 'I must go to Emma,' he said. 'I need to know that she is settled in with the Mortimers and does not lack for anything. It was good of that family to take her at such short notice but, all the same, this is a most unfortunate business for I have no doubt she will not be as easy and comfortable there as she was with us. I shall pass on her husband's message but I think it unlikely she will credit his promise to let her be in future.'

He caught sight of Cato, who, guessing his intentions, was lowering his head to receive the customary parting show of affection from his master. He give the bird a look of disapproval, and wagged a finger.

'There will be no fond farewells today, Cato,' he said, severely. 'You are in disgrace for your show of bad temper to our visitor.'

The bird watched him leave, looking as displeased as it is possible for any parrot to look.

'Silly old sod,' he said, quietly to himself.

Nine days after his traumatic visit to Darlington, Richard Forres set off on his customary Friday early morning ride to Stockton. Passage between the towns of Yarm and Stockton was facilitated by a well surfaced road, but the rider's preferred route, whenever time permitted, was along the somewhat longer scenic bridleway, which skirted the west bank of the Tees, on which river both towns were situated.

On this quiet backwater, he met with very few fellow travellers and his journey passed off without incident until he had passed the half-way village of Eaglescliffe, some distance off to the west.

Hidden in a bend of the bridlepath, and watching out for his approach, sat two horsemen. One, seated astride a fine grey stallion, was a young man of twenty years, or so, tall, fair-headed, and possessed of quick, alert features. The other, mounted on a less imposing chestnut gelding, was some fifteen years older than his companion and smaller of stature, although more powerfully built.

At the first glimpse of their intended victim, the younger man pulled up his neckerchief to a level a little below the eyes, and signalled his accomplice to do likewise. The action signified that, despite his lack of years, it was the younger of the two men who was calling the tune. It was a desperate venture which Peter Sinclair had embarked upon but one which he felt was long overdue.

Ignorant of the previous day's events, he had called on his sister the morning following the visit of Richard Forres, only to find the Jamieson household still in a state of confusion and Emma departed.

He had listened with a growing anger to the tale told by Agnes, an anger which had boiled over when he met with his sister at the isolated farmhouse three miles out of town. Here, he found a sad figure, pale and tearful, and withal a strange air of calm despair which made him deeply anxious on her account.

Gone was the cheerful sanctuary she had grown to know and love; gone, too, the creature comforts and pleasing situation. In their place was a rude, stone-built farmhouse, seated astride a lonely, windswept ridge, and the company of a group of obliging strangers.

He had always known it could happen. He had been conscious all the while that one day Sir Henry Forres might succeed in tracking down Emma, but it was a bitter pill for him to swallow that Thursday morning, all the same.

He rode back to his lodgings in Stockton later that day still seething with anger at what had taken place, and with a heart full of bitterness when he reflected on the fate of his unfortunate family. His mother and brother were dead, and the little family home sold to provide himself with a meagre capital. Now, he led a meaningless existence in a modest lodging house in Stockton, without family companionship, fortune, or prospects, existing on his dwindling savings and a small monthly allowance from his uncle in York.

Depressing as his situation was, he was forced to acknowledge that his sister's was far worse. He at least was his own master, but she had been reduced to the level of some wretched fugitive, without present joy, or future hope. There was no escape for her while her husband lived.

While he lived!

Not for the first time, the thought came to him that the only hope for both of them lay in their tormentor's death. In that event, Emma would come into possession of Grange Hall. She would be free to return there, and he with her. The two of them, along with a liberated Rachel, could regain a measure of happiness.

In the past he had quickly dismissed such thoughts as wishful thinking, but now, for the first time, they ceased to be idle fancies. Sir Henry Forres must die! He must be removed – eliminated – disposed of. Mentally, he shied away from the word 'murdered', but deep down he knew this was the correct expression for what he now contemplated.

Of course, there was an honourable alternative. He could issue a challenge and engage the man in a duel, which he would ensure would be to the death. Times had changed, and the authorities now frowned upon the practise, but not to the extent that the victor in a properly organised duel, freely entered into by both parties, would have to face the full rigour of the law, but there were difficulties, nonetheless, in this course of action. What if his adversary refused to take up the challenge? He would then have exposed his hand to no advantage. Worse still, what if the man took up the challenge and emerged the victor? He was keenly aware that his brother-in-law was at least as expert as he was with a pistol. Not that he was afraid for himself, but if he were to die while Sir Henry Forres continued to live he would have accomplished nothing save his own destruction and fresh misery for Emma.

No, it would not do. However much his nature shrank from the thought of an act of cold-blooded murder, the one *certain* way of solving at a stroke all of his sister's problems, as well as his own difficulties, was simply too tempting to pass up.

A little thought convinced him that he must enlist the aid of one other person to assist him. This superiority of numbers, plus the element of surprise, would, he felt sure, guarantee success. Just such an accomplice was readily at hand in the shape of Tom Hayle, a local ne're-do-well and petty criminal, with whom he was casually acquainted. The fellow knew nothing of the Sinclair family history, he was sure, which was all to the good. He would keep secret his true motive and pass off the proposed escapade as armed robbery, pure and simple, of a rich and easy target. He would carry out the killing himself and Hayle's protests at the turn of events would count for nothing once the deed was done. When the body of the victim was fished out of the river stripped of money and valuables, the authorities would, in all probability, put it down as a straightforward case of robbery and murder. He was aware of his brother-in-law's solitary, early morning ride into Stockton every Friday from one of the tradespeople whom the man regularly called upon. This would present the perfect opportunity. He would arrange matters with Hayle that coming weekend, the deed to be done the Friday following.

The moment for action had come.

Peter Sinclair moved forward to face the approaching rider with a carefully aimed pistol. His directions were bold and decisive, the voice a little muffled but perfectly distinct: 'Hold fast...... hold fast, I say. Dismount and stand away from the horse.'

He give a nod to Hayle. Dismounting, the man approached their intended victim with a confident, swaggering air. With his own pistol levelled at the head of a hapless Richard Forres, he began the pleasant task of relieving him of his money and valuables.

'Be quick,' urged Peter Sinclair, the first hint of anxiety creeping into his voice.

In truth, the young man's uneasiness was well founded, for the spot fixed upon had not been particularly well chosen. Although the bend in the path hid the little group from sight in both directions, the place was overlooked by rising ground to the west, between bridlepath and main highway. The sparsely wooded rise provided a screen of sorts, but there were clear gaps between the scattered copses and even the occasional sight of the brow of the hill itself.

So it was that Adam Fawley, making his way across country from highway to bridlepath, caught sight of the drama unfolding far below him. It was typical of the recent luck of the Sinclair family that the young horseman who now sat looking down upon the scene was no ordinary passerby but a parish constable from Stockton, out and about on an early morning call of duty. With one glance, his experienced eye had taken in the full meaning of the scene he had stumbled upon. Urging his horse forward, he moved to cover the intervening distance.

Meanwhile, down on the bridlepath, Tom Hayle was complaining bitterly to his partner in crime.

'Six guineas, a pocket watch, and a pair of gold cuff-links. Divided between the two of us, that's scant reward for the risks taken. You promised more, much more.'

To Hayle's astonishment Peter Sinclair's only response was to remove his mask.

'What are you doing, boy?' cried Hayle. 'Do you wish to have the finger pointed at you as soon as this fellow is free to do so?'

'This was done at your insistence,' said Peter Sinclair, rolling up his disguise and slipping it into his pocket as he spoke. 'I see no occasion for it now. But do not be alarmed, my good fellow. Dead men tell no tales, you know. As for the plunder, I want no part of it. Keep it all and be satisfied.' He paused, smiling. 'Surely the equivalent of ten guineas in coin and swag is no mean sum, even to the likes of a master criminal such as Tom Hayle?'

Furious at this casual use of his name, Hayle threw aside his own now useless disguise and glared at the speaker.

'What villainy is this?' he bellowed.

'No villainy, Tom, only a matter of simple justice. Now, stand aside. You are in my line of fire.'

'You fool! Would you get us both hung?' protested Hayle.

'My dear fellow, it is *already* a hanging matter. Now, are you going to shift yourself, or not?'

Sweating profusely, Tom Hayle gazed panic-stricken at his partner. In reality, this small-time crook, who specialised in sneak-thieving and the odd housebreaking from the weak and the vulnerable, was out of his depth, as he, himself, was beginning to appreciate. It came home to him that he had been duped into this escapade in order to serve the purposes of a young man whose real motive had nothing whatsoever to do with robbery and everything to do with some kind of personal revenge.

'You said nothing of murder,' he protested, still standing his ground.

With a gesture of impatience, Peter Sinclair dismounted. Holding a raised pistol in each hand, he moved towards his reluctant accomplice.

'I am asking you to step aside and give me a clear view of my prize,' he said. 'If you do not do so within the next ten seconds I shall put a bullet in your leg, which will shift you smartly enough, I fancy. That will still leave me my other pistol for our friend here.'

From the beginning, Richard Forres had been alert to the possibility of escape. An opportunity to do so now presented itself.

In the distraction of the falling out, he appeared to have been temporarily forgotten, at least by Tom Hayle. The man now stood with his back to him, pistol hanging by his side. Peter Sinclair stood half-a-dozen paces beyond, his eyes more on Hayle than on their hapless victim. He had reached 'five' in his count when Richard Forres made his move.

Launching himself forward, he succeeded in propelling Hayle with sufficient force for him to cannon into the arms of his criminal partner. In a twinkling all three ended up in a heap on the ground, with young Sinclair's brace of pistols cast harmlessly out of reach.

First on his feet was Tom Hayle, who was now heartily regretting that he had ever agreed to Peter Sinclair's proposition, and wished only to be away. Taking one swift look around, he scampered to his horse and bolted from the scene without further ado, leaving the two remaining antagonists to settle matters between themselves.

Locked together on the ground, things were going badly for Richard Forres. Not yet fully recovered from his recent injuries, he was proving no match for his fully fit and agile adversary, whose desperation at the sudden turn of events seemed to lend him a furious strength.

Frantically, Peter Sinclair tried to retrieve the situation by stunning his opponent long enough for him to recover a pistol and would, no doubt, have succeeded in doing just that had not the sound of rapidly approaching hoofs put an end to the struggle. A few seconds were sufficient for him to shrug off his hated relative, remount his horse, and flee from the scene, silently cursing his ill-luck.

Adam Fawley reined up his horse and, after a glance in the direction of the fugitive, looked down upon a face well-known to him.

'Are you injured, Sir Henry?' he asked, torn between a duty towards the prostrate victim and a desire to pursue the criminal responsible.

'Thank you, no. A little bruised and shaken, that is all,' said Richard Forres, getting slowly to his feet and dusting himself down.

With a curt nod of acknowledgement, Adam Fawley set off in pursuit of the mounted figure disappearing into the distance, leaving a troubled Richard Forres to stand gazing after him.

He had recognised his assailant the instant he had removed his disguise, and could easily guess the motive for this murderous assault coming so soon after his ill-fated visit to Darlington. However reprehensible Peter Sinclair's actions had been, he was forced to admit that they were understandable. He had no wish to see the young man suffer as a consequence, if only for Emma's sake. That being so, he began to regret not having detained his rescuer a little while longer by feigning injury, but a moment's thought was sufficient to ease his anxieties. Peter Sinclair had a good head start on his pursuer, and if he, Richard Forres, was any judge of horses, was mounted on a superior animal. His criminal relative would make good his escape, of that he had no doubt.

He unbuttoned and removed his coat and looked down at his left arm. His desperate struggle had reopened the scarcely healed wound of the previous week, leaving the shirt sleeve heavily stained with blood. Remounting his horse, which had been standing some little distance away contentedly grazing all the while, he turned its head back towards Yarm, and home. He would conduct no business in Stockton that day.

Had Peter Sinclair done the sensible thing and struck out across open country, there is every chance that he would, indeed, have effected his escape. Instead, he choose to put cover as well as distance between himself and the rider in pursuit by plunging into a wooded area on the southern outskirts of Stockton. He had barely covered a hundred metres over this new terrain when horse and rider came to grief on an exposed tree root lying across his path.

The horse, frightened but uninjured, was up in a moment, taking off in the direction of its fancy, but the rider could only lay motionless where he had come crashing down. In a very short while, Adam Fawley was kneeling beside his stunned and helpless prize.

'Now, my fine fellow, let us have a closer look at you,' he said, turning the groaning figure over onto his back. For a moment he stared in disbelief at the wretched face of his captive. 'Good God! Peter Sinclair! You fool! You damn fool!' he cried in dismay.

An hour later, with the prisoner safely under lock and key and the details recounted to a very surprised Chief Constable Hutton, Adam Fawley retired to a quiet place with his thoughts. Never had he performed a more onerous and unwelcome task than that of bringing in young Peter Sinclair to face the consequences of his crime. The fact that the unscathed victim of it all was none other than the odious Sir Henry Forres served only to add to the young constable's distress.

Having been born and brought up in Yarm, spending the first twenty years of his life there, he was well-acquainted with the Sinclair family. He held Peter Sinclair in no high regard, having always been of the opinion that he and his elder brother were a rather rash and headstrong pair, but he had a passionate admiration and regard, never declared, for

Emma. Though recently married himself, it was still the case that hardly a day passed during which she did not enter his thoughts, thoughts made more poignant of late by her recent tragic history. It grieved him that his duty had forced him to play a part in an event which could only bring Emma more distress and heartache, but if he could do no more he would at least send her word of what had taken place in the hope that somehow help could be brought to bear.

He wrote out the short message and saw it despatched with all possible speed to Vicar Sibley, whom, he felt sure, would know of Emma's whereabouts if anyone did. In less than an hour the note had been passed onto Colonel Palmer, within two hours it was in the hands of William Jamieson, and two and a half hours after the key had turned in the lock of Peter Sinclair's cell his sister was reading:

' STOCKTON, 10.00 A.M.

Lady Forres,

Your brother is taken and held here for the armed robbery and attempted murder of your husband. Sir Henry is uninjured, but it is a hanging matter for your brother, I fear.

Adam Fawley '

CHAPTER 19

Shortly before three o'clock in the afternoon of that same fateful day, the hired carriage which had brought Emma from Darlington entered the centre of Stockton. The ninety minute journey had been sufficient for her to collect her thoughts and strengthen her resolve.

She *must* save her brother. Everything else paled into insignificance in comparison to that. To achieve this she was determined to go to any lengths and employ every device within her power. She owed her brother nothing less in her estimation for she blamed herself for the perilous situation in which he was now placed.

Just short of two years before, flattered by the attentions of a handsome young man far above her station in life, but against her better judgement, she had placed her destiny and that of her family into the hands of a vicious and dissolute individual. The result of this wilful blindness on her part had been a tragedy, for herself and for all those she held most dear. Her mother and elder brother were lost, and her own life irretrievably ruined, but until today there had still been hope for young Peter. Restoring the fortunes of her one surviving brother was all that mattered to her now, her own blighted life of no consequence.

Of Chief Constable Hutton, on whom she was pinning her hopes, she knew nothing other than the few facts which had come to her secondhand. It was said that he was a gentleman of middle age, a widower, and a recent arrival to the town.

Five minutes after alighting from her carriage, through the good offices of her friend, Adam Fawley, she found herself being admitted into the presence of Benjamin Hutton, in his modest little office by the riverside in Finkle Street.

He was half-expecting a visit from the prisoner's sister and had been looking forward to it with more than a little curiosity. A native of Thirsk, a small market town some twenty miles distant, who had taken up his present post only three months previous, he was seeing Lady Forres for the first time. Notwithstanding, he had a fair knowledge of her circumstances and recent unhappy history, via his young assistant, Fawley. All that he had learnt in this respect tended to excite in him a deep sympathy for the unfortunate Sinclair family, and feelings of disapproval, bordering on disgust, for Sir Henry Forres.

That morning, he had listened in amused silence to his subordinate's praise of Emma, convinced that the young man's very evident partiality lay behind the glowing, and surely exaggerated, testimonial. Within a moment of the arrival of his beautiful visitor, however, he was forced to revise his opinion. The eye-catching beauty was there, to be sure, but with it came a certain presence – an indefinable *something* – which in an instant seemed to brighten and enrich, as never before, his rather drab little workplace.

To her, he appeared to be a gentleman of about forty-five years of age, of above average height, with dark-brown hair greying a little at the temples, and, overall, of a not unpleasing appearance. It could have been worse, much worse, she reflected. Idly, she wondered if his stomach was quite as flat as it looked.

It was to Emma's credit that she had never in her life sought to profit from her very evident charms, although there had been opportunities in plenty in years past to do just that, had she been so inclined. Now, the situation demanded otherwise. She had come to entice and to seduce and she intended to trade on those charms, shamelessly if need be.

She had come dressed the part. A military style pill-box hat – quite the fashion in certain circles – had been strategically placed towards the back of the head, leaving the peak to soar saucily skywards in a decidely unmilitary fashion. The dress, displaying neither a high neckline nor concealing lace-tuck, displayed just sufficient cleavage to tantalise but not shock. The unbound hair, a little wayward, give a vague impression of impending bedtime, but as if to counterbalance these several aspects the lady bore not the slightest trace of rouge, or make-up, and sported no jewellery other than a simple, gold chain necklace with plain crucifix, worn to lead the eye unwittingly downwards. To Benjamin Hutton the overall effect was almost breathtaking.

'I understand you have my brother in custody,' she began. 'May I see him?'

'What?' he said, staring at her.

She was happy to repeat herself.

Benjamin Hutton made an effort to concentrate on the matter in hand.

'For the present, I would rather you did not, my lady. One of my men is questioning him with regard to this most unfortunate affair and I would not have him disturbed in that task. If you would care to return here tomorrow I would be happy to accommodate you.'

'Has my brother admitted his guilt, then?'

'Such an admission is scarcely necessary, seeing that he was caught in the very act, but he had a partner in this crime whom we are anxious to identify and bring to account. So far, your brother refuses to say anything, and that is delaying matters.'

'Tell me frankly, sir: in the eyes of the law, how serious is this business?'

'Short of actual murder it could hardly be more serious. It would be cruel of me to pretend otherwise.'

'And what will become of Peter when you have finished with him here at Stockton?'

'Well, tomorrow is Saturday; by Monday we should be in a position to bring him before an examining magistrate. If it is found that there is a case to answer, which seems certain to be so, your brother will be transferred forthwith to the Durham jails, there to await trial at the next Assizes.'

'I understand the examining magistrate you speak of will be Sir James Palmer. He is the elder brother of Colonel Palmer of New Grange, is he not?'

'Yes, that is so.'

'May I ask if this business has been noised abroad much? Are there many people who are privy to what has happened?'

'No, very few, I imagine,' he said, a little puzzled by the question. 'My men know of it, of course, but I run a tight ship here, my lady, and do not encourage loose talk, or idle gossip, with the townsfolk. Naturally, I cannot say to whom your husband may have communicated this affair.'

'He has not been here, then?'

'No, which surprises me. I have been expecting him hourly.'

She nodded, gravely, before proceeding to give him a dazzling smile, one which seemed to linger on and on. There had been no hint of its coming, which made him all the more unprepared for it. He shifted uncomfortably in his comfortable chair, eyeing the out-of-context response warily.

'Forgive me for asking,' she said, at length, 'but would you say that you are allowed a degree of latitude in the execution of your duty?'

'Yes, much is left to my discretion,' he answered, reluctantly, sensing what was coming.

'So, it is in your power, is it not, to caution my brother and release him without charge?'

'Impossible!' he exclaimed.

'But why is it impossible? You have admitted that this business is not yet common knowledge, and have acknowledged the latitude extended to you in the exercise of your authority. For my part, I should tell you that Colonel Palmer has been a good friend to the Sinclair family over the years and I feel sure I can prevail upon him to smooth things over if any of this were to come to the ears of his brother.'

'But you forget that I am sworn to uphold the law in these parts. How can I reconcile that with doing what you ask? Really, madam, you ask me this favour as if you were pleading the case of a child found raiding a neighbour's orchard. Your brother is held for a most serious felony, and the law must take its course.'

She made no response to this except to lean forward across the desk which separated them. He found himself gazing, as if hypnotised, into two wonderfully expressive blue eyes, suddenly swimming with tears.

'Do not despair, I beg you,' he heard a distant voice say. 'Much can be put forward in your brother's defence: his youthful age; his social standing; his crime free past; the provocation which prompted his actions. These are all factors in his favour. In these enlightened days more and more capital sentences are being commuted to life imprisonment, or transportation.'

'But that is still a hard fate. Nor can you guarantee that it will turn out as you say,' she protested.

He felt a hand close on one of his as she leaned ever closer to him, her face now filling his whole vision, the warmth of her body reaching out to him, the faint scent of her hair enveloping him. He watched, fascinated, as her movements sent a lock of golden hair falling forward across her face. With a squint of the eyes and a puff of the cheeks, she sent it back to its proper place. Was it his imagination, or did the lips stay open and pursed a trifle longer than was necessary?

'If you will do as I ask I shall be forever grateful – how grateful I leave to your imagination,' she said, softly. 'I would refuse you nothing – nothing, you understand? You take my meaning?'

He did. He wavered. Benjamin Hutton, law enforcer for twenty years without fear or favour, wavered at this onslaught against his senses. Finally, he spoke: 'Emma – my lady – what you ask is impossible; you must see that,' he said, gently.

She renewed the attack, adopting different tactics, and he could only watch helplessly as she wept before him, not with her face in her hands, or bowed before him, but with a head held high and with eyes wide open, staring straight into his. She did no more than glance at the handkerchief he volunteered, and move her face towards it. Before he knew it, he was dabbing away her tears, all the while glancing nervously towards the door, praying no one would enter in upon the scene.

Benjamin Hutton was no fool, and while he saw clearly that the tears were real enough, he was not deceived by the manner in which this latest ploy was executed. This realisation did nothing to diminish his admiration for his visitor. On the contrary, he could only marvel at her feminine guile and resourcefulness.

'My lady, you have not thought this thing through,' he said, when he had contrived a measure of composure in his visitor. 'Are you not overlooking one person in all of this?'

'You mean, my husband?'

'Exactly. If I were to do as you ask, my leniency and the protection of Colonel Palmer would count for nothing if your husband is determined to pursue the matter. When all is said and done, he is the injured party in this affair. I can agree to nothing without his consent, but since you are, as I understand it, estranged from him, and there is a history of bad blood between your brother and him, I cannot see why he should want to fall in with your wishes.'

'Ah!' she exclaimed, visibly relieved, 'may I take it, then, that subject to my husband's approval you will release Peter?'

'Nay, my lady, you go too far,' he protested. 'I say only that it would remove the one difficulty.'

'Oh! but you would not have spoken of it if you, yourself, had not come around to my way of thinking,' she cried, clapping her hands together, and smiling through her tears. 'But I knew that in the end your goodness and compassion, writ plain in your face, would prevail over all other considerations.'

He opened his mouth to protest against this blatant flattery, but thinking better of it decided to give up on the unequal contest.

She was not yet done.

'Constable Hutton, I believe you to be the kindest and best of men and one incapable of failing a lady in distress. What say you?'

'I say you are a scheming, beautiful, devious, beautiful, manipulative young woman. What say *you* to *that*?'

'I would say...... I would say you have missed out a 'beautiful' – but I forgive you.'

He laughed with good-humoured resignation.

'Lady Forres, my advice is that you go to your husband and enlist his support. If – no, sorry, *when* you have done that, have him call here and the two of us will discuss the matter and see what is to be done.'

He got up from his chair, ready to escort her to the door.

'And now, I think it best if you were to leave before I find myself pleading your forgiveness for having locked up your brother in the first place.'

Low in spirits in spite of her achievement, Emma set off on the short journey from Stockton to Yarm.

She realised now, as she had not done before, that her hoped-for arrangement with Benjamin Hutton without reference to her husband was doomed to failure from the outset, and that his backing was all-important. She was confident that she would be able to persuade her husband to take a lenient view of her brother's crime, but only by an act of self-sacrifice on her part. She would have to volunteer her return to Grange Hall. That prospect filled her with dread, but the alternative, of returning forthwith to Darlington and abandoning her brother, was unthinkable. Mentally, she began to prepare herself for the ordeal which lay ahead.

She would call first on Colonel Palmer to acquaint him of her intentions, and then visit Mr. Sibley to enlist his support. He would accompany her to Grange Hall and ensure her a fair hearing and just treatment at the hands of her husband. If he proved stubborn and uncooperative, Sibley would lend his weight to her pleadings.

Such were her plans, and all went well until she made the second of her calls, only to find Sibley out on parish business. She gauged him important to her scheme and decided she must wait at the vicarage for his return. Here, she sat, restless and impatient, chafing at this unexpected delay. When an hour had passed and he had still not put in an appearance, she decided she could wait no longer. Nervous and fearful, but grimly resolved, she set off for Grange Hall on her own..

In fact, the first item on the Reverend Sibley's list of duties that morning had been to call at Grange Hall. Acquainted of the startling events which had earlier taken place by Adam Fawley's open letter to Emma, he had instantly resolved to obtain a fuller story at first hand. A sudden, unexpected call of duty, in the form of his attendance on a dying parishioner in an outlying hamlet, had prevented him from doing so until well into the afternoon. As it turned out, he was being received at Grange Hall at more or less the same time as Emma was making her entry into the Palmer's residence, scarcely more than a mile away.

It had come as a welcome relief to be able to verify Adam Fawley's note in one respect especially. He had found Richard Forres unharmed and seemingly unaffected by what had taken place. Almost as gratifying to Sibley was the young man's distress on learning of the arrest of Emma's brother.

A bare ten minutes after his arrival, he found himself back in the grounds of Grange Hall, nodding his approval at the hastily departing figure of Richard Forres. Further duties in and around town meant that he was not destined to meet with Emma at all that day.

With the arrival of Richard Forres coming little more than an hour after Emma's departure, Constable Hutton made the natural, if mistaken, assumption that this latest visitor had called at the prompting of his lady wife. In view of the indiscretions of the earlier meeting, he resolved not to broach the subject of Emma's visit in the hope that the new arrival would do likewise.

This was his first sight of the owner of Grange Hall, of whom he had heard so much, and he had to admit to himself that he would never have guessed the name behind the face if his caller had not owned to it. The friendly countenance and agreeable manner of the gentleman struck him as being strangely at variance with all he had been told about the man. To be sure, he had sufficient experience of the world to know that one could not always judge by appearances but, even so, he was more than a little surprised at the apparent contradiction.

'I am here in connection with young Peter Sinclair,' his visitor began.

'Of course, Sir Henry; I have been expecting you.'

'Sir Richard, or just plain Richard, but not Sir Henry, if you please, Constable Hutton.'

'Ah! my apologies. I fear I have been misinformed.'

Richard Forres, nodded. 'So,' he said, 'I trust the lad has not come to any harm?'

'He is a little bruised from a tumble from his horse, that is all. He looks well-enough, but says not a word.'

'A tumble, you say? So, it is probable, then, that the poor fellow is in a state of shock?'

'In a state of shock? No, I would not have said so. A sullen, uncooperative state of mind would be a more accurate description, I fancy.'

'No, I'm sure you are mistaken. Consider: he is enjoying an innocent, early morning ride when his horse stumbles and he takes a bad fall, but instead of the help and succour which he could reasonably expect in such a situation, he is led, stunned and confused, into your custody, where he is accused of a crime of which he has no knowledge. In such circumstances any confession he may have made is of no value.'

'He has confessed to nothing. He has yet to say a single word.'

'Well, there you are,' said Richard Forres; 'it is just as I say.' He slapped his thigh, as if the matter was settled.

'So, you are saying he is innocent but has not the wit to say as much?' said his bemused listener.

'I say exactly that. When he comes to his senses you shall have his testimony as proof of what I say. Now, may I see him?'

So you may coach him in what he is to say, thought Hutton. Openly, he said: 'Let me understand you correctly, Sir Richard. Are you seriously claiming that Peter Sinclair is innocent of this crime? If so, may I ask if you would be willing to testify as such under oath?'

'Indeed, I would. I had a good look at the principal villain and assure you that it was not...... that it was not my brother-in-law who robbed and assaulted me. You must own that I know my family relatives when I see them.'

'This is a novel approach to deal with your family's predicament, but I'm not sure it is a very creditable one,' said a disbelieving Constable Hutton.

His visitor shook his head. 'Did your man have a clear view of my assailant?' he asked.

'No, he was too far distant for that, but he took good note of the fellow's general appearance and that of his horse.'

'But plain grey horses are common enough in these parts, and you must admit that one rider looks much like another from the back. But there is another consideration: was Peter Sinclair taken at the scene of the crime?'

'You *know* he was not,' said Hutton, irritably. 'Fawley came upon him in Culvert Wood.'

'Yes, that hardly qualifies as the scene of the crime. Why, it is a full mile away.'

'Sir Richard, shall we put a stop to all this nonsense?' protested Hutton. 'I take it you wish to see the young man released, but you have yet to give me one good reason why I should oblige you in this matter. Forgive me for saying so, but it would be an understatement if I were to say I was sceptical of your testimony. You do realise, do you not, that if I were to agree to free your criminal relative I could well find myself in some difficulty should the true facts ever become public knowledge?'

'I have removed that particular difficulty by my testimony that you hold the wrong man. As I am both eyewitness and injured party in this business, you are duty bound to act on that testimony in spite of any opinion which you may hold to the contrary.'

'You must desire the release of this young man very badly,' said Hutton, quietly. 'Making amends, are we?'

'Yes, if you like, but there is more to it than that. Is it not a cruel fate for a young man of twenty years to end his days dangling at the end of a rope, or rotting away in some prison cell?'

'Indeed, it is, particularly when the young man in question is innocent,' said Hutton, dryly. 'But rest easy, sir. I have been giving the matter a little thought and have come up with a solution. Fawley tells me that Peter Sinclair is a first class horseman, besides being more than competent both with pistol and sword. There has been talk of him taking up a military career, has there not?'

This was news to Richard Forres, who contented himself with a nod in response.

'Our country fights on two fronts now – against Old Boney in the Old World, and our foolish American cousins in that New World over the water – and has need of young men of the likes of Peter Sinclair. I believe the Army would discipline that rash temper of his and put to good use the lad's pluck and daring. What is your opinion in the matter?'

'I believe you have hit on the perfect solution. Give me a little time and I shall arrange matters to everyone's satisfaction.'

'And do you guarantee his good behaviour in the meantime?'

'I think we may safely leave that in his sister's hands.'

'Very well, Sir Richard, I shall authorise his release, but in spite of your testimony I believe it will be no bad thing if he is made to cool his heels overnight in our little lock-up here, and he shall get the benefit of my tongue before he leaves us tomorrow morning.'

'What can I say? I am most grateful,' said Richard Forres, as the two men took their leave of each other. 'My young brother-in-law has had a very lucky escape at your hands, which I trust he will appreciate.'

'He is a very fortunate young man, so much so that I believe I may safely say without fear of contradiction that I know of only one other more fortunate.'

'Really? You intrigue me, Constable Hutton. Who is this luckiest of all men whom you have in mind?'

'Why, my dear sir, if you do not know the answer to that, it is not for me to enlighten you,' said Hutton. He bowed politely to his visitor. 'Please give my regards to your charming wife.'

Ten minutes after he had arrived back home from his meeting with Benjamin Hutton, Emma, hotfoot from her useless visit to The Vicarage, made her appearance at Grange Hall.

He received her in the drawing room. Very much surprised at this unexpected sight of her, he found himself lost for words.

'I am happy to see you, Miss Sinclair,' was all he could find to say.

This was the second time he had greeted her with words she regarded as fatuous, but decided she had no time to waste in raising the subject. Ignoring his greeting, she came directly to the object of her visit.

'My brother is held in custody for this morning's assault on you, as I think you must know by now,' she said, eyeing him apprehensively. 'I am here to plead with you on his behalf, for I believe it is in your power to secure his release. In return for this service, I am prepared to return to Grange Hall. I give you my word that I shall not desert you once my brother is free and clear of this business. What say you? Do we have a bargain, you and I?'

Of course! She did not know! How could she know of matters so recently arranged and in her absence? were his thoughts. To ease her fears concerning her brother, he knew he should inform her of the true situation, but he was also aware that if he did so there was a very good chance she would withdraw her offer and promptly leave him, if not now then at the first opportunity.

She saw his hesitation and misconstrued the reason for it.

'I come back of my own free will and with a promise to take up afresh all those duties encumbrant upon a loyal wife. I will not attempt to deceive you with an offer of my true affection. That is lost forever and it would be wrong of me to pretend otherwise, but in all other respects you shall not find me wanting.'

Still he hesitated, saying nothing, and with his continuing silence there came upon her a growing uneasiness. Had her confidence been misplaced? Was she destined to fail her brother after all?

'If you want me to beg on my knees, I will do so,' she said, in desperation. 'See how I abase myself.'

She began to sink to the floor and the sight of it spurred him into action.

'That will not be necessary,' he said, hastily, and moved quickly to raise her up. 'I agree to your offer on two conditions.'

'Name them,' she said in a quivering voice, fearful of what he had in mind for her.

'First, you are not to go unsupervised into the kitchen.'

'Into the *kitchen*?'

'Yes. Where the knives are kept.'

She studied his face and came to the conclusion that he was teasing her. Well, two could play at that game.

'I am sorry for the wounded arm, but I did not intend it so. My aim was at fault, you understand.'

He looked at her doubtfully, uncertain of her meaning. Deciding it would be best not to enquire further he went on: 'Second, we frown on spitting here at The Grange. I would ask you to respect that prohibition.'

She blushed, shamefaced.

'That was coarse and vulgar,' she admitted. 'I never in my life did such a thing before and am heartily repentant of it now.'

'Well, well,' he said, tolerantly, 'I would sooner have your hatred than your indifference. The first at least has a passion to it.'

'Will you go now and arrange matters with Constable Hutton?' she asked, anxiously.

'No, I think not, my dear,' he said. 'In the first place, I have had a tiring day and have no wish to be out on the road once more, and in the second place, it will do your brother no great harm to spend at least one night in his cell, reflecting on his criminal behaviour. Besides all that, I think I would be wise to put to the test these glowing promises which you make so readily before I fulfil my part of the bargain. I shall expect the performance of a lifetime from you tonight.'

He moved close to her and began to tidy her hair and fuss over her appearance.

'Rachel is away until tomorrow, so apart from the staff we have the house to ourselves,' he whispered, huskily. 'The long, still watches of the night will soon be upon two lovers, long parted. I am sure that for one of us at least those hours will pass pleasantly enough.'

This time, the teasing went unrecognised.

'You unfeeling brute!' she exclaimed, shrinking away from him.

'I must say, this is a fine beginning,' he said, smiling. 'You have scarce been here ten minutes and already you deal in insults.'

Light-hearted though his manner was, she took his words as a warning: her brother was not yet a free man and she would do well to remember that and act accordingly.

'Forgive me,' she pleaded. 'It has been an exhausting day and I am tired and overwrought.'

'Then, I insist that you rest before dinner. The last thing I want to hear from you tonight is that you have a headache.'

'But my brother!' she protested.

'I give you my word that by noon tomorrow he will be a free man, without a stain on his character. There, will that suffice?'

'Yes, I suppose so,' she said, reluctantly reconciling herself to the postponement of her brother's release.

'I will attend to the return of your carriage and shall send word of your intentions to those good people, the Jamiesons. Tomorrow, I shall arrange for your things to be collected and brought here. As for your room, I believe it to be much as you left it. Now, will you not rest quietly while you can? You will need all your stamina for the night ahead.'

'You have not *really* changed, have you?' she said, bitterly.

'No, I have to admit that you see me much as I was before. But if you are not happy with what you see you must change me for the better. Do you attempt to make a saint of me, and I shall strive to make a sinner of you.' He paused, smiling. 'But that is the way of things when boy meets girl, is it not?'

In a state of misery and fear, she sat, half-undressed, towards the head of her bed, her knees drawn up towards her chin. Her scheming had paid off. Her brother would be a free man again the next morning. Now came the reckoning, a reckoning which would never be paid in full but which would go on day after day, and night after night, until she could endure it no longer. When that time came, she would go down one quiet night to the small lake which lay in the grounds of the estate. Weighted down with anything she could find, she would wade towards its cold, dark centre. Like the water lilies at sunset, she would close in upon herself and slip beneath the surface, and a loving God would take pity on her and forgive her this mortal sin.

They had spent the evening quietly together until, with a few expressive yawns and pointed remarks, he had more or less forced her upstairs. Half-undressed, the lethargy of despair had come upon her, so

251

that now she crouched in this defensive, foetal position, listening to his approaching footsteps.

With a perfunctory knock, he entered in. With his coming, the darkness, her only friend, fled, for the lighted candelabra he had brought with him cast its perverted glow into every corner. She lifted her head as he came towards her, and stared, wide-eyed but unseeing, into the distance.

She would never have guessed his first words to her.

'Have you ever had a recurring dream?' he asked, as he seated himself close to her.

He seemed disposed to talk. Thankful for this brief reprieve, she turned her face towards him.

'I do not know,' she said. 'What exactly is a recurring dream?'

'Why, the same dream coming time and time again. You have no knowledge of such a thing?'

'No, I have never experienced anything of the sort.'

'I thought as much,' he said, nodding his head. 'I guessed it was all on my side.'

'All on *your* side? I do not take your meaning. Do you want to tell me about it?' she said, hopefully.

To her dismay, he did not seem to want to talk further on the subject. She turned her face away as he began a silent scrutiny of her.

He had intended to stay but a moment. A simple goodnight kiss would stand in sharp contrast to what he had threatened to do to her that night. This was to be the first of his little 'victories', hopefully just one of many in the days that lay ahead, and he had been determined that it should be seen to full effect. Hence his teasing threats, none of them really intended.

Now, however, sensually close to this extraordinary young woman, he could not rid himself of a shameful, swelling pride, akin to a collector gloating over an exquisitely beautiful butterfly in his possession. He could not put aside the thought that she belonged to him, and to him alone. The quick, goodnight kiss was forgotten. It was simply impossible for him to leave it at that. Could he do more than he had intended and still claim a 'victory'? Yes, he thought he could.

He showed her first his wounded arm, and then his damaged wrist, her teeth marks fading but still clearly visible. Finally, he touched his tongue with a finger and planted a little spittle on his face. Guessing the meaning which lay behind his actions, she began to cry.

'Yes, I shall now make you pay for these injuries,' he said.

She closed her eyes, bracing herself for the first blow.

'This is for the wrist,' he said, turning her face towards him and kissing her gently on the lips.

'And this is for the arm,' he said, kissing her a little more forcibly.

'And now we come to the worst injury of all. I think something more drastic is called for here.'

He made her lie down, and moved his mouth towards her neck. To her horror, he settled upon almost the exact same place as once before.

It was a step too far.

'No, not that,' she whimpered. 'Anything but that.'

'For old-time's sake,' he murmured.

Ten minutes were sufficient, after which he sat for a moment longer, looking down at her. He thought she had never looked more beautiful.

'You look terrible,' he said. 'Do try and compose yourself and get some sleep. I shall leave you now.'

Before she realised it, he was gone, and with him went the light.

Puzzled, she stared at the dim outline of the ghostly door through which he had passed.

He would return, she told herself, and continued to crouch waiting and expectant.

The minutes passed.

Surely, he would return? Surely he was not done with her?

A half-hour slipped by.

Was he *really* gone?

A distant clock chimed out midnight.

Still half-undressed, she slipped beneath the bedsheets and fell asleep.

Before she dressed herself the following morning, she spent a moment in front of the mirror studying his passion of the previous night. How different were her feelings this second time around.

'The mark of The Beast', were her words, as she gingerly touched the tiny puncture marks in the sea of red. 'Oh, Richard, my own dear Richard, forgive my broken promise,' she pleaded.

CHAPTER 20

'You will not forget your promise with regard to my brother?' she asked him, as they breakfasted together the next morning.

'No, of course not,' he had answered. 'I have given you my word on that score, have I not? I shall attend to it directly.'

But it had *not* been attended to, of that she was certain.

It was now well into the morning and all he had done since breakfast was to potter about the estate, occupying himself in odd jobs which were more properly the province of the gardeners. She had followed him everywhere, watching at a discreet distance. He, in turn, had viewed her out of the corner of his eye, smiling to himself at her growing frustration. Finally, her patience exhausted, she confronted him.

'You gave me your word yesterday that my brother would be released by noon today,' she said. 'Time is nearly up and yet you show not the slightest inclination to fulfil your promise. Is this to be but one more example of a pledge to me broken?'

'My dear Emma, you do me an injustice. Yes, I did promise you your brother's freedom, and I kept my word. I have secured his release and I'll wager that even as we speak he is drowning his sorrows in his favourite tavern.'

'Liar!' she cried. 'You may not be aware of it, but I have watched you all morning and I know for certain that you have not stepped outside the estate.'

He shook his head, sadly.

'It does not even enter your head, does it, that I may have made a special effort on your behalf yesterday afternoon while you rested in your room?'

'Forgive me,' she muttered, 'but you should have told me.'

'Told you? Told you what?'

'Why, that you went into town directly after we made our bargain.'

'But I didn't. I only said I *may* have done.'

He saw her draw a deep breath in an effort to control her emotions.

'More to the point, should I tell you that I sent a note with Simpson this morning to settle matters with Constable Hutton? You must have seen me talking with him after breakfast. No, I do not think I *should* elaborate. You deserve no such consideration. Oh! Emma, Emma, why do you always assume the worst of me?'

Once again, she found herself apologising.

'I'm sorry, truly I am. Is that what you did?'

'No, not at all.'

'Will you, or will you not, go now to Stockton?' she demanded, through gritted teeth.

'Not I,' he said.

She left him, breathing fire and fury. Ten minutes later, he watched as she boarded the carriage she had hastily commandeered.

'Remember your promise to return here,' he cried out to her. 'It is no small matter, you know, to break a pledge.'

A half-hour later she burst in upon a startled Benjamin Hutton.

'Forgive me, sir, but I must see my brother immediately,' she cried. 'I have spoken with my husband, as you advised, but it is hopeless, quite hopeless. He plays with me as a cat does with a mouse. He is the Devil, himself. You do not know what I suffer at his hands. Oh! what am I to do? My poor brother! My poor, poor brother!'

'Calm yourself, my lady,' he said, leading her to a chair. 'Now, what is all this? Your brother was released, a free man, some two hours ago.'

'Free? He is *free*?' she cried. 'But where is he now?'

'In his lodgings, I fancy, nursing his wounded pride.'

'I do not understand. I am confused,' she said, with a shake of the head.

'You are not the only one confused, although I had a clear enough head until your arrival. But you astonish me with your words. Did you not settle matters with your husband for him to call here and plead your brother's case?'

'Yes, certainly I did.'

'And did he not inform you that your brother would be released this very morning?'

'Yes! Yes!.'

'Then why are you here?' He looked at her in concern. 'You are overwrought, my lady. This business has affected you more than you realise.'

She began to shake her head again in frustration.

'Constable Hutton, tell me, when *exactly* did you meet with my husband?'

'Why, yesterday afternoon, a little more than an hour after you left – but you *know* that.'

'No, I do *not* know that. An hour after I left, you say? But that was before…… no, it is impossible.'

'I do not follow you. I am as confused as you appear to be. Why is that impossible? Did you not call on him directly after leaving here and persuade him to come immediately to see me?'

'No, I did not. That is the point. I was delayed and it was late into the afternoon by the time I arrived at The Grange.'

'But there is no great mystery here,' said Hutton, laughing. 'Clearly, your husband decided for himself that he must help your brother, although why he did not tell you that he had already spoken with me when the two of you met up, I do not know.'

'I believe I know the answer to that,' she said, her mind going back to the bargain she had struck with her husband, and his strange hesitation which had preceded it. 'What I do *not* understand is why he should have wanted to help Peter on his own account.'

'Perhaps he did it out of regard for you.'

'That is hardly likely,' she said, dismissively. 'No, he is up to something.'

He waited patiently while she thought the matter through.

'Oh, my God!' she cried suddenly. 'I believe I have it. He wants ready access to Peter so he may extract his own revenge.'

'Nonsense!' he exclaimed. 'What better revenge could any man wish for than to see his enemy languishing in prison, disgraced in open court, then hanged before a gawping public. What is a quick knife–thrust in the back to all of that?'

'Yes, you are right,' she said, thoughtfully, 'but there is a mystery here, all the same. Why would my husband act as he did?'

'I think you would do better to address that question to him.'

'I may well do so; but there is another matter. I am in your debt for the part you played in this business. I have not forgotten my offer of yesterday and I am fully prepared to discharge that debt to you.'

He walked across to the window and looked down into the busy street below.

'But your husband? What of him?' he said throwing a glance in her direction.

'He is of no consequence. Do not concern yourself with him.'

'It saddens me to hear you speak so,' he said, unhappily. 'Have you no regard for his feelings?'

'Why should I? He has no regard for mine, but let us not speak of him.'

She had begun to feel uncomfortable talking to the back of his head, but he now turned to look searchingly at her.

'Lady Forres, tell me plainly: do you desire this...... this thing which you are proposing?'

'No, I do not *desire* it, but I made a promise if you agreed to free my brother and I would not wish to go back on my word. I feel I owe you something.'

'No, you are wrong. You owe me nothing. I resisted your tempting offer, if you remember, and will not now take advantage of it.'

'You are a good man, Constable Hutton,' she said, softly.

He looked long and hard at the beautiful young woman seated before him and give a wry smile.

'I am a fool,' he said, 'but I hope I may be counted an honest fool.'

They parted at his office door.

'You should direct your gratitude towards your husband, my lady,' he said. 'Without his compliance in this business, all of your tears, and all of my sympathy, would have counted for nothing.'

'I am settled back at Grange Hall, so he has already been amply repaid,' she said. 'You would do well to remember that had it not been for his treatment of me over the years my brother would have had no occasion to act as he did. If, as you say, I owe you nothing, I owe him less than nothing.'

Her parting words were to disturb him long after she was gone. If love is blind, so, too, is hate, he reflected.

He listened as Adam Fawley conversed with their fair visitor in the passageway outside his door. After a moment, he took up a position by the window once more, where he was joined in due course by his young assistant. Together, they watched as the lady left the building and crossed the road to her waiting carriage.

'What a beautiful and bewitching young woman,' said the elder man.

'It is as I told you, sir,' said Fawley, with the self-satisfied air of one proven right.

'Yes, I believe I owe you an apology on that score,' acknowledged Hutton. 'I was convinced your wild-sounding praise of the lady had to be an exaggeration, but I see now that you painted an accurate portrait. One sees a face like that perhaps once or twice in a long lifetime.'

'And Sir Henry? What did you make of him?'

Benjamin Hutton paused a moment to consider the question.

'Fawley, there is something odd about that gentleman, something not quite right,' he said, frowning. 'I had the feeling all the time I was with him that he was concealing something, or, at the very least, holding something back.'

'It is very possible,' said Fawley, with a shrug of the shoulders. 'A man like that must have a lot on his conscience – always assuming he has one.'

'Now there you and I part company. Having seen the gentleman, and spoken with him at some length, I would have thought him utterly incapable of the misdeeds which you attribute to him.'

Elated at the release of their recent prisoner, Fawley was not disposed to forcibly argue the matter, but neither was he inclined to pass over this assessment in silence.

'Sir, in the short time I have known you I have come to believe that you are a shrewd judge of character, but here, at least, you are in error. The man is a monster.'

'Adam Fawley, in my twenty years of striving to uphold the law I have viewed wickedness in all its many forms, but I know goodness, too, when I see it and I know how to distinguish between the two. I also know when a fellow is putting on an act for my benefit, or trailing false colours. I tell you plainly, the man I met with yesterday is nothing like the man you described to me.'

It was late afternoon by the time Emma returned home. She found him relaxing by the side of the lake, his self-appointed chores seemingly completed.

'You've been away so long I began to grow anxious,' he said, rising to meet her.

'I have spent most of the afternoon with my brother,' she said.

'Ah! yes, of course. So how did you find my would-be assassin?'

'He is well-enough but suffers, all the same. It distresses him that his actions have forced my return here.'

'If that is the case, we must invite him to dine as soon as maybe. I would have him see for himself your happy situation.'

'He asked me to return these to you,' she said, placing a pocket-watch and a pair of cuff-links in his hands. 'It is not possible for him to recover the cash taken, but he says he will repay you in full, if you will give him a little time.'

'The lad is honest, I'll say that for him; but we must do something about that brother of yours. His way of life tends to bad company. He needs an occupation. Constable Hutton believes a career in the Army is the answer.'

'Yes, he has talked of it often enough, but the purchase of a commision and all that goes with it is beyond his means.'

'Can his uncle not help?'

'My uncle Johnathon is not a wealthy man, in spite of appearances to the contrary. He has a fine house, to be sure, left to him many years ago, but in all other respects his fortune is a modest one.'

'Then, the duty falls on me and I am happy to accept it,' he said. Taking her by the arm he began to lead her on a walk around the lake. 'So, you found Peter a free man, just as I promised you?'

'You tricked me on that score, as well you know,' she said, with more than a hint of bitterness and regret.

'Tricked you? How so?'

'You know full well. We struck our bargain *after* you had arranged for his release but said nothing of it at the time. It was a needless gesture on my part.'

'How you must hate me,' he said, with a sigh. 'I perform an unselfish act of forgiveness, one without pressure, or inducement, and am condemned on that account. Do you now consider yourself absolved from your promise made to me?'

'It *was* a kind thing you did, and I am still trying to fathom out the reason which lay behind it. As for the rest, I shall keep to my word. My very presence is proof of that. No, my brother is at liberty, which is all I asked of you, but it still grieves me to think I am now back in your power when it could have been otherwise.'

'My dear Miss Sinclair, it is not *you* who are in *my* power, but rather —.'

'And that is another thing,' she said, crossly, cutting short his words. 'Why do you persist in using my maiden name in that absurd fashion? You make me uncomfortable with your foolishness.'

What could he say? How could he begin to explain that this was another one of those little gestures he felt due to him? He had left her that balmy, star-spangled night as Emma Sinclair, and as such he still saw her.

'Very well, 'Emma' it is from now on,' he said; 'but in return you must address me not as Henry, but as Richard.'

The request came as no great surprise to her. When Rachel had last visited her she had spoken of this strange, self-effected change of names on his part.

'No, I cannot agree to that – Henry,' she said, firmly.

'But why not? Richard is one of my two given names, and I grow tired of 'Henry' – you do not know how tired.'

He met with a second refusal, as decisive as the first.

'But what is your objection? It is little enough to ask,' he persisted.

'Because...... because, if you must know, that name has a special meaning to me.'

'Ah! ah!' he cried, 'I do believe I have chanced upon a guilty secret. Can it be that I was not the first to explore your hidden charms? But who was this Richard fellow, he with the sacred name? What was he like?'

'He was loving, and kind, and gentle. In short, he was nothing like you, so there's a vast improvement,' she cried, furious at his flippant remarks.

'I doubt that,' he said, airily. 'If the truth be known, I fancy there is nothing to choose between the two of us.'

'You have a high opinion of yourself,' she said. 'God knows why that should be.'

'I only repeat what others say of me,' he said, looking full at her.

'What others?' she demanded. 'Your drunken cronies, perhaps? Or is it that some obliging whore has recently paid you a compliment?' She shook her head in contempt. 'You are not fit to lace up the boots of the man I have in mind.'

'Then, I must remember that when next I put them on, and call for assistance,' he said, smiling.

'Just what is that supposed to mean? Really! what nonsense you talk at times. Everything is a joke to you, is it not?'

'No, not everything, only life.' He caught her look. 'Sorry, only joking,' he said. 'But to return to the matter in hand. If you persist in using the name 'Henry', I shall no longer answer to it. Moreover, I, in turn, shall continue to use your maiden name, in public as well as in private. I'll wager that will embarass you more than it does me.'

'It would seem you leave me little choice,' she said. She shrugged her shoulders. 'Well, what's in a name, I suppose, and, who knows, I may even come to enjoy its use. It will be a daily reminder to me of the contrast between the two of you.'

They continued their slow circuit of the lake, he perfectly content, she struggling with herself to raise a certain subject.

'Why did you not stay with me last night?' she asked, all of a sudden.

She realised she was treading on dangerous ground. Her commonsense told her to steer clear of the subject, but her curiosity as to his reply won the day.

'Well, actually, I stayed longer than I intended, and I'm sorry for it.'

Casting a quick glance about her, she pulled back the high collar of her blouse to reveal his handiwork of the previous night.

'I assume you mean this,' she said. 'Well, you may be proud of it but I have no desire to show it to the world. Next time you feel the urge to give me one you would oblige me if you directed your attention to some more private part.'

For some reason she did not understand, he seemed to find her words hugely entertaining.

'Very necessary advice, I'm sure,' he said, laughing. 'But there will not be a next time in any shape, or form, until you say differently. I hereby resign my conjugal rights until you, yourself, feel inclined to reinstate them.'

She stood stock still, looking at him.

'No...... no, you cannot mean that,' she said.

He turned to face her squarely, his face suddenly serious.

'Do you really believe I could force myself upon any woman against her will? *That* is why I did not take matters further last night.'

'Do you honestly expect me to credit what you say?' she said. 'Why, you have forced yourself upon me a hundred times in the past.'

'Yes...... well...... that *really is* all in the past. No, my bedroom door will always be open to you, and I shall wait patiently for however long it takes you to come to me. I give you my word that I shall never again molest you. If I ever go back on my word you will be free to leave here without let or hindrance.'

'If you really mean all of that......'

'I *do* mean it. Have I not given you my word?'

'Then, I am safe for ever. I am safe!'

'For ever is a long time, my dear Emma. I shall give myself a month. Yes, I think you will sing a different tune within the month.'

He watched as she give him a somewhat furtive look, smiling to herself.

'Why do you smile so?' he asked.

'Should I tell you?' she said. 'Yes, in view of your promise I believe I owe you at least that. You must know that I am anxious to be away from here, and the sooner the better. I was just thinking of how easy it would be for me to tempt you beyond endurance. I really do believe that I could easily get you to break your word. There! I have put you on your guard against my better judgement. Is that not generous of me?'

She watched as the panic spread across his face and, in spite of herself, was touched by it.

'No, you would not be so cruel,' he said, huskily. 'I am only flesh and blood, when all is said and done. I have my limitations, as any man does.'

'Yes, of course you do. I dare say even the Devil, himself, has his limitations.'

'But there were good times, were they not?' he asked, hopefully.

'I cannot answer that, never being present on such occasions.'

The conversation was terminated by the arrival of Rachel's carriage, bringing her back home. He watched, happily, as the two young women ran to greet each other.

He continued to gaze over the waters of the lake, sparkling in the late summer sunshine, and as he did so he fell into a pensive mood. Given Emma's past treatment at the hands of Henry Forres, he had expected to meet a frightened, browbeaten young woman, who would shun his company at every opportunity, but that was proving not to be the case. For this he was grateful, but it puzzled him, too. It appeared that she did not care if she antagonised him, and was quite prepared to risk his anger with argument and confrontation. He sensed that something was giving her the courage to view her treatment at his hands with a degree of indifference.

Had he but known it, the explanation lay before his very eyes in the shape of the still, deep waters he looked out upon.

His spirits began to rise as he headed back towards the house. The mountain was there, sure enough, and as large as ever: huge, forbidding, discouraging, but in spite of her words of a few moments ago he sensed that it was certainly not immovable.

'I shall move this mountain if it kills me,' were his prophetic words to himself.

Late that evening he entered her room as she was retiring for the night.

'Don't be alarmed; I'm not going to bite you,' he said, producing a letter and handing it to her. 'This came by express messenger a couple of hours ago.'

She cast her eye down the single sheet of paper and read:

'The Manor, Richmond, Saturday.

Dear Sir,

With reference to your most recent communication, I beg leave to reaffirm that his Grace is unable to oblige you in this matter, but would wish to inform you that I am at your disposal and shall be pleased to receive you on Tuesday next, at three in the afternoon. An early reply would be appreciated if this is not convenient to you.

I remain, sir, your obedient servant,

James T. Dunstable,

principal secretary, H.G. the Duke of Marrick.'

'But what does it signify, and how does it concern me?' she asked, handing the letter back to him.

'It signifies a three hour journey to Richmond on Tuesday for the two of us. We shall set off mid-morning, partake of lunch in Richmond, and time our arrival at The Manor accordingly.'

'But why is my presence necessary? It scarcely reads like a social visit.'

'Indeed, it is not. It is a business venture, vital to the future well-being of the estate.'

'And do you really need me with you?'

'I believe your assistance could prove invaluable. Besides, having been apart for so long I would not relish the prospect of a further five or six days without you.'

'Five or six *days*?' she said, in surprise. 'We shall be gone five or six days? Is Rachel to accompany us, then?'

'No, my sister's presence is not necessary. Indeed, it could well prove a distraction to one and all.'

'Have you told her this?'

'Yes, I have just come from her room. She was none too pleased at the prospect of being left out of things, but I have already arranged for her to visit your uncle in York for a similar period of time, so she will not be left alone here. Rachel has not seen your uncle Johnathon these two years past, so a visit on her part is long overdue.'

'You seem to have everything planned, but will you not enlighten me as to the purpose of our journey?'

'The facts are very simply put. His Grace The Duke of Marrick has but two children, a boy of fifteen, who is meant to inherit, and a girl of nine years. The boy is in the final stage of consumption. The girl, so I'm reliably informed, looks tolerably well but carries within her the same seeds of destruction. There is a long history of the disease on the mother's side of the family, it would seem. We leave on Tuesday for the purpose of curing both children. In so doing, we shall restore the fortunes of both the Duke's estate and our own, but I shall tell you more on the journey there.'

'A youth in the final stage of consumption, and you are to cure him? What are you, then, some wonder of a physician?' she cried, wide-eyed with astonishment at his words. 'You are mad. You are quite, quite mad, and I will not join you on this insane enterprise.'

'If I do not succeed in this undertaking to everyone's satisfaction, your own included, I give you my word that I shall release you from

264

your obligation to me. On the day of our return, you will be free to leave here, for good if you wish it so.'

'I shall come,' she said, promptly.

'Yes, I thought that might change your mind.'

He observed with sadness the joy brought her by his unexpected offer, and noted with feelings akin to disgust the hope which now lit up her eyes.

'Yes...... well...... I shall leave you now,' he said, rising to go. 'I shall leave you in peace to pray for the deaths of these two children.'

An hour later she stole into his room and crouched by his bed.

'Richard!' she whispered. 'Richard!'

'What is it?' he asked, raising himself up on his elbow.

'I could not sleep after what you said. I am here to tell you I shall accompany you to Richmond, and I release you from your offer. In the circumstances, I do not desire it.'

'Then, I withdraw it, and am happy to do so.'

'There is one other matter,' she said, after a pause. 'You said earlier today that you would help Peter to obtain a commission. That would mean so much to me. Do you still stand by what you said?'

'Yes, of course I do,' he said. 'I love that young brother of yours.'

'You *love* him?' she said, startled by this claim on his part. 'Why, in the name of all that is wonderful, should you have cause to love him?'

'Really, Emma, you do ask the silliest of questions at times,' he said, yawning. 'I love him because you love him.'

It was as she made her way back to her room a moment later that the thought came to her for the first time.

'I do not know this man,' she told herself. 'But, no, this is all an act. It has to be. Well, he shall not fool me.'

CHAPTER 21

If the conduct of Emma, and that of Richard, puzzled both parties equally, Emma, alone, was mystified by Rachel's changed disposition. She was left to marvel at how the once shy and insecure girl now breezed through life with an easy confidence and playful assurance, and was forced to acknowledge that here, at least, no act was being put on for her benefit. Real enough, also, was the changed atmosphere and ordered life at Grange Hall, apparent to her within a few hours of her arrival back. The once subdued air and strict adherence to duty had given way to one of easy informality, marked by a cheerful performance of tasks amidst friendly household chatter. Indeed, in Emma's opinion the changes had gone *too* far in some respects. Her husband, she had noted, was now in the habit of addressing each and every one of the servants, however lowly their station, by their first name, and was even heard on occasions to greet Rogers and Simpson as 'my friend', behaviour which she held to be shockingly improper.

At her husband's insistence, on the Sunday following her return she accompanied him on a tour of the estate and found the changes here no less striking than elsewhere. The two of them were greeted at every turn not with the formally polite words of former times, but with a respectful warmth and affection and *genuine*-sounding enquiries concerning their state of health.

Their last port of call was on the Stilwell household, tenant farmers residing close to the southern boundary of the estate. Here, by all accounts, a happy event was imminent, if not overdue.

A few minutes after their arrival they were being ushered into the bedroom, where *two* very recent additions to the household were to be seen. When they made their entrance, the lady, propped up on her pillows, was frantically attending to her appearance, while the husband, dressed in his Sunday best, stood awkwardly by her side.

'Twins again, Mrs Stilwell?' said Emma, shaking her head and smiling down upon the two tiny bundles. 'This is the third pair in the past six years, is it not?' She knew there were two other matching pairs in the family, but was not altogether sure if there were any other, single, children. 'Tell me, do you always get twins?' she asked, in wonder.

'No, of course not, my lady,' replied the mother, laughing. She glanced at her husband. 'There are lots of times we don't get anything at all.'

Emma bit her lip in an attempt to control her emotions, but others present were less inhibited. She felt a pronounced dig in the back from Richard, who then proceeded to strike up a low, tuneless whistle, while the poor father stood blushing crimson at his wife's foolishness. With the greatest difficulty, Emma controlled herself during their short stay, but once outside she and her unmusical companion fell laughing into each other's arms. Within a moment, however, the knowledge of whose company she was in came to her, and with her composure regained she pulled sharply away.

They retraced their footsteps and had reached the edge of the lake before he made an oblique reference to their recent visit.

'I hope to be a father someday,' he said.

'Really? Then, you must tell me when it happens,' she said.

'I rather hoped you will be the very first to know of it. I would like a son and heir, of course, but, first, I think a little girl would please me more – a little girl who looks just like you must once have looked. Do you think any of that possible, Emma?'

'It is hardly likely,' she said. 'I have no twin sister –- not that I would recommend you to her if I had.'

'But you desire children, surely?' he said, refusing to be put off by her responses.

'Once I did, with a hoped-for partner in life whom I could love and respect, but it would seem it was not to be.'

The words were spoken with a genuine sadness, and he realised they were not intended to hurt him but were given out as a simple statement of fact.

'There maybe was once such a man,' she said, after a pause.

'Ah! yes, the mysterious gentleman whose boots I am unworthy to lace up, but tell me more of this flawless paragon, this man without a fault. What was his name? Where is he now? What was the exact nature of this dubious relationship?'

He had touched jestingly on a subject sacred to her, the details of which she had long ago resolved never to divulge to a living soul. It had never been her intention to acquaint her husband with the details, but his cavalier words so infuriated her that a wish to hurt and humiliate him overrode other considerations.

'I really know very little about him,' she said. 'We met only the once, and I never even had a proper sight of his face. I was very ill, my life despaired of – you know the time of which I speak – when he came to me.' She paused, and looked defiantly at him. 'We spent part of the night together...... the two of us alone...... in my bedroom, and on my bed.'

'Indeed?' he said, smiling. 'And what became of the gentleman, if I may properly give him such a title?'

'I do not know. I never saw him again.'

He should have left it at that, but didn't. In his enjoyment of the conversation, for once Richard Forres, ever considerate of the feelings of others, failed to appreciate that every teasing word of his was wounding Emma deeply.

'The man is a scoundrel,' he said. 'He is beneath contempt. He forces himself on a defenceless young woman, lying ill on her sickbed, and having had his evil way with her leaves without so much as volunteering a forwarding address.'

'It was not as you state it,' she cried. 'It was not like that at all. You degrade all that is fine and noble with your sordid words.'

Furiously angry that her story, which had been told with the intention of humiliating him, had rebounded upon herself, she give him a violent shove. They had been standing on the very edge of the lake, and it was enough to send him crashing into the water.

It was at this precise moment that Rachel, out and about in search of Emma and Richard, came upon the scene. Watching from a distance, she found the incident hilarious, her amusement heightened by the subsequent antics of her brother. He had surfaced, arms flailing and screaming for help. Was it possible that Emma did not know? she wondered. There was only one way to find out.

She rushed to Emma's side, her face suddenly very grave.

'Oh! good work, Emma,' she said. 'I see it hasn't taken you long to extract your revenge.'

'He is scarce ten yards away. Is the water so very deep?' said Emma, bewildered.

'There is a shallow shelf there,' said Rachel, pointing downwards, 'and then a sudden drop to more than eight feet. You've chosen your spot well.'

'He is screaming for help, and crying out that he cannot swim,' said Emma, horrified at the turn of events. 'Is that really so?'

'He cannot swim a stroke. Neither can I, come to that,' said Rachel.

'You must run back to the Hall and get help,' said Emma, panic-stricken.

'Are you mad?' cried Rachel. 'It will take me a good three minutes to get back there. Am I supposed to then hold a court of enquiry as to who can swim and who cannot before returning here? But we are wasting time. Every second counts. Look! he is going down for a second time. You, I know, are an expert swimmer. Good God! Emma, what are we doing standing here debating the matter? You must rescue him, there is nothing else for it.'

'But I have all my best Sunday clothes on,' Emma protested.

'You callous bitch,' screamed Rachel. 'Do you value your wardrobe above my brother's life?'

'No, of course not,' cried Emma, wide-eyed with terror. She began frantically fumbling at the buttons of her dress.

'There is no time for that,' cried Rachel.

Within seconds Emma was reduced to her somewhat flimsy summer underwear, her dress in tatters at her feet.

The lake now lay clear and placid.

'For God's sake, hurry,' screamed Rachel, as Emma edged her way out onto the underwater shelf.

Plunging into deeper waters, Emma covered the intervening distance with a few powerful strokes. Rachel watched with a set face as Emma disappeared beneath the surface, to reappear in less than a moment holding up the limp body of the victim.

With great difficulty she succeeded in bringing him safely to the bank.

'Oh, God! what a struggle,' gasped Emma, lying prostrate on the ground.

Meantime, Rachel was examining the rescued party.

'Oh, my God, Emma!' cried Rachel, 'he is not breathing.'

'What?' cried Emma, in alarm. 'Rachel, we *must* get help,' she said, beginning to weep.

'There is no time for that,' exclaimed Rachel. 'We must revive him here and now if we are to stand any chance.'

'Revive him? How do we do that?' asked Emma.

'Are you useless, or are you useless?' demanded Rachel. 'We must first get the water out of his lungs. Help me turn him onto his front.'

That done, Rachel began a vigorous pumping action below the shoulder blades.

'I think that will do,' she said, after a moment. 'Now, help me turn him onto his back.'

'What now?' cried Emma.

'We must get some air back into his lungs.' So saying, she opened wide her brother's mouth.

'And how do we do that?'

'Well, unless you have a pair of bellows handy, you must fill your lungs with air and blow forcibly into his mouth. Keep on doing that time and time again, and with God's help he may yet be saved. I shall now run for help.'

Emma looked down at the figure of the man she had grown to loathe and despise.

'No. No, you must do that,' she said.

'Emma, what I am asking you to do is vitally necessary,' cried Rachel. 'It is not seemly for a sister to do such a thing, but I would gladly throw convention to the wind if only Richard and I were involved. You are his wife, for God's sake, and are perfectly capable.'

She ran off, shouting back over her shoulder: 'I hold you responsible for this and, believe me, you shall be made to pay for it if Richard dies.'

After what seemed an eternity to Emma, Rachel reappeared with Simpson hard at her heels.

'Well?' gasped Rachel.

'I'm not sure,' said Emma. 'Where have you been? We have been mouth to mouth for what seemed to be an age.' She lifted a tear-stained face to Simpson. 'I had no idea the water was so deep so close to the bank.'

'It is along this small stretch, my lady,' said Simpson.

'Even so, although we have never touched on the subject, I would have thought that your master would have had no difficulty in reaching the bank safely. Did you know he never learnt to swim?'

'Yes, I was aware of that,' said Simpson, glancing a little sheepishly at Rachel.

It was at this point that a breathless Rogers appeared on the scene and proceeded to spoil everything.

'Heavens above! What has happened?' he said.

'That will do, Rogers,' said Rachel, hastily. 'We have the situation under control. You may leave us.'

'But what has happened, my lady?' repeated Rogers, ignoring Rachel's words.

'I...... that is to say, your master took a tumble into the lake. If he has not drowned, he has come very close to it.'

'My lady, if you will pardon me for saying so, that is nonsense. I know for a fact that my master is a proficient swimmer. Why, he could swim clear across the lake twice over without stopping, if he had a mind to. Miss Rachel will back me up in what I say.'

'*What? What?*' cried Emma. She looked balefully at Rachel, before transferring her gaze to Simpson.

'You must not blame Simpson,' said Rachel, looking at the ground. 'He only said what I ordered him to say.'

'*What? What?*' screamed Emma. Apart from the one word she give every indication of having lost the power of speech. She looked down at the prostrate figure of the man she had just plucked from the jaws of death and saw that he was fully conscious and smiling up at her.

'You...... you bloody lunatics!' she screamed. Enraged, she lashed out with her foot at the man on the ground.

It was not Emma's day. Shoeless, her bare foot made contact with a hard, solid hip-bone. He may have felt the shock of it, but it was she who felt the pain.

'Oh, God!' she cried, 'I do believe I've broken my foot. Oh, God! my foot.' For a moment she hopped about in the manner of some one-footed kangaroo, before taking herself off in the direction of Grange Hall. From a distance, they heard her rantings as she proceeded along in a series of hops and squelches.

'I think you had best steer clear of her for a few hours,' said Rachel to Richard. 'I shall run after her and do what I can to mollify her. And do get up, Richard. The show's over.'

Half-way to the Hall Rachel caught up with Emma.

'Emma, none of this was planned in advance,' she said. 'I was a witness to everything that happened. Richard's tumble into the lake was a genuine fall, I'm sure.'

'Yes, and everything that followed was deceit and play-acting on his part, was it not?' cried Emma; 'and you aided and abetted him in that deceit.' She held out her arms to reveal her sodden underclothes. 'Just look at me,' she stormed; 'not to mention my best dress ripped to shreds back there.'

'I'm sure Richard will make it up to you,' said Rachel, soothingly; 'and, look, here is Sarah with a blanket to see you decently covered. Emma, it was only a joke.'

'A *joke*? You dare to call it a joke?' cried Emma. 'I am soaked through, I have exposed myself in public, and am left with a broken foot. Oh, God!' she moaned, 'I'm crippled for life.'

'I'm sure the foot is not as bad as you imagine it to be,' said Rachel, reassuringly, 'but I shall send word to Doctor Hunter, and he will attend you. Just let me say ——.'

'No, not another word,' cried Emma. 'Rachel Forres, I am never going to speak to you again for as long as I live – and the same goes for that idiot brother of yours.'

'Well, how is the patient?' asked Rachel.

'Some of the toes are bruised and a little swollen, to be sure,' said Doctor Hunter, 'but there is nothing broken, I'm certain of that.'

'I'm glad to hear it,' said Rachel. 'Tell me, doctor, did she say what was the cause of it?'

'She was strangely reticent on that point, so much so that I must confess to being a little intrigued. One can hardly come by such an injury without the knowledge of what caused it. Are you able to enlighten me, Miss Rachel?'

'Yes, why not? There is no mystery here, doctor. Lady Forres pushed my brother into the lake. Thinking better of it, she was instrumental in his rescue. Once she had him back on dry land, she proceeded to kick him violently, but it was done with a bare foot – hence the injury.'

'Miss Rachel, you will have your little joke,' said Hunter, smiling, 'but you must learn to make your jesting credible.'

'Indeed, I do not jest,' said Rachel. 'If you doubt my word, you can verify the facts from Simpson, or Rogers. But I see I alarm you. There is no cause for that. It was merely a trifling falling out between Emma and my brother.'

'A *trifling* falling out, you say?' said Hunter, nodding gravely.

He left her only to reappear a moment later.

'Miss Rachel – a sudden thought, no more. If there is ever a *serious* falling out between your brother and his wife, pray do not hesitate to contact me immediately.'

Richard Forres, valuing his privacy, and deeming it totally unnecessary, had long since abandoned the custom of having servants standing rigidly to attention while he partook of his evening meal. A door slightly ajar, and a small gong was, in his eyes, sufficient to summon one or more of the staff when one course was finished and another due.

That evening, however, the practise he had instituted served no useful purpose. Apart from the occasional polite word passed between brother and sister, a full two courses had been consumed in almost total silence.

It was Rachel who spoke the first words of any consequence.

'I must say, you do not look at all well, Richard,' she said. 'You look positively ill, and have scarce eaten a thing.'

'Well! I like that,' exclaimed Emma, indignantly. 'It is I who have suffered by what happened today, but no one thinks to enquire after my state of health.'

'Hello!' said Rachel, cocking an ear. 'Richard, I do believe I've just heard a disembodied voice. It was a woman's voice, so it could hardly have come from you, and I know it was not Emma who spoke since she has vowed never to speak to us again.' She lifted up the tablecloth and peered into empty space. 'How very strange,' she said.

'Rachel, stop that,' said Richard, sharply. 'Emma has suffered enough without your further teasing. For myself, I am greatly in her debt for coming to my aid.'

'Would you mind repeating that – the last bit, I mean?' said Rachel.

'You were in no danger, none at all.'

'Well...... well, that's as maybe, but Emma did not know that. It was a brave thing she did.' He turned to Emma. 'Whether you are speaking to me, or not, will you at least answer me one question? In this day and age, there is not one female in a hundred who could have done what you did today. Who taught you to swim so expertly?'

'If you must know, it was my father, when I was a mere child. Living so close to water, he deemed it essential I should be taught to swim. He used to take me to some quiet backwater, and I soon became proficient. In later years, when they would allow it, I used to accompany my brothers, who both enjoyed that particular exercise. Rachel knew all of this, and I thought you did, too.' She paused to look doubtfully at him. 'This is not some device to simply engage me in conversation, is it?'

'No, not at all. I had quite forgotten,' he replied, glibly.

'Well, I think we should analyse the day's events and apportion blame where it is due,' said Rachel. 'You must accept one-third of the guilt, Richard, for your play-acting.'

'Yes, it was wrong of me. I freely acknowledge that.'

'So far, so good. For myself, I am willing to shoulder my one-third share for going along with your foolishness.' She paused, frowning. 'That still leaves one-third to apportion elsewhere. Do you know, Richard, I have quite forgotten: tell me, what was the start of this unfortunate affair? How came you in the lake in the first place?'

'We all know the answer to that, Rachel,' said Emma. 'Very well, then, I suppose I must take my fair share of the guilt, but I was sorely provoked.'

'How so?' said Rachel. 'Did my brother attempt to ravish you?'

'No, of course not,' said Emma, indignantly. ·

'Ah! I see you are annoyed,' said Rachel. 'Clearly, Richard provoked you by failing to ravish you. Far be it for me to censure you, Emma, but I would remind you that the privacy of the bedroom is generally considered to be a more seemly situation.'

'If you are going to talk nonsense, I shall leave,' said Emma. 'It was something your brother said which caused me to act the way I did.'

'Something he *said*? Well, I must learn to guard my tongue when next we two take a tour of the lake. I would not wish to suffer a similar fate.'

'Emma, is there anything I can do, or say, to make amends?' said Richard.

'Yes, two things,' said Emma, promptly – as if she had anticipated the question and had already answered it to her own satisfaction. 'First, I shall expect you to replace my beautiful dress lying in tatters out there.'

'You may go out into town tomorrow and choose the prettiest dress you light upon, and hang the cost.'

'Second, you must stop teasing me about a certain person. I will not have him censured, even in fun.'

'So be it. I hereby acknowledge his infinite superiority to my own poor self.'

'Of whom are you speaking?' said Rachel, intrigued.

'I do not wish to speak of it,' said Emma.

'We are talking of a gentleman whom Emma became briefly acquainted with a few years back. She holds him in the highest esteem, and rightly so,' said Richard.

'But Emma does not lightly bestow such unreserved approval on any man,' said Rachel. 'He must, indeed, be a very worthy gentleman. But tell me more, Emma. Does he live hereabouts? Do I know him? Is he married, or unmarried? Oh, Emma, if the latter would he do for me, do you suppose? If I am with you when next you see him, will you not oblige me with an introduction?'

'When next I see him?' sighed Emma. 'If only, Rachel, if only.'

Something was troubling Richard, so much so that the moment they were alone together he came straight to the root of the matter.

'Rachel, how did you come by the knowledge of mouth to mouth resuscitation?' he said.

He thought it likely that he might have to explain himself, for here was a potentially lifesaving act which by the mid-twentieth century had become recognised as the best aid one could give to a near-drowned person, but which was utterly unknown in the early nineteenth century. He found he had no need to elaborate.

He watched as she struggled to put her feelings into words.

'To tell the truth, Richard, I honestly do not know. I was, of course, aware that what I proposed to Emma would be a delight to you but, irrespective of that, I was also aware that in a real emergency it would have been the most effective course of action. I cannot explain why that should be so.' She shook her head, genuinely puzzled. 'Do you know, the strangest of thoughts and ideas have lately been coming into my head, and I have no notion from where they spring. I get the oddest feeling at times that I don't really belong to this time period. Standards and values which I once accepted without question now seem outdated, or even oppressive. Strange is it not?'

'Well, I dare say it is just a phase you are going through,' he said, lightly. 'It is of no matter.'

'And are you going through the same kind of phase?' she said. 'I might as easily ask you where *your* knowledge comes from.'

He had not anticipated the question although, perhaps, he should have done.

'Oh, I am a mine of useless, and not so useless, information,' was the best response he could come up with.

His reassuring words made to play down her state of mind were at odds with his thoughts when he left her: 'This is my doing. I only hope it is not all going to end up in tears'.

Emma was experiencing no such difficulties.

'How are the toes?' he asked, as he entered her room.

'Still attached to the foot, if that's what you mean,' she said.

'You still intend to accompany me to Richmond the day after tomorrow? Nothing has changed in that respect?'

'I shall be with you. To be honest, I am now quite looking forward to it. I am looking forward to you making a fool of yourself.'

'Well, we shall see,' he said, smiling; 'and thank you for your part in our little reconciliation over dinner.'

'I let you off lightly,' she said. 'Do you know, when I got back here I was physically sick at the thought of what I had been tricked into doing. In a sense, I suppose I have myself to blame. I should have guessed Rachel was talking nonsense. Whoever heard of anyone being revived by blowing air into their lungs?'

'Was that part so very terrible to you?'

'Yes, it was. Richard, I do not think you realise that, although I try not to show it, every time you touch me I cringe mentally.'

'You try not to show it, but you tell me about it. Thank you, Emma; you are a great comfort to me.'

'The remedy is in your hands. You may ask me to leave any time you choose, and I will gladly oblige you.'

'No...... no, let us both resolve to endure it for a few weeks longer, at least.'

'As you wish,' she said.

'And now, before I leave you, I would like to raise another matter. It is no pleasant thing to plunge fully clothed into a lake of cold water. Fair enough, you got a soaking, too, but at least you were prepared for it. It was not a pleasant experience for me, I assure you.'

'Yes, I can see that still,' she said. 'Rachel was right; you do not look at all well, and I am sorry for it.'

'Thank you for that, at least,' he said, 'but the point I am leading up to is this: if I fulfil the two stipulations you made of me, will you, in return, promise never to do such a thing again?'

'Very well, I promise,' she said.

Physically sick? Mentally cringing whenever he touched her were his thoughts after he left her. This is not just any mountain, he told himself, it is bloody Everest, itself. But he was grateful for her parting promise, if nothing else.

The fact was, Senior Technician Richard Travis could not swim a stroke, and the danger he had been in had been very real.

'Do you like it?' said Emma, holding wide her arms. 'It took me ages to find just what I was looking for.'

'It's very pretty, Emma,' said Richard; 'but, to be honest, I think you would look even better if you took it off.'

'Men!' exclaimed Emma, turning towards Rachel.

'Yes, good aren't they?' said Rachel, her eyes twinkling.

'I might have expected some such remark from you,' said Emma. 'You were no help at all today. In fact, you were a continual embarrassment. We were in town two hours and most of that time you spent trailing behind me, flirting with every young man we came across. It pains me to say it, Rachel, but I am rapidly coming to the conclusion that you are a lady no longer.'

'Well, at least I'm a woman, which is more than can be said for you,' retorted Rachel.

'And what exactly do you mean by that?' demanded Emma.

'I know that the sexual act before marriage is disapproved of, but I never yet heard of a so-called woman who disapproved of it *after* marriage. And do not look at Richard in that fashion. He has told me nothing. All our rooms are close together, and I am neither blind, nor stupid. Whatever the circumstances of the arrangement, I think it very hard on my brother.'

'None of that is your concern,' cried Emma. 'How dare you speak so?'

'Anything which touches on my brother's happiness *is* my concern.'

'What you need is a right and proper chastisement,' cried Emma, angrily.

'And what you need is a damn good seeing to. It would do you the world of good.'

Before Emma could respond to this Rachel had flounced out of the room.

'What did she mean by that?' demanded Emma; 'but no, do not answer. It was something coarse and vulgar, I have no doubt. I do not know what has gotten into your sister of late. She seems to have thrown propriety and decency out of the window. You should be taking steps to correct her behaviour, Richard.'

'I have no authority to do so,' he said.

'No authority to do so? You can say that as both brother and guardian?'

'Emma, listen to me. Three years ago, on her fifteenth birthday, she became of a marriageable age, and could have eloped at any time since then with some suitor, had she a mind to. In two weeks time she will be eighteen years and becomes a free agent. This authority of mine which you speak of, if authority I have, will end on that day.'

'Surely not? All of that comes on her twenty first birthday.'

'No, you are mistaken. She does not come into her inheritance until she is twenty one, but in all other respects it is as I say.'

'But she lives under your roof, does she not? You are due something for that, at least.'

'So, what would you have me do? Throw her out onto the street?

But you are a fine one to speak of authority. You live under the selfsame roof but I command very little authority over you. As long as Rachel is with us we can exert a moderating influence, an influence which will not be enhanced by confrontations of the like of which I've just witnessed.'

'I blame you for all of this,' said Emma.

'Yes, it would be a miracle if anything untoward happened around here which you did not lay at my door.'

'She has never been the same since you effected that change in her. Tell me, what exactly did you do to her?'

'You would never believe me if I told you – not that I'm going to.'

'Well, whatever it was, do not attempt the same feat on me.'

'It would be useless to try. Above all else, the subject must be a willing participant.' He covered his eyes with a hand, and sighed, wearily. 'Oh, God, how did I get myself into this situation? It need not have been so. I had a choice. It is at times like this that I really do believe I made the wrong choice. No, no, do not come near me,' he said, as she approached him. 'If you do, you may find yourself in danger of being physically sick, and there is no receptacle handy to accommodate you.'

'Yes, I'm sorry I spoke so, even if it was the truth,' she said, softly. 'Richard, believe me when I tell you, I do not deliberately set out to hurt you.'

'If that be the case you succeed remarkably well,' he said. 'But answer me this: have you ever been in love? The truth, now.'

'No, not really. I once had a high regard for you – in the days of our courtship, and for a short while after our marriage – but true love of the kind you mean? No.'

'Well, let me tell you that unrequited love is not at all a pleasant experience; quite the reverse, in fact. But there is something worse than that. Can you imagine the feelings of someone whose love is repaid with loathing and contempt?'

'No, I cannot imagine the feelings of such a person. Can you?'

She returned his silence with a tale he would sooner not have heard.

'As you say, it is Rachel's birthday in fourteen days time. Do you remember what happened a year ago to this very day? Being so close to Rachel's forthcoming birthday, I do. You came home in the early hours of the morning in a particularly vicious mood. You were much the worse for drink, as usual, but you had also lost a small fortune at cards. You bundled Rachel and myself out of our beds and flogged us screaming in our nightclothes through the grounds. You do not remember? No? Well, I have no doubt a small incident like that could easily slip your memory.'

She watched as the tears welled up in his eyes.

'A bit late for that, what?' she said, and left him.

'This is impossible,' he said, totally dispirited.

In spite of her recent words, Emma was feeling not in the least self-righteous. She had seen these bouts of contrition on his part several times in the past, sometimes real, sometimes faked, but never lasting, although she had to admit that she had never seen it quite on this scale before. It would not last, of that she had no doubt, but did any of that *really* matter?

Her thoughts were of Vicar Sibley and his Sunday sermon of the day before. By accident or design, it had been based on The Sermon on the Mount. Picking up her bible, she turned to the relevant chapters in St. Matthew and quickly found the words and phrases she knew full well: the exhortations to love her enemies, and to pray for those who had despitefully used her. As a good Christian she knew she should take those words to heart, and act upon them. For a moment she hesitated, but only for a moment.

'This is not possible,' she told herself, and cast the book to one side.

CHAPTER 22

'So, tell me more,' said Emma, as the carriage set off on its slow progress to Richmond.

'I gave you most of the details a few days ago. There is not a lot to add to that,' he said.

'Except to enlighten me as to how you propose to carry out this prodigious feat of healing you have in mind. For myself, irrespective of what you have to say, I believe this entire venture will prove to be a farcical waste of time.'

'You lack faith, my dear Emma, that is your trouble. Did you not know that it can move mountains?'

'Faith? You mean we are to pray for this miracle? Perhaps we should have brought Mr Sibley along to assist us,' she said, mockingly.

'I speak of a different kind of faith – a faith based on certainty and not on a mixture of creed and hope. As for prayer, the Christian believer would do better to order his God about in the confident expectation that his orders will be obeyed.'

'Listening to you, I am glad the good vicar is *not* with us. He would be more than a little shocked by your words.'

'I have no doubt of it,' he said, laughing, 'but I have scriptural authority for saying what I do: St. Mark's Gospel, chapter 11, if my memory serves me right – 'Whatsoever you ask for in prayer, believe that you receive it, and you will.' '

'That is meant to refer to spiritual matters.'

'Really? Who says so?'

'Why, The Church, of course.'

'I see. Redefining the dictionary definition of 'whatsoever', are we?'

'Better that than passing yourself off as a student of the Scriptures. I should have thought most of the sentiments expressed there were quite foreign to your nature.'

'Can we not declare a truce for the next few days?' he said, refusing to rise to the bait. 'We have a difficult enough task ahead of us as it is without spending time sniping at each other.'

'Very well, I shall do my best not to dent your own peculiar kind of faith.'

'You will never do that; but faith is not the only weapon which we take with us on this little enterprise of ours. Take a look at this.'

With these words, he handed her the plastic card with its encapsulated tablets, brought with him from his own time.

'What a strange object! I cannot make it out,' she exclaimed, turning it over and over in her hands. 'It looks like a piece of thick, lumpy, silver paper, but it does not *feel* like paper. What on earth is it, and how can it possibly be of help?'

'Buried beneath the surface are six small pills, which will effect a cure in the boy and promote the healing of the girl.'

'If you say so,' she said, shaking her head in disbelief. She handed the object back to him. 'How did you come by it?'

'It's a long story,' he said.

'No matter. We have a long journey ahead of us.'

Thus encouraged, he began his tale.

'Ten years ago, when I was little more than a boy, I served for two years aboard a small cargo vessel, plying a regular two way trade between Plymouth and The Azores. Now, a life at sea may sound a fine thing, but there is little enough to do much of the time, and boredom and tediousness are constant problems for the mariner. On one especially wearisome voyage, seven days out from Plymouth, we found ourselves becalmed for days on end. To relieve the monotony, the Captain and I took to gambling in his cabin. One particular evening, I had an extraordinary run of good luck, so much so that at the end of it I had reduced my opponent to his undergarments and wooden leg – everything he had of value had passed into my possession. So there we sat, he cursing his ill-luck, and I viewing him in his state of undress and wishing my adversary had been born a lady with a certain something still to wager.'

'I do not believe a word of this,' she said, 'but go on with your silly story.'

'Well, it was then he produced this card of tablets you see here – a sovereign remedy for tuberc -, for consumption, he swore to me. Apparently, he had picked it up on his wanderings years before from some wise, old lama – one of those Tibetan priest fellows, you understand, not that South American animal that spits. We gambled for it, my luck held, and it came into my possession.'

'It is a wondrous tale,' she said, gravely.

'Yes, but that is not the half of it. I retired to bed that night and when I awoke the following morning I found that my companion of the previous evening had taken to the long-boat and fled. He had decided to cut his losses by absconding with anything he could lay his hands on, including all of my winnings. Luckily, I had placed the tablets under my pillow before turning in for the night, but he had left me little else of value, for neither the vessel nor cargo were his to part with. The most amazing thing of all was that he had raided my wardrobe while I slept and stolen, amongst other things, all my left shoes and boots.'

'But that is not so strange. You said he had only the one leg.'

'Yes, the right one.'

'Then, it was no wonder you beat him at cards. So, what did you do?'

He shrugged. 'Well, what can a man with two sound legs do with an assortment of one-legged footwear?'

'I did not mean that, as well you know,' she said, smiling.

'Ah! I see. Well, he had left a skeleton crew aboard but, of course, being long dead they were no use at all. No, I was left to sail the vessel single-handed, and all went well for two days when I was suddenly attacked by a giant squid. Oh, my dear, I cannot begin to describe to you the full horror of that encounter: the dozen tentacles coiled around the gunwhale and reaching out to me; the eyes, as big as saucers, glaring at me; the parrot-like beak poised open to devour me. Seizing an axe, I began to hack frantically at the beast's tentacles, but though I severed three, or four, another half-dozen still bore down on me.'

He broke off to study the amused face of his listener.

'You may smile,' he said, shaking his head, 'but to me, a mere lad of sixteen years, the whole voyage was proving to be nightmare.'

'So, what happened next?'

'Why, then I woke up. I said it was a nightmare; but the strange thing was that, safe home in bed, I found underneath my pillow the next morning the same healing pills which I won in my dream, and which I still possess.'

He leaned forwarded, earnestly. 'So, there you have it, my dear. Now explain *that*, if you can.'

'Assuming this fantastic tale of yours is true, there are only two

283

possibilities, as I see it,' she said, frowning. 'Either, what you have there materialised out of nothing from some unreal, dream world, or......'

'Or, what?'

'Or, something very unusual happened.'

'Witty, as well as beautiful,' he said, laughing.

Reaching across to her, he picked up a strand of hair which had fallen onto her shoulders. Twirling it between thumb and forefinger, he fell silent and thoughtful.

'What is it?' she asked.

He stared at the long, golden strand.

'It is the stuff that dreams are made of,' he murmured.

After a leisurely taken lunch they had made their way to Richmond Manor, and now sat in the company of their recent correspondent.

James Traynor Dunstable, a pleasant, affable young man in his early thirties, had served his master, the 5th Duke of Marrick, for some five years, and was well capable as his private secretary of dealing with most matters which fell within his province. Now, however, he sat in a state of indecision, looking at first one and then the other of the two strangers before him. The handsome, friendly countenance of the gentleman had not escaped his notice, but it was his extraordinary female companion who really drew his eye, so much so that he was having some difficulty in concentrating on the matter in hand. With an effort, he fixed his eyes firmly on the gentleman.

'So, you are determined, Sir Richard, on a meeting with His Grace?'

'I must insist upon it, sir. I can only repeat that I am here on a delicate mission of vital importance to His Grace, the details of which must be for his ears only.'

He glanced at Emma, who, at this prearranged signal, give James Dunstable a nod of encouragement and her most winning smile.

'Very well,' he said, with a sigh. 'I shall see if His Grace will consent to see you.' He paused in the doorway, and turned to face the two visitors once more. 'Will you give me no hint concerning the purpose of this visit, which I may pass on to His Grace?'

'Tell him...... tell him I have come to make him a little poorer, but infinitely richer.'

'A little poorer, but infinitely richer? What the deuce does the fellow mean, James?'

His Grace the Duke of Marrick sat with his wife in the palatial lounge of their palatial home, he perusing, or attempting to peruse, his newspaper, she half-heartedly engaged in her embroidery. A short, stocky individual, with choleric features and a bristling moustache to match his personality, His Grace had a reputation for not suffering fools gladly. His wife, a timid, demure creature, eight years his junior, was in many respects the opposite of her husband, acting out her life of servile partner with a meek and uncomplaining acceptance. Recent family events, however, had changed the once placid and content face she was wont to show to the world into one careworn with anxiety and sorrow.

In this trying time, the Duke had no desire to meet with an uninvited visitor, especially a stranger who had all along refused to state his business in advance. He had left the matter in the hands of his secretary, or so he had thought.

'If it is a matter of business, and I fail to see how it can be anything else, I do not know why the fellow must needs drag his wife along with him,' he grumbled.

'Yes, that is a clue. The man obviously wishes to make a distinct impression upon your Grace. The lady is certainly an eye-catching asset.'

'James, you are talking nonsense. What is the matter with you today?' He put his newspaper reluctantly to one side. 'The man is persistent, if nothing else. I suppose you had best show them in.'

A moment later, James Dunstable was making the formal introductions. That done, he departed, more than a little curious as to what was about to take place but reflecting on the fact that his employer would, no doubt, enlighten him in due course.

'Once the ladies have left us, I would be grateful if you would quickly state your business, sir,' said the Duke.

'The ladies must remain,' said Forres, firmly. 'Forgive me, your Grace, but what I am about to say concerns your wife no less than it concerns you.'

'As you wish,' said the Duke, with no very good grace, 'but my wife and I are much preoccupied with family matters at present, so I would be obliged if you would come directly to the point of this visit.' This request appeared to fall on deaf ears. The Duke looked on in surprise as his gentleman visitor began to wander around the room, casually glancing at a painting here, nonchalantly picking up some antique there, and stealing an occasional look through the several windows overlooking portions of the estate. A minute into this performance, he began to speak in a flat, unemotional tone of voice.

'Consumption is a stubbornly resilient disease with a long and ignoble history. It was prevalent in the days of ancient Egypt and today, four thousand years on, we still struggle against it. It is a pitiless affliction, which strikes down without distinction kings and commoners, princes and paupers, old men and young women. At its worse, its prediliction for the young can rob a people of the flower of its next generation, while at the simplest level it blights every family it touches. A distressing disease, too, which leads to an emaciated body of little more than skin and bones, unholy sweats, a racking cough, rich in bloodsoaked sputum —— '

'You fiend! You devil! Have you come here to taunt us?' cried the Duke, his face crimson with indignation.

'You have a boy of fifteen years, your son and heir, who is in the terminal stage of the disease, with but a month, or two, to live,' said Forres, completely ignoring the other's outburst. 'You also have a young daughter, who is fated to tread the same path in due course. I can cure both children. I can give you back your hopes for the future, but there will be a price to pay. The boy's price is £20,000, half now and the remainder in six year's time when he comes of age. The girl I shall cure for nothing, out of the goodness of my heart, you understand.'

So that was it! It was all a sordid device to extract money by deception.

'You fraud! You charlatan! You scoundrel!' cried the Duke, rapidly loosing what little self-control he had left. 'Over the past year, the best physicians in the country, the most gifted men in their field, have treated with my son and now conclude there is nothing more to be done, yet you have the effrontery to claim pre-eminence over them.

You are a blackguard, sir, unworthy of your title, and if you do not leave this instant I shall call the servants and have you evicted.'

'So be it, your Grace,' said Forres, moving towards the door, and motioning Emma to follow him. He bowed politely to the lady of the house, who had risen to her feet, white-faced and trembling. 'I am sorry, my lady, that your husband has seen fit to seal your son's death warrant. I would not have had it so.' This said, he turned to face the Duke, who stood ten paces away with fists clenched in a barely suppressed rage. 'The greatest kindness you can now show your son would be to suffocate the lad while he sleeps,' he said. 'Believe me, it will be worth your trouble.'

The last vestige of self-control now fled the Duke, and he strode towards his tormentor in a boiling rage. In an instant, his wife had flung herself down at his feet, weeping and imploring, and he was forced to complete his short journey dragging her along in his wake. It only came later to the man how ludicrous he must have looked, stumbling forward in this fashion.

The blow when it came was a stunning one and Richard Forres reeled back into Emma's arms with the impact of it. She now stood holding him up, wide-eyed and rooted to the spot, and for an instant of time a stranger frozen tapestry of four actors in life's drama it would be difficult to conceive of.

For all his faults, His Grace The Duke of Marrick was at heart a kind man. With the dawning awareness of his wife's desperation there came concern and compassion.

She wanted above all else for their strange visitor and his beautiful companion to be allowed to stay and fulfil the promise made. How exactly this could be done did not trouble her, nor did she wish to analyse the whys and wherefores. All she knew was that after months' of resignation and despair there was now renewed hope, vague, uncertain, improbable perhaps, but hope all the same, where once there had been none.

The Duke sank to his knees beside his wife with words of sympathy and comfort, and down, too, went Richard Forres, speaking low and fast.

'Your Grace, give me but three days and I shall have done what I promise. On the fourth day have someone expert in this disease call and examine your son. Bring whomsoever you wish. I leave that entirely to you. If he does not conclude that your son is sound and whole you will owe me nothing –- *nothing*, you understand? Really, your Grace, what have you to lose? All I ask is accommodation for my wife and myself for four nights, so we are readily to hand.'

Lifting his head, the Duke looked long and hard into the eyes of the speaker, before shifting his gaze to embrace his wife's beseeching face. Finally, he glanced upward at the young woman who had come forward to join them, and received the same winning smile and nod of encouragement as his secretary before him.

'You may have your three days,' he said, at last, 'but I swear, if you have deceived me in this matter I shall see you horse-whipped from the estate.'

'There will be no occasion for that, I assure you,' said Forres.

Then came words at one and the same time strange and yet vaguely familiar to the Duke.

'Only have faith and believe, and all things are possible.'

'Who *are* you, sir?,' was his whispered, faltering question.

'Who am I? Why, your Grace, I am the man who moves mountains,' came the quiet, confident response.

Emma looked around in dismay at the bedroom allocated to the two of them.

'We have only the one room with the one bed,' she protested.

'So? It is a large enough room, beautifully fitted out, and the bed is enormous,' he answered.

'We should each have a room,' she said. 'Why do we not have twin rooms?'

'I imagine whoever arranged matters believed a young married couple such as ourselves would welcome each other's company through the night. Does it matter so very much?'

'Of course it matters. Am I expected to share my bed with you?'

He flopped heavily down onto the edge of the bed and viewed her through weary eyes.

'Do not distress yourself, my dear,' he said. 'My promise still holds good.'

'Go and arrange matters differently.'

'Not I. The present arrangement suits me, and as non-paying guests, here on trust, we are hardly in a position to start making demands. Besides, I'm not proud of the current state of our marriage and have no wish to proclaim it abroad.'

'This is your doing,' she said.

'No, indeed it is not. If it were, we would be sharing a much smaller bed.'

With a sigh, he picked up two of the pillows and set them down at the foot of the bed, lifting and arranging the covers to accommodate them.

'We shall sleep head to toe,' he said.

'That is a ridiculous arrangement, but if it must be I suppose it must be, only do not creep up the bed during the night.'

'Yes, turned towards each other that could prove interesting.'

Delving into his suitcase, he threw an item of night apparel across to her.

'Since it bothers you so much, wear these in bed. They will offer a measure of protection over and above what a simple, open nightshift can afford, will they not? I have a second pair with me to use myself.'

'What on earth are they?' she said, holding the garments up one in each hand.

'I had them specially tailored to my own design – three pairs in silk for summer, and three pairs in thick cotton for winter. I call them pyjamas.'

'And you actually sleep in these things?' she said, laughing. 'What is wrong with a plain nightshift?'

'A drab cotton nightshift does nothing for a woman and, more to the point, it looks ridiculous on a man. That is my opinion, anyway. My silk pyjamas will keep me cool in summer, and the cotton ones will ensure I stay warm and snug in winter. I offer them to you so as to give you a measure of protection in bed. Now, do you want them, or not?'

'They are hardly my size,' she said.

'Well, turn back the cuffs and trousers a little. No one save myself is going to see you in them.'

'Why do the trousers have this large slit in the front?'

'They are *gentlemens* pyjamas. Use your imagination, Emma.'

'Oh, I see; but very convenient for you if I was to wear them.'

289

'Oh, God! do you know, I have the feeling I could well die of old age before we reach the end of this discussion. Wear them back to front, if you must. I realise you must guard against giving me an opening but I have no aspirations in that direction, I assure you.'

'That will do,' she said. She half-turned away from him and he was astonished to see her attempting, not very successfully, to hide a smile. Apart from the one incident in Pine Tree Cottage, it was the first hint of a suppressed sensuality. Suddenly, he felt a little giddy.

She put the pyjamas underneath her pillow before turning towards him.

'If I had my way you would sleep on the floor tonight,' she said.

'And if I had my way you would scarcely sleep at all,' he replied.

'Yes, I know,' she said. 'I am only too sensible of all you would like to do to me.'

'If that be true, let me congratulate you on your powers of imagination. But I cannot believe it. You have yet to see my list.'

'List? What list?'

'Oh! it is nothing really. It is just a little list, well, not so little to be honest, of – how shall I put it? – of bedtime pursuits we can indulge in once we are fully reconciled to each other.'

'Am I hearing you correctly?' she said, outraged. 'You have compiled a list of...... of things you would like to do to me?'

'It occupies some of my leisure moments in a pleasant fashion. I keep adding to the list as novel ideas come to me. Anyway, it is not a list of things I would like to do to you, but, rather, things I would like us to do together. In point of fact, you take the more active role in much of it.'

'Do I, indeed?' she said, indignantly. 'Well, my advice is that you tear up your scribblings, much good they will ever do you. That aspect of our married life is over.'

'Oh, I think not. One day, you will come to me and release me from my promise made to you. One day, you will ask to study my little list, and then...... ' He moved close to her. Reaching out a hand, he traced the outline of her lips with a fingertip. 'And I on honeydew shall feed.' He dropped his hand to lightly touch her breasts. 'And drink the milk of paradise – Coleridge, 'Kubla Khan', a loose quotation.'

She brushed his hand away, and took a step backward.

'Do you imagine, husband or no husband, that I could ever willingly give myself to a man responsible for the deaths of my mother and my brother?'

Instantly deflated, he left her, to gaze, unseeing, out of the bedroom window.

'Well?' she said, after a moment's silence. 'Nothing to say in your own defence? My! My! and you with such fine words at your command.'

Having taken on the responsibility for the sins of Henry Forres, it seemed as if he would have to defend, however reluctantly, that gentleman.

'Your mother died of heart failure after a long illness. Everyone knows that,' he said, quietly.

'My mother died a good ten years before her time, and in abject misery at my own wretched state as your wife, but, in truth, I grieve more for poor Robert. Mother's life was, perhaps, nearing its natural end, but Robert had a lifetime ahead of him with everything to live for.'

'You *know* the coroner's court brought in a verdict of misadventure. I did not mean to injure Robert. Emma, it was an accident.'

In her heart she knew he spoke the truth, but unwilling to admit it, even to herself, she contrived to change the subject somewhat.

She pushed high the sleeves of her dress to reveal a whole series of old scars and fading blemishes.

'And I suppose these were accidents, too?' she asked, her voice heavy with sarcasm. She indicated a few of them in a matter-of-fact way. 'Burns, scaldings, and, oh! yes, puncture wounds done with your favourite cravat pin – a varied assortment of amusements, made as the fancy took you.'

Richard Forres could only stare in disbelief at what he was being shown. Vicar Sibley had spoken of beatings, but nothing more, and the revelation left him speechless. As he stood there, silent and distraught, there came upon him an almost overwhelming desire to reveal everything, to deny responsibility for these monstrous acts of cruelty and so absolve himself from guilt. To do that, however, would be to acknowledge he had no claim on her, or on Rachel, or on Grange Hall and its estate, and even on the very clothes he stood up in. He would be putting himself utterly in her hands with no certainty of what her reaction would be, and if all of that was not enough, how could he even begin to explain in terms meaningful to her the disappearance from the face of the earth of her husband?

In view of all she had said, she now proceeded to do what was to him an amazing thing. Pouring water into a bowl, she made him sit down beside her. Tilting his face towards her, she began to attend to his damaged cheek.

'I wonder you are able to bear my company for a single moment, let alone do what you are doing now,' he said.

'I am your wife and, as our good vicar is so fond of reminding me, I married you for better, or for worse – till death do us part, and all that.'

'I still wonder at your forebearance.'

'I wonder at it myself at times, but we struck a bargain you and I a short while back. You have honoured your part of it, and I shall do likewise. You have my willing company, but I never promised you a true affection. How could I in view of all that has gone before? So you see, you must not say the kind of things you were saying a moment ago.'

'Do they offend you?'

'They disturb me. Coming from you, I do not know how to deal with such sentiments.'

'Well, it would seem that all my past sins are coming home to roost,' he said, after an uncomfortable moment of silence. 'In the past few weeks I have been knifed, bitten, spat upon, damn-near killed with a warming pan, robbed and very nearly murdered, and now assaulted–

oh! yes, I nearly forgot: attacked by a South American parrot, for good measure.'

'An African parrot,' she corrected him. 'Yes, I heard about that.' She finished her work of healing before indicating his bruised and swollen cheek. 'But this latest injury you brought upon yourself. Did you have to antagonise the Duke so? I thought for a moment he was going to kill you.'

'I had been forewarned about the owner of this place and realised early on that a straightforward proposal on my part would have been dismissed out of hand. His lady wife was the key, I knew. I had to involve her in order to make any kind of impression on him.'

'That you did in the end, and he made a fairly good impression on you in return,' she said, gently touching his swelling bruise. 'I only hope you can fulfil your extravagant promises. How are you to proceed? You seem to set great store by those pills of yours, but will they really work? And if they are so wonderful, why has no one ever patented them?'

Ignoring the last of her questions, as ignore it he must, he outlined his plans.

'We have six of those pills to cure the boy. Four would probably do the trick, five certainly will. In effect, the sixth pill is superfluous. It is extra insurance, if I may put it that way, but hardly necessary. I shall take possession of that one, which will help matters with the girl. I shall attend to her, while you treat with the boy.'

'*Me?* I am to deal with the boy? Are you serious?'

'Emma, it is simplicity itself. All you have to do is ensure he has a pill morning and evening for the next two and a half days, starting tomorrow morning. Nothing else is required of you save to watch the lad's progress and see to his needs. His mother will assist you in that.

'I shall give my one pill to the girl tomorrow, after which I shall have to rely on my own powers. She will have to be confined to her room for three days, which will not go down well, I have no doubt, but there's no help for that. It is just as well that I deal with a trusting child, and not a doubting adult, and a child who has the disease at an early stage, but it will not be an easy task for me, all the same. Yet, I have no other choice than to proceed, for I could not contemplate the cruelty of restoring the boy to health while I turn a blind eye to his sister's future suffering.'

'If the girl really does have the disease, I do not see how you can possibly cure her,' she said.

'I shall do so. I *know* I shall,' he said, speaking with conviction in order to counteract her words.

'It is a hopeless task you set yourself,' she said.

'Do not say such things,' he cried, grabbing her wrist in a powerful grasp. 'No more, you hear? No more.'

'Richard, you are hurting me,' she protested.

'Forgive me. I did not mean to,' he said, releasing her. 'But you must not make me doubt. You *must not* make me doubt.'

Morning and afternoon –- pleasant and easy. Winning his young patient's confidence and trust.

Early evening –- the all-important single capsule administered.

Day Two

For the girl, a hypnotic-induced sleep. For him, a debilitating, exhausting, vital day. Using his long term memory cells as a convenient way to gain access to his subconscious self.

The family house, long ago, on a different world in a different universe...... moving through moonlit-filled rooms at the dead of night...... furniture, furnishings, pictures, viewed exactly as they were...... the cold touch of a *blank* mirror...... the sleepy pet cat stirring uneasily at the unnatural presence...... a ghostly treading of stairs...... his own bedroom, just as he remembered it...... viewing his sleeping childhood form.

A creeping numbness of limbs heralding *the* time...... self-argument, followed by total acceptance...... the two become as one...... employing the mind's eye...... the tiny shadow on the left lung – no! the *right* lung; get it right! get it right! this is important...... powerful, complex chemicals conjured up in the subject in miniscule amounts at a huge cost to himself...... an all-out assault...... die, you tuberculin bacilli, die!...... attack...... respite...... attack...... respite...... attack...... the passage of hours.

'*It taxes one more than it should.*'

'*Why am I so mediocre at this kind of thing?*'

A hard-won victory...... exhaustion, mental and physical...... the concerned look of Emma on his return to their room...... sleep before their evening meal taken in private...... some little recovery and renewal.

Day Two, Evening –- alone with Emma.

'You are in a sorry state,' she said, dabbing gently at his injured cheek. 'I believe this is getting worse, not better, and the wound on your arm has opened up again. It is a wonder you are able to cure others when you can scarce heal yourself.'

'Yes, I'm like the local builder whose house is always in need of repair,' he said. 'The man is so busy attending to other properties he has no time to deal with his own; but a few days of peace and quiet once we are back home will give me the chance to set matters right.'

'How did you fare with the girl today? With some difficulty, that much is obvious.'

'True, but I am nearly there. How did you leave the boy?'

'He is already vastly improved. Do you know, he kissed me earlier today – I mean a *proper* kiss – when I was bent over him. He claimed to be but half-awake, and said he thought I was his mother, but I believe he knew full well what he was about.'

'The little devil!' he said, laughing; 'but I cannot censure him. You must have sorely tempted him.'

'I did nothing,' she protested.

'My dear, you do not have to *do* anything, your mere presence is enough.'

She set aside the bowl and towel she still held, and looked at him steadily for a moment. Gathering up his pillows, she placed them beside her own.

'I am tired of waking to the sight of your toes peeping out at me,' she said. 'I believe I shall be quite safe tonight. You look too weary to trouble me.'

So it proved, although when she bent over him early the next morning to rouse him from his sleep, he startled her by kissing her full on the lips.

'Good morning, mother,' he murmured, in a not very convincing sleepy tone of voice.

Day Three, Morning and Afternoon.

The easier task of repair. Sealing off the area of past infection from the rest of the lung as an added precaution...... spinning the spider's web of fine adhesions...... thread upon thread – fragile; thread upon thread – firm; thread upon thread – strong...... the end of it all...... 'Alice in Wonderland' as a treat for his young patient.

CHAPTER 23

It was late in the evening of their third full day at Richmond Manor. He was undressing for bed when the door flew open and Emma burst into the room.

'Ah!, Emma, I was wondering where you had got to,' he said. 'What are the sleeping arrangements for tonight? Do you trust —- ' He broke off at the sight of her face. 'Good heavens! what is wrong?'

'This room! It is haunted,' she gasped.

'Rubbish!' he exclaimed. 'There are no such things as ghosts, well, not as people understand them. They are but another testament to the power of the mind, manifestering itself this time into deceiving —-.'

'Listen to me, just listen,' she interrupted. 'I have been speaking with Lucy – you know, that little chambermaid who services our room – and she has just informed me of the fact that this apartment of ours is most definitely haunted.'

'But that is nonsense,' he said. 'We have spent three nights here and seen, or heard, nothing out of the ordinary. You have been listening to foolish servant gossip and taken it all in. Really, Emma, I am surprised at you.'

She shook her head impatiently at these words.

'The girl gave me all the facts: names, dates, circumstances – the whole story. It seems that a hundred years ago, before the Duke's family came into possession of this place, the property was owned by a certain Squire Ebeneza Scrooge, a cruel, despotic man, who ruled with a rod of iron. One evening, in a fit of drunken rage, he savagely beat a young serving maid to death for some trifling offence. Richard, it happened in this very room. Once a year ever since, on the anniversary of the murder, she is said to come back and haunt the spot.'

'Indeed? And do we know the date of this spook's night out?'

'I do wish you would take this thing seriously. The date is well attested as September 10th.'

'Then, we have had a narrow escape,' he said, yawning. 'Today is Friday the 8th, and tonight is to be our last night here.'

'You are mistaken. Today is Friday the 9th.'

'Really? I seem to have mislaid a day somehow. Very well, then, we have had a *very* narrow escape, although......,' he paused, uncertain.

'Although what?'

'Well, I suppose if one thinks about it, at midnight tonight it *will be* September the 10th. I assume that is why little Lucy felt the need to tell you about it today of all days.'

'Oh, Lord! you are right,' she cried. 'It never occurred to me. My thoughts were all on tomorrow night.'

'No! No! It is all stuff and nonsense,' he said, airily, and resumed undressing.

'Go and arrange for another room to be put at our disposal,' she said.

'My dear girl, it is very nearly eleven o'clock. Half the household will be in bed, and the other half preparing for bed. I'm not wandering the corridors at this hour in search of a sympathetic servant willing to act on this ridiculous story. I dare say there isn't the one spare room which has been properly aired and stands ready to accommodate us. No, here we are and we shall just have to chance it.'

'What do you mean, we shall have to chance it?'

'It is just a figure of speech,' he sighed. 'Listen to me, Emma. You have me to protect you, do you not? I give you my word, no harm shall come to you tonight. In the morning, God willing, you will look back and laugh at these foolish fears. Now, what are the sleeping arrangements for tonight?'

'The same as last night if you promise not to take advantage of the situation. Do you promise to keep scrupulously to your side of the bed?'

'Yes, yes, I promise,' he sighed.

'Very well, I shall hold you to that.' She shook her head, unhappily. 'I shall be glad when this business is done and we are away from here. Do we know the name of the physician who is to examine the boy tomorrow?'

'A gentleman from Harrogate by the name of Sir John Barrow. Quite an eminent man in his field, so I am told, and well acquainted with the boy's medical history.'

'He will report favourably on the boy, will he not?'

'Certainly, he will. Both children are now perfectly sound.'

It was at this point in the conversation that at no great distance away a barn owl saw fit to shriek loudly. Emma sprang to her feet, trembling and agitated.

'What was that noise?' she asked, in a tremulous tone of voice.

'I don't know,' he said, going over to the window. 'It was probably nothing.'

'What do you mean '*nothing*'?'

'Well...... well, perhaps it was a bat.'

'A *bat*? Are you serious?'

'Oh! I'm off to bed,' he said, impatiently. 'Why not do likewise? Even by our dubious reckoning we have nothing to fear for an hour. Come to bed, and concentrate on getting to sleep before the midnight hour, after which, before you know it, it will be morning.'

She proceeded to act upon this advice with what he regarded as comic haste. Within a very short space of time she was between the sheets, separated from him by a comfortably wide margin of privacy.

For twenty minutes he listened to her tossing and turning, huffing and puffing. Finally, he spoke.

'Relax, Emma, and sleep will come naturally. You still have thirty minutes' grace.'

Ten minutes later, after a particularly heartfelt sigh on her part, he spoke again.

'Do try and compose yourself, my dear. You have only the twenty minutes left.'

'I *am* trying to compose myself,' she snapped back at him. 'And will you stop reminding me of the time? Far from easing my fears, I tell you plainly it is having the opposite effect.'

'Sorry I spoke,' he said, in an aggrieved tone of voice.

Within ten minutes he was lying very still and failing to respond to his whispered name. For her, however, sleep was proving to be an impossibility. She lay waiting, with a peculiar sinking feeling, for the faint chimes of the distant church clock to strike out midnight.

The witching hour found her still wide-awake. Events moved swiftly thereafter.

Her eyes, wide-open and staring, saw the pencil of corridor light, running the length of the bedroom door, blink abruptly out. Her ears, pricked for the slightest noise, caught the faint sound of movement in the corridor. Sitting bolt upright, she watched, petrified, as the door handle began slowly to revolve. She wanted to cry out, but found that an almost inaudible squeak was all she could muster. Paralysed with fear, the hairs on the back of her neck the only part of her in motion, she could only stare in horror as the door swung slowly open. In the now dim light of the corridor, she saw a vague, female form dressed in white. The apparition seemed to be looking directly at her. As if to confirm this, it raised its right arm and beckoned her with a finger.

For what seemed an eternity, but was in reality less than a moment, the waking nightmare continued until, at last, the door closed silently upon the unwelcome visitor.

Freedom of speech and movement returned simultaneously to her. With a shriek, she flung herself to one side, to land with a resounding thump on top of her bedfellow.

'I have seen it! It came here! It was horrible!' she babbled, above the barely articulate protests of her rudely awakened companion. 'Oh! I wish I were a million miles away from this place. Suppose it comes back?'

With a few soothing words, he attempted to calm her, but to little effect. Finally, he took her firmly in hand and made her listen to him.

'My dear Emma, you have had a nightmare, that is all. You have fallen asleep, dreamed this thing, and then woken up believing it to have been a reality. Look around you. There is nothing to be seen.'

'How could it have been a dream?' she protested. 'I have not closed my eyes in sleep for a single moment.' She indicated the bedroom door. 'Go and see if it is still out there, but do not go wandering off leaving me alone.'

Grumbling and protesting, he did as she asked.

'There is not a living soul to be seen,' he said. He took another long, hard look down the corridor, before turning back to face her. 'Emma, it's as silent as the grave out here.'

'Do not use phrases like that,' she wailed.

'Sorry; didn't think.' He grinned, sheepishly. 'I seem to be saying all the wrong things tonight. Do you want me to explore further?'

'No! No!' she cried. 'Come back to bed this instant.'

He got back into bed and began to settle himself. With a sigh, as if remembering something, he repositioned himself close to the edge of the bed.

'What are you doing?' she asked.

'Remembering my promise, and keeping my distance,' he said. 'Is that not what you want?'

'You may forget all about that,' she said, and proceeded to drag him bodily towards her. She held him in a tight embrace. 'You *promised* to protect me. You *said* no harm would come to me.'

'True,' he said. 'Very well, I shall watch over you until you fall asleep. Any ghost will have to deal with *me* first, I promise you.' He put a hand under her pyjama top, and curved it tight under her left breast. 'Good heavens! you really are frightened, are you not? Your heart is beating like a hammer.'

'I am petrified,' she admitted.

'Bodily contact is the answer – skin to skin contact, I mean.' His *free* hand began to stroke her back with long, calculated movements. 'There, is that not better?'

'It is a great comfort,' she acknowledged.

His hands now worked to their mutual, if differing, advantage. She raised no objection to what he was doing, seemingly oblivious to the liberties he was taking.

Within twenty minutes she had fallen asleep.

Tired though he was, he battled for a further hour to stay awake, not for her sake but for his own.

He soon came across an unexpected bonus. In her haste to get undressed and into bed, she had put her pyjama bottoms on in the opposite way she had intended.

'Do you think I should acquaint the Duchess of the night's events?' she asked him at breakfast the next morning.

The suggestion seemed positively to alarm him.

'No, I do not,' he said, emphatically. 'Emma, consider: we have been treated with every consideration and kindness since our first evening here. I believe it would be churlish to distress that good lady with a complaint that was none of her making and which is past remedy. In a few hours we shall be gone, with no plans to return here.' He waited anxiously for her response.

'Yes, you are right. I shall make no mention of it. For myself, I would like to thank you for not taking advantage of the situation in which I found myself last night.'

He coloured slightly, and looked away, discomforted.

'Why do you look so guilty?' she asked, in surprise. 'I invited your close intimacy so can hardly censure you for it.'

'Guilty? Do I look guilty? Yes, I suppose I am a little. I was thinking that I brought you here against your will, and the result is you have not had a particularly happy time of it. It was wrong of me to insist on you accompanying me.'

'You are mistaken, Richard. These few days spent together have been a not unpleasant experience for me. I'm glad I came. To own the truth, I have seen a soft and gentle side to your nature, which I never knew existed.' There was genuine regret in her voice as she went on: 'Oh!, why could you not always have been like this?'

'I have but the one face,' he said, softly.

'How can you say such a thing?' she exclaimed. 'Richard, that is simply untrue.'

Thinking over the events of the previous night in the silence which followed, she began to question, notwithstanding the circumstances, if she had not allowed herself to become a little too intimate, a little too free and easy, with her bed partner. Now, in the cold light of morning, she concluded that such was the case. She decided that their relationship must be restored to its former status.

'Tonight, we shall revert to our separate sleeping arrangements,' she said, firmly.

He merely nodded, and she sensed his pain and disappointment. Not for the first time, she felt a twinge of guilt, quickly followed by annoyance with herself for this irrational feeling on her part. Why should she feel guilty towards a man who had wrecked her life? Surely, if there was to be guilt it should be all on his side? She sought to justify his treatment at her hands.

'I must confess, I never believed that medication of yours would really work,' she said. 'It is a pity you cannot work the miracle of bringing the dead back to life – I am thinking of my mother and brother, you understand.'

She regretted the words almost as soon as they were out of her mouth. It was a silly, nonsensical thing to say, done for the one purpose of hurting him. Once again, he looked pained. Once again, she felt

301

guilty. She sighed, feeling trapped in a vicious circle of bitter resentment and irrational guilt.

He had that telltale look in his eyes which she was beginning to recognise as the prelude to some disconcerting little speech. He opened his mouth to respond to her words.

'Do not speak it,' she said, hurriedly.

They continued their meal in silence for a few minutes, but she decided in the end that he must have his say. She realised that she would have to learn to deal with his strange, new ability to conjure up telling phrases and unsettling sentiments.

'I'm sorry,' she said. 'What is it you wanted to say?'

'Only that you thanked me earlier, and I would like to thank you in return.'

'Thank me for what?'

'For honouring your side of our agreement, and perhaps a little more; for giving at least the impression that you care what happens to me; for being with me; for simply being who you are.' He paused, trying in vain to catch her averted eyes. 'You know, Emma, there is no real merit in showing consideration to a loved one. No, real merit is earned by treating someone whom you regard as quite the opposite in a kindly fashion. But you do not need me to tell you this – your very presence here with me is proof of that.'

Once again, with a few sentences, he had left her less than certain with regard to her feelings towards him.

'Do not make me out to be a saint,' she said. 'Heaven knows, I have failings in plenty. I am only doing my duty to you as your wife, and not all of those duties at that.'

'Doing what you do because you have to, or because you want to?'

'More tea?' she said, waving the milk-jug before him.

It was at best a noncommittal answer. It was a far cry from being a statement of affection, still less of love, but neither was it a contemptuous, outright rejection. He felt that after one short week it was a marvellous achievement on his part. He began to hum a little tune, which drew a glance of curiosity from her.

'Say when,' she said, milkjug poised in hand.

He did not so much as glance at his teacup.

'Oh, I judged a month. I shall stick to that,' he said.

She shook her head and made the decision for him.

'Foolish person,' she said, not unkindly.

A very perplexed physician Barrow had taken his leave an hour previous, at about the same time as the arrival of the carriage from Grange Hall. This now stood waiting to take Richard and Emma back home.

Richard was busy with the Duke, settling financial matters, while Emma was taking a last walk in the grounds of the estate in the company of the Duchess.

'It was quite an effort for my husband to say nothing of the events of the past few days but your husband was insistent on that point,' said the Duchess. 'Poor Sir John has left here totally bemused.'

'Yes, I understand from my husband that he has performed two cures he is not likely to be able to repeat, hence the need for secrecy,' Emma replied. 'If this business were to become public knowledge it could well end with a queue of very sick people at our door, whom my husband would have to cruelly disappoint.'

'Yes, I see that, and you have the Duke's and my own pledge of silence on that score.' She paused in thought, a hint of past anxieties returning to her face. 'Forgive my asking, but there is no danger of this sickness returning at some future date, is there? Your husband says not, but……'

'If Richard says not, you may be certain it is as he says,' said Emma, reassuringly.

'But this business of deferring for six years half of your husband's fee at his own insistence? What does it signify?'

'Richard believes that to be a fair and equitable arrangement to both parties but, I assure you, he has every expectation of collecting the balance in the course of time.'

'That is well,' said the Duchess, with a sigh of contentment.

A moment later, she began to weep quietly, releasing the pent-up emotion of past weeks.

'I bless the day you and your husband crossed our threshold,' she sobbed. After a moment, she composed herself, and the two of them resumed their walk.

'Your husband is a remarkable man, my dear Emma,' she said. 'You must love him very dearly.'

Emma was forced into a faltering reply.

'Oh!...... yes...... yes, of course.'

'He has a natural goodness, and I never saw such gentle compassion in any man. Caroline fair idolises him, and I fancy there will be tears from that young lady at the moment of their parting. Did you know, he has been entertaining her with a charming tale of a young girl by the name of Alice, who enters into a magical world of talking playing cards, near-human animals, and the like.'

'It all sounds a little silly to me,' said Emma, doubtfully.

'Well, in a way it is, of course, but it is a funny and delightful story, all the same, and just the kind of weird and amusing adventure story which children love to hear. But you have no children of your own, is that not so?'

'Yes, that is true,' acknowledged Emma.

'And are you long married?'

'Two years. Yes, very nearly two years.'

'Two unforgettable years for you, I dare say?'

'Unforgettable? Yes, that is the word,' said Emma, sadly.

She stood with an outstretched arm and clenched hand, and laughingly addressed her friend.

'Close your eyes,' she said.

Her fellow-chambermaid give the speaker an expressive look.

'Lucy Havers, what foolishness is this? I have duties to attend to, and so do you.'

'Close your eyes,' Lucy insisted.

With a sigh, friend Emily stopped what she was doing, and did as she was asked.

There came a brief silence.

'Now, you may open them.'

Emily Adams stared in amazement at the shiny gold coin which lay glinting in Lucy's open palm.

'Goodness me, how did you come by that?' she exclaimed. Gently, almost reverently, she took up the guinea piece. The occasional copper coin was all that she normally handled, although, rarely, the odd silver sixpence, or shilling, came her way, and once, on the death of her grandmother, she had come into the inheritance of a huge five shilling piece, but not once in her twenty three years had she experienced the touch and feel of a gold coin of the realm.

'Is it not heavy for its size?' she whispered. 'Is it yours?'

'Of course it's mine. Sir Richard Forres gave it me for services rendered.'

'For services rendered? Lucy, you don't mean......?'

'No, nothing like that,' said Lucy, laughing, 'although, to be honest, that gentleman would have no need of a gold coin for me to oblige him in that respect. Oh! Emily, is he not the most handsome man you ever saw?'

Emily could not help but blush at these words. Lucy had the disconcerting habit of saying exactly what was in her mind, a trait which embarrassed her friend all-too often.

Lucy had taken back the coin and for the tenth time that day was studying its image and inscription. After a moment's scrutiny, she pocketed it safely away and addressed her friend again.

'I know I can confide in you, so I shall let you into the secret of how I came by it. Our gentleman guest came to me after dinner yesterday evening with a proposition: frighten his wife with a tale of their room being haunted, and there was a guinea piece in it for me.'

'But there are no ghosts here at the Manor,' Emily protested.

'*I* know that. I'm only telling you what he asked me to do. He supplied all the details of a made up tale, a tale which I was to pass on as convincingly as possible to his wife.'

'Which you did?'

'Yes, but there is more. At the stroke of midnight, as we had arranged, I went along to their room and acted out the part. He told me that he would see to it that his wife would be awake to witness my visitation.'

'But why, for goodness sake, would he wish to alarm his wife in so cruel a fashion?'

'The very question I put to him. He explained that whereas he was a firm believer in the supernatural, Lady Forres was a confirmed sceptic. Apparently, they had a heated discussion on the subject the evening before and he had decided to pay her back for ridiculing his beliefs.'

'I must say, it sounds a very unlikely motive. Who in their right mind would wish to go to such lengths to score a hollow debating point?'

'I can only tell you what he told me. What other reason could he have had?'

'I'm sure I cannot guess,' said Emily. She shook her head in disapproval. 'Lucy, I can scarce believe what you are telling me. I have a high opinion of that young gentleman, but it seems I must need revise it downwards. Poor Lady Forres. She must have been frightened out of her wits.'

Lucy shifted uncomfortably from one foot to the other at these words. What had seemed like a harmless, amusing escapade the night before was appearing in a less creditable light the day after. The words of her friend served only to add to her guilt, which had been growing of its own accord all morning.

'The lady appeared perfectly composed at breakfast,' she said, defensively.

'No thanks to you two,' retorted Emily. 'You do realise, don't you, that if the Duke were to learn of any of this you would find yourself within the hour outside the Manor gates with your bags packed?'

Lucy scowled unhappily. She was beginning to wish she had kept the whole business secret to herself.

'I was merely obliging one of the master's guests in a matter relating to his lady wife. I did not undertake the prank for my own amusement. Anyway, Sir Richard said that if any of this came to the master's ears he would smooth things over and see I did not suffer by it.'

The striking chimes of the nearby landing clock brought an abrupt, if temporary, end to the conversation.

'Heavens! The time!' exclaimed Emily, throwing a feather duster across to her friend.

In spite of her words, Emily resumed her work with her thoughts very much elsewhere. Their recently departed guests had made a distinctly favourable impression on her. The unexpected visit had come like a breath of fresh air, the strikingly handsome young couple so very different from the staid and pompous guests who normally frequented the Manor. The gentleman's conduct, in particular, had been effortlessly considerate to one and all, as if that was the most natural thing in the world to him, and had carried with it not a hint of condescension. For the first time in she knew not how long, she felt as if she had been treated not as some unthinking asset of the Duke's estate, but as a human being with feelings and emotions. Moreover, if only half the rumours concerning the Duke's young son, currently sweeping through the Manor, were to be believed, the entire estate owned an immense debt of gratitude to the man responsible for the rumours. In view of all this, notwithstanding Lucy's tale, she felt very loathe to revise her high opinion of the gentleman in question. Within ten minutes of resuming work, she stopped what she was doing, and addressed her friend.

'Lucy, it's no good. I cannot think ill of our gentleman visitor. We are used to dealing with the Duke and his contemporaries, but that young man is from a different generation, and it shows in his manner. I am wondering if this tale of yours is but evidence of some playful, foolish pleasantry between that young couple. Their affection for one another is plain for anyone to see.'

This observation found instant acceptance.

'Emily, I'm sure you're right,' said Lucy.

Emily, her mind now quite made up on the subject, resumed her chores with gusto, but Lucy wandered listlessly over to the window, where she stood looking wistfully out into the distance.

'Emily, what would I not give to be Lady Forres for a week – for a mere twenty four hours, come to that? I would gladly give up my gold guinea, and fifty more if I had them, to make it so.' She sighed. 'I only hope his lady wife appreciates her good fortune.'

'I'm sure she does, Lucy. I'm sure she does,' said Emily

Still a little weary from his exertions of the previous four days, he had fallen asleep twenty minutes into their journey home but a conversation of sorts had preceded this.

'Ten thousand pounds!' exclaimed Emma. 'It will more than cancel out your debts at a stroke.'

'Not so,' he said. 'Half the sum is yours, you see, but my five thousand pounds will pay off more than half of what is due, and I have plans which, hopefully, will settle the balance in due course.'

'Five thousand pounds is to be mine?' said Emma. 'No, you cannot mean that.'

'Oh, but I do. What is mine is yours, and vice-versa, of course. That is how things should be between husband and wife, but I would hope that you use most of your share in settling a commission on your brother. That will leave precious little left over for your own pocket, I'm afraid.'

'I do not have such a pocket,' she said. 'I never did.'

'Well, you have one now,' he said, smiling.

'Ah! I see. You seek to *buy* my affection. Well, if that be so you are wasting both your time and money.'

'Yes, I thought you might say that. It seems I cannot do right for doing wrong in your eyes, but I'll wager you will accept your share, notwithstanding. You do want to help your brother, don't you?'

'Of course I want to help him, but I'm not too happy about this business of what's yours is mine. Am I to be held personally responsible in future for some of your gambling debts?'

'It is six weeks since I gambled anything at all.'

'Yes, so Rachel informs me. Well, that will not last. She also tells me that you have stayed sober for a similar period of time. That *certainly* will not last. A leopard cannot change its spots. I understand your restraint. It is done to act out the part of penitent husband, but there is one change in your lifestyle I do not understand, and one I have been meaning to ask you about. Why this sudden aversion to meat, for goodness sake?'

In the age in which he now lived his true answer would make no sense to her, he realised that. He would have to come up with some white lie, however implausible.

'Yes...... well, I believe red meat is not good for a person. It has certainly started to disagree with my digestive system.'

'I always know when you are lying,' she said, shaking her head. 'I can read it plain in your eyes.'

'Really? A walking lie detector. Now, there's a novelty. Always, you say?'

'Always,' she said.

'Very well, let me test you out. I shall come out with some statement, and you shall tell me if I speak the truth. Ready? Looking full into my eyes are you?'

She walked unsuspecting into the trap he had set.

'I'm ready,' she said.

'So, here goes. I love you Emma Forres.'

She had not expected this, and was sorely tempted to say that what he had said was a plain untruth, but gazing into his eyes she found, in all conscience, that she could not make such a claim. He appeared for all the world to be sincere.

She averted her eyes, and found herself looking at the floor.

'Maybe 'always' was overstating the case,' she said.

'Ah! is that it?' he said. 'Do you know, for a moment there I thought you were afraid of the truth.'

'I'm not afraid of the truth. Are you, I wonder? Tell me truly: when I provoke you, and I admit I deliberately set out to do so at times, do you ever get the urge to hurt, or injure me?'

'Oh, there are times when I would like to do far worse than that,' he said. 'There are times when I get this almost irresistible urge to eat you.'

She watched as he closed a pair of sleepy eyes.

'I must remember to put that down on my list,' he murmured.

Together with Rachel, they sat together after their evening meal before a blazing lounge fire. He had given an account of their stay at Richmond Manor to Rachel, and with the benefit of her own remarkable experience at the hands of her brother she did not doubt his explanation for all that had been accomplished. Emma, however, was more sceptical.

'It is difficult to credit the power of the mind to the extent you claim,' she said. 'I can scarcely doubt that you effected a remarkable cure in the boy since I was party to it, but I am sceptical with regard to the girl. She appeared all along well-enough to me. As for the boy, that remarkable medication of yours is, in itself, sufficient explanation for your success. You say, amongst other things, that a believing mind is able to influence physical objects. Very well, let us put that to the test. Stop yonder timepiece and I shall be convinced.' Here, she indicated a handsome bracket-clock perched atop the mantelpiece.

Richard was no expert practitioner in the difficult and unpredictable art of psychokinesis. The expenditure of a vast amount of mental energy in an otherwise simple physical task of moving an object from 'A' to 'B' in order to perform a mere parlour trick had never claimed his interest. He had to smile to himself, however, at Emma's challenge, for the stoppage of a small mechanical clock was one of the easiest of all such exercises.

'Very well, my dear, I accept the challenge,' he said, 'but let us add a little extra interest with a wager between the two of us: five guineas to you if I fail; a single kiss for me if I succeed. What say you?'

'You offer poor odds,' said Emma, 'but I shall accept, if only to teach you a lesson.'

'I shall act as judge, since I am impartial in the matter,' cried Rachel. 'Do it, Richard! Do it!'

Within a moment of fixing his eyes on the object in question, he was smiling and relaxed once more. 'It is done,' he said. 'The clock is still, is it not?'

Rachel approached the timepiece and put an ear to it. 'It is true,' she said, addressing Emma.

'No, it cannot be,' said Emma. 'Let us leave it a little while and observe the minute hand.'

'It is stopped,' said Rachel, emphatically, after the passage of a further few minutes. 'Emma, you can see plainly it is stopped.'

'I believe the victory is mine,' said Richard.

'Forfeit! Forfeit!' cried Rachel in delight.

Emma went up to the victor with a good grace and presented her cheek to him, but before she was aware of what was happening he had clamped a hand either side of her head and was extracting a breathtaking payment. She struggled in vain to free herself, finally lifting up her eyes to the heavens in a frantic, desperate appeal.

'Give it to her,' urged Rachel.

Emma's lips parted slightly in an involuntary gasp of surprise at Rachel's words. Straightaway, she felt a strange tongue enter her mouth and begin to explore its inner recesses. With a supreme effort, she succeeded in breaking free, to stand breathless and trembling before him.

'You...... you...... you animal!' she cried. 'I was never kissed like that in all my life.' She turned furiously on Rachel. 'And you, young lady. Your vulgarity astonishes me.' With these words, she stormed out of the room.

Laughing to himself, Richard picked up a newspaper. Sitting himself down, he began to idly scan its pages. He was soon disturbed by Rachel, peeping over the top and peering down at him.

'What did you do to her?' she whispered.

'I merely kissed her. I was only extracting my reward.'

'No, you did more than that. Tell me exactly what you did.'

He made no reply, which brought forth an angry remark: 'I'm not a child, you know, Richard.'

With a sigh, he put his newspaper to one side.

'I put my tongue in her mouth,' he confessed.

A hand flew to her mouth in horror. 'Oh! poor Emma. Oh! how beastly for her.'

'Thank you, Rachel,' he said, dryly. 'We *are* supposed to be man and wife, you know.'

'Yes, but even so.'

He looked at her, frowning all the while. There were times, he reflected, when he was apt to get a little tired of the strict moral code of the period, and now was just such an occasion.

'Let me tell you something, Rachel,' he said. 'Nothing a husband and wife may do together to show their love for each other is sinful, or immoral. Let no one tell you differently.'

'Nothing? Nothing at all?' she asked, wide-eyed with surprise at this statement.

He went over to the lounge clock, reset the time, and shook it gently until it ticked back to life. For the time being at least he was done with parlour tricks. Glancing down at Rachel, he saw that she had reseated herself, and now sat deep in thought, a heaving breast and a pensive look in her eyes mute testimony to some inner turmoil.

'Rachel?' he asked, uncertainly.

She turned her eyes towards him. 'I wish I were married,' she said, huskily.

His look of surprise at these unexpected words provoked another irritated response: 'I keep telling you, brother, I'm not a child. I do wish you would stop treating me as one.'

'Yes, of course. Forgive me.' He indicated the clock before them, now ticking away steadily and rhythmically. 'Eleven o'clock,' he said. 'Time for peepy-byes.'

He had slipped between the bedsheets and was about to blow out the candle when Emma, dressed only in a nightgown and shawl, made a surprise appearance.

Saying not a word, she seated herself on the edge of his bed and began to study him intently. As once before, at York, this silent scrutiny began to unnerve him. With each passing second he felt a growing uneasiness.

'It is my husband I am looking at?' she said, at length.

'What a question,' he said, forcing a laugh, and running a finger down the well-known small scar on his cheek.

She nodded in acknowledgement, but continued to voice her doubts.

'How is it possible to live with a man for two years and at the end of that time still not know for certain his true nature? Still not know what he is going to say, or do, from one moment to the next? Still not know the depth of his talents? Still not know what tomorrow will bring?'

'You might say the same of Rachel,' he suggested.

'Indeed, I might. In some respects, the change in her is even more startling. She doesn't even *look* the same. I worry about that girl, though. She has swung from one extreme to the other. I see trouble ahead, Richard, mark my words.'

'But you would not wish to see either of us as we once were, surely?'

'No, of course not, but the two of you constantly bewilder me. It is as if I have returned home to find myself in the company of two complete strangers.'

'I apologise for what took place earlier this evening,' he said, anxious to change the subject.

'I overreacted, perhaps, but you took me completely by surprise. You made me bite my tongue, you know,' she said, accusingly. She showed it to him as evidence, squinting to view it for herself.

He gazed at the pert and pretty picture before him and swallowed hard.

312

'Kiss it better?' he asked, hopefully.

'To do that, you must first mend a broken heart,' she said. 'Tell me, is this talent for healing you suddenly seem to have acquired up to that?'

He blew out the candle, and his voice came to her out of the darkness.

'Oh, broken hearts are my speciality,' he said, 'and you shall be a witness to it.'

CHAPTER 24

Four days after returning from Richmond Manor, Richard Forres came close to losing Emma.

She had come to him after breakfast with a request.

'I believe you know that my dear friend Colonel Palmer has had a cancerous growth these three months past,' she said.

'Yes,' he answered, 'but I'm not acquainted with the details.'

'He took ill a little over three months ago and the disease has progressed steadily since then. A week ago he took a sudden turn for the worse, and is not expected to last beyond two or three weeks. Nothing can be done. It is a hopeless case. I called on Elizabeth yesterday and was shocked by his appearance after a mere ten days' absence on my part. He suffers a great deal and my heart goes out to him. I come with a request from him. He wishes to make his peace with the world and is anxious to be reconciled to you above all men. Out of regard for me, I know he has been a bitter enemy of yours these past eighteen months, and I shall not condemn you if you refuse to see him, but will you not do so for my sake?'

'Yes, of course,' he said. 'I shall be with him within the hour. Are you to come, too?'

'I think it best if you see him alone.'

'Yes, I understand,' he said. 'I shall go directly.'

'There is one thing more I would wish you to do,' she said. 'He is in great pain and has made plain his wish to die sooner rather than later, even to the extent of refusing all nourishment. In spite of his suffering, I cannot condone that. God, alone, must decide the day and the hour when He takes my dear friend to Himself. Will you not use your powers of persuasion to get him to acknowledge that fact and act accordingly?'

'No, I will not,' he said. 'I believe he has every right to make that decision for himself. No, Emma, no arguments, please! I shall go and make my peace with Colonel Palmer but I will not oblige you in this other matter.'

He entered into the sickroom to find the patient sleeping fitfully, and with Doctor Hunter in attendance. Pulling the doctor to one side, he began a whispered conversation.

'You are quite certain of your diagnosis?' he asked.

'Oh, yes, he is riddled with the disease. It is only a matter of time, Sir Richard.'

'And is his pain so very bad?'

'Undoubtedly. I do what I can, of course.'

'But you could do more if you had a mind to. I am told he has made his wishes very clear in that respect. Those sleeping draughts you prescribe may not be very effective in relieving pain, but a few massive overdoses would ease his passage quickly into the next world, would they not?'

Hunter scrutinised the speaker's face in silence for a brief moment before replying.

'You see no wrong in such an act?' he said, at length.

'None at all. I'm only surprised you seem to.'

'I believe I can safely trust you, Sir Richard. I see plainly you are sincere. During the past twenty years, in truly terrible situations which we have here, I have done exactly what you suggest, more times than I care to count.'

'Then, why not now?'

'Because the Colonel has made his wishes a little *too* often and a little *too* public for safety's sake. I simply dare not risk it. We are talking of a criminal act, although in a more enlightened age such an act of mercy may be viewed altogether differently. I have dropped some broad hints to Miss Elizabeth and I believe her to be sympathetic, but it is quite the opposite with regard to the mother. I said on one occasion that I would not wish to see a dog suffer as her husband does.'

'Well said, doctor. What was her response?'

'She said that a dog does not have a soul, whereas a human being does, and that soul is in God's hands, and His alone.'

'And how did you answer that?'

'I didn't. I could not.'

'You might have said that what she was saying was a statement of opinion, or a statement of religious belief if you like, but not a statement of fact.'

'I made mention of a dignified end, and she replied that dignity comes from within.'

'Oh! that old chestnut. Yes, dignity *does* come from within – it comes from within the person who is suffering and only he, or she, can be the judge of what is dignified and what is not. I have to confess it infuriates me. What right does any person have to impose their religious beliefs on another? I thought we had done with that a century ago.'

'I think he is waking,' said Hunter, indicating the bed at the far end of the room.

'Before I go to him, tell me, who is in the house at present?'

'Most of the servants, of course, together with Miss Elizabeth. The mother is visiting a sick aunt at Egglescliffe – not one of my patients. I understand she will be back here early this afternoon.'

'That is all to the good. Would you bring Elizabeth to me? I propose to end this obscenity, but you have no cause for alarm, doctor. You will observe nothing amiss, I assure you.'

'Ah! it's you, Sir Richard,' said Colonel Palmer, as he approached the sickbed. 'Good of you to come.'

'I am happy to be here, but distressed to see you in such a sorry state, Colonel. Is the pain so very great?'

'I never knew what pain was until this illness came upon me. I *thought* I did, but I was wrong. How can a body endure so much and still function? But enough of that. Let us talk of you for the moment. These days, I hear nothing but good of you from all quarters. Quite a change from the old days, what? But will it last? I ask myself. Emma is very dear to me, you understand. Make a promise to a dying man. Promise me that she will never again be made to suffer as she has suffered in the past.'

'I promise. The bad old days are gone for good, I swear it.'

'Then, let us shake hands on that.'

'With all my heart,' said Richard, extending a hand.

'Oh, God! the pain,' whispered Palmer. 'It is suddenly on its way back with a vengeance. Perhaps it would be for the best if you were to leave now.'

'No, I should like to sit with you a little longer; and, look, here is Elizabeth come to join us.'

'Do you take one hand, Elizabeth, and I shall clasp the other,' he said, quietly. 'Now, Colonel,' he said, turning back to the patient, 'why not try and compose yourself? Please do try, and with my help you may be surprised at the result.'

A moment later the sufferer was resting easy, and was saying so openly.

For her part, Elizabeth was somewhat taken aback at the huge beads of perspiration clearly visible on their visitor's forehead. Holding her father's hand in a union of three, she listened to what he had to say.

'Now, Colonel,' he said, 'try not to dwell on the present moment, or on what the future holds, but take your thoughts back to some happy experience of the past. Tell me, what comes to mind?'

'Boyhood days, forty years ago in Scotland. In those days we had a second, small, estate in the Highlands, where I used to spend my summer holidays each year. I would roam those wild and beautiful moors for hours at a time. I have never known such quiet contentment in all my life.'

'And did you have a favourite walk?'

'Yes, along the coast for a little while, and then I would make my way inland, following the course of the stream at Inverie.'

'And do you have the picture in your mind?'

'Oh, yes, perfectly so. Is it not odd how sometimes scenes and images of half a lifetime ago come clearer to the mind than those of half a year? I can *feel* the spring in the heather beneath my feet where it encroaches on the sheep-path. I can *smell* the salt air as the mist comes drifting towards me across the moors.'

'You are very good at bringing past sensations back to life, that much is plain. Not everyone has the ability to such a degree; but let us walk together for a little while.'

'Yes, join me if you wish. Let us walk towards the setting sun.'

'My dear Colonel, you are surely mistaken,' said Richard, laughing. 'It is early morning, the dawn of a new day. The sun is rising, not setting. Surely, you see that?'

'Yes, of course,' chuckled Palmer. 'How stupid of me.'

'You are the expert in these matters, so tell me: what is that strange, liquid, bubbling call from over yonder?'

'Ah! you mean that curlew calling away in the distance? They breed in these moors, you know, but they will soon take themselves off to winter on the coast.'

Both men fell silent for five minutes, continuing their separate journeys together, until Richard finally spoke.

'I don't know how you fare, but I must confess to feeling a little tired. Shall we not rest awhile beside the brook? There is a moss-covered knoll over there which looks very inviting.'

'Yes, I see it. To own the truth, I shall be glad to join you. Suddenly, I feel so very weary. I do believe we've come a good mile too far the pair of us.'

'Then, let us both take a little nap before we start back.'

'It is over. He has slipped away,' said Richard, after the passage of a few minutes. Gently, he disengaged his hand from that of the dead man.

'No, it cannot be,' said Hunter, moving hurriedly to join the little group. After a brief examination, he turned to address Elizabeth. 'Sir Richard is correct. All signs of life are gone. I was certain he would linger on a few weeks more, but perhaps it is for the best.'

'Of that I have no doubt,' said Elizabeth. 'Thanks be to God for putting an end to his suffering.'

'Try not to distress yourself, Elizabeth,' said Richard. 'Come, dry your tears. Believe me when I tell you that your father has embarked on the most exciting adventure a man may experience. And now, I shall leave you. Please extend my deepest sympathy to your mother.'

'I understand you walked here, Sir Richard?' she said.

'Yes, it is but a mile, and the weather is fine.'

'Then, may I accompany you at least part of the way? Doctor Hunter and the servants will attend to matters here, and mother is not due back for another hour at least. Or would you rather make the return journey in our carriage? It would be no trouble. I must say, this business seems to have affected you deeply. Please forgive me for saying so, but you look awful.'

'I am well-enough to make the journey home on foot,' he said. 'Indeed, the walk will do me more good than harm, but come with me by all means, if that is what you wish.'

'I suppose my father was wandering in his mind,' said Elizabeth. 'Towards the end, I mean. You encouraged him in his flight of fancy to take his mind off his suffering. Is that not so?'

'No, not exactly, Elizabeth. In a sense your father *really* was back in the Highlands. You may call it all imagination, or make-believe, if you wish, but there is not quite the sharp distinction between imagination and reality as many people suppose.'

'Really? You think so? Tell me more. You begin to intrigue me, truly you do.'

'Well, of one thing I am certain. Lovelace was right. 'Stone walls do not a prison make, nor iron bars a cage'. If only people would learn to free their minds from the shackles of convention a whole new world would open up to them. Next time you feel wearied, or dispirited, go to your room, draw the curtains, and lie down. Take yourself off, as your father did, to a favourite haunt, or relive some happy event, and see what happens. You will be surprised at the peace and comfort which will come to you.'

'But I would have thought that pining for the past, or wishing oneself elsewhere, would have quite the opposite effect.'

'Not if the thing is done properly. Not if one enters into the spirit of the thing. You must put yourself truly *into* the scene. You must *feel* the wind in your face, or the heat of the sun on your back, as your father did. You must *experience* the touch of a loved one lost. You must view your conjured images as a *reality*. To the prisoner caged as some animal, to the bedridden invalid, to all those people locked in a life of drudgery, all the world remains open to them.' He paused to reach out and touch her forehead. 'There are no locked doors in there, no barriers, no sickbeds, and no horizons. You have not *really* lost your father, Elizabeth, not as long as your memory of him survives. Do what I advise and you may meet with him in spirit anytime you wish and relive the past, or fashion the present moment to your heart's desire.'

She had stopped walking as they talked together and now stood staring at him.

'What an extraordinary man you have become of late. Who would have believed it?' she said. 'Others may say you are talking nonsense but I sense the truth of your words. I have the feeling that, unasked for, you have handed me something beautiful and precious. I shall do as you advise, and I shall do it with all the sincerity I can muster.' She looked about her. 'I believe I have come far enough. I must turn back in case mother returns early. It is I who shall have to break the news to her.' She held out her hand and grasped his firmly. 'I never thought the day would come when I would be doing this. I never thought there would come a time when my eyes would look upon you with gratitude and affection. I never thought that death could be beautiful, but you have made it so today. I am left to marvel at the change in you. I must go, but give my love to Emma, and keep some back for yourself.'

Elizabeth's words were in sharp contrast to Emma's when he arrived home.

'*Dead?* So soon? So suddenly? But how can that be?' she said.

'The Colonel passed away while I was with him,' he said.

'I find that very odd,' she said. 'Why, you were scarcely with him an hour. But why do you skulk in the doorway like that? Come closer.'

One close-up look was sufficient.

'I know that look,' she cried. 'I saw the same look on the second day of our stay at Richmond Manor after your dealings with young Caroline. My God! what have you done?'

'I did what had to be done,' he said.

'Dear God! you stopped his beating heart as surely as you stopped that ticking clock a few days back. I send you on an errand of reconciliation and you pay me back by doing this.'

'I do not wish to discuss the matter further,' he said. 'I'm going to my room.'

For a few minutes Emma paced the floor, deeply agitated, before rushing upstairs to accost him once more. She found him resting on his bed.

'What will you say on The Day Of Judgement, I wonder?' were her opening words to him. 'How will you plead away this murder along with all your other misdeeds?'

'In that unlikely event, I shall simply say: I have done my best, now You may do your worst.'

'I hope you are satisfied with your morning's work,' she said, bitterly. 'You now have three deaths on your conscience.'

These words were the final straw to the accused man. It was rare for him to lose his temper, but he did so now.

'You sanctimonious fraud! What did I ever see in you, I wonder?'

320

he shouted. Leaping off his bed he grabbed hold of her. 'You have made it plain all along that you wanted only to be away from here. Very well, you may leave here first thing tomorrow morning, and I shall make it easy for you. I would not wish you to leave without feeling fully justified in doing so.'

With these words, he began to roughly remove her clothes, tearing at the material when he met with a button, or a catch. He pushed her, half-naked, onto the bed and threw himself on top of her.

She tried to detach herself from the situation, to put herself elsewhere, in spirit if not in body, and for a while succeeded. The only problem was, he was doing the unexpected. He seemed more intent on satisfying her than himself – a prelude, no doubt, but one she was not used to, and one which seemed to go on and on. Never before had she been made love to in this fashion. In spite of her best efforts, in spite of her hateful situation, she began to experience a measure of pleasure and passion. Frantically, she tried to fight back – to say, or do, something which would stop him dead in his tracks.

She give an expressive yawn, which in no way reflected her inner feelings.

'Are you going to be long?' she said. 'I have things to do.'

It was a clear affront, and one he could not ignore. He rolled over onto his back and stared at the ceiling. His voice when he spoke was calm and detached.

'You want me to change the past, Emma,' he said. 'You are wanting me to do the impossible.'

'All I want is for you to leave me alone,' she said, getting off the bed and gathering up her scattered garments.

'Very well, you have your wish,' he said. 'As for what I did today, I shall only say this: I believe in deeds, not creeds.'

'It *is* possible to believe in both,' she answered. 'This afternoon, I shall go to see Elizabeth. I may not be able to undo what you have done, but I can at least offer my sympathy and support.'

'Don't forget to cry,' he said.

She was on the point of leaving when he called out to her.

'Was what I did to you just now so very hateful to you, Emma?'

'I loathed every second of it,' she answered.

Closing the door behind her, she leant back against it.

'Oh, Emma Forres, you liar,' she whispered.

Clearly much agitated, Emma greeted Elizabeth with a great outpouring of words. After a full two minutes of this, Elizabeth silenced her.

'Yes, mother was, of course, much affected by the news when she arrived back here, but I think secretly she is relieved that father is at last at peace. Doctor Hunter prescribed a sedative, and she is resting in her room. No, you may not see father until tomorrow, when we expect him back here. It was mother's wish that he be removed immediately to the morticians, there to be made 'presentable', as she put it. I understand those people can work wonders with a ravaged body. I did not agree to that, but mother overruled me. I suppose from tomorrow we shall get an endless stream of visitors paying their last respects, but it is my belief that if they could not gladly come and view my father as he really was at the end, they had better stay away.

'Moving on to your twentieth sentence, I have to say that I am more than a little surprised at this bitter condemnation of your husband. You say that he willed my father's death, but to be honest I was willing it, too. I see that shocks you. In my defence, I would only say that it was I, not you, who was forced to witness my father's decline these three months past. Towards the end I could not bear to watch his pain, so I do not know what he was doing with it.'

'But you do not understand,' protested Emma. 'He more than willed your father's death, he actually brought it about. I know that must sound fantastic to you but it is true.'

'It was God who ended my father's life,' said Elizabeth, 'but even if it was as you say, I could not condemn your Richard.'

'I see we shall have to differ on that score,' said Emma, 'but he is not 'my Richard' anymore. I am leaving Grange Hall tomorrow but shall, of course, return to Yarm for your father's funeral.'

'I can scarce believe this,' said Elizabeth. 'You are actually leaving him for what you believe he did here this morning?'

'That is partly the reason, but there is more to it than that. Today, he went back on the agreement between the two of us which I told you about. He forced himself upon me.'

'Emma, listen to me. There is not one husband in a hundred who

322

would have volunteered such an arrangement out of regard for his wife's feelings, and even fewer who would have kept to it for this length of time. Tell me, did he...... did he go all the way?'

'No, thank God,' said Emma, laughing. 'I stopped him short with a few well-chosen words.'

'Yes, I can just imagine it,' said Elizabeth, coldly; 'but you must have provoked him, I'm sure.'

'Well, perhaps I did antagonise him with a few words of criticism, but in the circumstances I believe I had every right to do so.'

'What *exactly* did you say to him?' said Elizabeth, looking critically at her friend.

'I said he now had three deaths on his conscience to contend with.'

'Meaning, I suppose, your mother, your brother, and my father?'

'Why, yes. In my view, he murdered your father, and I told him as much.'

Angry and indignant, Elizabeth turned her back on Emma, and went across to the window.

All along, Emma had failed to spot the warning signs emanating from Elizabeth. Blithely, she continued on her way.

'Anyway, enough of that. I am here to tell you that as soon as I am settled elsewhere I shall write to you. We shall then be able to resume the correspondence which we had when I was at Darlington. Your letters meant so much to me when I was there.'

Elizabeth turned back to her with a face pale with anger.

'You may write if you wish but do not expect a reply. Our friendship is at an end,' she said. 'Now, I must go to mother. See yourself out. You know the way.' She paused in the doorway to say what was meant to be a few final words to a shocked and distraught Emma. 'You know, Emma, your fervent admirer Adam Fawley always used to say that you did not deserve your husband. I begin to think he was right, but not the way he intended it.'

'How can you say such a thing?' cried Emma. 'You of all people *know* what that husband of mine is capable of.'

'After today, I'm not sure that I do,' said Elizabeth; 'but I shall tell you something for nothing Emma Forres: if you had not a prior claim on him, and given the opportunity, I would be willing to risk everything to find out.'

'You have a short memory, that is your trouble,' cried Emma.

'And you have a long one, and that is your tragedy,' said Elizabeth, quietly.

Deeply unhappy, Emma made her way back to Grange Hall. It should come as no surprise to the reader to learn that she blamed one person above all others for her state of mind. She did not hesitate to tell him as much the moment she arrived back.

'You steal away all those who are dearest to me,' she said. 'Rachel has entirely forgiven you, and she is closer to you now than to me. My uncle will not have a word said against you, and even Peter has been here more than once when there was a time he shunned the place completely. Now, I have lost my oldest and dearest friend to you. Elizabeth has made that very plain.'

'Perhaps the fault does not lie entirely with me,' he said, 'but I am sorry for it, all the same. I did not intend it so.'

She did not linger at the scene, and neither did he. Once she had left him, he set out, a little wearily, for the Palmer residence.

Feelings of guilt and self-reproach occupied his thoughts as he walked along, and not simply because of the day's events.

How could I have been so unthinking, so selfish, in the pursuit of what *I* wanted? he asked himself. Not content with usurping the title and position of another man, from the beginning I have assumed that I am entitled also to his wife. Emma has made no marriage vows to *me*. She owes me *nothing*. So, I saved her life, but that was only done as part of a scientific experiment. Have I at any time considered what is best for her, or had any regard for her feelings, other than how those feelings touched upon my own interests? To think, I damn-near raped her today, there is no other word to describe what I did, and she is right in saying I am taking from her the few loved ones she has left in the world. I may be doing it unwittingly and without malice, but I am doing it all the same. I should have made my way quietly to London at the outset and left her to rebuild her life as *she* saw fit. Perhaps it is too late for that, but I can at least restore her friend to her, and see to it that she leaves tomorrow with not a shred of self-guilt and with not a single pang of conscience.

Late that afternoon, Emma received a short message from Elizabeth, delivered by hand.

'I got your note an hour ago,' said Emma. 'It told me little more than you wished to see me once more.'

'Yes, I should really have come in person, but mother needs me here. Emma, I asked to see you in order to plead your forgiveness. I did not mean to censure you, and am heartily sorry for some of the things I said. I still feel that your condemnation of Richard is unjustified, but that should not be allowed to spoil a friendship which extends back to the days of our early childhood. As you, yourself, said, it is possible for us to differ on that score without rancour, or enmity. I only wish to say that I hope you find the happiness you are looking for after you leave Yarm tomorrow, and I look forward to hearing from you very soon.'

'Oh, my dearest Elizabeth, I am overjoyed to hear you speak so,' said Emma, coming forward to embrace her friend. 'Oh, but this is one in the eye for my husband. He shall discover that I have at least the one true friend whom he cannot entice away from me.'

'Oh, God!' exclaimed Elizabeth, covering her eyes with a hand. 'It's no use. I cannot hear you speak so and hold to my promise. I just cannot.' She paused for a moment before continuing. 'Emma, I am going to do something which I never did before in all my life. I am about to go back on my word. Would it surprise you to learn that Richard called here a second time today, barely an hour after you left?'

'No, it would not surprise me unduly,' said Emma. 'Come to plead his case, did he?'

'On the contrary, he spent half of the time singing your praises and marvelling at your forebearance in letting him near you. The remainder of the time he spent pleading with me to make it up to you. He asked me to try and understand your feelings in the light of all that has happened these two years past. He reminded me forcibly of all that you were made to endure at his hands throughout that time, pointing out that if I had been made to suffer as you have suffered I might not find it so easy to forgive and forget. I have to say that there was much truth in what he said, and I did not find it at all difficult to agree to his suggestion of this meeting of reconciliation. Finally, he made me promise faithfully not to make any reference to his visit. This reconciliation was to be my doing, and mine alone. That is the promise I have now broken. I believe if you and I are justified in condemning him for his past conduct, it would be less than honest of us if we were not to give credit where credit is due.'

'I do not know what to say,' said Emma, after a moment of stunned silence. 'At every turn he does the unexpected these days. As you say, his meeting with you reflects to his credit. Why, then, would he wish to keep it a secret from me?'

'I believe he is doing his best to make it easy for you. He does not want the credit because he wants you to leave tomorrow still thinking ill of him, and with no feelings of self-reproach on your part. He told me as much himself. I begged him to reconsider. I asked him to take back my promise, but he would not. I told him not to do anything which he would later regret. He said: "Elizabeth, I am doing what is right and proper, and I shall regret it all the days of my life." '

'I do not understand any of this,' said Emma. 'I have thought all along he has been play-acting, but now I'm not so sure. What is your opinion?'

'I think if he is acting he should be on the London Stage. Remember, too, how he effected Peter's release from prison without reference to you. Even now, neither of us can come up with a satisfactory explanation for that. Of course, we both assumed it could not possibly spring from a natural goodness on his part, but was that assumption wrong? Recall, also, those changes for the better at Grange Hall, which you noted on your return there. Emma, I know for certain that they were done weeks before your return.'

'Yes, all of that is true,' acknowledged Emma. She shook her head in despair. 'Oh, I do not know about anything anymore. Are you able to help me? Can you explain this apparent transformation in him?'

'Perhaps he has found God,' said Elizabeth.

'No, that cannot be,' said Emma. 'I know that from some of the things he comes out with.'

'If that be the case, I can offer you no explanation,' said Elizabeth. 'It is almost as if we are dealing with two entirely different persons.'

'Yes...... yes, I get that sensation at times.'

'And there is more I have to tell. I imagine you thought he would now withdraw his offer to help Peter?'

'Why, yes. I took that for granted.'

'Not so,' said Elizabeth, 'although he did say that he expected a reward from you in the shape of one last kiss – the French way, he said. Do you know what he meant by that?'

'Yes, I believe so,' said Emma, flushing a little.

'There is still more you should know,' said Elizabeth. 'He made mention of some invention of his, which would bring him a vast amount of money, although I must confess that I did not understand what little he told me concerning it. Once he is sure of its success, he is going to hand Grange Hall over to you in its entirety, all legally done and above board.'

'But I have no right to Grange Hall,' said Emma in amazement. 'That never was the property of the Sinclair family. Why should he want to do such a thing?'

'Well, for some strange reason, he seems to think you have the better claim to it,' said Elizabeth. 'He did not say as much openly, but that was the strong impression I got.' She shook her head in disbelief. 'It is all beyond me.'

'And me,' said Emma.

'One thing you must promise me before you leave here,' said Elizabeth. 'I would die of shame if he were to learn that I had gone back on my word. Whether you leave him, or no, is up to you, but if you stay you must promise not to give the true details of this meeting between the two of us as a reason for doing so.'

'Yes, you have my word on that,' said Emma.

'I have one thing more to tell you, and I have a feeling you will not thank me for doing so. As he was leaving, I said: you *really* do love Emma, don't you? He give a wry smile and said: "dear Elizabeth, I'm afraid it's worse than that. I more than love her, I'm *in love* with her.".'

'Oh, dear God! what am I to do?' cried Emma, burying her head in her hands. 'Yesterday I placed fresh flowers on mother's and Robert's grave, and came away bitterly regretting every kind word and every kind deed between the two of us since I returned here. I felt so guilty. How can I set aside the past as if it never happened? But there is more to it than that. It is one thing to suffer at the hands of a husband for whom one has little or no respect, and from whom one expects nothing better, and it is quite another matter to suffer the same terrible treatment from a person one has grown fond of, which, in spite of appearances to the contrary, is the direction in which I am heading. So you see, my worse nightmare is that one fine morning I shall wake up to find he has changed back to what he always was. After a mere two weeks back here I am already beginning to live from day to day riddled with feelings of guilt and in an agony of suspense for what tomorrow will bring. But, Elizabeth, I have learnt one thing since returning home, if nothing else. From personal experience, I can testify that it is simply impossible to return continual affection with unremitting hatred.'

'Ah! that explains it – this inner turmoil of yours, I mean,' said Elizabeth. 'I wondered at the time what he meant by it.'

'I do not understand,' said Emma. 'To what do you refer?'

'I believe Richard senses this terrible struggle within yourself, and is fearful on your behalf of the outcome. Out of the blue, without reference to what had been said before, he suddenly said: "you know, Elizabeth, there is an old Indian saying to the effect that when a man catches a rare and exquisitely beautiful butterfly, he is left with a choice. He may either release it back into the world, or claim it as his own, hold it close, and watch it die." '

Emma returned home late that evening to find Richard alone in his room.

'You have made it up with Elizabeth. I'm glad of that,' he said.

'Yes, we are friends again, but how did you know of it?'

'Oh, I guessed as much when I got your note saying you were to take dinner with her. You would hardly do that unless the pair of you were fully reconciled.'

'Were you forced to eat alone?' she asked.

'No, Rachel returned from her excursion in time to join me. She is in her room if you wish to see her.'

'Yes, I must speak with her.'

'If it concerns her leaving with you, I'm afraid you will be wasting your time. I have done my very best to persuade her to join you, but she will not.'

'I never expected she would want to accompany me. I wish to speak to her on another matter.'

'So, where will you go?' he said.

'Initially, to my uncle. I expect I shall get a lecture from him when I arrive there. After that, I'm not sure.'

'I shall write him a conciliatory note, which you shall take with you. That may help matters. But I'm happy that your friendship with Elizabeth is restored. Tell me,' he said, casually, - a little *too* casually, she thought – 'did Elizabeth give a reason for her change of heart?'

'Only that, having thought it through, she decided our friendship must continue at all cost.'

'Did she speak of me at all?'

'We touched on you, naturally, but not at any length. We talked mostly of my plans for the future.'

'Good – I mean, yes, I understand.'

It was her turn to attempt to sound casual.

'I suppose it is no use asking you for the five thousand pounds you promised me when we left Richmond Manor? I'm not thinking of myself, you understand, but of my brother, and his commission.'

'I know a promise is a promise,' he said, 'but, all the same, I believe you will owe me something if I keep to my word.'

'Yes, I suppose so,' she said. 'Do you wish to continue where you left off this morning? I would not be averse to that, if only for Peter's sake.'

'No, I do not think anything so drastic is called for. I had a special kind of parting kiss in mind. The French do it all the time, you know.'

'I believe I know what you mean. So be it. I can hardly refuse in view of your generosity.'

'Then, shall we get it over and done with now?' he said.

'If you like, but I would have thought tomorrow morning, just before my departure, would be a more appropriate moment.'

'True, except I shall not be here to see you off. I have some urgent business in town to attend to early tomorrow morning.'

'Urgent business, my foot!' she said. 'You cannot bear to witness my departure. Is that not the truth of it?'

'Yes,…… well, 'parting is such sweet sorrow', and all that.'

'Then, do what you have to do now,' she said.

He kissed her lightly on both cheeks, before stepping back a pace.

'Oh, Emma, you do look funny standing there with your eyes closed and your mouth open,' he said, laughing. 'It is a good job the summer flies are gone.'

'Is that it?' she asked, in surprise. 'Is that all you had in mind?'

'But, of course,' he said. 'What else? Is that not how the French do it? They say that even the *men* there greet each other, and part company, in just such a way. I must say, that would not appeal to me in the least.'

'You are unreal,' she said, shaking her head in disbelief. 'You are too good to be true.'

'Yes, you are quite right in what you say. It has all been show and effect on my part these few weeks past. It signifies nothing. I see you have realised that at last. You do well to leave tomorrow before my true character reasserts itself. Still, my little piece of foolishness just now has given you something to remember me by for all time. You will leave here tomorrow, and in time will meet with a man who has not a past to live down. You will marry, and have children, and one day you will gather them about you and say: "children, did I ever tell you of the time I sold a kiss for five thousand pounds?" and they will say: "five thousand pounds for a *single* kiss? but no woman in the history of the world has done such a thing"; and you will tell them the details, and the story will be remembered, and handed down in the family from one generation to the next. But, Emma, why do you look so solemn, so serious? Worse things happen at sea, you know.'

'Such as giant squids?' she said.

She watched as the smile faded from his face.

'Yes,' he said, and turned away.

Rachel proved to be of no help to Emma.

'Before I leave here, I would wish you to give me the answer to one question,' she said. 'How is it that you can so easily forgive Richard all his past sins when I have such difficulty in doing the same?'

'To be honest, I do not rightly know,' said Rachel, frowning. 'I can give you two explanations, one silly, and one sensible. I shall give you the silly one first. I sense that Richard is not responsible for the sins you speak of.'

'But that is nonsense,' exclaimed Emma. 'If he is not to blame, who is?'

'Well, I did say it was silly,' said Rachel, 'but let me give you a more sensible explanation. I do not have your difficulties because, in inward essence as distinct from outward show, I am a much better person than you.'

'Thank you for that,' said Emma, dryly. 'Really, Rachel, you grow more like your brother every day.'

'Oh, Emma, do you really think so?' said Rachel, coming forward to embrace her. 'Do you know, that is the nicest thing you have said to me in a long time.'

Emma spent a sleepless night. Her freedom beckoned. It was all she had ever wanted for two years, and yet......

Early that morning she came to a decision.

'He has said more than once that I bring out the best in him. Why does he bring out the *worst* in me?' she asked herself. 'Well, no more.'

She came down early to breakfast but found in spite of that he had already eaten and left for Yarm. Half-an-hour later she was disembarking from the carriage which was meant to take her to York, and was sending it on its way back to the stables at Grange Hall. Straightaway, she began to search the highways and byways of the town. Within ten minutes she caught sight of him. He was window shopping in the desultory manner of a man killing time.

Silently, unobserved, she approached him from behind, and wrapt an arm around one of his.

'Emma, what are you doing here?' he asked, in surprise. 'You should be on the road to York by now.'

'Oh, you shall not get rid of me as easily as that,' she said. She turned and indicated in the direction of Grange Hall. 'Going my way?' she said.

Even as she spoke, she felt his arm tightening around her own.

CHAPTER 25

Emma had not been back at Grange Hall very long before she became aware of the frequent presence of Nancy Gibson within the estate.

'Nancy calls at the stables and paddock twice a week and is an occasional visitor to the house,' said Rachel, in response to Emma's enquiry.

'But there is bad blood between my husband and the Gibsons,' said Emma.

'Oh, that is all in the past,' said Rachel, and proceeded to bring Emma up to date with some recent history.

'Nancy seems greatly changed,' said Emma. 'She is much more sedate, more ladylike, than I remember her.'

'Yes, that is Richard's doing. He has an affect on people.' She looked pointedly at Emma. 'Well, an affect on most people, that is.'

'They seem on friendly terms, the two of them,' said Emma, ignoring this last remark.

'True,' said Rachel, casting a sly look at Emma. 'He addresses her as 'Beautiful' when he believes no one is within earshot. She scolds him for it, but I think secretly it pleases her.'

'Indeed?' said Emma, raising an eyebrow.

'Oh, there is nothing improper in the relationship, I'm sure,' said Rachel. 'Richard has a petname for most of those close to him.'

'Really? So what is his petname for you?'

'Sometimes, he addresses me as 'Slim'.'

'Slim? You did say 'Slim'?'

'Yes,' said Rachel.

'Well, that is not particularly flattering.'

'Oh, I do not mind. It is just a little foolishness on his part,' said Rachel. Eyes twinkling, she looked at Emma. 'Incidentally, in case you are wondering, you are 'Blondie'.'

'He has never called me that to my face,' said Emma.

'I believe he would like to on occasions but I suspect he is a little afraid of how you would respond.'

'So, a friend warrants the name of 'Beautiful', while I, his wife, have to make do with 'Blondie',' said Emma, not looking best pleased.

'I asked him about that. He replied that Nancy's petname would not sit well on you.'

'I see,' said Emma. Much to her surprise, she found herself distinctly unhappy at this latest turn in the conversation. To add to her annoyance, Rachel chose to burst out laughing.

'Oh! Emma, you do look cross. Let me put you out of your misery.'

'It is of no consequence. It is all childish nonsense,' said Emma, with a toss of her head.

'Yes, of course,' said Rachel, smiling, 'but I should tell you that Richard went on to say that Nancy's petname applied to you would be far too unimaginative. Much too obvious, he said.'

'Oh! I see,' exclaimed Emma.

'Still, as you say, it is all nonsense.'

'Yes...... yes, certainly,' said Emma in a less than decisive tone of voice.

'Nancy calls on average once a week to instruct Richard in the finer points of dancing, although absent as he was at Richmond it is a full two weeks since she has been with us. She is quite expert in the art, which I never knew. On occasions, the three of us turn the event into a full-scale music evening.'

'Dancing lessons! Music evenings! Whatever next?' said Emma. 'So, what exactly takes place when the three of you are together?'

'Oh, nothing of special note. Richard and I amuse ourselves on the pianoforte, and Nancy sings a song, or two. She has an exquisite voice, you know – quite lovely. From time to time, Richard plays and sings to us.'

'Richard sings! Yea gods! What is he like?'

'He is terrible. I can only liken his singing to the sound you hear when you accidentally tread on a cat. Of course, we both applaud at the end of it, Nancy for politeness sake, and I out of gratitude he has finished. We are due to meet up tonight. Has Richard not made mention of it?'

'I believe he did say something the other day, but my mind was elsewhere and it did not really register.'

'You will join us, will you not?'

'I would not miss it for the world,' said Emma; 'but you know, Rachel, every day seems to bring some new surprise. I sometimes ask myself if I have returned to the same Grange Hall I left a few months ago, or did I dream the past two years and have woken up from some nightmare? Everything is different.'

'Not everything is different, and not everyone has changed,' said Rachel. 'If you doubt that, spend a little time with Martha, if you can bear to. Richard calls her 'Tarzan', you know. Now *that* I don't understand.'

They were coming to the end of an enjoyable evening. Rachel and Nancy, first singly and then together, had spent an hour on the pianoforte, playing and singing before an appreciative Emma and Richard. Next, Emma had displayed her modest talents before an encouraging trio of listeners. Finally, at Emma's coaxing, Richard had agreed to do likewise. His partiality was for late twentieth century popular ballads, a selection of which he performed tolerably well. He would have been the first to admit, however, that this type of music was totally alien to early nineteenth century ears, and so it proved.

'It is an unusual sound. It is a novelty, at least,' whispered Emma to Rachel, half-way through the performance.

'A crowing donkey would be a novelty. Did you have to encourage him so?' hissed Rachel.

When he was done, Richard took the floor with Nancy. Together, they went through the motions of a few modest dance routines, which the gentleman was still to fully master. At the end of it, a little flushed and breathless, he sought Emma's opinion.

'You must admit that my dancing has improved,' he said.

'Yes, but at what cost to poor Nancy's toes?' she said.

Studying the playful, teasing face of the speaker, a thought came to him.

'I own you are a much superior dancer,' he said, 'but I have the advantage over you with regard to one little jig.'

'Indeed? What dance is that?' she said.

'A new diversion from across the seas, still to find its way to these shores. I happen to be expert at it. Come, my dear, let me instruct you.'

He led her into the centre of the room, turning his head to address Nancy as he did so.

'When I give the signal, beaut -, Nancy, dear, strike up some slow and easy tune – some quiet melody, gentle on the ear.'

He positioned Emma close to him and began to manoeuvre her to his liking.

'You must put your arms around my neck...... no, not your hands, you wicked girl, your arms...... yes, just so. I hold you close, one arm around your waist, and my free hand in the small of your back. Now, we are ready.'

'What do you mean, "we are ready"?' she protested. 'How am I supposed to partner you when I am ignorant of the steps?'

'The steps are unimportant at this stage. We shall come to those later. I shall lead and you must shuffle your feet and follow as best you can.'

'This is all beginning to sound very unlikely, but I shall humour you. Tell me, does this strange dance of yours have a name?'

'It is called 'smooching'.'

' 'Smooching'? That is an odd name for a dance.'

'Yes, isn't it? Now, hold tight.'

At his signal, Nancy struck up a slow, pleasing melody. The two partners began to shuffle their way around the floor. Out of the corner of her eye, Emma could see Rachel laughing. Nancy, looking up from her playing from time to time, appeared decidedly embarrassed.

'Getting the feel of it?' he asked, at one point.

'You could say that,' gasped Emma. 'Must you press me so tightly? Is it really necessary for you to cling to me so?'

'Oh, yes. That is the most essential part,' he assured her.

Emma endured it for a little while longer, but when he tilted her head onto his shoulder and began to nibble at her ear, and when his free hand began to drift down below her waist, she decided to call a halt.

'Enough! More than enough,' she protested, disengaging herself from him. 'This is no dance. It is some novel way of procreation. I believe you concocted the whole performance.'

'It took her a long time to come to that conclusion,' whispered Rachel to Nancy.

'Yes, I was thinking that,' said Nancy. 'Would you allow a young man to do that to you?'

'Yes, but I think the horizontal position would be more to my liking,' said Rachel.

335

Meanwhile, Emma was complaining to Richard.

'Your hands were everywhere,' she said.

'Ah! if only that were true,' he said.

'You nearly crushed the life out of me. You and that giant squid of yours are two of a kind.'

'Yes, 'feed' and 'breed' – the two great driving forces of nature. I shall leave you to decide upon our respective motives.'

With an expressive shake of the head, Emma acknowledged defeat.

'I am off to rejoin the girls. I shall leave you to your own devices.'

'I have tried that,' he said. 'It is not the same.'

'To the pure, all things are pure', so it is said. This last remark, at least, was lost on her.

The evening's entertainment was over. Nancy had departed, and Rachel had retired to her room. Emma was thinking of doing the same when the distant sound of music drew her elsewhere. For a full twenty minutes she stood quietly outside the slightly ajar door of the music room.

He had returned there, and now sat playing and singing tunes and songs even more uninhibited to her ears than before. As previously, she judged the performance uneven and disjointed, the words lacking proper diction, and the notes jarring on the ear on occasions. In spite of all that, she felt herself strangely drawn to the singer and his songs. Standing motionless and unobserved, she listened to a performance at the one and the same time wild and subdued, raucous and tender, ugly and yet beautiful – an assortment of haunting melodies, which in the days that followed she found herself quietly humming in vacant moments.

'We must raise more money,' he said to her, as they sat together the following evening.

'So you keep telling me,' said Emma. 'Do you have anything in mind?'

'I believe this will serve our purposes,' he said, producing a small sheaf of papers, covered with detailed drawings and copious notes.

So this is the invention which Elizabeth spoke of, thought Emma, as she sifted through the papers. After a few moments, she give a despairing shake of the head.

'I can make no sense of it,' she said. 'What exactly is it? Clearly, it is a machine of some kind, but what purpose does it serve?'

'It is a new scientific invention, which I intend to christen a 'phonograph'. Put simply, it is a device to reproduce sound recordings. Let me explain its workings. Believe me, the machine is not as complicated as it looks to be on paper.'

In this Richard Forres spoke the truth. Simple in both design and construction, and involving very little in the way of new technology, the hand-cranked phonograph, or gramophone as it later came to be known, is characterised by its extreme simplicity. Indeed, it would be no exaggeration to state that, armed with the inventor's design drawings, any competent ancient Greek, or Roman, engineer would have been able to construct a working machine out of materials readily to hand, the only marvel being that the invention was so long delayed. It was also what may be termed 'a self-contained' invention in that it brought with it no great breakthrough in any other scientific field.

These factors weighed heavily with Richard Forres in his choice of the phonograph as the ideal invention to secure his financial future, but the decision to proceed had, all the same, caused him much heart-searching. He was only too well-aware that his premature invention was destined to rob a certain Thomas Edison of some well deserved glory, but he consoled himself with the thought that this would still leave several noteworthy inventions to stand to the credit of that talented American.

If Emma was amazed at the potential of her husband's invention, as explained to her, she was not a little surprised to learn that he had been secretly working on the project for several weeks past and had involved her uncle in the undertaking from an early stage.

'Your uncle Johnathon, working from a second set of plans, is very near to completing a prototype machine,' he told her. 'Once the machine is duplicated and on the open market, I have no doubt it will bring us vast sums of money.'

'How much money?' she said.

'Oh, in the course of time, millions of pounds,' he said.

'*Millions of pounds?*' she exclaimed. 'Are you serious?'

'Perfectly serious,' he said. 'The invention is already going through the process of being patented. We shall have a worldwide market, and without a single competitor.'

'But what shall we do with such a vast fortune?' she said.

'Oh, I dare say that in the course of time I shall give most of it away,' he said.

'Give it away? Give it away to whom?'

'To the poor and needy, of course. To all those less fortunate than ourselves. Do you know, Emma, I love this world I find myself in, but there are aspects of it which I hate. I hate the squalor and deprivation which abounds. I hate the grinding poverty, the inequalities, the injustices, and the cruelties.'

'If you are bent on curing the world's ills, even a million pounds will not go very far.'

'But because one can do so very little does that mean one should do nothing at all? In my own small way, I shall do what I can.'

'But you will not give everything away, surely?' she said. 'That would be madness. You will at least ensure that Rachel and I shall want for nothing?'

'But, of course,' he said. 'You shall have everything that money can buy, although I have to say that from the first instant I saw you I would have taken you together with nothing but your shift. Come to think of it, I could happily have dispensed with that.'

'And at the first opportunity, I dare say,' said Emma, smiling. 'Tell me, is that the only sort of thing which occupies your thoughts these days?'

'Not at all,' he said. 'Sometimes when we are together whole minutes pass by without it even entering my head – well, seconds, at least.'

'Poor Richard,' she said. 'You can if you want to.'

'Do you want to?' he said.

'No; no, not really,' she said. 'I do not want to fully commit myself only to be hurt afterwards.'

'Yes, I understand,' he said. 'Well, that settles the matter, but I hope that you have at least forgiven me for loving you.'

She turned her head away and closed her eyes. 'Oh, God, where did *that* come from?' were her thoughts.

'I feel that as your wife I have a duty…… that is to say, I owe you……'

'Emma, you owe me nothing. *Nothing*, do you hear? You have nothing to reproach yourself for. But, we were speaking of my invention, remember? Let us return to that.'

'You do what you see fit with the money it brings you. If a sizeable portion of it is to go to the deserving poor, you shall hear no complaints from me.'

'You mean the deserving poor, as distinct from the undeserving poor? Yes, I suppose you are right, although I must say that there is often a fine line between the two. But why do we never hear talk of the undeserving *rich?* Odd, is it not? Most of those living in the lap of luxury have never done a day's work in their life. They were born with a silver spoon in their mouth, their land, property, and money, all handed down to them.'

'At the risk of offending you, is that not the case with you? You owe all that you have to your father, and his father before him, do you not?'

'If you mean I am not really entitled to any of this,' he said, sweeping a hand towards the window and the estate which lay beyond, 'I could not agree more. That troubles me at times, more than you can imagine. I don't deserve it. Least of all, I don't deserve you.'

'Yes, everyone seems to be saying that these days, although they do not always mean the same thing by it. Well, I, and I alone, shall be the judge of that. But, as you say, we were speaking of your invention. You have your machine, or will have very soon. What next?'

'I shall need financial backing to manufacture and market it on a large scale. The money to do that is way beyond my pocket. London is the only place in the country to secure that. I have already made tentative arrangements for a stay of some duration there. We shall travel down a week from today, breaking our journey at York. We shall need to make some recordings for demonstration purposes, and shall do that at your uncle's house, after which all five of us will travel onto London.'

'Five of us? Whom do you have in mind, apart from uncle and ourselves? Is Rachel to come with us?'

'Yes, and Nancy, too.'

'Nancy Gibson?' she asked, in surprise.

'Of course. What sweeter songbird for our recordings? And since she must needs travel to York and will be involved in that part of the project, I believe it is only right that she accompanies us to London. Indeed, it is in our own interest that she does so. An intrigued audience may well wish to view the charming singer behind the voice they hear.'

'Will her father release her into your charge?'

'I have already spoken with him and he is more than agreeable. He sees this venture as a rare opportunity for Nancy to improve herself, and I agree with him. That young woman is wasted closeted away on a small hill farm.'

'The pair of you are very close these days,' Emma observed.

Was there a hint of jealousy in the remark? he wondered. He hoped there was. It was true that they still kept to their separate rooms each night but apart from the one incident concerning Colonel Palmer he had sensed a definite softening in her attitude towards him of late.

'Yes, I admire her greatly,' he answered, 'but there is only the one woman in the world whom I would wish to spend the rest of my life with, and if you cannot guess who that is I shall think you a blockhead.'

'A blockhead I am not,' she said, 'but before I leave you there is another matter I wish to raise. Would you please stop calling me 'Blondie' behind my back?'

'Ah! I see Rachel has been speaking out of turn,' he said. 'It is merely a term of affection, Emma, but if it offends you I shall do as you ask.'

'It does offend me,' she said, giving him a contradictory smile. 'It offends me that you do not choose to use that name to my face.'

Emma's participation in the London venture was put at risk by an incident which took place two days before the party of four were due to set off for York. It was an incident which was to have far reaching consequences for Richard Forres.

He had come down a little late to breakfast to find Emma and Rachel partaking of their meal in the company of a rather odd third party. Richard gauged the young girl seated at the breakfast table to be about fifteen years of age, and was somewhat surprised that Rachel should cultivate the friendship of a girl nearly three years her junior. That she was a friend of Rachel, he did not doubt. No other possibility presented itself. It was typical of Rachel, he thought, that she should invite a guest to the Hall and leave him in ignorance of the fact.

He stood waiting patiently for an introduction, but none came. Rachel appeared to be engrossed in her meal, pointedly ignoring everyone present. If anything, he judged, she seemed ill at ease, her indifference to her surroundings a little too studied to be natural. Emma, he noted, was being kind and attentive, plying their young visitor with food and drink. After a glance at Rachel, she give him a terrible look, which he interpreted as deep disapproval of her sister-in-law's conduct. Early in the day though it was, he surmised that there had been some falling out between Rachel and her young friend, but that was no excuse, none at all, for Rachel's appalling rudeness.

'Rachel,' he said, reproachfully, 'will you not introduce me to your friend?'

Her response was to lift her eyes to his with a look of silent contempt. Emma put down her teacup and said quietly, to no one in particular: 'This is *too* much. This is not to be borne.' Without another word, she left the room.

Richard stood transfixed, eyes darting from their strange visitor to the closing breakfast room door, and back again, a look of total confusion on his face. Slowly, it began to dawn upon him that, as once before in attorney Buckland's office, he was guilty of some terrible faux-pas. Glancing at Rachel, he saw that she was studying him intently. He felt himself floundering, at a loss as to what to say, or do. Hurriedly, he left the room to seek out Rogers, or Simpson, only to bump into Mary on her way down to the kitchen.

For once, his little friend proved unhelpful, denying any knowledge concerning their morning's visitor with a patent insincerity. Dismissing the girl, he moved on, finally coming upon Rogers on the upstairs' landing.

Throwing caution to the wind, he said: 'Rogers, who is that girl in the breakfast room, and why is she here?'

Rogers coughed, discreetly. 'Really, sir!' he murmured.

'Be so good as to answer me, Rogers,' he said, quietly.

It was then that the sauve, imperturbable butler did a most out-of-character thing. He give a slight but perceptible shrug of the shoulders.

'The Jessel boy was taken last night,' he said.

'What do you mean, he was 'taken'?' said Richard.

Rogers give a barely audible sign.

'The boy was caught red-handed poaching on the estate again. He was taken into custody in the early hours of the morning. Has Mr. Smilie not acquainted you with the night's events?'

'I have not seen Mr. Smilie as yet, but what has any of this to do with our guest at breakfast?'

There followed a deafening silence.

'Rogers, I asked you a question. Have the goodness to respond when I speak,' he said, angrily.

Rogers could not begin to imagine the reason for the absurd charade which was taking place. It was true that Elizabeth Jessel had not been a visitor to the Hall for six months, but six months is not six years, he reflected. It was also true, he knew, that his master was attempting to put such shameful episodes behind him, but he felt that this was carrying the exercise to ridiculous lengths. Still, his master was demanding, for some obscure reason, that the full, sordid story should be recounted to him.

'Sir, your visitor is Elizabeth Jessel, that young criminal's sister. I have no doubt that she is here at the prompting of her mother. Elizabeth has come to...... has come to secure her brother's release in the only way she knows how.' He paused. 'By obliging you with her favours.' Another pause. 'As on previous occasions.'

The words were plain enough, and Richard was left to wonder if there was no end to his predecessor's list of misdeeds.

'She is just a child,' he said, huskily.

'As you say, sir,' said Rogers, coolly.

'But did you have to admit her into the presence of Lady Forres and Miss Rachel?' he said, irritably. 'Why did you not come to me directly the girl put in an appearance?'

'Sir, you have given specific instructions in the past that on occasions such as this the girl is to be given a free run of the house, without reference to yourself. "She is to come and go as she pleases, irrespective of who is present", were, I believe, your exact words.'

Yes, of course, thought Richard. Emma and Rachel were both well-acquainted with the girl, that much was obvious from the scene at the breakfast table. Rachel had been embarrassed and angry. Emma, clearly, felt sorry for the girl, little more than a child, and attached all the blame to him. That terrible look was meant for him, not Rachel. He could well understand that. Not content with cheating on his wife with a mere slip of a girl, Henry Forres had obviously derived some sadistic pleasure in flaunting her before his long-suffering wife.

For a moment he felt anger against several people all at the same time: at the girl, irrespective of her youthful age and seemingly selfless motive, for consenting to the arrangement; at the mother, for prostituting her own daughter in this fashion; at the Jessel boy, the cause of it all; at Rogers, notwithstanding any instructions to the contrary, for allowing the girl into the breakfast room that morning; and, collectively, at a society which saw fit to look the other way when a person such as Sir Henry Forres, baronet and *gentleman*, was involved.

His thoughts turned to Emma. Once again, irrespective of the arrangement made between the two of them, he was left to wonder at her forebearance – that she allowed him the degree of intimacy that she did; that she consented to let him touch her, listened to his words, spoke to him, *laughed* with him on occasions. People have short memories in matters which do not directly affect them, he reflected. Already, in the space of seven short weeks, he was fast becoming the 'agreeable and pleasing' owner of Grange Hall, while Emma, he was aware, was beginning to attract the first voices of criticism for what was believed to be a resentful and unforgiving attitude towards him. It was all so unfair, he thought.

His thoughts came back to his present predicament.

'Rogers, those past instructions with regard to Elizabeth Jessel are now cancelled. *Cancelled*, you understand? That girl is never again to be allowed within this house.'

Rogers looked at the somewhat weary and disconsolate face of his master and ventured a rare opinion.

'I am happy to hear you speak so, sir,' he said. 'With your permission, I shall send her packing forthwith.'

'Yes, do that, but before you do enlighten me in one respect. How old is the girl? Do you know?'

A superficial glance had told him she was, perhaps, fifteen years of age, but she could easily be a little older. That at least would be something.

'Elizabeth is thirteen years of age,' said Rogers.

'No! Are you certain?'

'Quite certain, sir, although I grant you she has all the appearance of being a year, or two, older.'

'I see. Now, humour me, Rogers. My memory fails me. How often has she been here in the past?'

'On two occasions,' replied an unblinking Rogers. 'The most recent six months ago. Before then, about a year back.' He paused, doubtful. 'No, it must have been a little more than a year ago. If my memory serves me right, there was some talk of her forthcoming twelfth birthday.'

'This is getting worse by the minute', thought Richard. He shook his head in anger. 'There is a law against this sort of thing,' he said, as if to himself.

Rogers raised his eyebrows at these biting words of self-criticism, but said nothing.

He voiced his manservant's thoughts for him.

'But it is not a law which applies to the landed gentry, that much is clear,' he muttered.

He had spent a fruitless half-hour searching the estate nearby for Emma and Rachel. His circuitous route brought him back to the front portico of the house, where he stood for a little while pondering what next to do. It was then that a horse and rider came into view at the far end of the long, gravel drive, and began to head towards him. A moment later, he found himself looking up into a familiar face.

'Constable Dukinfield, good morning to you,' he said. 'Tell me, how fares the prisoner?'

The new arrival dismounted, and give him a rueful look.

'That is why I am here,' he replied. He give a nervous cough, visibly embarrassed. 'Sir Richard, I hardly know how to tell you this. The fact is, that young rascal the Jessel boy has got clean away from us.'

Richard smiled to himself at the use of the word 'us', as if he, himself, had somehow been involved in the debacle of a lost prisoner.

'I see,' he answered, mildly. 'Lose many prisoners from your little lock-up, do you?'

'The first in all my time,' protested Dukinfield. 'No, it's that fool of a lad of mine. One cannot trust him to do anything. He had the keeping of the prisoner while I was off attending to another matter. When I got back I found the lock of the cell door forced, our bird flown, and my young assistant running hither and thither like some headless chicken. Claimed he heard and saw nothing, and him barely twenty feet away in an adjoining room. I've already sent word to my colleague, Hutton, to be on the lookout – Nathan Jessel is well-known north of the river, of course – but I have to say that I'm not very optimistic in that respect. Well, I would not blame you if you decide to make a formal complaint. It's a bad business all round, and there's no mistake.'

'Well, I dare say you might yet recover him,' said Richard.

'To be honest, sir, I very much doubt that. He is nothing if not sharp that one, and he has a good head start on us.'

'But he must return here eventually, surely? All his family remain in Yarm.'

Dukinfield shook his head.

'Reckon he's gone for good this time. Bristol, more likely than not.'

'Bristol, you say? Now there's a journey and a half. Why should he make for Bristol, of all places?'

'The family hails from there. Not been in these parts beyond six years, and still got a dozen relatives in that city. Fact is, things have finally got a bit too hot for Nathan hereabouts. Besides, richer pickings by far in Bristol than around this neck of the wood. Surprised, really, he's lingered here as long as he has after the death of his father.'

'Would he really abandon his family like that? I understand he is their sole means of support.'

'If one can call it 'support'. He's emptied a few purses and cash boxes these three years past – nothing definite proved against him, you understand – but the family has seen precious little of it. He's kept them out of the poorhouse, and that's about as far as it goes.'

'I see. The father is dead, you say?'

'Yes, 'afore your time, sir. Drunk himself to death these three years back. A bad lot, the Jessels – the menfolk, at least. Like father, like son, and there's no mistake.'

'And you feel sure he has gone for good?'

'Reckon so. The word hereabouts is that lately he has been talking more and more of returning south. Reckon this latest business has given him the necessary nudge, which was all that was needed.'

'It may be as you say, but, for myself, I find it hard to believe he would abandon his family and leave them to shift for themselves. Elizabeth apart, I understand there are three young children, including a sister not above three years old.'

'No, he has gone for good,' said Dukinfield, firmly. 'Believe me, sir, the father was a selfish, uncaring wastrel, and the son is just the same. "A bloody millstone around my neck" were his very words to me this morning, speaking of his sisters and young brother. No, he has stayed this long because it suited him, but now it suits him to be away.'

'Yes, I see, but there is one thing that puzzles me still. Why should he take to his heels in such haste? He has been apprehended twice before for poaching on my estate and each time I have arranged for his release. Clearly, he believed his luck would not hold a third time. Why is that?'

The question appeared to present some difficulty to the constable. His reply was a long time in coming.

'Truth is, that is down to me,' he said. 'That young scoundrel was so cocksure of his release when first I took charge of him that I could not refrain from pointing out that the sequel was likely to be altogether different this time, and that he would be made to pay for his offence.'

'You were right to say as much. I sent Elizabeth packing.'

'I guessed you would this time round,' said Dukinfield, nodding his approval. 'That arrangement...... that arrangement......'

'That previous arrangement was not a very creditable one. Yes, I freely own to that. But what of the girl's mother? How could she thrice offer up her own daughter in such a way?'

'Do not be too severe in judging Annie Jessel, sir. She has had one hell of a life, first with the husband, and then with the son, but I have to say that with all his faults Nathan still contrived to keep a roof over the family's head. Plainly, the woman was desperate to keep the lad with her.'

'So, what will happen to the family now?'

The constable shook his head with an air of resignation.

'I have no doubt the family are behind with their rent – they always are. Once word of Nathan's flight becomes public knowledge I imagine old Josh Cohen will have them out of their cottage in no time at all. With the only breadwinner gone he must know there is very little prospect of any money forthcoming from the family.'

'So, the family will be torn apart, the mother into the poorhouse, and the children into some orphanage?'

'Elizabeth is of an age to be gainfully employed, but for the rest, it is as you say.'

'Perhaps Mr Sibley will prevent that? Perhaps he will come to their aid?'

'I doubt that, sir. Five years back, his predecessor, the Reverend Hutchinson, did his level best for the family. I mean, he *really* put himself out. And what was the outcome? Father and son caught thieving from the vicarage. *From the man's own house!* He would not let us prosecute, but from that time on the church authorities washed their hands of the family.'

'But that was father and son. Surely, Sibley would not hold that against the mother and little ones?'

'Well, perhaps not, but there are many more deserving claimants on the church's slender resources. This is for the most part a rural parish, Sir Richard, and none too prosperous on that account, as you are well-aware. Lots of poverty. Plenty of hard-luck stories.'

The conversation was interrupted by a noisy altercation not far from the main entrance to the estate. Both men turned in that direction and watched as one of the gardeners attempted to bar the progress of the very subject of their talk. Annie Jessel had come visiting, bringing with

347

her the remnant of her family. A small, fair-head girl nestled in her arms, while an older girl and a young boy clutched at her skirt. Behind the little group, Elizabeth hovered, uncertain, just within the gates of the estate.

'Well I never! Speak of the Devil!' exclaimed Dukinfield. 'Come to plead Nathan's cause, I have no doubt.' He looked questioningly at Richard Forres. 'She should be acquainted of the true situation and told Nathan is out of everyone's reach. Would you like me to do that?'

'No, I shall see to that. I'm sure you have other duties to attend to. Thank you for calling, constable.'

The two men separated, Dukinfield riding past the little knot of struggling figures with an air of complete indifference, and Richard Forres striding purposefully into the middle of it all.

Her daughter Elizabeth's early return home had thrown Annie Jessel into a panic. Her tried and tested ploy to secure Nathan's release had failed this time. It seemed that the owner of Grange Hall had lost interest in her eldest daughter. It was not to be wondered at, she reflected. That gentleman's new-found devotion to his wife was the talk of the district, and she now acknowledged to herself that she had been foolishly optimistic in expecting the arrangement to carry on as before. Not that she had ever been happy with it. On the contrary, she felt a deep sense of shame whenever she allowed her thoughts to dwell on the subject, but Elizabeth had been a willing participant – *too willing,* in truth – and it had effectively served to keep her little family together, which was the most important thing in the world to her. Now, complete and utter ruin stared her in the face and filled her with despair.

If, however, the sins of the flesh no longer tempted the master of Grange Hall, perhaps the man could be moved by pity. Hastily, she organised the children, so that within ten minutes of Elizabeth's arrival home the group of five had set off to walk the short distance back there.

Richard Forres moved quickly into the middle of the little mêlée, which was threatening to get out of hand. Ridley, one of the under-gardeners, was sent about his business, while Simpson, hurrying from

The Hall to assist, was turned back. That done, he approached Annie Jessel.

'Madam,' he said, 'I believe I can guess why you are here, but there is something which I think you should know at the outset.'

Before he had time to say more, the lady had set down her small bundle on its feet and was on her knees before him, an outcry of words accompanying the action. He glanced apprehensively towards the Hall. The sight of a little group of servants drawn to the scene and watching in curiosity served only to add to the embarrassment which he was feeling. To make matters worse, the two youngest children broke into a series of loud, wailing cries, the trio of voices making an indescribable din. He was forced to shout in order to make himself heard.

'Madam! Really! There is no call for any of this. Calm yourself, I beg you.' This said, he went down on his haunches and with some difficulty raised up a grovelling Annie Jessel.

He looked full into a face grey with anxiety, and careworn with years of unending struggle. He knew the woman to be not yet forty years of age, but to him she looked at least ten years older, the hair prematurely grey, and the face etched with half-a dozen deep furrows. The hands he clasped to raise her up had the feel of sandpaper. Yet, the threadbare clothes had been carefully patched and repaired in a dozen places, he noted. The woman's hair had the appearance of having been recently washed and brushed, while the white face and red hands were patently clean. In spite of their bare feet, the three young children all presented a similar picture.

This is a woman who is doing her level best against impossible odds, were his thoughts. Looking at the ravages of ceaseless toil, the last remnant of anger left him. He realised that in all probability Annie Jessel would from the beginning have offered up herself in preference to Elizabeth if there had been any possibility that such an offer would have tempted Henry Forres.

He gathered up the youngest child in his arms, and pointed to a cloudless blue sky.

'Remarkably fine weather for the time of year, is it not, Mrs Jessel?' he said. 'What say you to a picnic here on the lawn?'

Looking towards the estate gates, he caught sight of Elizabeth flitting in and out of the trees which framed the entrance. Alone of the family, Elizabeth was nicely dressed, he noted, no doubt in clothes bought by her criminal admirer. In spite of his recent prohibition concerning her, he could not bring himself to send her away to an empty house.

'Go and tell Elizabeth to stop playing peek-a-boo and to come and join us. I shall organise matters with my staff, half of whom seem to have nothing better to do than stand and gawp at us.'

An incredulous Annie Jessel wandered off to do as she was bidden, while the gentleman began to make his way towards the house.

'Do you like cake, little Rebecca?' he asked the three year old in his arms. 'What a silly question! Of course you do. So, we shall have a cake, and biscuits, and jelly, and cream, and honey, and lemonade. It is high time things were livened up around here.'

Emma and Rachel had been walking together in a secluded part of the estate, discussing the morning's events. On their return, they had approached the house from the rear and entered quietly by a side entrance, all the time unaware of the impromptu picnic now in full swing on the front lawn. In the privacy of Rachel's room Emma give vent to her anger once more.

'What really infuriated me was that feeble attempt on Richard's part to feign ignorance of that Jessel girl. He must take us for a pair of fools.'

'His behaviour was strange, to be sure,' said Rachel.

'Strange is not the word, it was pathetic,' replied Emma.

Rachel made no reply. During their walk together the strangest of notions concerning her brother had occupied her thoughts, but after due consideration she had all but dismissed them from her mind. No, it cannot be. It is too ridiculous for words, she had told herself.

She moved idly over to the window, and cast her eye over the gardens, which stretched away into the distance. For an instant, she overlooked what was taking place on the lawn directly in front of her, but only for an instant. Calling Emma over to her, she pointed out the scene below.

'That is the Jessel family,' said Emma, stating the obvious. 'Rachel, what on earth is my husband up to now?'

Rachel caught a glimpse of Rogers passing the open bedroom door and hastily called him to her.

'Rogers, just what exactly is going on down there?' she asked, indicating the little gathering.

'It is the master's doing, Miss Rachel,' replied Rogers, stiffly. 'He is entertaining guests.'

'The Jessel family are invited guests?' asked Rachel, disbelieving.

'So it would seem,' said Rogers. There was a distinct hint of disapproval in the tone of voice.

'You sound as if you do not approve,' said Emma.

'Forgive me, my lady,' said Rogers. 'It goes without saying that it is not my place to approve, or disapprove.'

'But you clearly have an opinion in the matter,' said Emma. 'Come, let us hear it.'

Rogers hesitated a brief moment before replying with some reluctance: 'Well, since you press me on the matter, I believe it is hardly fitting for the master to be entertaining that particular family in so public a fashion.'

'Very proper, Rogers,' said Emma, 'but let me assure you in confidence that Sir Richard's recent conduct, including the events of today, baffle me just as much as they seem to puzzle you.'

'I do not see Nathan,' said Rachel, still engrossed with the scene from the bedroom window. 'Presumably, Constable Dukinfield still holds him?'

'Not so,' said Rogers. 'That young criminal has made good his escape, so I am informed. The general opinion is that we are not likely to see him again in these parts.'

'If that be so, it is a bleak future which stretches before Annie Jessel,' said Emma, 'yet one would not think so to look at her.'

'Yes, what a merry scene down there!' exclaimed Rachel.

'I believe I can offer you an explanation, my lady,' said Rogers. 'The master has already arranged for the family to take possession of Worsall Cottage, which has been empty these three weeks past – rent free, so it would seem.'

'So they are to come and live on the estate?' said Emma, frowning.

'Yes,' said Rogers; 'and to ensure they have an income of sorts, Annie Jessel is to undertake a little needlework, as and when time allows, and the master has asked me to find a position for Elizabeth in the kitchen here at The Hall.'

Emma stiffened at these words.

'That should be a convenient arrangement for him,' she said.

'Well, that is subject to your approval,' said Rogers. 'If you would have it otherwise, the master will do his best to find a position for her on some nearby estate. Those were his words to me, my lady.'

Rogers looked keenly at his mistress. The fact was, he was feeling somewhat responsible for the distressing event at the breakfast table that morning. Due to his thoughtlessness, the family he served had been made to endure an unnecessary ordeal. His master was right. He *should* have been consulted before the Jessel girl had been given permission to enter the house. He was anxious now to make amends for his error of judgement.

'My lady, may I speak freely?' he said.

At a nod from his mistress he said: 'This morning's unfortunate business was none of the master's doing. The fault is mine, and mine alone. He was both distressed and angry to find the Jessel girl here. Do not condemn him, I beg you, for my unthinking carelessness.'

'Thank you, Rogers,' said Emma, with a warm smile. 'I have kept you from your duties long enough. You may go now.'

'I do not believe what I am seeing,' said Rachel, after Rogers was gone. Emma joined her at the window and looked in the direction of Rachel's pointed finger. Little Rebecca had climbed onto Richard's lap. He had circled her with an arm and was in the process of wiping some very sticky fingers with a large handkerchief.

'He does not care for children,' murmured Emma. 'I shall not embarrass you with the details of how he has ensured against that so far in our marriage.' With a shake of her head, which summed up her perplexity, she turned to face Rachel. 'These past few weeks I have looked in vain for the sly glance in my direction when that brother of yours performed what I took to be some *calculated* act of kindness done for my benefit. I have studied him intently on numerous occasions when he has had to deal with some offence against himself, always expecting to see a forced smile, or some momentary hesitation, but seeing neither. I have deliberately tried his patience, or tested his temper, on a score of occasions, and all I get in return is that patient, indulgent smile of his. I have seen him lose his temper just the once when I provoked him beyond the endurance of any man. He punishes my offences not with blows, but with kisses. Rachel, he rings true every time. I do not understand it. I simply do not understand it.'

Rachel listened in silence. The weird notion which had troubled her earlier now returned in full force. This time, try as she might, she found she could not so easily dismiss it as a fantasy.

'We are now going down there to put him to the ultimate test. You will back me up in everything I say,' said Emma.

She approached him, all smiles, and planted a kiss on his cheek.

In view of the morning's events, her warm greeting took him by surprise.

'Blondie, you are a saint,' he said.

'Indeed, you are mistaken,' she said. 'You should more properly call me a hypocrite. So, you have cheated on me time and time again, and Elizabeth Jessel is but one example, but I am far from being guiltless in that respect. You should know, you have a right to know, I cheated on you during my stay in Darlington, as Rachel, here, can testify.'

His response was immediate, but not along the lines she had expected. He appeared anxious and concerned, rather than angry.

'Well......,' he said, aimlessly shifting a stray pebble which lay at his feet. 'Well, I shall not condemn you. I perfectly understand the situation you were in. You met a young man who give you the love and respect so long denied you. Does he......? Do you......?'

'I'm afraid it was nothing so fine and noble,' she said, sighing. 'I had several casual affairs in Darlington – a string of them, in fact.'

Rachel, standing close to Emma, was horrified at these words.

'Emma, you go too far,' she whispered in her ear. 'It's all lies. What are you trying to do? Destroy him?'

Rachel's words of caution and censure were unnecessary.

'Oh! that *is* good news,' he said, elated.

Four small arms began to tug at him.

'It seems I am needed elsewhere,' he cried, cheerfully.

'I doubt there is a husband in the world who would not have been outraged by such an admission from his wife,' said Emma, staring back at the reunited party. 'I half-expected him to go beserk, and why should

353

he not? Rachel, he is an enigma to me. His words and deeds are inexplicable at times. I sometimes wonder if he still retains his sanity.'

'Oh, I am certain of his sanity,' said Rachel.

. 'If that be so, how do you explain what took place a moment ago?' said Emma.

'I cannot explain it,' said Rachel. 'But wait...... wait. Yes, of course. Of course! That must be it. Emma, he does not condemn you because he does not feel he has the right to do so. He knows he has no claim on you.'

'You mean, he has forfeited a husband's rights by his treatment of me these two years past? Yes, I suppose that is a possibility.'

'That is not what I meant,' said Rachel, staring into space.

'What then?' said Emma. 'Rachel, for goodness sake don't you start speaking in riddles. I have difficulty enough in dealing with your brother's responses.'

The little picnic on the lawn had run its course. He had not headed off with the Jessel family, so Emma had been told, but neither had he returned to The Hall.

She found him lying on his back beside the little stream which fed into the lake. She sat down beside him, saying nothing. He acknowledge her presence with the briefest of smiles.

'Come back home,' she said, after a moment of silence.

'In a little while,' he said. 'The feeling has all but past.' He opened his eyes and indicated the little stream a few feet away. 'This is my favourite place. It is the perfect spot. For a dozen yards, or so, the stream shallows hereabouts. If there is any sound in the world more beautiful than the quiet murmur of water as it pushes its way over shingle and pebbles, I have yet to hear it. I come here when the loneliness becomes unbearable. I think it was the garden party which did it, or to be more accurate the ending of it. Have you ever returned to an empty house after a long holiday? Oh, one may be glad to be home, but as one wanders through rooms at the one and the same time strange and familiar, there comes a feeling of deflation, or anti-climax. I experienced the same sensation when I stood alone on that empty lawn. For me, it does not take much to trigger a sadness which borders on depression. So, here I come, as I always do at such times, and listen to what the waters have to say. They say, 'you and I know each other. I am the one familiar spot in a strange world'. There was just such a place as this back home, you see. I have only to close my eyes and I find myself back there.'

'You mean, back home in Lincolnshire?'

'What? Oh! yes, Lincolnshire.'

'Richard, there is something I must know,' she said. 'Why did the news of one affair make you look anxious, while a tale of a string of infidelities restore your spirits?'

'Selfishness, pure selfishness on my part,' he said, getting to his feet and extending a hand. 'I thought at first that I had a rival for your affections, but then you went on to speak of several *casual* affairs. Clearly, those lovers mean nothing to you. The moral dimension did not, does not, concern me. I leave that to you. Selfishness, you see.'

'You may call it that if you wish, but I shall not,' she said. 'Richard, I am ashamed to admit it, but I was merely testing you. There were no lovers. I give you my word on that.'

'Even better,' he said, smiling.

'Give me time,' she said.

'I shall give you time if you will give me hope,' he answered.

'Agreed,' she said.

On the eve of their departure south came the news that everything was ready to receive them at York. Both phonograph and recording machine lay gleaming new in the doctor's workshop, aside the soft wax discs on which the recordings were to be made.

Nor had the creature comforts been overlooked. Rarely used rooms in the doctor's house now stood opened up. Beds seldom slept in lay aired and made up. A normally sparsely filled larder, perfectly adequate for the frugal doctor and his modest household staff, now bulged at its large seams.

The little party arrived in York at noon after an uneventful four hour journey from Yarm, and set to work immediately after lunch. By the afternoon of the following day, five recordings had been made to the satisfaction of the inventor.

The recordings were intended to reproduce a variety of sounds, which would show to full advantage the potential of the invention. The voice of Nancy featured in most of them, together with some pianoforte playing by Rachel, and a performance of violin playing, on which musical instrument Johnathon Sinclair excelled. One disc was vocal only. It carried the voice of Richard and was meant to explain the workings of his invention. One of Nancy's discs consisted of a love song of unknown origin. Richard had written out the musical score, but refused to acknowledge it as his own composition. The song rejoiced under the title of 'Danny Boy', and Emma deemed it a particularly beautiful and haunting melody, perfectly suited to Nancy's lovely voice.

To all save the inventor, the first testing out of the phonograph was an unforgettable moment – an eerie, magical experience. Richard gave the appearance of being highly satisfied with the result of all his labours, but no more than that. It was just one more show of emotion, or, to be more accurate, lack of it, which Emma found inexplicable.

Four days after leaving York, the party of five arrived in London, their home for the next few weeks being a fine town house, generously put at their disposal by an old friend of the Doctor.

Their entry into the capital marked the beginning of Richard Forres' own magical experience. This was London, the hub of an empire which covered nearly a quarter of the known world. This was London in the Year of Grace 1813, and he was there *in person*. The many images of that city viewed in retrospect on the monitors at London Complex were to prove as nothing to him in comparison to the reality.

CHAPTER 27

Their stay in the capital got off to a disappointing and inauspicious start.

It had been arranged through a third party that Richard Forres and Johnathon Sinclair were to be guest speakers at the forthcoming meeting of The Royal Society, where the new invention would be unveiled. The Doctor had left their lodgings the morning after their arrival to finalise matters, only to return in dismay within the hour.

'The meeting is cancelled at short notice,' he told a disappointed Richard. 'There has been an outbreak of influenza in the capital, and though the illness is now fast declining, it was deemed best that the meeting should not go ahead. Our contact here has been attempting to reach us with the news these three days past but, of course, we have been on the road all that time. It is all very vexing. There will not be another such meeting for a month.'

'We cannot delay here a month, that much is certain,' said Richard. 'Perhaps we should have been a little more forthcoming concerning our invention. I warrant the meeting would have gone ahead, sickness, or no sickness, if The Society had known with more certainty what was planned, but it is all too late for such thoughts now.'

'Then, what is to be done?' said Johnathon.

'Well, it seems we are in need of some other public gathering which will serve our purposes. Give me a little time to consider the matter.'

Later that day, he sought out Johnathon.

'This is a copy of today's 'Times' newspaper,' he said, leafing through the pages. 'See here this column of court engagements and social events for the next few days. Lady Chessington is holding a ball two evenings hence, at which The Prince Regent is expected to put in an appearance, so we are told. We must secure an invitation, and take our phonograph along with us.'

'A ball!' exclaimed Johnathon. 'Announce our scientific invention at some social gathering?'

'Why not? It will give us the publicity which we seek. What better occasion than a gathering of the most influential citizens of the capital? A ball is not an event solely devoted to dancing. There is conversation. There is entertainment. There is a variety of amusements and diversions.'

'It will be some diversion, I grant you that,' said Johnathon.

'Yes, I, like you, would have rather gone public before a scientific gathering, but it seems that is not to be; and consider: is a ball so very out of place for a machine which is primarily designed for entertainment? No, Johnathon, this social event will serve us very well and has the added advantage of allowing us to bring Emma, Rachel, and Nancy along with us.'

'But we have no invitation,' protested Johnathon.

'Leave that to me,' said Richard. 'Tomorrow morning, before she has time to take herself off somewhere, I shall call on Lady Chessington. Given the opportunity, I intend to startle that fair lady out of her wits.'

At thirty eight years of age, Lady Chessington still retained much of the beauty of her younger days, and was generally held to be the most eligible widow in town. A lady of some influence, with a wide circle of friends and acquaintances from The Prince Regent downwards, she refused to be hidebound by the strictures and conventions of the time. So it was that she viewed the calling card in her hand not with an air of disapproval, or of censure, but with a mixture of amusement and curiosity. For the third time, she read the short, handwritten message penned on the back of the card:

'Immortality in exchange for twenty minutes of your time. Is that not a most generous offer?'

'What is our early bird like?' she asked.

'Young, personable, and unconventional,' answered the footman.

'Oh? Why do you say 'unconventional'?'

'He asked concerning my health, and enquired after my family, my lady.'

'Did he, indeed?'

'Almost as if I were his equal.'

'Yes, I do take your point, Manners.'

'He is a very handsome gentleman, to be sure,' broke in the maid in attendance, who had made a point of taking a peep at their caller.

'That will do, Susan; you may go. Very well, Manners, have him come in.'

Lady Chessington held up the visiting card as Richard Forres entered the room.

'Now, sir, explain yourself. What is the meaning of this impudent message of yours? I am not accustomed to receiving communications of this nature. You do realise, do you not, that if you had called barely an hour earlier you would have found me in bed?'

'Then, you have had a narrow escape, Lady Chessington,' he said. 'Five minutes after the hour you might well have found *me* in bed.'

'Why, you impudent rascal,' she said, rising to her feet.

The joke had not gone down well, he realised. Something else was called for on his part. Stealing inventions from the future was one thing, but the purloining of witty remarks was another matter. It was Oscar Wilde who came to his rescue.

'Forgive me, my ladyship,' he said. 'It is a failing, I know, but the sad fact is I can resist everything except temptation.'

It was a quotation he was later to regret somewhat, but for the moment it served its purpose.

The frown of disapproval disappeared, to be replaced by an outburst of laughter, a laughter which was cut short when a servant – not one of *her* servants – entered the room and at her visitor's directions deposited a large wooden box on a nearby occasional table. The man departed, leaving the two of them alone.

'Please excuse me, Lady Chessington,' he said. 'This will take but a moment.' He turned his back on her and, having emptied the box of its contents, began to tinker with she knew not what. She caught a glimpse over his shoulder of some strange mechanical device, at which point she found her voice.

'I hope you have not called here in an attempt to sell me something,' she said, testily.

'I would like an invitation for a party of five to attend your ball tomorrow evening,' he said, glancing back at her while he continued with his work.

'Would you indeed?' she said, surprised by his boldness.

'And it is important that the dance floor be cleared for half-an-hour at midnight.'

'Oh, quite! Quite! Anything else?' she said.

'Yes, one more thing. I understand the presence of His Royal

Highness is by no means certain tomorrow evening, but I would have him there, if at all possible. You are not to inform him as to what you are about to witness, but a few broad hints from you should pique his curiosity sufficient for him to wish to attend.'

Before she had time to respond, he had turned to face her and was indicating the strange object he had brought with him, and with which he had been occupied.

'A machine such as this will enable you to listen to the voice of a person going about their daily business on the other side of the world. In the fullness of time, the voices of people long dead will come to life again. For the moment, the voice of a young lady a mere three miles away and very much alive will have to suffice.'

Lord, help me! I am closeted with a madman, she thought, greatly alarmed by these wild words.

Turning back to the machine, he made a simple hand movement.

'Listen, my lady,' he said. 'Listen and wonder.'

Would she ever forget that moment? No, never! Within the span of a few seconds, an odd, unaccountable soft hissing noise had given way to the clear, beautiful sound of a young woman singing the sweetest of melodies:

'Oh, Danny boy,
The pipes, the pipes are calling,
From glen to glen
And down the mountain side......'

'She had the appearance of a woman paralysed,' an amused Richard Forres was later to say when retelling the incident.

'Do not be afraid, my lady. It is only a machine and nothing more than that,' he said, reassuringly. Taking her by the hand, he led her towards it. 'See here,' he said, stretching out a hand. 'We can turn down the volume of sound – so. We can turn it back up again – thus. We can move on in an instant to another part of the song – like this. We may put a stop to it, if we wish,' he said, lifting the needle clear of the recording. 'We may restart it, if the fancy takes us – so. You see, it is but a machine, which will do nothing except at one's bidding.'

'But it is a machine that *speaks*,' she gasped. 'How is such a thing possible?'

Having stopped the turntable, he removed the recording disc and showed it to her.

'These hundreds of very fine lines you see are, in fact, circular grooves made when the disc was plain and soft. They were etched by a needle, vibrating to the sound of a voice. Place the *hardened* disc onto the turntable, set it in motion, and allow a second needle to retrace the grooves, and that needle will ride into and over every tiny bump and blip, and every pit and hollow. In so doing, it will emit the exact same sound waves as those which caused its making in the first place. In other words, it will excite the air so as to reproduce exactly the original sound.'

'Are you saying that there is a human voice in there?' she asked. She stretched out a hand to touch the disc but, thinking better of it, hastily withdrew it.

'Not a human voice as you mean it,' he said, patiently, 'but rather the programmed *capability* to *reproduce* the one song.'

'It is a miracle,' she breathed.

'It is no miracle, my lady. It is science,' he said.

'It is a miracle,' she reaffirmed, with a shake of the head.

'We shall compromise and call it a miracle of science,' he said, smiling.

'But why come to me with this wonder?' she asked.

'I have to confess, you were not my first choice,' he said. He proceeded to tell her of the abortive meeting of The Royal Society.

'Well, The Society's loss is my gain. Your little contraption will make tomorrow's gathering an evening to remember.'

'Yes, for all time, I dare say. You must forgive my foolish note, my lady. No one is immortal, but the memory of a person may be reckoned so. Your name, and mine, and those of others intimately involved in this business will be recorded in the history books for all time. That is immortality of a kind, is it not?'

She had produced a printed invitation and now began to fill in the details by hand.

'Lady Denby will be green with envy,' she said, with evident satisfaction.

The name meant nothing to Richard Forres, but he guessed the lady in question was some rival whose social gatherings competed in splendour with Lady Chessington's.

'Poor Lady Denby,' he said, taking his cue from her.

. She found herself warming to her unconventional visitor. Still engaged upon her task, she give him a sly, sideways glance. Susan was right, she thought. He *is* a very handsome fellow.

'I have made it out to Sir Richard Forres, plus a party of four,' she said, handing over the completed invitation. 'Satisfy my curiosity by telling me who is to accompany you tomorrow evening.'

'My uncle, Doctor Johnathon Sinclair, together with three young ladies. The gentleman built the machine you see here, working from my own plans, and all four of the party had a hand in the recordings which I shall be bringing with me.'

'Is there a Lady Forres?' she asked. In spite of her best efforts, the words did not come out in quite the off-hand tone of voice she had intended.

'Yes. Emma is her name. She will be one of the party.'

She nodded, not in the least discouraged. She preferred married men. In her experience, they were more considerate, more discreet, and less demanding than the average unmarried male.

'Why have we not seen you in these parts before now? Yorkshire is not so very far away.'

'My estate occupies much of my time. I am happy there.'

She waved a hand towards the phonograph. 'That will change things,' she said.

'I think not. I am determined not to let it rule my life.'

'You *are* a strange fellow,' she said, smiling. 'If it were my invention, I would glory in it. I would want to shout it out from the rooftops. What are your future plans for your machine?'

'Ultimately, to market it. Ten years from now, I would hope to see it in every household of consequence in the kingdom and, indeed, far beyond, but the first step is to secure financial backing for the enterprise. That is why I am here in London.'

'But I hope business matters will not occupy all your time. Tell me, how long do you plan to remain with us?'

'I hope to be in a position to start back home in two weeks.'

'But you will return again directly, surely?'

'Yes, with business interests here in London I expect I shall be a frequent visitor in future.'

'Your card carries no London address. Can I take it you have no house of your own in town?'

'I have never felt the need of one until now. That must needs wait a little while longer.'

'Well, until that time comes, I would be happy to accommodate you on any future visit, here at 'High Gables',' she said. She paused briefly before adding: 'Of course, you may bring Lady Forres – if you must.'

'You are very kind, Lady Chessington,' he said, smiling.

'Oh, I do assure you, kindness does not enter into it,' she said, gravely.

Lady Chessington did as he had asked.

A sufficiently intriguing note to her royal friend served to guarantee his presence at her ball. She also took it upon herself to ensure that most of her close friends were made aware of the fact that this was to be no ordinary gathering, and that a very unusual event was to take place at the midnight hour. Gossip did the rest, so much so that when Richard Forres and his companions made their appearance at 'High Gables', the loud hum of social conversation quite died away, and all eyes turned in the direction of the newcomers. Soon, a fair flock of curious strangers were clustered around the little party, the whole gathering augmented at regular intervals by the steady trickle of young men, and not so young men, requesting the pleasure of a partner for this, or that, dance.

The three ladies in question each dealt with these requests in their different ways. Rachel eagerly accepted every offer until Richard felt the need to whisper in her ear: 'Rachel, you must learn to say no on occasions, otherwise you will be on your knees before the evening is half-over.' To which Rachel had replied: 'And on my back, I would hope, shortly after. Where are the guest bedrooms in this place, anyway?'

Nancy was more discriminating, although she never refused anyone absolutely, Richard noted, but left every applicant with at least the prospect of future accomodation.

Emma received far fewer invitations, which, perhaps, is not to be wondered at – beyond a certain point beauty intimidates rather than attracts. Many more requests were to come her way, however, as the evening wore on and strong drink began to bolster faint hearts.

At an early stage in the proceedings, Richard secured dances with half-a-dozen plain, middle aged dames. In response to Emma's amused enquiry on this point he replied: 'I've not come here to dance, but I can hardly stand around like some wallflower all evening.'

'But it is a strange selection you have made, all the same,' said Emma. 'There is a host of pretty young women here.'

'Yes, but the ladies of my choice will make more allowance for my indifferent dancing. Besides, why antagonise a lover when one may please a husband?'

'This is a world apart from Yarm,' said Emma, looking about her.

'Oh, yes, that much is certain. I've already been propositioned.'

'Propositioned? What do you mean?'

'Lady Rochester, over there, simply came up to me and asked outright if during my stay in London I would like to sleep with her sometime in return for five hundred pounds.'

'The brazen young hussy!' exclaimed Emma. 'I was always of the opinion that London is a sink of iniquity but not to that extent. Was she serious, do you think?'

'Frankly, I do not know. She may have been joking but I had the feeling she was not.'

'Then, how did you respond?'

'I simply said: but Lady Rochester, do you *have* five hundred pounds? She took my response in good part and contrived to secure a dance with me.'

'Well, I shall be watching the pair of you when you take to the floor, and shall be on the lookout for any hint of smooching.'

In addition to his own selection and that of Lady Rochester, three more dances were more or less forced upon him at the outset. Lady Chessington, apologising profusely, had declared that she could only oblige him with *three* dances since, as hostess, she was expected to circulate more than most. Any serious designs harboured by that lady were, however, abandoned at her first sight of Emma. Such a wife! Men are fickle creatures, to be sure, but not *that* fickle, were her thoughts. Now, she merely looked forward to a little innocent flirtation and drew comfort from the fact that, for once, the handsome, irritating Lady Denby and her beautiful, tiresome daughter would not be the centre of male attention at yet one more of *her* balls.

The one sour note of the evening came early on.

Lady Denby, sweeping across the room with a regal dignity, and trailing her daughter in her wake, accosted Richard Forres and his party. She did not wait for an introduction, but contented herself with a curt nod of greeting to Lady Chessington and to Richard. It was visibly apparent that the attention normally paid to herself and her daughter which had so far failed to show itself that evening had ruffled her feathers somewhat. She quickly turned her attention to Emma as the most culpable and vulnerable person in the group of strangers.

'I understand that in years past your father was in trade, and with some family connections more humble still,' she said, viewing Emma disdainfully through a pair of pinze-nez held a few inches before her eyes.

'What of it?' said Emma, indignantly. 'I am not ashamed to admit to my humble origins, Lady Denby.'

'Really? How brave of you,' said the lady.

Lady Chessington opened her mouth to protest at this cruel, unwarranted jibe, but was cut short by Rachel.

'Leave this to me,' whispered Rachel.

She took a pace forward, smiling sweetly as she did so.

'Lady Denby, we are all delighted to make your acquaintance, but will you not introduce us to your grand-daughter?'

Lady Denby drew herself up to her full height.

'Young woman,' she said, 'when you have been in society a little while you will learn propriety dictates that a person of your age stays silent in the company of her elders and betters until she is spoken to. You would do well to remember that. As for Lady Harriet, here, for your information, she is my daughter, not my grand-daughter.'

'Ah! had her late in life, did you?,' said Rachel. 'I apologise for my error, but it was a natural mistake on my part, as I think everyone here would agree.'

'Insolent girl,' said Lady Denby, bristling with anger. 'Come, Harriet, let us seek out some more agreeable company.'

Harriet, however, chose to stand her ground, glancing back at the retreating figure of her mother.

'Did you have to be so rude with mother?' she demanded, angrily.

'Indeed, you are mistaken, Lady Harriet,' said Rachel. 'I was rude *to* your mother, not with her. I am only ever rude *with* men.'

'Yes, you look the sort of girl who dispenses her favours widely and freely,' said Harriet.

In the context of the conversation, there could be no doubt as to the meaning of this remark. Once again, Lady Chessington felt the need to protest but found she had no need to.

'It is true that I dispense my favours freely,' said Rachel, 'but to own the truth, I have been having second thoughts on that score of late. Why should I not profit from my favours? I ask myself. The trouble is, I am in need of some expert advice on the matter. Tell me, Lady Harriet, how much do *you* charge?'

'You have made an enemy there – two, in fact,' said Lady Chessington when the incident had passed.

'Oh, I can suffer that,' said Rachel. 'Indeed, it will come as a welcome change to everyone fawning over me all the time.'

'What a delightful creature you are,' said Lady Chessington, hugging her. 'I am tired of Lady Denby's sarcastic, cutting remarks. The trouble is, I can never think of a suitable response until hours later.'

'I believe you suffer from what the French call 'Staircase Wit' '

' 'Staircase Wit'? What on earth is that, Miss Rachel?'

'The ability to come up with some witty, suitable response only when one is climbing the stairs to bed hours later.'

Lady Chessington turned to Richard.

'I intend to claim your sister for myself,' she said. 'She shall come to 'High Gables' as often as she likes, and stay as long as the fancy takes her. She shall be the daughter I never had.'

If Rachel could readily and wittily offend when provoked, she also possessed the talent to charm and flatter with an equal ability.

'Lady Chessington, you are very kind, and I shall certainly take advantage of your offer in the future, but your daughter? No, that will never do. No one will credit it. You must pass me off as your younger sister.'

It was late into the evening before His Royal Highness The Prince Regent put in an appearance. Lady Chessington lost little time thereafter in introducing him to Richard Forres and his party.

Richard and Johnathon rose to the occasion with an easy assurance, but Emma could not hide her nervousness, while Nancy was quite overwhelmed. Rachel, however, showing not the slightest trepidation, did not scruple to shamelessly exploit the informality of the occasion.

'We are happy to make your acquaintance, Miss Rachel,' said the Prince. 'Pray, what age are you?'

'I am but eighteen years, your Royal Highness,' she replied.

'You cut a fine figure for one so young, if I may be so bold.'

'You have yet to see the whole of it, your Royal Highness, and I give you leave to be as bold as you wish.'

The Prince was drawn irresistibly back to Emma.

'Tell me, how did you come by this Jewel of the North, Sir Richard?' he asked.

'Ah! thereby hangs a tale,' he replied. 'Let us just say that I was in the right place at the right time.'

'I understand Lady Chessington has been more than kind during her short acquaintance with you. I have to tell you, Sir Richard, that is her nature, given half a chance.' He turned to the lady in question, smiling all the while. 'Give up the unequal contest, Lady Chessington, that is my earnest advice.' He indicated Emma with a nod in her direction. 'You are out of your depth on this occasion, I fancy. What man would want to stray from *that*?'

'I had already come to the same conclusion,' said Lady Chessington, while an uncomprehending Emma looked on in silence.

With a shake of his head, the Prince turned to his aide-de-camp standing at his side and said: 'Colonel Morton, I believe you and I would do well to pay a visit to this county of Yorkshire. If this bevy of beauties is an accurate sample of the fair sex to be found there, I believe it is high time I made a tour of that shire with a view to exercising my royal prerogative, or whatever it is I am supposed to exercise.' He turned to Richard Forres. 'And you, sir, what say you to an exchange of places for a period of time? You may deal with my troublesome subjects, treat with my vexatious ministers, and meet with the Turkish ambassador the day after tomorrow, and I shall take over your duties as husband, brother, and friend. What say you to that? But no, I shall save you the trouble of a reply. I see plainly from your expression that the offer is not to your liking, but I shall have my way in one matter, at least. I expect to see you and your fair companions at Court very often in the future. Lady Chessington, you shall attend to it.

'Now, to other matters. I understand we are all to be entertained in a novel way later this evening. Our hostess, here, refuses to elaborate, and so I shall be patient and not press you for enlightenment.'

'You are very forebearing, your Royal Highness,' said Richard, 'but let me reassure on one point, at least. The spectacle will be worth the waiting, of that I am certain.'

After a further few minutes of conversation the little group broke up, leaving Richard, in particular, to enjoy the rest of the evening's entertainment. Of all the many people in attendance it is doubtful if there was one who thrilled more to the occasion. Nor was this based solely on the knowledge of what would happen at midnight. He had watched such gatherings often enough in the past in another reality, but this did not bear comparison to the actual experience. The music, the dancing, the colour of it all, the fair female sex, so different in appearance and character from those of his own time, the rubbing of shoulders with historical personalities whose future destinies were known only to him – all of this in the shimmering light of a thousand flickering candles went to make up what was to him a wondrous, breathtaking experience. How far had he not come in space of nine short weeks, he reflected, when he stood alone as a stranger in a strange land, owning little more than the clothes on his back, and contemplating the prospect of a night spent under some wayside hedge.

It was a little after midnight, and Richard Forres stood with his four companions within the cleared space at the centre of the ballroom. A little to one side, and attracting many a curious glance, was the phonograph machine, placed on a small table of convenient height. Lady Chessington had made a short speech by way of introduction, and the assembled company crowded, hushed and expectant, in a huge semicircle around and about.

With a few brief words, Richard brought forward his companions one by one, detailing the assistance of each one in the enterprise. The preliminaries over, he set up the first of the recordings.

Set at full volume, the phonograph came to life before a startled audience.

The whole performance was over in little more than thirty minutes, producing in this short span of time a range of emotions perhaps without parallel in history. Shock, alarm, fear, apprehension, consternation, awe, bewilderment, a sense of wonder, amazement, delight, exhilaration – each ran their course in turn.

In the long history of man's inventions from stone axe to sophisticated computer, there has been many an artefact more significant than the humble phonograph, but there have been very few to match its novelty. Anticipated by virtually no one, it surprised a world of 1878, and stunned a world of 1813.

Within seven days of the machine's first public showing, Richard Forres had all the financial backing he needed.

'I suppose the notoriety was only to be expected, but speaking for myself I find it irksome.'

It was two weeks after the events at Lady Chessington's ball, and Richard was speaking to Emma.

'Notoriety is hardly the word for it,' said Emma. 'You are a cause célébre, which is not to be wondered at. How far advanced are the business arrangements?'

'They were completed today. The Corbitt Brothers, a first class engineering concern, are to manufacture the machine, and Sir George Banks is to provide all the necessary funding. I shall be responsible for all future research and development, and the three of us each have a third holding in the enterprise.'

'And you are sixty thousand pounds to the good, I understand.'

'Yes, thirty thousand pounds from each of the other two parties to buy their way into the enterprise. That will be more than enough for us to purchase and staff a substantial property here in London. It is only fitting that we should have a second home in the capital now that the Forres family fortune is tied to the place. It goes without saying that the future prospect of Grange Hall and its estate is now secured for all time.'

'You have no plans to sell Grange Hall, then?'

'Certainly not. I would not forfeit the peace and quiet of Yarm for a permanent existence in London. I assure you, Emma, that my visits to London shall be as infrequent as I can make them.'

'We both know Rachel holds a different point of view. She has made that very plain, and yet......'

'And yet, she turned down the opportunity to remain in London for a further month in the care of Lady Chessington. Yes, that was odd. The two of them get on wonderfully well together, and yet she has refused that lady's offer, on this visit at least.'

'She is preoccupied with some matter, but I do not know with what,' said Emma, thoughtfully. 'Have you noticed that she has taken to harping on about your early days together in Lincolnshire?'

Richard give a helpless shrug of the shoulders.

'I do not pretend to understand Rachel much of the time,' he said. 'I am but seven years her senior, but on occasions she is apt to make me feel as if I were from a different generation.'

Emma looked at him in surprise.

'Seven years? You are her elder by a full nine years.'

'Ah! ...... yes, of course. Stupid of me,' he said, forcing a smile. He felt a pressing need to change the subject. 'I wish I could persuade your uncle to retain a financial interest in our phonograph invention – he is fully entitled to do so, and at no cost to himself – but he will not. He tells me he is happy in his present situation, that he lacks for nothing, and that the securing of our future and that of Peter's is reward enough for his work.'

'You said yesterday that we are to leave for home on Thursday. Does that still stand?'

'Yes, everything is settled, so we shall leave the day after tomorrow. I am pressed on all sides to extend our stay, but I am determined to be away, if only for your uncle's sake. He makes no complaint, but I believe he is anxious to return home as soon as possible. He misses old friends and acquaintances, hearth and home, and a well-loved daily routine. There is also Nancy to consider. I promised her father that she would be back home within the month.'

'A month,' mused Emma. 'That period of time strikes a not too distant chord.'

'I know to what you refer,' he said. 'Well, perhaps I was overconfident in that respect. How am I doing, Blondie?'

'I wanted to see how you would conduct yourself in London, with its many enticements and temptations. You have passed the test with flying colours; but this is not the time, nor the place. Can you wait until we get home? I have a proposition to put to you, better done there than here.'

'A *proposition?* Very well, I agree,' he said.

'How can you agree to something without knowing what I have in mind?' she said.

'Oh, I know full well what you have in mind, and I know from whence it springs,' he said. 'Well, thank goodness for my phonograph machine and the money it will bring me.'

'What on earth are you talking of?' she asked.

He appeared not to be listening. He appeared to be mentally engrossed with something.

'Richard!' she exclaimed.

He shook his head, impatiently.

'I nearly had it before you distracted me. Blondie, what is five hundred pounds times three hundred and sixty five?'

A week later saw the party of travellers returned to York, the Doctor arriving back to news of the sudden death of an old friend and near-neighbour. Having missed the funeral, he was anxious to pay his respects by a visit to the grave of his friend in the nearby churchyard of St. Olave.

'It is a fine day. Allow me to accompany you,' said Richard.

Twenty minutes later they were standing in silence by the mound of freshly turned earth.

'It is a stark reminder of one's own mortality,' said Johnathon, after a moment of silent contemplation. He turned a troubled face to his companion. 'Was Shakespeare right, Richard?' he asked. 'Is life a tale told by an idiot, full of sound and fury, and signifying nothing? If that be so, what, then, is left to us?'

'What is left, Johnathon, is the only thing that any of us *really* possess: the present moment. As for life, that is all things to all men.

To the thinker, life is an enigma; to the sensitive type, it is a tragedy; to those who never concern themselves with such matters, it is simply an experience; to the lazy fellow, it is an effort; to the bold, it is a challenge; to the cynic, it is a bad joke on a cosmic scale. Yes, life is what one makes of it. Perhaps, thinking about it, that is the best of all possible answers. At least it has the merit of offering a *chosen* purpose to life, rather than an *imposed* one.'

'We are skirting around the problem,' said Johnathon. 'None of what you say gets us to the heart of the matter. Why does the Universe 'bother' to exist? Why are we here at all? is the question.'

'Well, perhaps at some time in the distant future some clever fellow will prove from scientific first principles that it would be impossible for there to be nothing.'

'And where does all of that leave us? Do we live out our three score years and ten, and that is the end of the matter? I suppose that is the obvious philosophy. What say you?'

'I say it is an impoverished way of looking at things. It is simplistic. It is banal. I know for certain it is wrong. Let me just say that things are rarely what they seem to be in matters as profound as this.'

'These are deep waters,' said Johnathon, shaking his head.

'Indeed they are,' said Richard, 'but I believe a man may concern himself too much with the meaning of life, to the detriment of living it. Let us ponder the matter no more. Let us return home to a cheerful fireside and to the company of three beautiful young women, whose natural inclination is not to ponder, but to love.'

CHAPTER 28

Early the following morning, having said their goodbyes to Johnathon Sinclair, they set off on the last stage of their journey home.

Within two hours of their arrival in Yarm three events of consequence had taken place.

At Rachel's insistence, the carriage had travelled on into the centre of the town to pick up a passenger.

'My word, he has certainly grown in twelve weeks,' said Richard at the first sight of Charlie in Rachel's arms. 'I take it you now trust me to deal kindly with him?'

'Knowing you, I think there is a good chance you will spoil him something rotten,' said Rachel. 'I suppose if he misbehaves it will be left to me to correct him.'

The second surprise came when Emma followed him into his room even before she had entered her own.

'Shall I unpack here?' she said. 'Shall I go further, and transfer some of my effects from my room to yours? We have always had our separate bedrooms. Do you want to change that? Would you like this room to become *our* room from now on?'

'Need you ask?' he said, huskily, 'but I know you expect something from me in return. Just what is this proposition you spoke of in London?'

'I now know why you are a different person from the man I once knew,' she said. 'It is a mystery to me no longer.'

Was it possible she had hit on at least part of the truth, and it did not matter to her? he asked himself. If only that were so.

'Go on,' he said, not trusting himself to say more.

'Drink,' she said.

'What?' he exclaimed.

'I spent some time in London speaking to a specialist physician who devotes his time to the affliction. I give him a full history of our marriage, sparing no details. He confirmed what I had begun to suspect for myself. There are two Richard Forres: one sober, kind, and considerate, and the other intoxicated, vicious, and selfish. Drink, intoxicating liquor – call it what you will – has been your downfall these two years past.'

373

'Emma, that is nonsense,' he said. 'Drunk, or sober, I have but the one face.'

'How can you say such a thing?' she protested. 'Do you deny that my worst moments, and Rachel's, too, have come when you have arrived home drunk almost out of your senses? Do you claim there is no connection between the two? Long ago, shortly after my return here, Rachel informed me that your change for the better coincided with a sustained period of abstinence on your part. Doctor Morrell is of the opinion that no other explanation fits the facts.'

'Doctor Morrell?'

'The physician I went to see. He was full of admiration for you when I told him how you have conducted yourself these three months past. He says it is difficult enough to give up the addiction when expert help is at hand, let alone to do so alone and unaided, but he was disturbed when I told him that you had not totally abandoned the habit.'

'I have the occasional glass of wine, or sherry, that is all,' he protested. 'Really, Emma!'

'Yes, I acknowledge that, but *total* abstinence is the only answer, so he told me. The demon inside you is not dead but merely sleeping. Richard, you have come nine-tenths of the way yourself, and I give you credit for that, but will you not take this final step for my sake? Promise me faithfully to do so and I shall abandon my room in favour of yours.'

It was a very tempting offer to Richard. He had no great liking for strong liquor, although he was partial to a drink from time to time, especially a glass of wine with his main meal. So, it would have been easy to have said yes - easy, but wrong in essence.

'No, I cannot agree to your proposal,' he said. 'I cannot agree to it on principle.'

'Principle? What principle?' she said.

'Emma, your request tells me plainly that you still do not fully trust me – *that* is the material point in all of this, at least to me. I am nearly there. I sense it. I *know* it. As for this other business, I can only say that an excess of liquor makes me foolish, not vicious. I see you doubt that, and with good cause, I have to admit. Very well, it is up to me to furnish proof of what I claim, and I shall do so. Tell me, how much did you pay this Doctor Morrell for his advice?'

'Ten guineas,' she said; 'but Richard — .'

He held up a hand to stop her in mid-sentence.

'Blondie, write and ask him for your money back. That is my advice to you. As to me, give me a few days more, that is all I ask.'

The third incident came later that same afternoon.

Richard had returned, furiously angry, to Grange Hall after an hour long tour of the estate.

'That is it,' he proclaimed to Emma. 'I have suffered that man long enough, but no more.'

'Of whom are you speaking?' asked Emma.

'Why, our esteemed estate manager, Mr. Smilie, of course. We have returned a day early and I caught him unawares. The mantraps are back, or rather they were. I caught him red-handed in the process of removing them. You will not believe what he has done in my absence. Our pair of breeding buzzards have been shot out of the sky, and I have it on good authority that he has allowed the obscene practice of badger baiting to resume in Scar Wood. All those involved have been given a final warning, and Smilie has been summarily dismissed. I have given him until five o'clock to remove himself from the estate.'

'But what will he do? Where will he go?' said Emma.

'I do not know, and I do not care,' he said. 'Perhaps he will take himself back to Lincolnshire, there to find a situation more to his liking.'

'Richard, the estate cannot function without a steward, especially now with your commitments in London.'

'I am well aware of that, but I have the ideal replacement in mind. Hopefully, he can be with us within the week.'

'And whom might that be?' said Emma. 'Do I know him?'

'I would be surprised if you did, since I have yet to clap eyes on him myself, but I have had very good reports of him from his sister, with whom I am acquainted.'

'Tell me more,' said Emma.

'His name is Edward Gaskell, and he hails from Leeds. His sister, Jane, is a friend of the Harker family, here in Yarm. I met with her a few months back, and we have conducted a correspondence of sorts since then. Shortly after her last visit to Yarm, her father died suddenly. The mother died many years ago, when Jane was a small child, so she is left alone in the world apart from Edward, and his wife and child. Jane is but seventeen years of age, Edward is twenty eight. For the past six years he has had the running of an estate such as ours outside Leeds, but has recently forfeited his position through no fault of his own. For the past two months he has been endeavouring to find another post, but without success. I shall send an express messenger to Leeds this very day in the hope that he will be with us before too long. The estate is perfectly capable of running itself for a week, or two. I have no doubt he will bring Jane with him, together with his wife and child, of course.'

'But what little you know of him has come via his sister,' Emma pointed out. 'How can you be sure he will be to your liking?'

'Well, he comes highly recommended from his previous employer, so I understand. They only parted company because the estate was sold on and the new owner has his own steward. Jane speaks highly of him, which is enough for me. He is young, agreeable, sensitive to the needs of those under his charge, and has a love of nature in all its many forms. In short, unless I have been grossly misinformed, he is the very opposite of the late, unlamented Smilie.'

'And Jane? What of her?' said Emma.

'You will like her Emma, I'm sure – one cannot fail to do so – and I have the feeling that Rachel, too, will instantly take to her. I cannot speak for Edward's wife, but Jane is the most captivating girl I have ever met. It will be a delight to have her here on the estate.'

'I see,' said Emma, frowning. 'Well, let us hope she gives you as much satisfaction as you hope for from her brother.'

'Blondie, you are a blockhead,' he said.

'Do you think so?' she said, returning his smile.

'I *know* so,' he said.

An ideal opportunity for Richard to become intoxicated came three days later when, together with Emma and Rachel, he fulfilled a long standing invitation to a dinner-dance at the nearby village of Egglescliffe.

Anxious not to embarrass the assembled company, he had planned to render himself inebriated but not hopelessly incapable, although as events were to turn out in this he was not entirely successful.

He was, and never had been, a heavy drinker, and was not looking forward to the event on that account, but he had a point to make, which could not be avoided. The point in question was that whereas Sir Henry Forres had been a belligerent, highly aggressive individual when drunk, Technician Richard Travis had a tendency to veer off in the opposite direction of foolish affability. In view of his recent conversation with Emma, he had been left with no other option than to make that distinction abundantly clear to her.

Within a short time of their arrival, Emma was viewing with consternation this seemingly eager return to his former ways. After the passage of an hour, with him well and truly 'into his cups', she began to absent herself from his side for longer and longer periods of time. She had attempted to entice him onto the dance floor, but without success. It appeared that he had abandoned his interest in dancing in favour of increasingly frequent visits to the large, communal punch bowl. Unutterably depressed at what she was witnessing, she, too, began to drink more than was her custom.

It appeared that her worst nightmare was coming true. Or, was it?

As the evening wore on, she saw plainly that the expected change in his disposition was failing to materialise. On the contrary, the affable, easy-going behaviour, which had characterised him of late, was deteriorating merely into a rather garrulous foolishness.

No less surprising to Emma was Rachel's conduct. Appearing perfectly at ease, she had stayed close to her brother for much of the evening. It was plain to Emma that she shared none of her own feelings of apprehension.

Late into the evening, Emma had watched from a distance as Rachel, after a discreet look about her, concluded a long and particularly friendly spell of tête-à-tête by giving the gentleman a most unsisterly-like kiss. It was at this point that she decided to rejoin the pair.

They welcomed her appearance in marked contrast to each other. He greeted her wildly, as some long-lost bosom friend. Her welcome was more restrained, the smile warm and friendly, but the eyes challenging and with a hint of defiance.

'You are drunk, Richard,' said Emma, mildly reproving.

The foolish smile disappeared momentarily. 'That is true, my dear Blondie,' he said, soberly.

'I believe our little gathering is beginning to break up,' said Emma, looking about her. 'Perhaps it is time we, too, left.'

With some difficulty, she and Rachel got him to his feet. Taking an arm each, they began to guide him towards the exit.

'I believe the sooner Rachel and I get you home, and have you in bed, the better,' said Emma.

Emma was immediately to regret this somewhat carelessly worded statement.

'Oh, good! An orgy!' he exclaimed, loudly. 'A menagerie a trios, as the French say. Bags I piggy in the middle.'

'Will you lower your voice?' breathed Emma. 'People are looking at us. They can hear you.'

Emma had hoped that they would be able to take their leave unobserved, but it was not to be. Their host and hostess had, in fact, already taken up a position near the door in order to bid farewell to their departing guests. There was no escape.

'Ah! Sir Richard. Leaving us so soon?' said the lady. 'Can I not persuade you to stay a little while longer?'

Now it is an undoubted fact that the merry reveller the world over loses the ability to conduct a quiet conversation. As now.

'You are very kind, madam,' he declared, his voice carrying to the far corners of the room, 'but I fear we must take our leave. Emma is eager to get the three of us home and into bed together.'

Emma cringed as she saw her hostess' jaw drop open. She blushed crimson as a dozen heads turned in her direction. Distinctly, she heard a male voice proclaim: 'That Sinclair girl! Still waters. I always said so.'

'Some fellows have all the luck,' muttered their host to himself, and received a dig in the ribs from his wife for his pains.

Wishing the ground would open up and swallow her, Emma helped propel their burden through the open door and in the direction of their waiting carriage.

'Did you have to say that to Mrs Barton?' she hissed.

'Say what, my dear Blondie?' he said.

'That I was eager to get the three of us into bed together. I nearly died of shame.'

'Ah! meant to be a secret, was it?'

'Yes – I mean, no – that is to say – oh, blow!'

'You sound a little confused, my dear,' he said. 'Wine gone to your head, has it?'

'Gone to *my* head!' she exclaimed. 'Well, I like that.'

'Do not worry, I shall look after you. I shall see no harm comes to you,' he said, treading on her toes.

It was at that moment they saw the rapidly approaching figure of Vicar Sibley.

'What is he doing here?' Emma whispered to Rachel.

'He has his nephew and neice staying with him,' Rachel whispered back. 'They were at the dance. I can only think he is here to escort them back to the vicarage.'

'It's rude to whisper,' said Richard, loudly.

'Be quiet,' Emma urged him. 'If you must speak, you will confine your remarks to the weather. *To the weather*, do you understand?'

'Sir Richard – Emma – Miss Rachel: good evening to you,' said Sibley. 'I trust you have had an enjoyable time?'

'Very enjoyable, thank you,' Emma interposed, hurriedly.

'Richard, I need to speak to you on a certain matter,' said Sibley. 'When would be a good time to call on you?'

Confine yourself to the weather – to the weather, Richard told himself.

He looked up to a glowering sky.

'Looks set to piss down, Mr. Sibley,' he said.

Leaving an astonished Sibley staring at them, Emma bundled Richard into the carriage.

'Drunk as a lord,' said Rachel to Emma.

'No!' exclaimed Richard, looking back at Sibley. 'Really, what is the world coming to? And him a cloth of the man, too.'

Emma seated herself and took off her left shoe.

'Oh! my poor toes,' she said. 'You trod all over them. Really, Richard!'

'I shall give them a gentle massage,' he said, leaning forward towards her. 'I have a healing touch; you must grant me that.'

'I shall probably regret this, but go ahead,' said Emma, extending her leg and resting her foot between his open knees.

'It would help before I begin if Matthews was to slow down a little,' he said. 'Rachel, lean out of the window and tell him to do so. The carriage is swaying about all over the place.'

'We haven't set off yet,' said Rachel.

'Ah! that explains it,' he said. He began to flex his fingers. 'Now then, let me see if I can repair the damage Rachel has done.'

For a few moments he worked sensibly and effectively before his inebriated foolishness began to reassert itself.

'This little piggy went to market,' he said, taking a gentle hold on Emma's big toe.

'I have never, ever, seen him like this before,' Emma said to Rachel.

'And this little piggy stayed at home,' he said, moving on to the next toe.

'Frankly, Rachel, I have given up trying to understand him.'

'This little piggy had corned beef.'

'I only hope Mr. Sibley has come to the conclusion that he misheard his views on the weather.'

'And this little piggy had none.'

'Look at him, Rachel. Just look at what he is doing. Can that possibly be the man I married? I ask myself.'

'And this little piggy went –'

Emma gave out a shriek as his hand shot swiftly from her little toe, under her dress, and up to the top of her leg.

'—wee, wee, wee, nearly all the way home.'

'Come and sit between us, and behave yourself, Richard,' said Emma, opening up a space between herself and Rachel.

For a few moments he did as he was told, only to eventually shatter the silence by loudly proclaiming: 'I have a pronouncement to pronounce, which will shock all present.'

'I believe we have had more than enough shocks for one evening,' Emma said. 'Save your pronouncement until the morning.'

'No, I can keep silent on the matter no longer,' he cried. He paused marshalling his thoughts with difficulty. 'Emma, Rachel, you are two woman, each one of the two of you, while I am a ...... I am ......'

'A man?' volunteered Rachel.

'Yes, exactly so. Thank you, Rachel. You read my thoughts very well. So, I am a man, and you are not men.'

'I have long suspected it,' said Rachel, gravely.

'So, to continue,' he said.

Emma groaned.

'Why do I get the feeling we are on the brink of one of those interminably long and pointless discussions during the course of which one longs for sudden death?'

'Pardon?' he said, blinking.

'Never mind,' sighed Emma. 'Carry on if you must.'

'Thank you, I shall.' He paused, perplexed. 'I've lost my thread now. What was I saying? Oh! yes. I have an announcement to pronounce.'

'Oh, Lord! we are back at the beginning,' gasped Emma. 'You are a man and we are two women,' she reminded him.

'Yes...... yes, I would not dispute that,' he said, 'so what exactly is your point, Emma?'

'Oh, my hat!' exclaimed Rachel.

'I suppose the point you are trying to make is that you both have something I do not possess,' he said. 'I think we can all guess what that is.'

'A brain?' suggested Rachel.

'It was a measure of Richard's state of mind that he considered this suggestion in perfect seriousness for several seconds before responding.

'No, not a brain, Rachel. I believe Emma is speaking of your feminine charms as opposed to my gentlemanly feelings. I could not agree more. In fact, I was going to raise the same point myself before Emma anticipated me.'

Rachel shook her head in disbelief.

'Is that the sum total of our discussion for the past five minutes? Your gentlemanly feelings as distinct from the feminine charms of Emma and myself?'

'What do you mean by that?' he said, indignantly. 'Emma and I at least hold them in high regard. *They*, of course, hold a different point of view. *They* look upon every gentlemanly act as an aberration. *They* would have the sexes equal in every respect.'

'Richard, what *are* you talking about?' Emma demanded. 'Who are these 'they' which you speak of?'

'Why, my own people, of course,' he said.

With an expressive sigh, and a shake of the head, Emma give up on the conversation and turned her eyes to the ghostly scenery flashing past the carriage window. Not so, Rachel. She scrutinised the pleasant, foolish face next to her own.

'So, we are getting to it,' she said. 'Who are your people, my strange and wonderful friend?'

'You may well ask,' he said. With a secretive, knowing look, he raised a finger to tap the side of his nose, but with his aim at fault succeeded only in poking himself in the eye. This reduced him to silence for a moment before he broke out once more.

'Emma! Rachel! I have been thinking and wondering. Are you partial to 'Dick'?'

'Oh, Lord, Rachel! he is off again,' said Emma.

'I have a petname for each of you. May I not offer you one in return? 'Dick' is the obvious contraction of Richard, and although I have no great liking for it myself, the name has a long history and tradition.'

'There is Dick Pearce, landlord of 'The George and Dragon',' Rachel pointed out.

'Hardly a celebrated figure, Rachel, but, yes, we may fairly count him as an example.'

'There is Dick Purcell, from the stagecoach office in town.'

'True, but what of more celebrated persons in history? What of Dick what's-his-name, and the Lord Mayor of London Town, his cat?'

'A clever pussy. Almost human,' said Rachel.

'Nor should we forget Dick Van Ryn of Rigel 7 fame.'

'Dick *who*?' said Emma, drawn to the bizarre conversation.

'Never heard of a Dick Hoo,' said Richard, frowning. 'Chinese, was he? Chinese father, English mother – that kind of thing? Really, Emma, when Rachel and I are doing so well, is that the best name you can come up with? Some Chinese fellow no one has ever heard of?'

'Oh! I say,' protested Emma.

'Now, I shall give you a *real* household name,' he said. 'I give you Dick Turnip, the celebrated highwayman who rode to York to get hanged.'

'I often wonder why he did that,' said Rachel, thoughtfully.

'*Turpin*, Dick *Turpin*,' Emma corrected him.

'Yes him, too. Well done, Emma. So, let me see. That makes nine in all, not counting Emma's Chinaman.'

'Oh, crumbs!' exclaimed Rachel.

'Listen to me, Richard, listen to me,' pleaded Emma. 'Watch my lips. *TURPIN*, Dick *TURPIN* – *he* was the man who rode from London to York.'

'Yes, there's another, which makes twelve, I think.'

'Not counting the Chinaman,' said Rachel, gravely.

'Not counting the Chinaman,' he agreed. He paused, frowning. 'Hold on, Emma, we have already counted Turnip, I'm sure. Really, my dear, do try to pay attention.'

This was too much for Rachel, who broke out into an outburst of laughter, but Emma, suddenly grave and silent, began to weep quietly, the tears welling up in her eyes and coursing down her cheek.

This show of emotion was not lost on either Richard or Rachel.

'We shall count this Dick Hoo fellow,' he said, patting her hand reassuringly. 'I can't say fairer than that.'

The sensible response came from Rachel.

'What is wrong, Emma, dear? What is the matter?' she said.

'I was thinking of the old days. I much prefer all this nonsense to a beating,' she sobbed.

'Those days are gone for good,' said Rachel, quietly.

'Do you know, Rachel, I believe you may be right. And now I am going to do something which, perhaps, is long overdue.'

Having dried her eyes, and composed herself, she moved closer to where he sat, now quietly holding a conversation with himself. She turned his face towards hers. He opened his mouth to speak to her, but she laid a finger on his lips.

'Now, Richard, since words seem to have no affect on you, I see that I shall have to silence you in another way.' So saying, she moved a pair of lips restlessly onto his. Finding the sight unbearable, Rachel turned her back on the scene.

After a moment, she broke free to pause for breath, and he seized upon this opportunity.

'Dick Whittington – he was another,' he exclaimed.

'We have already counted Whittington,' she said, smiling. Her mouth moved once more towards his. 'Really, Richard, do try to pay attention,' she murmured.

It was a blessed relief to Rachel when their carriage arrived home. With some difficulty, she and Emma managed to get their burden upstairs to his room, and onto his bed.

Together, they viewed him as he lay helpless and prostrate.

'I shall attend to him. It is my duty,' said Emma.

'Oh, it is no one's duty,' said Rachel, 'but for this little while longer I shall leave him in your charge.'

Emma thought this such an odd remark that she was lost for a response as Rachel made her way out of the room.

Turning her attention back to Richard, she saw that he had opened his eyes and was looking at her.

'Has Rachel gone?' he asked.

'Yes, just a moment ago,' she said.

'Perhaps it is for the best,' he said. 'I fear we would, in any event, have had to postpone our plans to spend the night together. The truth is, I lack the wherewithal and would doubtless have disappointed you both.'

'There were no plans for the three of us to spend the night together, except for those which existed in your own muddled imagination,' said Emma, indignantly. 'How can you speak in such terms with regard to Rachel? She is your *sister*, for heaven's sake, or had you forgotten?'

'She is not my sister,' he answered, boldly.

'Oh, very well, she is your half-sister. Do you plead that in mitigation?'

'I have to confess, there are times when I do not look on her as a sister, whole, or half.'

'Yes, that much has become obvious of late, but to be honest, Richard, I could not really blame you if you were drawn to another.' With a sigh, she seated herself beside him, her expression softening all the while. 'I know I have been less than a wife to you since my return, and you have been more than patient in that respect.'

'That aspect of our life together is not so important as it once was,' he said. 'The truth is, there was a time – and not so long ago at that – when your body would have sufficed. Now, I want more. Emma, it is your soul I seek.'

She give a little laugh, in tone both affectionate and embarrassed.

'I am not sure you should speak so. My soul belongs to God.'

'Oh, Blondie, He will not begrudge me the loan of it, I'm sure. I only want it for a lifetime.'

There it was again, she thought: the striking turn of phrase, beautifully expressed – a combination of sentiment and command of words which until recently had never shown itself. She felt a stirring within herself as her self-imposed inhibitions began to evaporate, but this was not the time, or situation, she acknowledged to herself. She got to her feet, and addressed him in a light-hearted tone of voice.

'Shall I undress you, or would you rather I summon Simpson?'

'I think that is quite the silliest question ever put to me,' he said.

'I shall take that as meaning you wish me to help you,' she said, smiling.

She started on her task, talking all the while.

'I have never seen you like this before. Here you are, very much the worse for drink and yet as gentle as a lamb. So, here is another wonder to add to all the rest. But your fondness for liquor this evening was out-of-character of late and —.' She broke off in mid-sentence, struck by a sudden thought. 'Can it be that all this was done for my benefit? Give me a few more days you said on the day we returned from London. Did you want to show me that your character holds good whatever your state of mind? Is that the truth of the matter, Richard? Is it?'

'I keep telling you, I have but the one face,' he said.

'Yes, I believe you,' she answered.

Having undressed him to his underclothes, she got him, grumbling and complaining, into bed. She was in the act of leaving him when he reached out a hand to draw her back.

'Do not go,' he said. 'Stay a little while longer, and let us talk. I believe my head is clearing somewhat.'

'If you wish,' she said, taking a seat beside him. She looked at him expectantly. 'So, what shall we talk about?'

'Tell me of this other Richard fellow. Tell me about that night. Tell me what you felt and thought.'

She looked at him in surprise.

'I should have thought those details would pain you,' she said.

'Believe me, they will not,' he said.

. With his encouragement, she began to tell in her own words the story of their first meeting.

'It is strange,' was his verdict when she had finished.

'That is surely an understatement,' she said. 'Looking back, it seems but a dream, and, yet, here I am, alive and well, and still lacking my father's ring.'

'Emma, you mistake my meaning,' he said.

He was back to Emily Brontë again. As in the snowbound graveyard of his dream, the associations were unmistakable. What did it all mean? Did any of the connections have a meaning, or was it pure coincidence? He began to voice his thoughts.

'You say this man came to you one dark and starry night, on the wings of a warm, gentle wind. You tell me he brought with him a great sense of peace, which awoke in you a burning desire to have done with this world of tears. At the same time, he brought you a great pain, an agony of brain and body, so that you were left uncaring as to whether you were bound for heaven, or bound for hell.'

The liquor had left him forgetful and confused, his concentration gone, but racking his brains and his store of knowledge, and with the occasional slip and many a stumble, he recited, as follows:

'He comes with western winds, with evening's wandering airs,
With that clear dusk of heaven that brings the thickest stars;
Winds take a pensive tone, and stars a tender fire,
And visions rise and change which kill me with desire –

Desire for nothing known in my maturer years,
When joy grew mad with awe at counting future tears;
When, if my spirit's sky was full of flashes warm,
I knew not whence they came, from sun or thunderstorm;

But first a hush of peace, a soundless calm descends;
The struggle of distress and fierce impatience ends;
Mute music soothes my breast – unuttered harmony

That I could never dream till earth was lost to me.'

He paused, uncertain.
'Oh! yes,' she breathed; 'go on. Go on if there is more.'
'I forget,' he said, closing heavy eyes.
'Think! Think!' she urged.
After a moment, he resumed:

'Oh dreadful is the check, intense the agony,
When the ear begins to hear, and the eye begins to see;
When the pulse begins to throb, the brain to think again,
The soul to feel the flesh and the flesh to feel the chain.

Yet I would lose no sting, would wish no torture less;
The more that anguish racks, the earlier it will bless;
And robed in fires of Hell, or bright with heavenly shine,
If it but herald Death, the vision is divine.'

'Is that all of it?' she asked.
'I think I may have left out a verse,' he said, sighing. 'Emma, I do not feel very well.'
'But where does the poem come from?' she said. 'I never heard its like before. It is so true to my own experience, it might have been composed for me.'
She saw that he was struggling to say something, his face full of anguish. She bent over him, an ear inches from his lips, her loosened hair mingling with his. She sensed that what he was trying to say was of vital importance to them both.
'What is it, my love? What is it?' she urged.
'Oh! Emma,' he groaned, 'I think I want to be sick.'

CHAPTER 29

The next afternoon, Emma made her weekly visit to the churchyard of St. Mary Magdalene, there to place fresh flowers on the grave of her mother and elder brother.

It was a mistake.

Even now, she could not rid herself of the feelings of guilt and bitterness, which had been the inevitable consequence of each and every visit since her return to Grange Hall. She was quiet and subdued at the evening meal, and had retired early to bed – her own bed.

'What more can I do?' Richard asked himself after he watched in silence as she ascended the stairs to her room.

Had he but realised, the time had come for him to return a gift.

Sleep eluded Emma, which is not surprising in view of her state of mind. Tormented by emotions which tugged at her heart-strings, first one way and then the other, she wrestled with her situation for a full two hours before arriving at a decision.

'Mother, brother, forgive me. I love him,' she said.

Wrapping a shawl around her shoulders, she made her way to his bedroom, where a shock awaited her.

She was about to enter when she heard the low murmur of his voice. The female voice was louder. Hardly daring to breath, she noiselessly turned the handle of his door and eased it slightly ajar. Now, his voice came louder to her ears, although still indistinct, but hers fell clear upon her. She was teasing him, laughing and joking all the while, and through the gap in the door, and by the light of the single candle which burned in the room, she saw, and recognised, the girl's naked body kneeling astride his own. She closed the door as silently as she had opened it, and stood there for a moment, shocked beyond measure.

She had been deceived and betrayed. For goodness knows how long, he had deceived her. They had both deceived her. Little incidents, snatches of conversation overheard, knowing smiles and looks, particularly on her part – all came back to mind and now found a ready explanation. It was the ultimate act of cruelty towards her. It was unforgiveable.

The tears when they came were not so much for herself, but out of shame for the pair of them.

Returned to her room, she quickly dressed and bundled together a few necessities. Twenty minutes after her discovery, she was rousing a sleepy coachman from his bed close by the stables. Urging him to make haste, it was not long before the estate was receding behind her.

'There are times when I do not view her as a sister,' he had said. Recollecting his words, Emma was forced to admit that she had been blind all along to what had been happening under her very nose.

In truth, she *had* been blind, and in more ways than one, but it was a blindness born of a hatred dissipating but not yet fully spent.

He had retired for the night at his normal time of a little before eleven o'clock. At half past the hour he awoke out of a sound sleep to find a naked form pressed tight against him.

'Emma?' he whispered, turning towards his nocturnal visitor.

'Not Emma; Rachel,' came a voice.

In an instant he was out of bed and relighting his candle with a shaking hand.

'Rachel, have you taken leave of your senses?' he demanded.

'No, say rather I have come to them at long last,' she said.

He opened his mouth to protest, but she silenced him with the briefest of declarations.

'I *know*,' she said.

The words were spoken with a conviction which brooked no denial but, all the same, he found himself saying: 'What do you know? Rachel, what is all this?'

She smiled, a patient smile.

'Very well, if you wish me to spell it out, I shall do so. *You* are not Sir Henry Forres. *I* am not your sister. *We* are in no way related to each other.' She paused for a moment to view the effect of her words before adding with a voice charged with emotion: 'You do not know how happy all of that makes me.'

'How long have you known?' he asked, conceding defeat.

'With certainty, about a week or two, but I had my first suspicions more than a month ago. You remember that business with the Jessel family? In particular, Elizabeth Jessel's unexpected appearance at our breakfast table? Your look of total bewilderment as events unfolded suggested to me that you had no knowledge of Elizabeth, and no notion as to what her presence with us signified.'

'Yes,' he sighed, 'I had a feeling at the time I had not handled that episode well.'

'These past few weeks in London I have been testing you, dearest. I have tested you and found you wanting. Do you recall our little conversation concerning my cousin George? Well, there is no such person. I made him up, and inwardly was more than a little amused when you agreed with me as to how tiresome he can be on the rare occasions we meet with him. Do you recall our conversation of ten days ago concerning the kitten which you gave me for my fourth birthday? Needless to say, there was no such gift, although plainly you thought otherwise. There was no lake in the grounds of our estate at Grantham, there were no family holidays at Cromer, no old family tutor by the name of Ryan. Need I go on?'

He shook his head. 'I have been asking myself of late, why this sudden preoccupation with ancient family history, for it was subtly done on your part. I must confess, those conversations presented me with more than the odd difficulty.'

'They were meant to. I have to say that you were not very forthcoming in your responses, but the little that you *did* say, the little I *forced* you into saying, more than confirmed my suspicions.' She paused to scrutinise his face, shaking her head all the while. 'You are the spit and image of Henry. It is almost beyond belief and, yet, it is not truly a perfect match. There is a subtle difference in the outline of the mouth, and you have the general appearance of being his junior by a couple of years – yes, two years, I would say. You have the same tiny scar on the cheek – that was the result of a slight fencing mishap years ago, by the way – but do you have the same strawberry-coloured birthmark high up on the left arm? I wonder. Ah! I see from your expression that you do not. I wonder how you would have explained that to Emma when the time came? I suppose you would have thought of something to say. The most amazing thing to me is that you have most of Henry's mannerisms and little peculiarities. Self-taught, were they? The least convincing aspect is your manner of address and tone of voice – if you remember, I spotted that fairly early on. Still, I suppose to imitate a man's voice convincingly and consistently is the most difficult thing in the world, and I must give you credit for a remarkably good performance. In another situation you would have made a first rate actor. All in all, I must congratulate you for fooling me as long as you did, I who have known the man you set out to impersonate all my life. It does not greatly surprise me that Emma, who is a recent addition to our family, is still in ignorance of the truth.'

He had sat listening to her in silence, and with a growing astonishment which sprang not from what she was saying, but from what she was *not* saying.

'Rachel, this conversation has gone on for a full ten minutes, during which time you have done most of the talking,' he said; 'yet, I have still to hear you enquire after your brother.'

She shrugged her shoulders with an air of indifference.

'I took it for granted that you had disposed of him in order you might take his place.'

These words, and the casual way in which they were spoken, horrified him.

'Rachel, I give you my word that I never so much as harmed a hair on his head. Believe me when I tell you that he met with...... he met with an accident, which was entirely unforeseen on my part.' He looked at her uneasily. 'I have to tell you that you will never see him again.'

'I am glad to hear it. He was a monster, and I do not regret his passing one bit. As for the details of what took place between the two of you, they are of no consequence to me.'

'But we are speaking of your *brother*,' he protested.

'In point of fact, he was my half-brother, and if you had suffered one-tenth as much at his hands as I have you would not look at me as you do,' she cried, angrily.

'You were ready enough to forgive and forget when I first appeared on the scene,' he pointed out.

'Forgive? Yes. Forget? No. Anyway, it was *you* who earned his forgiveness. There is no merit to be laid at *his* door, I see that now. But do not suppose I hate his memory. I am simply happy to forget him.'

'Well, I can understand that, and I do not condemn you for it,' he answered, after a moment spent in reflecting on her words; 'but do you not want to know who it is who is talking to you – who I am, and how

I came here? Have you no questions concerning me?'

'Are you married?' she asked.

'Is that the most important thing on your mind?' he said.

'Actually, yes, it is,' she said, laughing.

'I am not married,' he said.

'Good! Neither am I,' she said. 'As for the rest of it, I shall allow you to enlighten me in your own good time.'

He found this statement incredible, and said as much.

'What you are is more important to me than what you once were,' she said, shaking her head at his words.

She was propped up on her elbow as she spoke, the flickering light of the single candle lending a soft and shimmering outline to her features.

'Rachel, you are a remarkable young woman,' he said, falteringly. 'One day, you are going to make some fortunate young man very happy.'

'Let us talk about that,' she said, smiling.

Before he knew it, she was out of bed and standing with his hand in hers.

'Come to bed,' she said, softly.

Reluctantly, he allowed her to pull him onto the bed. She rolled him flat onto his back, and knelt astride him.

Unnoticed by either one of them, the door in the far corner of the room inched open.

As once before, on his second night at Grange Hall, he was tempted. Here was an attractive and vivacious young woman, a sister in name only, of whom he had grown very fond, and one who was prepared to accept him for what he was, irrespective of his origins. There was only the one flaw in all of this, and that was his feelings towards Emma. The tender, protective affection for the one would, he knew, be no substitute for the passionate longing which he felt for the other.

'Rachel, this is folly,' he protested. 'In the eyes of the law we are brother and sister, and nothing can alter that. This new relationship between the two of us which you are proposing can lead to nothing but grief.'

She shook her head, impatiently.

'Grange Hall is not some ancestral home, and neither of us has any special attachment to the place. You could dispose of your interest in your new invention, and sell up here. We would then be free to settle elsewhere – any place where we would not be known would suffice. We could go to America, or to one of the Colonies. We could start a new life as man and wife. It *is* possible, Richard. It *is* possible. I know it is asking a lot of you, but I also know I could make you happy. I could dispel that loneliness which still lurks in those eyes of yours, if you but let me.'

'And what of Emma in all of this?' he asked.

'Emma has had her chance with you,' she answered, scowling. 'Give her what she has always wanted – a divorce – and let us both be rid of her.'

Silently, unobserved, the bedroom door, so briefly ajar, closed shut once more.

'Rachel, I can offer you nothing more than a brother's affection,' he said, firmly. Angered by her show of callous disregard for the feelings of Emma, he pushed her away, and threw her discarded nightshift back to her.

Without a protest, she covered her naked body, and retreated to the centre of the room. Here, she began to pace the floor, her face pale with suppressed anger and mortification, her eyes shooting darting glances in his direction.

'Emma does not love you. Do not delude yourself on that score,' she said, at length.

'You are wrong,' he answered. 'You were with us in the coach bringing us home yesterday evening. You saw for yourself how her feelings towards me have changed of late.'

'I saw clearly that you were *both* the worse for drink. What happened yesterday signifies nothing on her part.'

'You see only what you want to see. I believe Emma now has a true affection for me.'

'Affection! Affection!' she cried, scornfully. 'If that be so, and what happened on our way home has any significance, answer me this: why is she not with you now? Why did I find you alone tonight?'

'Things will change in time,' he answered. 'I shall not always be alone.'

'Well, I suppose that is just possible,' she replied, grudgingly, 'but only if you continue to deceive her, and work on her. Oh! yes, I saw your look of disdain when you rejected me a moment ago, but let us examine your conduct in this whole affair. All along, you have deceived Emma and me. In so doing, you have cheated Emma what was due to her, for she is the rightful owner of this estate, not you. In addition to all of that, you lay claim to Emma's affection as if you were due them as her husband. Not a very creditable performance, wouldn't you say? You are a liar, a cheat, and a thief.'

Somewhat to her surprise, he did not attempt to defend himself.

'Yes, you are right,' he acknowledged. 'Believe me, the same thoughts have come to me often enough. Perhaps it is time Emma learned the truth. It is possible she may accept me for what I am, as you have done.'

'Do you honestly believe that?' she said.

'No. No, not really,' he sighed.

'No, indeed. Emma is not as I am. She will be horrified to learn that some stranger has duped her into a degree of intimacy due solely to a husband. Yet, if she is to accept you on the same terms as I have done, she *must* be told. If you are unwilling to do the telling, I shall do it for you. I give you three days. For the rest, be assured your secret is safe with me. Come what may, I could never do anything which would expose you to danger.'

She paused at the doorway before leaving him with words soft and gentle.

'I am all you have, you know, Richard. There is no one else, however much you would wish it otherwise. In time you shall come to realise the truth of what I say. When that time comes, I shall be waiting for you. Oh! and one final thought for you to contemplate: do not condemn me for my conduct this night. Remember, you made me what I am.'

The following morning brought to light Emma's flight, confirmed by a terse two line note she had left for him. It read: 'I am taking advantage of your offer of a few weeks ago to release me. Why did I delay, I wonder?'

'I do not understand it,' he said. 'I had every reason to believe matters were progressing well between the two of us. Why should she up and leave in the middle of the night, leaving such a cruel message?'

'Who knows?' said Rachel, with a shrug of the shoulders. 'I suspect you have been in the middle of a tug-of-war, with Emma at one end, and Robert and her mother at the other end. I guess you've just lost. Where has she gone, do you know?'

'Matthews says he conveyed her back to the Jamiesons. The fact she has not attempted to conceal her destination suggests that is but a temporary refuge, and she plans to remove herself elsewhere at the first opportunity. I believe it also shows that she trusts me to keep to my word and not pursue her. That at least stands to my credit, although I have to say it brings me little comfort.'

'Richard, she is a lost cause. If, believing you to be her husband she chooses to leave, what chance is there she would have stayed if she knew what I know? In truth, none at all.' She laid a comforting hand on one of his. 'It is as I said. I am all you have. Richard, there is no one else.'

'I do not know how I shall live from day to day without her. Suddenly, nothing else seems to matter anymore.'

'You were reconciled to her leaving a while back,' Rachel pointed out.

'Yes, but it is the manner of her leaving which distresses me,' he said. 'I had hoped that if we must part we could have done so on terms of friendship.' He picked up the note once more. '"Why did I delay, I wonder?" ' he quoted.

'I have an outing to Stockton arranged, but I would gladly cancel it if you wish me to stay with you.'

'You would find me poor company, I fear,' he said. 'No, keep to your arrangements.'

'I do not like to leave you like this,' said Rachel. 'May I not stay?'

'Rachel, I prefer to be alone. Please! just go,' he said, distractedly.

Reluctantly, with more than the one backward glance in his direction, she left him.

In spite of the presence of Charlie to keep her company, Rachel was fated not to enjoy her day out in Stockton. The blame for that lay entirely with her conscience.

'He has given me so much, this stranger, and asked for nothing in return save a sisterly affection,' she told Charlie. 'When I think of my life before he appeared on the scene! Charlie, did I do right last night? My heart tells me I did, but my conscience tells me I did not.'

, Charlie's only possible response was to cock his head in the manner of any dog trying to make sense of unfamiliar words.

Later, Rachel began to worry over the state of mind of the man she had come to love. Although she had tried to make light of it at the time, she had to admit to herself that he had taken the shock of Emma's leaving very badly. At his insistence, she had left him alone with his thoughts. Concern for his well-being began to pray on her mind to such an extent that she set off for home a full two hours before she had intended. On her arrival, she found herself confronted by an appalling situation.

Miserably inclement weather, fully in keeping with his mood, was to keep him indoors for much of the morning, but a little after eleven o'clock the driving rain, which had beaten against the window panes for two hours, began to slacken.

In vain, he applied himself to half-a-dozen tasks, each in turn taken up with determination, only to be abandoned in despair. When, therefore, a pale, watery sun put in an appearance, casting the first ghostly shadows of the day, he was glad to take himself off outdoors.

He had hardly set foot outside when he was startled by the sudden appearance of a bedraggled Harold Gibson. He listened in dismay to the tearful giant's tale of a riding accident to a sister, who now lay close to death in an upstairs' room of the little farmhouse which was her home.

Stopping only to scribble a short message to Rachel in the event of her early return, he made his way with all speed to Fold Farm.

He burst into the sickroom to find a stunned father keeping a solitary vigil by his daughter's bedside. Approaching, he saw the deathly pale, unconscious form of his beautiful friend.

'Good God, Samuel! what has happened?' he cried, aghast at the sight. 'Harold spoke only of some kind of riding accident before he rushed off elsewhere.'

Samuel Gibson lifted a distracted face and began to speak in a curiously detached tone of voice.

'I thought you should know how things stood. It was good of you to come so promptly. I can add little to what Harold has told you. It happened an hour ago. Nancy's horse shied and threw her to the ground. Exactly why, we do not know. Fortunately, her friend Julia Castleton was riding with her and raised an immediate alarm.'

'But what has been done? Why is Doctor Hunter not here? Where has Harold gone?'

'Doctor Hunter has been and gone. He left here just a few moments ago, with a promise to return later in the day. Short of cleaning the wound and seeing to her comfort, he said he could do no more. The skull is badly fractured, you see. She is slipping away from us, Richard, she is slipping away. Hunter says it is only a matter of time – twenty four hours, perhaps. Harold has gone in search of Mr. Sibley. I understand he is away on parish business in Kirkleavington.' His eyes drifted back to his daughter. 'I feel so helpless sitting here,' he whispered.

Richard felt his world falling apart. Of the three people nearest and dearest to him, one was a sister no longer, consumed with a jealous possessiveness, another had abandoned him, and the third lay dying – and all this in the space of twelve hours. The memory of that happy little band which had taken London by storm such a short while back now seemed but a distant recollection.

It was, he resolved, time to stop the rot. It was time to make a stand. No, more than that, it was time to fight back against adversity. He would not, he *could not*, accept this latest disaster. He set his teeth. He would tackle this one last mountain, and if need be go down fighting.

'Samuel, my friend, do you trust me?' he asked.

'Yes, of course,' came the reply he was hoping for.

'Will you trust me for a little while against all your sense and reason? Will you give me an hour alone with Nancy?'

'Gladly, but to what purpose?'

'Do not ask me questions, only give me your trust.'

'Very well, Richard, you may have your hour.'

'If Harold returns with Sibley, or Doctor Hunter puts in another appearance, please detain them if my time is not yet up.'

'Very well,' said Samuel. He looked thoughtfully at Richard. 'I suppose you wish to be alone with Nancy so you may concentrate your mind in prayer?'

'Concentrate my mind? Yes, that is exactly it; but one last thing before you go, Samuel: it is Nancy's birthday next week, is it not? I seem to remember being told that Nancy's and Emma's birthdays are but a few days apart.'

'Yes, that is so. It will be...... it would have been her twenty first birthday in five days time.'

'And do you have a present for her?'

'I have a fine new bonnet which she saw and admired a while back in town.'

'Does she know this? Has she tried it on?'

'No to both questions. It was meant to be a surprise.'

'Excellent!' exclaimed Richard, delighted by this information. 'Now, listen to me. I want you to go downstairs, take hold of the bonnet, and picture Nancy in it as clearly as you can in your mind's eye. Hold that picture in your mind for as long as you can. Picture her in it laughing and smiling. Picture her in it vibrant and full of life.'

'I shall do as you ask,' said Samuel; 'but I haven't the least idea what you have in mind.'

'That is not important. Just do as I ask. Samuel, you said you would trust me against all sense and reason. Were those mere words on your part?'

They were not. A moment later and he was alone with the unconscious Nancy. He began to brace himself for the coming ordeal.

His mind's eye had seen a brain swimming in blood, and fear and doubt had come irresistibly upon him. This task is beyond me, he thought. These unspoken words were dismissed in an instant from his mind.

Too late! The thought *had* come, and it had come with firm conviction. The fatal seed of doubt had been truly sown.

He fought on, refusing to acknowledge defeat, with a face now paler than his beautiful friend. Recklessly, he entered into forbidden, dangerous territory, spurred on by a growing awareness that his efforts were, indeed, meeting with some success. Onward, ever onward, he went, summoning up resources which he never knew he possessed. Old wounds, long-healed, reopened, and new ones took form and shape as the secular stigmata came upon him. 'This is my death', he thought, and with the knowledge of it came a great weariness. A weariness but not despair. If it was to be a life for a life, so be it. As for himself, he had done his utmost in all things, in all challenges, since his first entry into his new world, and no man could do more than that, he acknowledged. Perhaps it was time to admit defeat and move on. He had met his Everest and had fallen within close sight of its' summit. There was no disgrace in that.

Emma was not in the least surprised when Vicar Sibley put in an appearance at her lodgings late that same afternoon. She had been expecting some such ploy on the part of her husband.

She went forward to meet him, determined to pay no heed to any criticism which he might utter, or to be swayed by any message which he may have brought from her husband. Her mind was made up. She would leave for York early the following morning. If she did not find a ready welcome at her uncle's hands, she would move on to London, where several new friends and acquaintances awaited her. She felt the coldness of Sibley's curt greeting, and sensed the supressed anger which prompted it.

In words which he was later to regret, Sibley came straight to the point of his visit.

'I must congratulate you, Emma, on a well-thought out revenge. You have had to wait a long time for it, but perhaps you derive extra pleasure from the old saying 'revenge is a dish best eaten when cold'; but come and see the fruits of your handiwork.'

She thought these words harsh to the point of wildness, but contented herself with saying: 'I suppose you have listened and taken in only the one side of the argument, as usual. Well, I shall not enlighten you except to say that if you knew the true reason for my leaving last night you would not speak to me as you do.' Suddenly, she was weary of what she judged to be his one-sided partiality, based on his interpretation of the faith he embraced, his prejudices, and his ignorance of the true facts. It had always been so in her opinion. 'What do you know, what have you ever known of my sufferings?' she said, bitterly. 'My husband —.'

'Your husband is dead,' he interrupted, 'or perhaps it would be more accurate to say he was dying when I left him – and you have played a part in the tragedy. I saw that spiteful note you left behind. How could you desert him in so cruel a fashion when he has treated you with so much affection and consideration since your return to him?'

Nothing but his first few words registered on her senses.

'*Dead?* What do you mean, he is *dead*?' she gasped.

'Why, Emma, I would have thought the word was plain enough,' he replied; 'but come, come just as you are, and I shall tell you the whole story on the way.'

He told her the day's events, as far as he knew and understood them, and was surprised at the sheer anguish this produced. He had not expected this, and he began to feel uneasy about his calculated indifference to her feelings when they had first met. The truth was, the sight of the note which she had left had convinced him that her sole concern at the news he was bringing her would be for herself and her future prospects. This mistaken conviction had left him seething with an uncharacteristic anger.

'I do not pretend to understand the half of it,' he concluded, shaking his head all the while. 'As I say, although still not conscious, Nancy is unaccountably improved, and the cause of Richard's present condition is an even bigger mystery. It appears for all the world that he has bought her improvement by forfeiting his own state of health, but such a thing is surely nonsensical.'

It was not nonsensical to Emma. Drawing on her experience at Richmond, and his words to her on the subject, she felt she had a fair idea of what had taken place at Fold Farm. Sick at heart, she stayed silent on the subject.

'Rachel is beside herself with grief, and blames herself for her brother's situation. She says had it not been for her Richard would not have risked himself as recklessly as he did today – whatever that may mean. But I do not wonder at her feelings of guilt, if only in respect of her shameful and revolting conduct towards her brother last night, the sordid details of which she felt the need to confess to me. There is a word for what she planned, and it is not a pretty one.'

'*Her* shameful conduct towards *him*?' said Emma. 'Surely, you are deceived. Their shameful conduct towards each other is closer to the truth.'

'You know of that?' said Sibley, in surprise.

'I was an accidental witness to it last night.'

'So, is that why you left as you did?'

'But of course. Why else?'

'If that be so, I have grievously misjudged you, my dear, and I can only ask forgiveness for my unfeeling words when first we met. I had attributed your desertion, and the manner of it, to the base motives of hatred and revenge – a desire to make your husband suffer for his mistreatment of you over the years. But if I have erred, unless I am very much mistaken, so, too, have you. Rachel forced herself upon her brother. He spurned her advances, and nothing came of it. Richard is entirely blameless in this matter.'

'But...... but I thought I was witnessing just the one incident in some sordid affair between the two of them,' cried Emma, wildly.

'An *affair*? No, you are mistaken. Nothing could be further from the truth. Oh! my dear child, it appears we have both been blind.'

'It is a failing of mine,' said Emma, through her tears, 'and the blame for all of this falls squarely on my shoulders. Had I been by his side last night, as any true and loyal wife would have been, Rachel would have had no opportunity to disgrace herself. I should have been with him today. I could have been by his side to counsel caution with regard to poor Nancy.'

He could only watch helplessly as she broke down completely.

'Oh, dear God! what have I done?' she wept.

Nothing he could find to say seemed to bring her any comfort, and looking at her weeping uncontrollably before him, he could only wonder at the way of things. Lord God, how you do try a poor man's faith at times, were his unspoken, heartfelt words to himself.

CHAPTER 30

He was poised, motionless, at the mouth of the tunnel, which stretched away into the distance. At the end of it, far distant, he saw the pinprick of light conjured up in his brain.

The view before him came as no great surprise. There was strong evidence, for the most part anecdotal but compelling for all that, which, he knew, pointed to a kind of self-reassurance at the end, as if the deepest recesses of an all-knowing, all-seeing mind was telling itself that this was not really an irrevocable extinction.

Yet, for all that, something was wrong. At this late stage, with his life ebbing away, consciousness should be fading rapidly, with hopes, fears, and memories, melting and dissolving. Such was not the case. He continued to remain in perfect awareness of his situation, the memory of how he had got there sharp and poignant. More than this, although both he and the tunnel remained at perfect rest, the light, no longer a tiny speck, was racing towards him. He saw that it had become elongated, and was taking on a human shape.

She stood in silence before him, smiling condescendingly.

'Mother?' he asked, in wonder.

'No, not mother,' she said, 'but I think you'll agree it's a happy medium between a disembodied voice and a burning bush. I considered putting in an appearance as Emma, but came to the conclusion that would only serve to confuse things. You must be wondering who I am. Well, let me enlighten you. I am from a civilisation many millions of years in advance of your own. We have achieved near-immortality, and discarded the frailties of a human body aeons ago. My name would be unpronounceable in your language, but you may call me Wanda, as a close proximation. I am your designated case officer, for want of a better term.' She shook her head in the manner of one reproving a small child. 'So, technician, you have been attempting to set your new world to rights, and a pretty fine mess you've made of things in the process. You take too much upon yourself but, then, that was ever your way. The task you set yourself with regard to Nancy was way beyond your powers. It was an act of madness to even attempt it.'

'So, where does all of that leave me?' he said. 'Am I alive, or am I dead?'

'You ought to be dead. You *would be dead* if I had not stopped the process in its tracks. Your current status is that you are in a state of limbo.'

'I see,' he said. 'So can I take it you have been playing the part of Peeping Tom for the past few months?'

'Peeping Tom? I must say that's rich coming from you. Why, you and people like you at London Complex spend all their working lives prying into the lives of people in other realities. In point of fact, I haven't been keeping a constant watch over you. I have simply been looking in on you from time to time, something which you should be grateful for in the light of recent events.' She paused to indicate the tunnel behind her shoulder. 'Your next reality. Do you want it?'

'No, not if I have any choice in the matter,' he said. 'It will come soon enough.'

'Very well, technician, put your hand in mine and let us leave this place,' she said.

In an instant, he found himself back in his flat at London Complex. She seated herself and watched as he wandered from room to room. Everything was in its place, just as he remembered it.

'The real thing?' he said.

'Certainly,' she said. 'This is no illusion, or purpose-built copy on my part. We *really are* here. Your people have kept things just as they were on your last day here. It has become almost a shrine.'

He resumed his wandering tour until she began to grow impatient.

'I do wish you would come and sit beside me and settle yourself. You are making me uneasy with your restlessness.'

'I'm surprised you suffer from such a human trait as uneasiness,' he said, taking up a position close to her.

'Normally, I don't,' she said, 'but this outward shell seems to bring with it feelings and emotions strange to me. It is not the first time that has happened to me.'

'So, everything that took place here at London Complex a few months' back is down to you and your kind,' he said. 'I suppose it was my people's tinkering with time, reality, and the Cosmos, and in particular my own contribution to that, which prompted you to take action?'

'Tinkering is hardly the word for it. You and your people do not realise what you are getting into. You may continue to shape your own destiny with your puny efforts in the exploration of space, but other universes are out of bounds. Out of bounds, technician, do you understand?'

'But what gives you the right to lay down what a civilisation may, or may not, do?' he said.

'And what gives *you* the right to go blundering around the Cosmos meddling with other realities?' she retorted. 'As for us, we may view with equanimity, if not with indifference, the self-destruction of an entire civilisation, or the catastrophic effects of a supernova, but we cannot stand idly by while a race of people set out to tamper with the very fabric of the Cosmos. Oh! I know what you are going to say: why do we not announce ourselves to your people so that a compromise solution may be agreed upon? Well, when the time is right we shall probably do just that. It may be a hundred years from now, or a hundred thousand years, but now is not the right time. I doubt your civilisation could withstand the culture shock. Technician, we have powers beyond your comprehension. I tell you plainly that, standing here, I could destroy your entire civilisation with a passing thought, if I had a mind to.'

She had been pacing the floor as she spoke, clearly agitated. It was plain to Technician Travis that the body she had assumed was beginning to assert itself. Human emotions were clearly taking over. Suddenly, a great fear came upon him, a fear not for himself but for his own homeworld. A passing thought comes so easily to mind, he reflected. He moved quickly to her side. She resisted half-heartedly as he led her back to the couch.

'Damn this useless body,' she muttered, as she took her place beside him. 'I do believe your mother's personality is taking over. A crochety old bag of bones, wasn't she?'

'Why not change into someone young, agreeable, and well known to me,' he said, ignoring her insult. 'Why not assume Emma's form and shape?'

'Well......,' she said, clearly uncertain.

'I promise not to take advantage,' he said.

He watched as she capitulated.

'Emma,' he began.

'Do not call me by that name,' she said, sharply.

'Sorry – Wanda. The whole purpose of that transporter of ours is to restock our planet with all the diversity of nature lost to us in the past millennium. Why does it trouble you so?'

'That is not entirely true,' she said. 'You know there are plans afoot to eventually transport talented people from the past who can be of service to you. It is what I believe is called the 'thin end of the wedge'. Where will it all end? Give a small child a box of matches to play with and it will most surely burn itself in time.'

'But the transporter is still here,' he said, indicating the vista of London Complex outside the window. 'All you have succeeded in doing is separating me from it.'

'Oh, we have succeeded in more than that,' she said. 'The transporter no longer functions – we have seen to that – and no one can fathom out why. We hold the one man capable of putting it back into working order.'

'But another Technician Travis will come along eventually. It may take a generation for that to happen, but happen it will.'

'Then, we shall deal with that when the time comes – and again, and again, if need be. Eventually, your leaders will give up on the unequal contest and spend the vast sums of money involved on more practical projects. Already, in the light of what has happened, there is a growing demand that the transporter project be abandoned.'

'But in this infinite Cosmos of ours you shall have to deal with an infinite number of Technician Travis'. Their very numbers will overwhelm you. You are dealing with an infinite number of realities.'

'But, but, but,' she said, smiling. 'Richard, is that all you can say?' She patted his hand, affectionately. 'Let us not get into technicalities. What you say is true, but there are ways around the problem, believe me.'

'What I do not understand is why you opted for such a complicated scheme to damage our research programme when far more simple methods were open to you. For example, why did you not simply do away with me at some stage?'

'We are not barbarians,' she said, indignantly.

'Well, then, you could still have achieved your end goal by a simple act of sabotage. You could have wrecked any one of a dozen pieces of scientific equipment vital to us.'

'True,' she acknowledged, 'but that would have been difficult to do without leaving telltale signs of outside interference. No, your people were dead set on those transporter trips of yours. We thought it best that they went ahead whilst making very certain it would all end in a disaster. You say our method was complicated, but it worked didn't it?'

'But why bring me back to Yarm two years adrift? What advantage did that serve?'

'That was none of our doing,' she exclaimed. 'That was *your* transporter that malfunctioned. We had nothing to do with it.'

'And Emma served as the bait in all of this?'

'Yes. We had long-noted the beauty of that lady – by the comic standards of you human beings, that is – and we were well-aware of your partiality for that type of woman. As for Sir Henry Forres, he is not a creature of our making. We could not fail to see the amazing resemblance between the two of you. We simply took advantage of a very lucky coincidence. Lucky for you, that is. If he hadn't existed, I have to confess we wouldn't have bothered about a change of places. We would simply have left you stranded and alone in your new reality. We put it into his head to pay a visit to Pine Tree Cottage at the crucial time, and the rest you know.'

'Yes, and that dream of mine was your doing, too. It served to draw me irresistibly to Emma; but there is something here which does not add up. No one can see into the future, not even you, because it doesn't exist in any given reality. Just to take one example, if I were to ask you exactly what Rachel will be doing in five years' time you couldn't answer me. Is that not so?'

'True,' she said. 'So what exactly is your point, Richard?'

'That dream of mine. That dream of the graveyard, Pine Tree Cottage, and Emma and me. It was a recurring dream, stretching back to my childhood. How could you foresee that one day you would have to deal with me, long before the transporter was up and running, long before I joined London Complex?'

'There was only the one such dream – the last by your reckoning – and at a time when we knew full-well what was about to take place.'

'No, you are wrong. You *have* to be wrong. That dream, I *know,* came to me on ten different occasions spanning fifteen years.'

She shook her head, impatiently.

'I tell you there was only the one dream centred on Pine Tree Cottage on the one occasion. There were no childhood dreams. When we put it into your head we planted a false memory of previous occurrences.'

'Why would you want to do that?' he said.

'To heighten the effect. A one-off dream, however bizarre, may be dismissed as of no consequence, but a dream which has seemingly haunted one since childhood cannot be so easily set aside. So it proved. Off you went in pursuit of that dream.'

'That was a clever ploy,' he said.

'Yes, wasn't it?' she said, laughing, 'but, then, we *are* clever. We have even circumvented The Uncertainty Principle up to a point. That is why I am able to return time and again to the same reality. We cannot backtrack, mark you. Changing the past will forever remain an impossibility.'

He made no response to this, other than to walk across to the window, where he stood in silence looking out onto the bright moonlit scene. His eye took in the vague outline of London Complex proper, away in the distance.

'Why have you brought me here?' he asked.

'Let us say it is for old times' sake, plus the fact that it is a good place for us to talk, here in your former lodgings at the dead of night.'

He continued to stare out of the window.

'I have no regrets,' he said. 'For all my abilities, I never really fitted in here. This microscopic examination of the past is, in the final analysis, introspective and unhealthy. I believe, deep down, I have always known that. So, we do not locate and recover all the lost treasures of the past, but do we really have need of them all? So, we would have to live with a measure of unsolved crimes. Very well, we could respond to that by making the forces of law and order more proficient. So, we do not solve all the mysteries of the past, but the best part of any mystery thriller is not the ending, but the plot. Moreover, is it not more important to live the present rather than relive the past, and is not what is to come of more consequence than what has gone before?'

'I'm glad to hear you speak so,' she said. 'I'm glad because even if you felt differently, there is no way I would be allowed to let you return here.'

'So, mission accomplished on your part,' he said, smiling. 'That being the case, I am wondering why this continuing interest in me. Why did my 'case officer' feel the need to intervene at the point of my death? I ask myself. After all, I brought that upon myself. You had no hand in it. Why do I get the feeling that you are no longer acting under orders, but are taking a *personal* interest in me? Will that not bring trouble down upon your head?'

These series of questions appeared to fluster her. The reply, when it came, was hesitant and halting.

'As long as you remain in the world we put you in, that is all that matters to my superiors. As for the rest of it, I must confess you intrigue me, Richard. I do not really want to let go of you, but let go of you I must. An age ago, when I still inhabited a physical body, I knew and loved a man not unlike you: gentle, caring, sensitive, and, strange to tell, bearing a physical likeness to you. There, does that answer your question?'

She had ceased to call him Technician, and was now using his first name, he noted. Could he now safely respond in kind? he wondered.

'Take me home, Emma,' he said. 'Restore me to health once more, and take me home.' He paused, waiting for some words of censure, but none came. 'I know the problems I have there still remain, but so be it.'

'You are wrong, Richard,' she said. 'Rachel has learnt her lesson – the fact that one cannot always have what one wants in life. I believe you will have no further trouble from that quarter. As for Emma, she knows the true situation between Rachel and yourself. She is full of remorse, and is on her way back to you. But Rachel is right in one respect. You cannot continue to live a lie with Emma. She must be told the truth. Take care how you do that.'

'And what of Nancy?' he said.

'You have effected a partial healing, but have not delayed her final decline beyond a few weeks,' she said.

'Then, you must do the curing for me,' he said.

'No, you ask too much,' she said. 'I shall not help you there.'

'But why not?' he exclaimed. 'Emma, I don't understand.'

He appeared visibly distressed by her refusal, and she was moved to lay a comforting hand on his cheek.

'Listen to me, Richard,' she said. 'I know we are dealing with only the one reality but we do have *some* obligation to it. You belong to this new reality, but you do not own it, and neither do I. As it is, your presence in it has already induced a massive reality change and curing Nancy would be yet one more instance of that, and an unnecessary one into the bargain. As Technician Richard Travis you must know that Nancy is simply moving on naturally to another reality. Oh, dearest Richard, do try and understand.'

Dearest Richard! Dearest Richard!

It was now plain that Emma's personality was gradually asserting itself, he reflected, although Wanda, or whatever her true name was, appeared not to be aware of the fact. Determined to have his way with regard to Nancy, he would bide his time until the right moment presented itself.

'Come, Richard, give me your hand and we shall return home, as you put it,' she said. 'There is still one factor which I want to discuss with you.'

He did as she asked and in the twinkling of an eye he found himself tucked up comfortably in bed, she sitting by his side.

'Fold Farm Cottage?' he said, glancing around the tiny attic bedroom.

'Yes. Nancy is in the room below. Her brother watches over her. You were moved here some little time ago, and have been given up as lost by everyone.'

He began to probe his body, his hand seeking out old injuries, before moving on to check pulse and heartbeat.

'You are essentially sound,' she assured him.

'I do not truly feel fit and well,' he said.

'I have left you convalescent. It will take a few days before you are fully recovered. I believe that is all to the good.'

'Now, why should that be?' he said, in surprise.

'Oh, I think that will be to your advantage,' she said, with a knowing smile. 'You will require careful nursing for a day or two – loving care, in fact, and a closeness and a bonding together. I think you can guess with whom that will be.'

Before he could reply she had gone on to speak of the subject uppermost in her mind.

'I believe it would be best for all concerned if you were relieved of some of that potentially dangerous knowledge which you possess. I am referring to your memories of time spent at London Complex, this scientific knowledge a thousand years in advance of the time, and your awareness of forthcoming historical events, based on the history of the reality you have now abandoned. Oh, my dear Richard, it would be better so. There will be no possible regrets for the life you have given up, no looking back, no second thoughts, no more doubt and confusion as to which is your true homeworld.'

'And no possible temptation to take advantage of a scientific know-how vastly ahead of this world of 1813?'

'Yes, that, too. A phonographic machine, indeed! Well, I suppose that at least is harmless enough, but there must be no more such enterprises.'

'What of this meeting between the two of us?' he said.

'The memory of that will begin to blur and fade away in time. But do not be alarmed. I shall be selective in what I blot out and much will be left to you, including all those things which make you what you are, and which makes you so dear to me. It shall be done very gradually over a period of weeks, and I guarantee you will not even be aware of the process.'

A moment spent in thought convinced him that she was right in what she had said. He drew a deep breath. 'Very well, make it so,' he said.

'Then, I think that's just about everything,' she said. 'Time for me to leave you.'

This said, she bent over him and kissed him long and lovingly.

It was now or never, he thought.

She relinquished her hold on him but he continued to hold her tight. His lips began to roam her face as he started speaking.

'I have only the one regret, and that is the loss of my beautiful Nancy,' he murmured in her ear. 'What you said a while back may be true, but how shall I bear the happiness of my time here at Fold Farm knowing all the while that a few feet below me Nancy's life is ebbing away before the eyes of her suffering family?' His lips reached the nape of her neck. 'Emma, loving you as I do, I could refuse you nothing. Can you truly claim the same on your part?'

He watched as she hesitated. It was for little more than an instant, but it was enough. The potent force of a passing thought, which she had spoken of earlier, had taken full effect.

'I did not mean to do that,' she said, breaking free of him. Her true self reasserted itself. 'You tricked me, technician. You said you would not take advantage of the situation, but that is exactly what you've done.'

'Nancy is healed?' he asked.

'You know very well she is,' she said.

'For pity's sake, don't take back your gift of life,' he said. 'I have never begged for anything in my life before, but I am doing so now.'

'Oh, you may have your indispensable friend,' she said, with an air of resignation. 'I suppose the sky is not going to fall in as a consequence, but I think it's high time I left here before I find myself in bed with you. Besides, in a moment your beautiful Nancy will probably be sitting up in bed, indignantly demanding to know what her brother is doing in her room. A few seconds later, I have no doubt, one will hear that noisy giant of a brother bellowing down the stairs for his father. Since I have a headache coming on – at least I think it's a headache – I have no desire to be here when all hell breaks loose.'

She left his side, and walked to the foot of the bed, adopting as she did so the guise of his mother once more.

'Fare you well, Senior Technician Richard Travis, alias Sir Henry Forres, alias Richard Forres,' she said. She lifted a warning finger. 'Take heed, my friend. One day this naïve, disinterested goodness of yours could well prove to be your undoing, only I shall not be there to pick up the pieces. So, please, technician, in your own interests, try not to attempt anything which would be beyond my own powers.'

She left him staring into space.

Try as she might, Emma could not find it in herself to join in the noisy celebrations which marked the recent very dramatic recovery of Nancy. Her thoughts were elsewhere. After the briefest of congratulations on her part, she slipped quietly away, the eyes of

Sibley viewing her departure with silent sympathy.

Fully expecting the worst, she pushed open the door of the second of the two sickrooms and entered in.

Her immense relief at finding him alive and conscious was short-lived as she took in the sight of a pair of glazed eyes peeping out through half-closed lids. The face was pale and drawn, with a peculiarly mournful expression hardly inspiring confidence in her. The hands clasped and unclasped the bedclothes in jerky, feverish movements.

She took her place beside him with a sinking heart.

'Mother? Is that you?' he croaked.

'No, dearest, it is Emma,' she said, miserably.

He give a bitter, pain-wracked laugh.

'No, that cannot be. Emma has deserted me. She hates me.'

'No!' she protested.

'She loathes me,' he said, sadly.

'No!' she cried.

'She despises me,' he insisted.

'No! No! She loves you. *I* love you,' she cried.

'What, both of you?' he said. 'Does Emma know of your affection for me?'

'Listen to me, Richard,' she said, taking hold of his hand. 'I speak only of Emma. It is, I, Emma, who sits here.'

He lifted up his free hand to stroke her cheek, squinting up at her all the while.

'Is it really you?' he asked, wonderingly. 'Yes...... yes, I see plainly it is.' He paused to study her face, noting the puffed and swollen eyes. 'Dear Blondie, I seem destined to bring you nothing but pain and sorrow.'

'Do not speak so, dearest,' she said. 'These past few weeks have been a revelation and a joy to me.'

'And yet, you left me,' he said, accusingly.

'A foolish misunderstanding on my part,' she pleaded. 'Say that you forgive me.'

'How could I not when you have forgiven me so much?'

'Sibley told me you were dying. Tell me that is not true. Tell me I have you always.'

'God has spared me for a little while longer so we may say goodbye,' he said, shaking his head. 'For that I am grateful.'

'No! No! I shall not let you be taken from me. I shall not,' she cried, fiercely.

'The shadows are closing in. I shall be gone soon,' he said, mournfully. 'Emma, will you do one last thing for me?'

'Anything! Anything! You have but to name it,' she said.

'Take off your clothes and come to bed. Let me embrace you in death.'

He saw her hesitation and, with a melodramatic sigh, turned his head away from her.

'Richard, there is a room full of people just the one floor down,' she pointed out. 'What of them?'

'Dear Blondie, do be sensible,' he protested. He indicated the vacant space beside him. 'There simply isn't the room.'

'I can refuse you nothing,' she said. Quickly discarding most of her clothing, she slipped in beside him.

'How dark it is in here,' he said, glancing around the sunlit room.

'Hush, dearest, hush,' she said, softly.

'Do not distress yourself, my dear. Do not be sad,' he said, stroking her cheek. 'I have no regrets. It is a far, far better thing I do, than I have ever done; it is a far, far better rest that I go to, than I have ever known.'

It was at this point that the door opened, and an unsuspecting clerical gentleman poked his head into the room. His eyes took in the trail of discarded female garments scattered across the floor, before they drifted over to the bed.

'Who is it?' asked the 'dying' man of Emma.

'God!' she gasped, before burying her head under the bedclothes.

'Really? So soon?' he said. 'I suppose it is a honour, Him calling in person, but I had hoped for a little while longer.'

'It is Mr. Sibley,' came a muffled voice.

'So it is,' he said, lifting his head from his pillow. 'Ah! vicar, it's you. Will you not join us?'

Confused, embarrassed, doubting his senses, their visitor beat a hasty retreat.

'Oh, Lord! I shall never be able to look him in the face again,' wailed Emma. Her dying husband temporarily forgotten, she bounded out of bed, and hastily began to dress herself. That done, she turned to face him and was horrified to see that he now lay deathly still, his upturned eyes fixed on the ceiling. There came a faint whisper of 'Quickly, Emma, before it is too late; kiss me.'

Summoning up all her willpower in a grim determination not to break down while he still lived, she did as he asked.

She had expected the soft and tender pressure of a pair of near-lifeless lips, but that was far from being the case. He took hold of both of her arms and gripped them with a surprising strength. The kiss which followed was long, forceful, and passionate. It was a full moment before she could break free, literally gasping for breath. Of one thing she was certain: this was *not* the kiss of a dying man.

Calmly, he began to prop himself up on his pillows, looking beyond her to the door.

'What time is tea?' he asked in a matter-of-fact tone of voice. 'I had no lunch, you know,' he added, plaintively.

There came a dawning realisation, followed by an emotional outburst. Just in time, he was able to catch hold of the two clenched fists poised threateningly above him, and she was left to pummel empty space. Emotions violent and varied fought for possession of her, but it was relief, sheer, blessed relief which won the day.

'I suppose I had that coming to me,' she acknowledged. She scrutinised a face still drawn and haggard. 'But you are not well. I can see plainly that you are not well.'

At that precise moment, as if to prove the point, a long and painful-sounding bought of coughing, alarming to her ears, seized him. It was a full two minutes before, gasping and wheezing, he was able to sink his head back onto the pillow. He looked to her exhausted, the beads of sweat standing out on his forehead. Plainly, this was no act. Gently, she rebuked him.

'What a foolish fellow you are, acting the goat like that when you should be resting.' She looked at him, anxiously. 'Tell me you shall be well again. I could not bear it if it were otherwise.'

'I shall be well in a few days, really I shall. I expect Doctor Hunter will advise that I not be moved in the meantime, so I suppose this will be my home for a little while.'

'Then, it shall be my home, too. I shall nurse you back to health. But, tell me, what exactly happened here this morning? No one seems to know.'

'I was attempting to help Nancy. I overreached myself, and that is putting it mildly.'

'I guessed as much. Well, you will be happy to know that your efforts were not in vain. I have already looked in on Nancy, and I can tell you that she looks remarkably well, although her father is insisting that she stays in bed until Doctor Hunter can be sent for to check her over.'

'A good fellow, that Doctor Hunter,' he said, thoughtfully. 'I have heard he is the man to see you safely through every crisis except for the last one.'

'Always the little jest,' she said, smiling. 'Oh, dear! whatever am I going to do with you?'

He was still thinking of a saucy response when she added, huskily: 'I know what I would like to do to you.'

Rising to her feet, she began to busy herself with his creature comforts. That done to her satisfaction, she resumed her place close beside him.

'Comfortable?' she asked. 'Can I get you anything?'

He gazed upwards into a pair of shifting blue eyes and heard himself saying: 'I could murder a kiss – a proper kiss, not a little peck like last time.'

'A little peck!' she exclaimed. 'You call that assault on me a few moments ago 'a little peck'?'

'It was a little peck in my book,' he said, studying his finger nails.

Smilingly, she bent low over him, filling his present and future horizons. It was a strange turn of phrase he had used, to 'murder a kiss', but she was more than willing to enter into the spirit of things. Her lips moved towards his.

'Come, then, kill me slowly,' she urged.

She cosseted and nursed him for the best part of the following two days. By an unspoken, mutual agreement, she had hand-fed him his meals long after it was really essential to do so, an arm draped around his shoulders to lend a scarcely needed support, her bright eyes inches from his own to still his chatter while he ate.

Apart from her more or less constant attendance, he was to receive a steady flow of visitors during this period of time.

Aside from several folk from town, come to enquire after his health, there was the reassuring presence from time to time of a benign Mr Sibley, blithely ascribing the happy ending of all concerned to the benevolence of God, and the occasional appearance of a self-satisfied Doctor Hunter, who was disposed to claim at least a measure of success for his doctoring, insignificant though this had been. There were short but frequent visits from a fussing Samuel Gibson, who was honest enough to view recent events with incomprehension, and there was a clumsy Harold, who give the matter not a moment's thought and whose visits were characterised by sixty seconds of conversation, followed by nine minutes of awkward silence. There was a tearful, penitent Rachel, eager to make amends, and a glowingly healthy Nancy, anxious to show her gratitude.

It was on the afternoon of his third day at Fold Farm that he received an unexpected visitor. It was the first time Emma had left his side for any length of time, and he was quite alone in the house, apart from the two servants, Meg and Flora. He had fallen asleep after lunch, only to awake an hour and a half later to find a 'foreign body' in his bed.

'Why do I keep waking up to find some strange woman in my bed?,' he said, peering down on the tousled mop of fair hair pressed against his chest. 'It seems to be the story of my life these past few months. Jane, just what do you think you are doing here?'

'I'm glad you are awake at last,' said Jane Gaskell. 'I really didn't want to wake you myself – that would have spoilt everything – but it was getting to the stage where I would have been left with no option but to do so. A full hour was more than I bargained for when I did what I did.'

He watched as she got out of bed and began to smooth out the creases in her dress.

'Well, that's done,' she said. 'I can rest easy now. Just do not ask me to do the same thing again, that's all.'

'Jane, I haven't a clue what you mean by any of that,' he said.

'I always pay my debts,' she said.

'If you refer to this business with young William Harker a few months back, may I remind you that it wasn't your debt at all.'

'I do not look on it in that light. I took the debt upon myself in a way. You cheated yourself out of your due, but I have now settled the score for good. Still a virgin,' she added, grinning. 'Glad you woke yourself up. Happy to have fulfilled that lifelong ambition of yours.'

'I'm only glad Emma didn't walk in upon us. *That* would have required some considerable explanation on my part.'

'Oh, do stop complaining,' she said. 'I've been fully dressed all the time, and if you care to look towards the door you will see I took the precaution of wedging a chair under the handle.' She paused to study him intently. 'Now, what is all this business of a brain fever Peter told me about? You look well-enough to me.'

'Peter? Peter Sinclair?'

'Yes. I should tell you that I arrived in Yarm late yesterday and stayed overnight with Ruth and her family. My brother, and his impedimenta and baggage, so to speak, will not be here until Monday. He asked me to pass that message onto you. The fact is, he has still to settle some of his affairs in Leeds. This morning I went to Grange Hall and apart from Peter found the place deserted – except for the household staff, of course. It is the same here. Where is everyone?'

'I insisted Emma take herself off for a few hours. She has been with me every minute of the day since Monday afternoon. She and Nancy are doing a little leisurely shopping in Stockton. Rachel left yesterday morning to stay with friends at Stokesley for a few days. Peter is staying at Grange Hall until Monday, when he leaves to join his regiment down south. As for Mr Gibson and his son, I dare say you will find them at work somewhere on their farm. There, does that answer all of your questions?'

'All but one,' she said. 'If I were to marry Peter Sinclair I would, in effect, become Emma's sister. Would it be stretching things a little too far if I was to claim you as a brother when that time comes? I would like that very much.'

'I would be happy to have you as a second sister but, Jane, you astonish me. I never knew Peter and you had an attachment for each other, and I think I may safely say that Emma is in the same state of ignorance.'

'You are perfectly correct, and I have to tell you that Peter, himself, qualifies in that respect,' she said, smiling. 'The fact is, I never set eyes on Peter Sinclair until today, although I knew of his existence from Ruth. I understand there was a time when the two of you did not see eye to eye, and that is understating the case, but Peter spoke well of you today, so I assume all of that is in the past?'

'Indeed, it is, but Jane, Jane, you have still to explain yourself.'

'I spent four hours in his company this morning. That is why I am a little late in calling on you. I could not drag myself away from him. I found him more than agreeable. I have to say that he seems to possess all those qualities which I find most appealing in a man. I found him handsome, dashing, and spirited to the point of devil-may-care.'

'Oh, he is all of those things, to be sure, Jane.'

'Then, he is the man for me. I felt that instinctively within a short time of meeting with him.'

'But, Jane,' he protested, 'how can you be so certain of your feelings after so short an acquaintance?'

'I *am* certain,' she said. 'I happen to believe in love at first sight.'

'Very well, but have you any grounds for believing that he is ever likely to want to return your affection?'

'Indeed, I have. We had been speaking of his future prospects, and I complained at one point how restricted were a woman's options in life in contrast to a man's. I said I wished I had been born a man, and he responded by saying that he was exceedingly glad that was not the case. He was helping me over a stile at the time, and he took an unconsciously long time in releasing my hand.'

'A stile which you were perfectly capable of negotiating yourself, I have no doubt. Yes, I get the picture, but I am surprised at such an easy capitulation on his part. As I understand it, he has had several female admirers in the past few years, but the partiality has all been on the one side.'

'The horserace stood me in good stead. The horserace between the two of us, I mean. My suggestion, of course. He rode that fine looking animal of his, whose name I forget, while my choice from your stables was that stallion called Star.'

'Ladies do not ride stallions, they ride mares,' he said. 'Jane, dear, you never cease to amaze me.'

'Yes, Peter was taken aback at my choice,' she said.

'I am surprised Star let you so much as mount him. There are very few *men* he will tolerate in the saddle.'

'Yes, he give me the evil eye when I began to saddle him up, but I wasn't going to stand for any of that. I give him a good verbal dressing down, but made up for it at the end by bonding with him. Carrot and stick technique, don't you see?'

'I'm almost afraid to ask you this, Jane, but how does one bond with a horse?'

'By blowing gently into the animal's nostrils. It is a show of affection few horses can resist. Didn't you know that?'

'No, I did not,' he said, 'but tell me more. How did it all end?'

'Well, Peter give me a hundred yards start, which is only fair since I was riding sidesaddle and we had most of the park to cover. I let him beat me, of course, but only by a short head. He was very impressed, I can tell you.'

'As well he might be,' he said, shaking his head. 'Jane, you are a wonder but even you will have your work cut out to secure young Peter. He leaves for his regiment in just five days time.'

'Yes, I know. A public commitment on his part within that span of time is, I realise, too much to hope for, but a firm understanding between the two of us before he leaves will suffice.'

'And how do you hope to achieve that?'

'I know Peter Sinclair's type. A meek, simpering female would repel him, but I also know that he would welcome a show of frail femininity should the occasion demand it. I have a plan in mind. I shall entice him to some secluded spot, on foot, that is. I need an area of ground which is broken and uneven, and beyond the reach of immediate assistance. I shall find such a place, not *too* far from Grange Hall, of course.'

'And then what?'

'Why, I shall contrive to stumble and fall. I shall plead a sprained ankle, which will force him into carrying me home in his arms. I shall lay my head on his chest, my arms around his neck, and play the part of frail womanhood. If he is not mine by the time we arrive back at Grange Hall, my name is not Jane Gaskell.'

'Poor Peter,' he said, laughing. 'He is already ensnared without even realising it. I can visualise the picture you paint, and have no doubt it will work out exactly as you say.'

'And what of your lovelife?' she said. 'Your wife has returned to you, so I am told. Do you know, I have yet to see her? Is she as beautiful as people say?'

'You will meet her soon, I have no doubt, and you shall judge for yourself,' he said, smiling.

'And may I ask how things stand between the two of you?' she said.

'Very well,' he said, 'but one thing still needs to be done. I shall be as bold and decisive as you have been, Jane, and then, hopefully, our union shall be complete.'

He must tell Emma the truth immediate upon their return to Grange Hall tomorrow, he had decided. There was also a certain ring to show her.

'I would advise against it, brother-to-be,' she said, as if reading his thoughts. 'It does not work with human beings.'

'What doesn't work?' he asked, puzzled by her words.

'Why, blowing up people's noses, of course,' she said.

CHAPTER 31

The most tension-filled few hours of Richard's life began the following morning, when Emma and he made the short journey home from Fold Farm.

Prompt upon their arrival, Emma began to move many of her personal effects into his room, making her intentions abundantly clear to him. Even as she did so, he was engaged upon an increasingly frantic search for the ring she had bestowed on Technician Travis. In point of fact, a search of any kind should have been unnecessary. He was quite sure in his own mind that he had hidden the ring at the back of the top drawer of the small chest in his room, but the ring was not to be found. Also missing were a few other items of value, including a pair of gold cuff-links, and a jewelled cravat pin. Increasingly desperate, he began to look in the most unlikely of places, prompting Emma in her comings and goings to ask the obvious.

'Looking for something?' she said.

'Nothing of consequence,' he lied.

Cursing his carelessness in not locking the ring safely away in the bottom drawer, he went directly to Rogers to acquaint him of the situation.

'Then it is true,' said Rogers, as if to himself. Visibly shocked, he went on to explain himself. 'Miss Rachel was complaining to me a week ago on your return from London of a few items of jewellery which had disappeared from her room. I must confess I did not take the matter very seriously. She has made similar claims in the past, only to announce a week or two later that the said items have 'turned up', as she puts it. If you will forgive me for saying so, sir, she is not the most tidy of persons. One has only to glance into her room to see that, but your own losses changes everything. It pains me to say it, but I believe we harbour a thief here at Grange Hall.'

'So it would seem,' said Richard. 'Do you have any notion as to whom that might be? It is Margaret who has the task of cleaning the family rooms, is it not?'

'That is so,' said Rogers, 'but I would stake my life on her honesty. As you know, she has been with your family for nigh on twelve years and has never given me a moment's cause for concern on that score.'

He shook his head, despairingly. 'The difficulty is we have a score of possible suspects. During a quiet period, any one of the staff from the kitchen upwards could make their way unobserved to the family rooms and be back at their post within five minutes. I shall, of course, begin an immediate and thorough investigation.'

'Rogers, I must have that ring I told you about back at all costs,' said Richard, earnestly. 'Although I should not say so, everything else is of no consequence to me. We are speaking of a gold finger ring with a cornelian bezel, on which is engraved the crouching figure of a lion. The ring is of...... of great sentimental value to me.'

The loss of the ring had come as a real body blow. It was meant to proclaim to Emma whom he really was. The return of it to her would have served to mitigate his subterfuge and deceit of the past few months. She had made it plain to him in more than one conversation on the subject that long ago she had given her heart away to her mysterious nocturnal visitor. The sight of the ring, with all its associations, could not fail to move her, of that he was certain. It was true he would still have been left with some difficult questions to answer, but the ring could have spoken for him to a degree. The trouble was, it was his one and only proof of his true identity. There was nothing he could relate concerning his visit to Pine Tree Cottage, nothing secret between the two of them, which she had not already divulged to him. For that reason, he began to regret his inquisitiveness concerning her feelings towards Technician Travis, which had prompted her to reveal all. No, in the absence of the ring, he could lay no claim to her affections. A confrontation which he had not been looking forward to now filled him with dread, but his conscience told him that the moment of truth had arrived and could not be put off a day, still less a night, longer.

The moment of truth came later that morning when, together, they took a walk beside the lake. She had addressed him casually in conversation as 'husband', giving him the opening he both sought and wished to avoid.

'I am not your husband,' he said, quietly but firmly.

He had to repeat the statement twice, earnestly and with conviction, before she would take his words seriously. Even then, she would not credit it as the truth.

'Take off your coat and shirt,' she demanded.

He did as she asked.

'Good God! it's true,' she said, aghast.

'Yes, I know what you are looking for: Henry's birthmark. As you can see, it is not there. It never was. Because it is not openly visible, it was not thought necessary to reproduce it.' Avoiding her eyes, he busied himself with his shirt and coat. 'You told me that when you were reconciled with Rachel three days ago she said at one point that her offence was not as bad as you supposed it to be. I know you found that remark of hers inexplicable, but do you not see the truth of it now? Rachel is no more related to me by blood than you are to me by marriage. Rachel has known the truth for weeks past. It explains so much, does it not?'

Indeed, it did, she acknowledged to herself: the gift of healing; a scientific knowledge which had dazzled her uncle; a technical ability which had produced a machine set fair to astonish the world; a character, once vicious and debauched, seemingly changed out of all recognition but, in truth, not changed at all. In short, virtues and abilities which her husband had never possessed and was never likely to. Rachel's recent behaviour could now be seen in its true light: it was all part of a determined effort on her part to win the man who stood before her.

She had stepped back from him, and now stood in fear and trembling, staring at him in silence.

'Are you afraid of me?' he asked, gently.

'No,' she said, after a brief hesitation. 'No, I am not afraid of you.' As if in a daze, she came slowly back to him.

'This is incomprehensible to me,' she stammered. 'Why, you are the very image of my husband.'

'Yes, those were Rachel's words. The similarity is but a coincidence.'

'And is this a coincidence, too?' she asked, reaching out to touch the scar on his cheek.

'No,' he acknowledged, 'that was made deliberately to complete the picture, so to speak.'

'So, you stand there calmly telling me that I have lived these past few months with...... with an imposter?' she said, appalled at the memory of their many intimate moments spent together.

He cringed at this description of him, but made no protest. He could not deny that the word 'imposter' summed him up perfectly.

'Thank you for not having a fit of hysteria,' he said, meekly.

'Do not speak too soon. I may yet do so,' she cried. 'But who *are* you?'

'My name is Richard Travis,' he said.

'That tells me nothing. Who *exactly* are you? How came you here?'

'I would prefer not to answer that.'

'Good God! my husband. Where is my husband?'

'I may not answer that, either.'

'But is he alive, or is he dead?' she demanded. 'I have a *right* to know.'

'In one sense, he is dead, but in another sense, he is alive,' he said, floundering.

'*Sense?* What kind of sense is any of that?' she retorted.

'It is the only response open to me, but this I can tell you with certainty: he can never return here.'

She drew back from him once more, stunned by his words.

'He is dead,' she cried. 'He is dead, but you have not the courage to say as much. You have murdered him, that is the truth of it. You have murdered him in order to take his place.'

'Knowing me as you do, do you *really* believe me capable of that?' he said, indignantly.

'I do not know what to believe any longer,' she said, helplessly. 'I only know you will not tell me plainly what has become of him.'

He had rehearsed the true explanation once before, he reflected. 'He was accidentally transported to another reality, divorced in time and space from this one', was his unspoken explanation. The sheer nonsense of such words were he to utter them in this world of 1813 forced him into silence.

'Well?' she persisted. 'I am waiting for your reply.'

He sighed, and made a feeble attempt at some kind of response.

'It was never my intention to take your husband's place, but after he...... after he disappeared...... that is to say, after he met with an accident and disappeared from the scene, well, it seemed the logical thing for me to do.'

'Do you take me for an idiot?' she said, quietly. 'You say that it was never your intention to take his place but your tone of voice, your mode of speech, and even some of your mannerisms, are all identical to those of Henry. Do you deny that all this has to be the result of previous study on your part? Do you deny that they were all in place long before the substitution took place?'

'No, I cannot deny it,' he acknowledged.

'That scar of yours was also in place in good time, was it not? Made to complete the picture, you said. And what of Henry's birthmark? "Because it is not openly visible, it was not thought necessary to reproduce it" – those are your words, not mine.'

Once more, he was lost for a response. For her part, she stood, ashen-faced and wide-eyed, staring at him.

'What gave you the right to force yourself upon me, playing the role of injured husband?' she demanded.

'That was wrong of me, but I could not help myself for never was a man more tempted. Emma, you ask who I am. I answer: I am a man who loves you, and one who would gladly lay down his life for you. Is that not enough? Can you not accept me for what I am? For what you know me to be?'

He watched the struggle taking place within herself. She resolved it with a despairing cry of: 'No, I cannot. I cannot.'

'Why not? Rachel has.'

'I am not Rachel, and for that I am grateful. That girl lives only for the present moment. She may be eager to climb into bed with every agreeable stranger who takes her fancy, but I am not so disposed.'

'Is that all I am to you – some agreeable stranger?'

She shook her head, dismissively.

'In spite of your words, I remain a married woman. That may mean nothing to Rachel, but it means something to me. Nor can I easily forget how you have deceived me all these weeks past. How do I know you do not deceive me still in some way? What basis is that for a relationship meant to last a lifetime?'

She paused to look frantically about her.

'I must leave this place,' she said.

'Why? Why must you leave?' he said.

'You ask me that? Do you imagine that I could spend the rest of my life with some mysterious stranger? I could not live with the doubt, the confusion, the uncertainty. You say my husband will never return to me, but what guarantee do I have of that? If he *were* to return, what then? What would the world think of me?'

'I do assure you he has gone for good,' he said. 'Believe me when I tell you that it is impossible for him to return here.'

'Then, prove it to me,' she said.

'I cannot,' he said, sighing.

'Oh! this is impossible,' she cried, wildly. 'I do not know if you speak the truth because I do not truly know you. I do not know who you are, where you are from, why you are here, or how long you will remain.'

She turned her back on him and began to hurry away.

'Where are you going?' he shouted after her.

'I shall go to my uncle and consult as what is best to be done. Do not attempt to follow me. I need time to be alone. I need time to think.'

'How much time?' he cried. 'Shall I see you again?'

Her outstretched arms waved frantically either side of her.

'I do not know. I do not know,' she cried.

'By rights, it is I who should be leaving,' he shouted.

These words stopped her in her tracks momentarily. She turned to face him one last time.

'You are welcome to the place,' she said, casting a look about her. 'It has brought *me* precious little happiness over the years.'

Within a short space of time he was watching the flutter of activity away in the distance. He saw the small carriage brought out of the stables and made ready, the scurry of servants to and fro from The Hall, and the luggage loaded onto the waiting vehicle. Shortly thereafter, he caught sight of her leaving the house to board the vehicle. She did not so much as glance in his direction. The carriage began its journey into town, and within a moment it had disappeared from view.

He was not left alone for long, being soon joined by Jane Gaskell, breathing heavily from her dash towards him from The Hall.

'What is happening?' she said. 'Why has Lady Forres taken herself off, baggage and all?'

'She has left me, Jane,' he said.

'Not again!' she exclaimed. 'Why, for heaven's sake?'

'We have had a serious disagreement. That is all I can tell you,' he said.

'Ah! caught you cheating her at cards, did she? A bad habit that of yours.'

'Jane, I am in no mood for jokes,' he said, wearily.

'Well, she may have made an effort to say goodbye to me before she left. I saw her for the first time this morning and have scarce spent twenty minutes in her company. And what of her brother? Peter leaves here tomorrow to join his regiment, only she will not be here to see him off. Could not she at least have waited until he returns from Stockton?'

'She is bound for her uncle at York, by the noon Post by the look of it. If you recall, Peter breaks his journey with an overnight stay in that city. I have no doubt they will meet at their uncle's house tomorrow evening.'

It was at that moment that Annie Jessel and her brood appeared on the scene in the company of Simpson.

'Forgive me, sir,' said Simpson, 'but Mrs Jessel called at the Hall a few moments ago, insisting she must see you immediately.' He looked disparagingly at the lady in question. 'I hate to disturb you at such a moment, and told her as much, but she will not take no for an answer.'

'What is it, Mrs Jessel?' said Richard.

Her reply was simply to unclench her right hand to reveal several items of jewellery, in the midst of which was a certain gentleman's finger ring.

'Heavens above!' he cried, 'I can scarce believe it.' Taking the jewellery from her, he pocketed away all but the ring. 'I think you owe me an explanation, Mrs Jessel. How did you come by these things?'

'This is Elizabeth's doing, sir,' she said, quietly. 'I was cleaning her room yesterday when, quite by chance, I came upon what you have there hidden away. Of course, I knew instantly how she had come by them. On her return home from work I confronted her with my discovery. I understand there is talk of a thief amongst the household staff, identity unknown. Well, to my everlasting shame, you may now put a name to that thief. I know I should have marched Elizabeth straight back to Mr. Rogers to reveal her wickedness, but she pleaded with me to grant her a little time to make good her escape. She left at first light this morning to join Nathan in Bristol. I gave her all my savings, all that I have scrimped and saved since coming here, to see her safely to Bristol, but have now washed my hands of both her and Nathan.' She paused to glance down at her remaining offspring. 'Children! They are a blessing and a curse,' she said, smiling through her tears. 'Still got hope for these three little mites, though. As for me, I know I have aided and abetted the escape of a thief, and am ready to face the consequences of that. No doubt you will want to see my family and me evicted from our home and the property handed over to a more deserving party, and I would not blame you if you were disposed to take the matter up with Constable Dukinfield, but I implore you not to have him pursue Elizabeth with a view to bringing her to account.'

She had said all that was to be said with a calm resolve. That done, she felt free to give vent to her anguish.

'Oh, God!, what is to become of us?' she cried, clutching at her children.

'Evict you? Pursue Elizabeth?' said Richard. 'Mrs Jessel, I would not do either thing for the world. On the contrary, I have a good mind to kiss you.' He glanced at the ring he had been clutching all the while, the ring which meant so much to both him and Emma. 'Damn it, I *shall* kiss you,' he said, and proceeded to do so with more than mere ceremony. 'And do not concern yourself about the loss of your savings. I told Rogers to inform everyone that there is a reward of ten pounds on offer to anyone who recovers my ring, and I shall see you have the money directly. That will more than compensate you for your loss, I fancy.' He turned to the rest of the party. 'Come Jane – Simpson – let us hasten back. Time presses and we have lingered here long enough.'

Annie Jessel watched in silence as they hurried away. Her spirits restored, she knelt down to face her three little ones.

'Children, if you grow up half as good as Sir Richard I shall be proud of you,' she said. 'Listen to your mother when I tell you that there goes the best man by far whom I have ever known.'

Meanwhile, Simpson was expressing his surprise.

'Sir, Mr. Rogers has acquainted all the staff of this most unfortunate business, laying particular stress on the recovery of your ring, but he said nothing about such a princely reward as ten pounds.'

'Did he not?' said Richard. 'Dear me, how very remiss of him.'

Half-way back Jane and Simpson had to come to his assistance.

'I still do not feel one hundred percent,' he confessed. 'I sometimes wonder if Wanda got it right.'

'I do not know who this Wanda is,' said Jane, 'but whoever she is it is hardly fair to blame her for your double affliction of age and infirmity.' She looked at him, sympathetically. 'It must be awful to be old.'

Having dismissed Simpson on their arrival back, Richard took Jane up to his room.

Sitting himself down, he took pen to paper and began to write.

'Ah! good, good,' said Jane.

'What?' he said, looking up at her.

'I thought for a moment there you were going to produce a pack of cards.'

He shook his head, bemused, and resumed writing.

'How are things between you and Peter?' he said, not looking up from his task.

'As I foretold you,' she said. 'We intend to announce our engagement before he leaves tomorrow. We have not settled on a date for the marriage – that rather depends when he returns home from Spain – but I hope it will not be beyond a year. I am only sorry that Lady Forres will not be here tomorrow to share in the occasion.'

'I hope this will change all that,' he said, sealing up the small package and handing it to her. 'Will you see that Matthews gets this immediately? He is to make all speed into town to the stagecoach office, where he should find the noon Post set to embark for York. I have no doubt but that he will find Emma on board. He is to hand it to her personally.' He glanced at his watch. 'Twenty minutes to the hour,' he said. 'Impress upon him the urgency of this errand. He *must* be there before the coach leaves. I would go myself but I really do not feel up to it.'

'Matthews is in Stockton with Peter,' she pointed out.

'Oh, drat! I had quite forgotten,' he said, in dismay.

'No matter,' she said, gaily. 'I shall attend to it myself.'

'You will?' he said. 'Jane, this is important.'

'I shall be there in time, depend upon it,' she said. 'I shall take Star, of course. I shall dispense with a bridle and saddle, which will save time spent in getting him ready.'

'You propose to ride Star bareback into town?' he said, in amazement.

'Why not?' she said. 'I rode him the same way to Kirkleavington yesterday.' She tapped his head with the package. 'You worry too much, that is your trouble,' she said.

For whatever reason, Jane found Star in a truculent frame of mind. It was a full fifteen minutes before she succeeded in calming him sufficient for her to mount him and point his head obediently in the direction of town. Conscious of the fact that she now had to cover a mile of busy road in under two minutes, she did not attempt to conceal her displeasure.

'Star, if it proves to be the case that you have let me down, I swear I shall never blow into your nose again,' she said.

'Room for one more, is there, Joe?'

Joe Bagley, stagecoach driver on the Newcastle to York section of the Edinburgh to London Post, was not disposed to give a favourable response. He had brought his coach into Yarm on time, but a slight lameness to one of the horses had necessitated the unscheduled change of the animal in question. He was now running late and the knowledge of it irritated him.

'You know the company rule, Mr Blenkinsop,' he said. 'Maximum seven paying passengers, children counting half, inside, and the same number up top. I already carry a full complement inside, and with all the extra luggage we carry on this trip there isn't room for a mouse topside, let alone a passenger. Of course, I could always step down and give way and leave the horses to find their own way to York.'

Company Clerk James Blenkinsop was not to be put off so easily, especially with regard to such a person as Lady Forres.

'But one of the seven inside *is* a child, besides which the clerical gentleman only travels as far as Thirsk. The fact is, I have here a young lady who must get to York as soon as possible.'

From his vantage point, Joseph Bagley cast a curious eye over the said lady. Although there was no company rule which forbid it, it was generally considered not *quite* the done thing for a lady to travel Post unaccompanied, and such passengers were rare in his experience. He saw at a glance that here was a lady of rank and breeding; young and more than pretty, she appeared to be in some distress.

Grudgingly, he nodded his agreement.

'Very well, Mr Blenkinsop. I dare say the horses will manage well-enough – assuming that is we ever get the full complement of them.'

Emma took her seat next to a family of three – man, woman, and small girl. Directly opposite her sat a clerical gentleman, small of stature, grey haired, and bespectacled. A sturdy, ruddy-faced farmer, and a strangely contrasting couple, consisting of a thin, pale-faced husband and his amply proportioned, rosy-cheeked wife, completed the complement of passengers.

Deeply preoccupied with her own thoughts, Emma hardly noticed her travelling companions, although several of them were casting mildly curious looks in *her* direction. She came back to the present moment with the opening of the carriage door and the sound of a voice first heard only that morning.

'For you, my lady, from your husband,' said Jane Gaskell, reaching across to thrust the small package into Emma's hands.

'From my husband?' said Emma.

'Yes, your husband,' said Jane. 'You know, that man you have condescended to sleep with on a couple of occasions. May I add my voice to his letter? Little William is wailing his head off at your abandonment of him, and we are trying desperately, but so far without success, to find a wet-nurse for the baby. Is their misery worth the pleasures of the flesh which you shall enjoy in the arms of your lover in York?'

'Dear God!' said the clerical gentleman, horror-struck by these words.

'Miss Gaskell, that is anything but funny,' cried Emma, angrily.

She glared around at her travelling companions, who were staring at her in stunned silence.

'None of that is true,' she cried; 'none of it.'

From up top they heard the voice of Joe Bagley bellowing down at Jane.

'Young lady, would you kindly shut the carriage door and remove yourself and that animal of yours away from my coach? We are ready for the off, fifteen minutes late as it is, and you stand there jawing.'

'All right, baldy; keep your hair on,' cried Jane. 'I'm just leaving.'

Within a moment, to the sound of a posthorn, the carriage was in motion and picking up speed.

Emma was left to ponder her situation.

Her decision to leave had seemed at the time to be the right and proper thing to do but now, seated in a vehicle which would soon take her far away from the little town of her birth and from well loved, long familiar scenes, the decision appeared less clear cut.

No, there is more to it than that, she acknowledged to herself. Why do I not admit to the truth? It is him I shall miss. How shall I fare without him?

A glance out of the window told her that they had traversed the High Street and were now passing through the southern outskirts of the town. Soon, the carriage would sweep past the borders of Grange Hall Estate. She must not be a witness to the sight, she told herself. As a distraction, she turned her attention to the letter she had been handed, and saw that the double sheet of paper, sealed at both sides, displayed a small, circular bulge at its centre. Mechanically, her thoughts elsewhere, she broke the first seal.

Where are you, Richard – my other Richard? she asked herself, not for the first time in the course of the past two years. Does the same sun which warms me warm you, too, I wonder? Do the same cold winds of winter chill you also? Am I never to see you again, not even for a fleeting moment? Would that you were here to advise and counsel me.

Distractedly, she broke the second seal.

The package strove sluggishly to open of its own accord, before it abruptly discharged itself of its contents.

She heard the sound of a small, metallic object strike the floor and roll away from her under the seat opposite. Obligingly, the frock-coated, clerical gentleman strove to recover it for her, speaking all the while.

'My child,' he said, 'reassure me once more concerning that incident before we left. Was there any truth in what that young lady said?'

'Very little,' said Emma. 'I have no children, or anyone else dependant on me. I am on my way to visit my uncle in York. I suppose it was Jane's idea of a joke.'

'Young people today!' he exclaimed, shaking his head. 'You must take her to task when next you see her. Ah! yes...... yes, I have it.'

Smilingly, he placed the object in her hand, and she was left staring in disbelief at the sight of her father's ring.

The message which accompanied it read:

'He comes with western winds, with evening's wandering airs,
With that clear dusk of heaven that brings the thickest stars;
Winds take a pensive tone, and stars a tender fire,
And visions rise and change which kill me with desire.

Then it was that the scales fell from her eyes. There came a dawning realisation that the clues to his identity, his *real* identity, had been there all along, at times almost carelessly discarded by him, as if he half-hoped that she would guess the truth.

There was his preference, until she had put a stop to it, for addressing her as Miss Sinclair, as if he refused to acknowledge the fact of her marriage. There was his insistence on having her, and others, address him as Richard, rather than Henry. *His* name had been Richard. The name was a very common one and she had failed to make the connection, a connection which now appeared to be blindingly obvious. Rachel, who knew nothing of this other Richard, had hit upon half of the truth, while the whole of it had passed *her* by. There was his abiding interest in her memories of that night of nights at Pine Tree Cottage. There was the same wonderful healing touch which had brought her back from the brink of death. Above all else, there was the same patient, gentle, compassionate goodness.

Yes, the clues had been there in plenty, but consumed by a blind prejudice she had failed to spot them.

'I have been as blind as a beetle,' she whispered to herself.

This was a man who had never raised a hand to her, except in love.

This was a man who had rescued her brother, *his own would-be murderer*, and gave him back his freedom, his self-respect, and hope for the future. This was a man to whom she owed her very life.

The passionate longing of old, long kept in check as a necessity, returned to her in full force. Instinctively, her hand moved to her neck to probe in vain for long-healed wounds. The first had been lovingly cherished for as long as it had lasted, the second regarded with loathing as 'the mark of The Beast'. The recollection of those words and a hundred others of a like kind, not to mention hate inspired deeds, now consumed her with shame.

The reasons she had stated for leaving were still valid. In particular, he remained a mysterious stranger, of whom she knew very little. Suddenly, however, none of that seemed to matter anymore. By some means, he had returned to her in the guise of her husband. He had returned, as she always hoped he would one day, and she was *fleeing* from him!

The carriage was now clear of the town, and with the driver anxious to make up for lost time was picking up speed. Glancing out of the window, she saw the countryside flashing past. The sight threw her into a panic. She got to her feet, her body swaying with the motion of the coach.

'What am I doing?' she cried out to a startled audience. 'Oh! what am I doing?'

The clerical gentleman had risen to his feet, and was doing his best to restrain her. She shrugged him off. 'Let me out of here,' she cried.

The vehicle was now in full motion, the carriage wheels eating up the ground and spitting out a shower of gravel and small stones. With flashing hoofs beating out a solo rhythm, and necks arched forward probing the near distance, the six horses pulled together in perfect unison. The dizzy, panoramic view through the carriage window was eloquent testimony to a headlong flight.

A headlong flight! At the thought of it, her cries became a continuous wail, taking on that strange element of wild abandon which comes only with total, abject regret.

Pandemonium now reigned about her. The little girl passenger, eyes wide in alarm, sought the protection of her astonished mother, while

434

the buxom lady's fan worked overtime in an attempt to calm its startled owner. All four gentlemen were on their feet, two locked, rocking and swaying, with the maniac in their midst, and two offering verbal encouragement from a safe distance. With an effort, Emma cast off her would-be rescuers and flung herself at the carriage door, frantically trying to open it, but desperate hands dragged her back to safety.

Risking life and limb, one of the men passengers leaned perilously out of one of the carriage windows and succeeded in attracting the driver's attention. Conscious now of the uproar within his coach, and thoroughly alarmed by it, Joseph Bagley made a supreme effort and contrived to bring the vehicle to a sickening halt.

Luggage carefully stowed up-top cartwheeled its way into grassy verges. Passengers who a few moments earlier had sat neatly spaced out and at their ease, now formed a jumbled, breathless heap. Particularly ill-favoured was our clerical friend, who found himself spread-eagled under a certain lady twice his size.

Quickly on her feet, Emma flung open the carriage door and took to her heels, abandoning her luggage, and disregarding the oaths and curses of the driver, and the outraged cries and imprecations of her fellow passengers. She had barely covered a hundred yards before the heavens opened and a violent autumn shower began to rain down upon her.

Leaving the highway, she struck out across country, seeking the bridlepath which ran north into Yarm. Across fields ploughed and fallow she ran, scrambling over stiles and forcing her way through clumps of bracken and briar until, panting breathlessly, she reached the bridlepath. The deluge was now petering out but the fifteen minutes soaking had left her drenched to the skin, the clothes clinging to her, and her hair in total disarray. Her shoes had been an early casualty of her scamper across country, one snagged and discarded in a deceptively dense thicket, the other lost in an unavoidable small quagmire. Wearily, she turned her face homeward and ran on until she could run no more. Exhausted, she sank down by the side of the path for a moment's respite.

Help was at hand, however, in the form of Constable Hutton, pursuing his business south of the river.

'For God's sake, what has happened?' he cried, dismounting from his horse and coming quickly to her side. 'How came you here all alone and in such a sorry state?'

'Constable Hutton, I was never more pleased to see anyone in all my life,' she gasped. 'I must get home as soon as possible. Will you help me?'

He remounted his horse and held out a hand to her. With effortless ease, he lifted her up to sit sidesaddle in front of him.

'Bob can easily manage the two of us, it is but two miles we have to cover,' he said. 'Do you hold on firmly.'

True gentleman that he was, the constable would never have dreamed of satisfying his curiosity with a string of prying questions, even in the novel situation in which he found himself. The weather was a safe topic of conversation, he thought.

'That was quite a downpour we had. I was able to take shelter beneath an accommodating tree, but you seem not to have been so fortunate; but I believe the afternoon is now set fair.' He indicated a bright sun, already having its effect on a sodden countryside, and pointed out a rainbow arcing a kaleidoscopic sky away in the distance.

A fifteen minute ride brought them to the outskirts of the estate. He expressed a wish to take her the whole way home and see her safely inside, but she declined his offer and had him leave her at one of the postern gates which fronted the bridlepath. Nodding his goodbye, he watched as she ran on her way.

'Good luck, my lady,' he shouted, on an impulse.

He had left her once before, she reflected. Terrified that in her absence he had done the same, she lost no time in an attempt to dispel her fears. She raced towards the Hall, ignoring the stares of several of the gardeners and, having reached her destination, flung open the front door. In the hallway she confronted a startled Simpson.

'Where is your master?' she cried.

'He is in the drawing room with Mr. Sibley,' he said, his eye taking in her bedraggled appearance, bare feet and all. 'But, my lady,' he protested, as she headed off in that direction.

Sibley was in the middle of explaining the reason for some very necessary repair work to the roof of his church, with a view to extracting the promise of a generous contribution towards the cost, when Emma burst in upon them.

'Merciful heavens!' he cried, at the sight of her. 'I was told you were on your way to York to visit your uncle. Has there been some terrible accident to the coach?'

Her only response was to briefly shake her head and stare past him at Richard.

'My dear child, you will catch your death standing there,' said Sibley. 'Go to your room, change your clothes, and I shall see you before I leave here.'

Once more, his words fell on deaf ears. She was paying not the least notice of him, or his words. He turned his attention to the gentleman.

'Richard, you will support me in this, I'm sure. Tell Emma to do as I advise.'

To his surprise, Richard made no reply. More than that, he, too, appeared to be oblivious of his very presence.

Bewildered, he turned back to Emma once more and was startled to see that the liquid coursing down her cheeks stemmed not from her sodden hair but from her eyes – and the look which accompanied them! Oh! such a look!

Never in his life had Sibley felt so intrusive, encroaching upon the privacy of a man and a woman who wished only to be left alone together. His business at The Hall could wait a while longer, he decided. Without a word, he slipped quietly away.

He approached his waiting pony and trap with a spring in his step. He had seen the look on both Emma and Richard's faces on a number of occasions in the past, and had recognised it for what it was. He had seen it in the eyes of a mother when she first took her newborn baby into her arms. He had seen the same look in the eyes of a loving husband when it had first dawned upon him that his desperately ill wife was not destined to be taken from him after all. It was a look of pure, unadulterated love of the deepest kind. Whatever the circumstances of the scene he had just witnessed signified, and irrespective of all the trials and tribulations of the past, of one thing he was now certain. Love had come to stay and flourish at Grange Hall.

As he mounted his little carriage, he so far forgot his calling as to break out into a loud and jaunty whistle.

CHAPTER 32

'Where have you been since that night at Pine Tree Cottage?' she said, staring fixedly at him.

'Well, for the past two months I have been with you,' he said.

'Yes, I know that now,' she said, 'but what of the previous two years? Why did you make no effort to contact me?'

'It was impossible for me to do so,' he said. 'You could say I was unavoidably detained elsewhere. I had no knowledge of your marriage, and the pain and grief it brought you, until very recently.' He sighed, wearily. The conversation was beginning to follow the pattern of the previous one, he thought. 'I suppose you still wish to know who I really am?'

She went over to the fireplace and began to warm herself before the brightly flickering flames.

'I know who you are,' she said, casually. 'You are my husband, Richard.'

'Do you really mean that?' he said.

'I do,' she said. 'As you say, Rachel has accepted you for what you are, so how can I fail to do likewise? I who owe my very existence to you.'

Loathe as he was to raise the subject, he felt duty bound to point out one fact of which, surprisingly, she seemed oblivious.

'Remember, Emma, that although we may be counted as a married couple in the eyes of the law, we are not married in the sight of God.'

'That is not true,' she protested. 'I never want to hear you say such a thing again. Does the truth still escape you? This is all God's doing. It has to be. We have the best of all unions. We have a marriage made in heaven.'

He thought these words pure nonsense, but would never have dreamt of saying as much.

'I have only the one question,' she said. 'Why did you not show me the ring this morning?'

'I hate to admit it, but I lost it for a short while. I only recovered it shortly after you left.'

'So, that is what you were frantically looking for this morning?'

'Yes, exactly.'

'Even so, you could have revealed yourself to me much sooner. We have been together for two months. Why did you not do so?'

'Initially, I was not certain of your true feelings. Remember, as you rightly said this morning, I am nothing short of an imposter, with no legal claim on you, or any part of the estate; but perhaps you are right. I should have acted earlier but with the passage of time a kind of stubbornness came over me – I can explain it no other way. I set my sights on winning you by my own merits, without recourse to reminding you of what Emma Sinclair owed to Richard Travis.'

'I feel so ashamed,' she whispered. 'I feel so guilty. You have given me so much, and I have treated you abominably in return. When I think of our confrontation in Darlington! My God! I could have killed you.'

'None of that was your fault. You were not to know. Besides, if I saved your life at Pine Tree Cottage you returned the compliment when you saved me from drowning. I wasn't play-acting that day. To own the truth, I cannot swim a stroke.'

'Dear God!' she exclaimed, shocked by this admission. 'I wish you had not told me that. I can claim no credit for what happened that day. On the contrary, it was I who pushed you in, remember?'

'Did you? No, you are mistaken, I'm sure. I seem to recall the fault was mine. I slipped and fell.'

'I shall make it up to you, I swear, starting from this very day, this very hour.' She took hold of his hand. 'Come, we have talked long enough. Let us go upstairs.'

He watched as she began to shed herself of her wet clothes. He started to do likewise.

'No, I want to do that,' she said, 'but first I think I should ask to see this famous list of yours.'

Somewhat sheepishly, he brought it to her.

She sat on the edge of the bed and studied it for a moment before screwing it up and throwing it away.

'Too tame,' she said, 'much too tame.'

She held up the ring before him.

'Shall it be 'till death us do part', or shall it be a case of five hundred pounds on each occasion?'

'Till death us do part,' he said.

'I was hoping you were going to say that,' she said, slipping the ring

439

onto his finger. 'How I could possibly come up with thousands of pounds every week, I really do not know.'

She woke from a sleep of deep contentment to find his eyes fixed upon her.

'I was just about to wake you,' he said. 'You've been sound asleep for more than an hour. We really should get up and dress for dinner. It's very nearly half-past six, and we do not want to keep Peter and Jane waiting.'

'In a moment,' she murmured, sleepily. 'After you have done one more thing for me.'

She rolled over onto her back. Touching her neck with a finger, she began to pull him towards her.

'Ah!' he exclaimed, 'this will bring back memories.' He brushed aside a lock of hair and fixed upon a spot. 'I know, I know,' he acknowledged; 'low down, where it may not be readily seen.'

'No, indeed,' she said, smiling; 'high up, for all the world to see.'

'Little William and the baby are quiet this evening,' Emma said to Jane, as they took their places at the dinner table.

'Sorry about that, Lady Forres,' said Jane, blushing. 'I do not know why I said what I did. There is a mischievous streak in me, I own to that.'

'Well, I am in a very forgiving mood today, so we shall say no more about it, provided that you stop addressing me as Lady Forres. We do not stand on ceremony here at Grange Hall. My name, at least to you, is Emma.'

They had barely started on their meal before Jane was digging Peter in the ribs.

'That is how it should be done,' she whispered, indicating Emma's neck. 'Really, Peter, I have had bigger bites from a midgee fly.'

'What have you two been up to?' said Emma, who unfortunately for Jane had overheard these words. 'Show me to what you refer, Jane.'

'I cannot really do that without...... well, without well and truly exposing myself,' stammered Jane.

'Peter!' exclaimed Emma, lost for words.

'It is not as bad as what Jane says,' said Peter.

'No?' queried Emma.

'Indeed, not, sister,' he said, grinning. 'Not as good as yours, I have to admit.'

'We meant to tell you tomorrow before Peter left,' Jane interposed.

'Tell me? Tell me what?' said Emma.

'Jane and I have reached an understanding,' said Peter. 'I would not go so far as to call it a formal engagement, but rather an attachment and a firm commitment to each other.'

'But you have known each other less than a week,' Emma protested. She turned to Richard. 'Did you know about this?' she said.

'I must confess, I did,' he said.

'But they have known each other less than a week.'

'Emma, you are repeating yourself,' he said. 'Listen to me. You lost your heart in the course of a single night, remember? They have my blessing, even if they do not have yours.'

'The matter is a simple one. We love each other,' said Peter.

'Then, if that be the case, you have my blessing, too,' said Emma, smiling.

Later that evening, however, Emma was still expressing her doubts to Richard.

'Do you really think they are suited to each other?' she said.

'I believe they are ideally suited,' he said, 'although I have to admit that they are each of a strong-willed and impetuous disposition. I foresee a relationship which, although stormy at times, will prove in all essentials to be a happy one.'

'Yes, I believe you are right,' Emma conceded, 'but I have to say that I find Jane's behaviour very odd at times. Do you know, one of your under-gardeners, Ridley, tells me he has twice come upon Jane half-way up a tree. Why would she want to climb a tree, for goodness sake?'

'Why, to get to the top, silly,' he said.

The following morning, Emma, Richard, and Jane said their goodbyes to Peter, during the course of which a few tears were shed.

The three became four again with the arrival back a few hours later of Rachel after a self-imposed exile of several days. 'Too ashamed to face everyone. Putting it off,' had been Emma's verdict at the first news of her intended absence, but with a little prior prompting from Richard she greeted her warmly enough.

'How are you, Rachel?' she asked.

'I am well-enough,' answered Rachel, as she alighted from the carriage with Charlie in her arms. 'I see you are in a perfect state of health and happiness. You look absolutely ravished.'

'I believe, dear Rachel, you mean I look absolutely ravishing,' said Emma, laughing.

'No, no, ravished is the word,' said Rachel.

Emma flung wide her arms to embrace her.

'Dearest Rachel, welcome home,' she said, tearfully.

'Where is Richard?' said Rachel, after returning Emma's embrace.

'He is in the drawing room, waiting to see you,' said Emma. 'He wishes to have a word in private with you.'

'Are you going to take me to task?' said Rachel at her first sight of him. 'I thought I had earned your forgiveness at Fold Farm.'

'And so you did,' he said, smiling. 'I only wanted this to be a private moment between the two of us. I have yet to speak to Emma about your stated intention at Fold Farm to leave here for London. Will you not reconsider?'

'No, I believe it would be for the best. I only returned from London when I did to be with you. There is nothing to hold me here now. It will be no exile, Richard, believe me. Some of my happiest moments were spent there, and I long to be back. I have had three letters already in the space of two weeks from Lady Chessington urging my return.'

'Yes, and a fourth arrived just a few hours ago. I recognised the lady's handwriting. I am only sorry to lose you so soon after your return. You are to leave the day after tomorrow, I understand?'

'Yes, I sent Lady Chessington word express of my intentions five days ago. I imagine the letter you hold is in acknowledgement of that.' She moved close to him and kissed him lightly on the cheek. 'You are not about to lose me, not really. You plan future trips to London yourself, do you not?'

'Why, yes, I must return there within the month.'

'Then, I expect to see Emma and you very often at 'High Gables' in the future, and for my own part I shall be a frequent visitor to your new house in Chelsea whenever you are in town. And you talk of losing me!'

'But I wish I could persuade you to stay here just a little while longer. You will miss Emma's birthday in five days' time.'

'I cannot linger that long,' she said, shaking her head. 'I would leave tomorrow were it not for Nancy's birthday. It is her twenty first, and it would be churlish of me if I were to leave on the very day of that. Which reminds me, I have been meaning to ask for future reference: when is your birthday?'

'Oh, not for the best part of four months – the 10th of March, to be precise.'

'How very strange,' she exclaimed. 'How very odd that it falls a mere two days before Arthur's.'

'Arthur? Who is Arthur?' he said.

'Oh, no one special,' she said, coyly, as she turned to leave him.

'Rachel, one more thing before you go to your room,' he said. 'My secret is safe with you, I trust?'

She returned to his side and began to tidy his cravat.

'Secret? What secret is that, brother?' she said.

To Emma, Rachel was a little more forthcoming.

'It was very wrong of me, I realise that now. With all his talents, Richard is destined for great things, of that I have no doubt. How could I expect him to abandon a life full of promise by skulking with me in some far-flung corner of the Empire?'

'Dear Rachel, I hope you find true love and perfect contentment in London,' said Emma. 'Oh, yes, Richard told me of your intentions an hour ago. Believe me, there *is* such a man somewhere out there for you.'

'Richard is truly unique,' said Rachel, 'but I believe there is some merit in what you say. In fact, I may already have lighted upon a very agreeable alternative. Let me tell you about him.'

The morning after Nancy's enjoyable but fairly uneventful birthday party, Emma and Richard waved their goodbyes to Rachel.

'It is a pity Jane's acquaintance with Rachel should have been of such short duration,' said Emma. 'They got on famously together yesterday evening.'

'Yes, didn't they just.'

'I wonder if we are doing the right thing in leaving Rachel in the care of Lady Chessington,' she said, as the carriage disappeared from sight. 'She could so easily be led even further astray.'

'Oh, I believe Rachel is quite capable of looking after herself.'

'You mistake my meaning, husband,' she said. 'My concern is for Lady Chessington.'

She responded to his laughter with some surprising news.

'Actually, I do not know why I said that. I have the feeling that Rachel's stay at 'High Gables' may prove to be a fairly short one. She told me that it is not only the lady which draws her back to the capital. In short, on our recent visit there she found herself strongly attracted to a certain gentleman, and he to her.'

'Really? You do surprise me,' he said. 'Who is the gentleman in question? Did I meet with him?'

'I believe we both did on a couple of occasions, although speaking personally I have no clear recollection of him, and I fancy it is the same with you. Rachel, however, was in his company very often, I understand.'

'What do you know of him?'

'Only what Rachel has told me. His name is Arthur Forrester. Strange that: Forres – Forrester. He is twenty four years of age, and is the eldest son of Sir William Forrester. The family do not lack for money, that much is certain, and Sir William is held in high regard at court.'

'And what of the son? Is he a handsome fellow?'

'The general opinion, so Rachel informed me, is that he is the most handsome man one could wish to meet.'

'What? More handsome than me?' he said, smiling.

'Oh, I believe there are many who would say so,' she said, teasingly.

'Tell me more. Tell me all you know,' he said, 'but please! Emma! do try and keep the details credible.'

She proceeded to do so, at the end of which he began to speculate about the future.

'We must hope for the best,' he said. 'Yes, let us hope that everything turns out well. Rachel Forrester! Yes, I like the sound of that. It has a nice ring to it.'

Abruptly, he fell silent, deep in thought.

'What is it, my love?' she said, gently.

'That name – Rachel Forrester. It strikes a distant chord. I have the strangest feeling that it is a name already known to me.' With a shake of the head, he dismissed the matter from his mind. 'No, it's gone,' he said.

At noon the next day Edward Gaskell, his steward to be, put in an appearance, together with his wife and child.

'You do not object to their living with us here in The Hall, rather than The Lodge?' he said to Emma. 'No second thoughts on that score?'

'No, indeed,' said Emma. 'With Peter and Rachel gone, and the two of us sharing, the family quarters are all but deserted. It is absurd to have so many rooms standing idle. Besides, I am looking forward to spending some time with the baby.'

'Good experience for you?'

'I hope so,' she said, smiling.

'We have yet to make a tour of the estate, but I have already spent half-an-hour in the company of Edward, giving him a detailed description of it and outlining his duties. I must say, Emma, I took to him instantly. I am sure I have made the right choice and we shall get on very well together.'

'What did you make of Catherine?' she said. 'My first impression was that she appeared to be a rather timid creature, not at all like her young sister-in-law.'

'No, but a second Jane would have been too much to hope for. I found her reserved but pleasant enough. Jane tells me she is one of those Christian types who take their religious beliefs seriously, but in all other respects she seemed to me to be a sensible lady.'

'I shall pray for you,' she said, shaking her head at his words. 'I shall pray for your continuing health and happiness. Someone has to.'

'I shall attend to my health,' he said. 'My happiness I leave to you.'

'That is hardly a fair division,' she said, smiling. 'I have the easiest part by far.'

Late that afternoon, a small cloud appeared on the horizon.

'Oh, Lord!' he said.

'What is it?' said Emma.

'A message from Mr. Blenkinsop, which has just arrived,' he said, waving it in front of her. 'I was half-expecting something of the kind when you told me of that abortive trip of yours to York the other day. It seems that several of the passengers, not to mention the driver, have made an official complaint concerning your conduct. Although he does not expressly say so, I think Mr. Blenkinsop is expecting some kind of explanation from you.'

'But what explanation can I give him?' exclaimed Emma. 'I can hardly tell him the truth, can I?'

'No, I suppose not, nor can you tell him that you took fright at the sight of a rogue elephant charging the carriage. I shall accompany you into town tomorrow. My presence may bring some influence to bear, although lord knows what excuse we can offer him.'

'Remember what I told you,' he said, as they approached the stagecoach offices. 'You were badly stung by a wasp which had flown into the carriage, and took fright.' He pointed to her neck. 'At least you can show him that in evidence.'

'I believe he will know for a fact that wasps do not have teeth,' she said.

'Yes, but I dare say he will not scrutinise it too closely.'

'I have to say that even supposing he believes us, it scarcely justifies my conduct.'

'True,' he said, 'but can you come up with anything better? For the life of me, I cannot.'

James Blenkinsop was not disbelieving, but only mildly sympathetic. It was clear that he judged Emma's conduct on the day in question to be out of all proportion to the provocation.

'There is more to it than that, Mr. Blenkinsop,' said Richard. 'A word in your ear, if you please.'

The two men withdrew to one side and began an animated conversation. Even from a distance, Emma could sense the other man's coldness evaporating. She smiled across at him at one point, which provoked him into producing a large, red handkerchief, with which he began to mop his brow.

His manner was markedly different on his return: 'a most distressing incident for the lady'...... 'deepest sympathy extended'...... 'no blame could possibly be attached to her'...... 'great pains taken to ensure the comfort and safety of passengers but impossible to guard against every eventuality'...... 'company proud to count the lady and gentleman amongst its patrons'.

Emma could only nod, uncertainly, at every declaration. To her, the speaker appeared somewhat flushed and agitated, and she shifted uncomfortably under the man's penetrating gaze.

'What in heaven's name did you say to affect him so?' she said, after they had taken their leave.

'Do you really want to know?'

'Yes, of course I do.' She looked at him, suspiciously. 'What yarn did you spin him which so excited his sympathy?'

'Excited his imagination is nearer the mark, I fancy. I said that after stinging you on the neck, the insect somehow contrived to get inside your underwear and stung you a second time, on the bottom. I pointed out that you could scarcely be expected to disrobe in public in order to rid yourself of the creature, so off you went in a tearing hurry to some private spot, where you disposed of it. Ingenious, what?'

'You told him all *that*!' she exclaimed.

'I said you were not in the habit of stripping naked in front of strangers.'

'Oh, Lord! this is getting worse and worse. What did he say to *that*?'

'I'm not sure. He mumbled some word, or other. It sounded suspiciously like 'pity'.'

'Richard, you really are outrageous at times,' she exclaimed.

'Well, I had to come up with *something*,' he protested. 'We were in danger of becoming persona non grata with his company. As it is, you have had a very narrow escape.'

'*I* have had a narrow escape? What do you mean by *I* have?'

'Well, I thought at one point he was going to ask to see the evidence of this supposed second injury.'

'What people hereabouts are going to say about me, I cannot imagine,' she said, shaking her head.

447

'Do not concern yourself on that score,' he reassured her. 'I have no doubt that Mr. Blenkinsop will look upon this business as a private matter between the three of us, but I must say the fellow surprised me. I have engaged him in conversation on several occasions before today and would never have guessed he possessed a ready wit.'

She groaned at these words.

'I suppose you had best tell me,' she said. 'Why do you say that? What else did he say?'

'Well, his parting words to me were: "It is a comfort to know that the insect died happy".'

Emma's mortification was complete an hour later in the premises of 'George Kennedy, Gentleman's Outfitters'. The establishment stood at the far end of the High Street, as far away as it was possible to get from the stagecoach offices, be it noted.

She stood, a little restlessly, while he examined a selection of cravats, newly arrived. The cause of her restlessness came in the shape of the Kennedy twins, two fifteen year old boys, who served behind the counter of their grandfather's shop.

The pair were sniggering together – sniggering at her, she felt sure – and casting knowing looks in her direction. Was it possible they knew? she wondered. No, it cannot be, she concluded. The Kennedy pair had always been two foolish, ignorant boys, had they not? She glanced at her dress to see if anything was amiss.

Old Mr. Kennedy appeared on the scene. One severe look on his part was sufficient to silence his grandsons. Ever conscious of the comfort of his customers, he carried with him a chair to offer to Emma. He paused, uncertain, a few feet from her, the chair poised a few inches above the floor.

'Are you able to sit down, Lady Forres?' he asked.

'You are going to pay for this,' she said, as they began their walk home. 'I intend to suspend your conjugal rights for twenty four hours.'

'Blondie, that is hardly fair, and certainly not sensible,' he protested. 'We are never going to have that baby at this rate.'

'Yes, you are right. Twelve hours, then.'

'From the time the offence was committed – nine-thirty this morning?'

'Naturally. That goes without saying.'

'Early night tonight?'

'Yes, if you like.'

The following morning he came down a little late to breakfast to find her in the process of opening a small pile of letters, and several packages of various sizes.

'From absent friends and loved ones,' she said. 'Rogers has had the keeping of them as and when they arrived. There will be more during the day, although I should not say so. People are so kind.'

'They are never that kind to me,' he said, staring at the beautiful pair of fur mufflers she held in her hand. 'Blondie, dear, what is all this?'

'It is my birthday,' she said, brightly. 'Twenty three years! Dear me, I feel quite old. I intend to put a stop to it for as long as I can when I reach twenty nine.'

'But...... but, I had no idea,' he said. 'Why did you not tell me?'

'One does not go about dropping hints about one's birthday,' she said, 'although I am a little surprised that Rachel did not think to mention it before she left. I have yet to open her present.'

'I feel terrible,' he said. 'I feel awful. I haven't a thing for you. I shall have to go into town and buy you something.'

'You shall do no such thing,' she said. She took hold of his hand and pressed it against her cheek. 'These trifles are nothing to me in comparison to a lost love found. Besides, the first of our visitors will be arriving within the hour, and they shall expect to see you here.'

'Visitors? What visitors?'

'The Jamiesons are coming for the day, and I expect Elizabeth this afternoon, and Nancy, too, of course. Harold and his father will put in an appearance this evening, and I dare say Mr. Sibley will drop by. They are all invited to the party this evening, along with our new steward and his family. I only wish Peter and Rachel could be with us, uncle Johnathon, too. He sends his regrets and this lovely brooch, and I shall have to be content with that.'

'A party? There is to be a party this evening, and not a single soul thought to mention it to me. Well, really!'

'Oh, it will be a small affair compared to Nancy's. I shall never see twenty one again, that much is certain.'

'No one is to stay over then?'

'There is no occasion for that,' she said. 'I dare say it will all be over by ten o'clock.'

It worked out just as Emma had predicted. Enjoyable as they were, the festivities came to an end prompt at ten o'clock with the departure of the last of their guests, the Gibson family.

'What a lovely day,' said Emma, 'and the pleasure is not yet over. Ten o'clock – time for bed, I think. In the absence of a present I shall expect a special performance from you tonight.'

'Yes, I shall just get our coats,' he said. 'Stay where you are, and occupy yourself in opening this.'

'Why, you sly thing,' she exclaimed, looking at the gift-wrapped, small package thrust into her hand, 'you had a present for me all along; but why the show of ignorance this morning? And why should we need our coats to go to bed, for heaven's sake?'

'If I had owned to the knowledge of your birthday this morning that would have left me little choice but to give you your present immediately.' He pointed to his gift. 'I fear *that* would have proved a constant distraction to you throughout the day, which would hardly have been fair to our guests. I wager the Jamiesons would have arrived to find no one here to greet them, servants apart. Open your present and I shall be back in a moment. We really do have need of our gloves and coats.'

He returned to find her picking her way through his present of well used, well remembered keys.

'The keys to Pine Tree Cottage. I recognised them instantly,' she said; 'but, Richard, I do not understand. What are they doing in your possession?'

'It would be a strange thing if a man did not have the keeping of the keys to his own property,' he said, 'except, it is not my property any longer, it is yours. I see it is all a mystery to you, so let me explain. A few weeks ago Mr. Buckland informed me that Pine Tree Cottage was about to come up for sale once more. I understand that Mrs Williamson never took to the place, finding the situation a mite too quiet for her liking, and that she and her husband have removed themselves to a town house in Stockton.'

'I never knew any of that,' she said.

'No, but, then, why should you? You never did become acquainted with the Williamsons, in spite of their proximity to Grange Hall, and Pine Tree Cottage was never openly on the market. My purchase of it was a private arrangement between the owners, Mr. Buckland, and myself. With your birthday in mind, I forced the purchase through in double-quick time, and came into possession of the place three days ago. In short, my dear Blondie, Pine Tree Cottage is now back where it belongs – in the keeping of the Sinclair family. Mr. Williamson appears to have made very few alterations to the place, and I believe you will find it pretty much as you remember it. Now, let me help you on with your coat and we shall pay a nocturnal visit to the place of your birth, and the site of our first meeting. As you know, it is but a fifteen minute walk, and since the weather holds good I think we can dispense with a carriage.'

Emma said very little on the short walk to Pine Tree Cottage, seemingly dumbfounded by what she had been told.

'We should have brought a lantern,' was her only remark of note.

She give a visible start when her former home came into view.

'The place is all lit-up,' she said. 'Is that your doing?'

'Patience,' he said. 'Have the front door key ready.'

'Good God!' she said, as they entered into the fully furnished and brightly lit hallway. Through the open door of the drawing room she saw the fire burning cheerfully in its grate. She stepped into the room and stared about her in amazement.

'The past is staring me in the face,' she said. 'There is mother's favourite chair, and see there the table where I used to work at my embroidery. The same pictures hang on the walls. Why, even the ornaments remain the same,' she said, picking up a porcelain figure of a shepherd and his dog.

'Not everything is *exactly* as it was, I'm sure,' he said. 'I had to guess where everything went, and it would be too much to hope that I got everything right. If you like, you may make a tour of the place tomorrow, correcting my mistakes, but, come, let us go upstairs.'

He had to help her up, the shock of it all-too much for her.

'I do not understand,' she kept repeating over and over again.

'There is no mystery,' he assured her. 'Believe me, I have no magic

451

wand at my disposal. Did you know that all of the furniture from Pine Tree Cottage, and most of the smaller items, down to the most trifling of ornaments, were removed by Sir Henry before Mr and Mrs Williamson took possession of the property? No, I suppose you did not know that. I only came across them by chance a week ago, in a half-forgotten lumber room at Grange Hall. During the past few days Simpson has seen to their return here, and I have put the finishing touches to everything. It was no small feat to keep the whole thing secret from you. Most of the work was done in your absence, some of it under the cover of darkness. In years to come this place shall be our little hideaway whenever we wish to be alone for a while. I thought we might make a start by spending the night of your birthday here. The place is fully aired and warmed, there is food in the larder, and, in short, we lack for nothing.' He opened her bedroom door, and pointed inside. 'There is that bed of yours on which a certain gentleman made himself at home one memorable night a few years back.'

The sight was too much for Emma. She flung her arms around him and began to weep.

'Oh, God! what have I done to deserve such happiness?' she said. She lifted her face to his. 'And I have nothing to give you in return save myself. So be it. Freely – willingly – gladly, I give you back the life I owe.'

After the tender embrace of a few moments, he gently freed himself.

'Undress, and get into bed, and I shall join you shortly,' he said. 'This is an emotional experience for me, too, and I need to be alone with my thoughts for a little while.'

He left her and went downstairs. Opening the rear door, he took a few paces out onto the lawn. The scene before him brought his thoughts irresistibly back to that evening, when only a few yards from where he stood the link with his own world had been so abruptly severed.

There was the same little plot of lawn and trees stretching before him, dim and shadowy under a star-studded night sky. The same gentle breeze, albeit some ten degrees colder, lazily stirred the branches of the same trees, now gaunt and bare but otherwise not so very different.

In his hand he held the very same bundle of keys which he had held before, the faded, tie-on label, which served to hold them together, still proclaiming 'Pine Tree Cottage – James Buckland, Attorney at Law'.

If the scene was more or less as before, his emotions four months on were very different. Then, he had stood, bewildered and afraid, contemplating an uncertain future in a friendless world. Now, there was happiness, and hope for the future, and love beyond anything he had ever known.

He allowed himself a brief moment of swelling pride. Had he not done what the poet of old had urged one to do? 'To strive, to seek, to find, and not to yield'. The mountain had been levelled, and before him there stretched the unbroken vista of a promised land.

He turned his eyes to a vaulted sky, spangled with ten thousand specks of light. Some things would never change in a billion years, he reflected. Mercury, Venus, Mars, Diana, and the nine outer planets would continue to rise and set this Earth just as surely as they would rise and set the Earth which was his birthplace. This Earth's solitary moon would continue to arc the night sky in precise unison with his Earth's moon, except it was no longer *his* Earth – this one was. On a non-cosmic scale, however, the two worlds were beginning to diverge. Identical in every respect in the year 1813, they would be very different a thousand years from now, he knew. The signs were already there in some recent world events which did not tally with the history he had been taught at school.

Of little significance on the world's stage, but striking to him nonetheless because it was happening close to home, was a diverging local history. A case in point were the extensive repairs and alterations currently being carried out at the local Methodist chapel. If his memory of parochial events he had researched served him right, this work was not due to begin until 1815.

If his memory served him right!

Therein lay the difficulty, for in the recent past his memory had been playing him false in some very odd ways. His knowledge of things to come seemed to be fading away, so much so that he was fast losing the ability to distinguish with certainty the expected, anticipated event as opposed to the unexpected, unforeseen event.

Similarly at fault was the memory of his own *past*. In particular, although many memories of a personal nature from long ago were as vivid now as ever was, other aspects, such as the purpose and content of his work at...... at London Centre, was it? and his scientific and technical 'know-how', were almost a blank to him.

Thinking the matter over, he could only attribute all of this to his recent illness, when he had overreached himself in the healing of his friend, Nancy. Not that he regretted for one moment doing what he did. Single-handedly, he had brought his friend back from the brink of death, and, relying on those same powers, had contrived to save himself, too. With his thoughts dwelling on that event, a picture of his mother's face came to mind, which he thought the oddest thing.

Close at hand, the screech of a barn owl, very possibly the selfsame bird as before, he thought, pierced the night air, bringing him back to the present moment with a start.

That sound is where I came in, he said to himself; but what was he doing? What was he doing standing there minute after minute, wrapped in his own thoughts? On this night of all nights, too. Fully expecting him to join her shortly, Emma would be waiting for him, waiting and wondering where he had got to.

He made his way back to her, and heard her give a sigh of relief as he made his appearance.

'What have you been doing all this time?' she said. 'I was just about to go looking for you. I began to fear that you had left me, as you did once before.'

'*Left you?*' he said. 'Blondie, you are...... what are you?'

'A blockhead?' she ventured.

'Right in one,' he said.

Quickly, he undressed and slipped in beside her.

It was then, with a few brief words, that she dispelled for all time the last lingering regrets he had for the life he had given up.

'Left you, indeed!' he exclaimed. 'Always remember, Emma, that however much you love me, I love you more.'

He studied her face as she considered this statement for a moment. Finally, she answered him.

'No,' she said, with a shake of her head, 'no, that is just not possible.'